Glacé F

Glacé Fruits

STORIES

ROBIN WALTON

PANDORA

London Boston Sydney Wellington

Published in the UK by Pandora Press, an imprint of the trade division of Unwin Hyman Ltd, in 1989.

Originally published in Australia by Allen & Unwin Australia Pty Ltd.

Allen & Unwin Australia Pty Ltd
An Unwin Hyman company
8 Napier Street, North Sydney NSW 2059 Australia

Pandora Press
Unwin Hyman Limited
15-17 Broadwick Street, London W1V 1FP England

Allen & Unwin New Zealand Limited
60 Cambridge Terrace, Wellington, New Zealand

Unwin Hyman Inc.
8 Winchester Terrace, Winchester, Mass. 01890 USA

A CIP record is available from the British Library

Printed in Maryborough, Australia by the Australian Print Group

Contents

On Easy Street

On our street, anything is acceptable. You may booze, litter, argue, whistle, spit, play a radio or tambourine, harangue or fondle, solicit, proselytise, sulk or sunbake. Our street is our living room. Everything and everyone is tolerated. The crazies are known by name.

Don't mistake me. You will not be welcomed. Indeed, you'll be ignored, shoved, menaced, or knocked sideways by a lout on a skateboard. But you will have perfect freedom to do the same back. Our shibboleth changes from week to week, and we have no written laws.

There are men and women here who sleep, sponge and cough in single rooms and take their sustenance on the bus seats. Others live nowhere and everywhere, pacing out their patches and hoarding their carrybags in sacred nooks, in alleys and sidings and between the buttress roots of Moreton Bay figs. Bats watch over them as they dine on pizza rinds and barbequed chicken carcasses.

Others share houses. There is a constant ludo game of room swapping. Every renter has lived in every side street at one time or another. They say: 'Oh, that house. I had the back bedroom. Is it still . . . ?' Others squat like unsaleable imports in warehouses classified for preservation or the torch.

Each room is a hundred years old and its layers of paint sprinkle flakes on those few fixtures which furnish the means of existence. Flicking paint from our hair, we pull chairs outside into the sun.

Ours is an uninhibiting street. People change and nobody cares. One day you may discover yourself prancing about naked at the lights. A woman who would never breastfeed in public will yank out her tit. A solicitor will eat on the run, dribbling gravy. There are always dogs to snout the refuse.

Kids operate electronic gadgets on the pavement. Toddlers waddle out from behind shop counters. Two-year-old Danielles and Gabrielles whine and pull at the scrawny arms of their junkie parents.

This is not a boulevard of dreams. We do not cherish broken hearts, or nurture fantasies. Your little drama will be forgotten five minutes after it buffeted you, whirled aside by another more complicated and loud.

It is no use shuffling along here peering in gutters for clues to your life. Nor in garbage bins. The deros will have got there first. The wrapping of our lives is washed away every morning by the council watertruck.

This is a place of new starts, no matter how tentative or eccentric. Your past failures will not show up any more than anyone else's. A restaurant fails—well, what could you expect? Another Greek stocktake—you could see that coming.

This is a firezone, a place where conflagrations eliminate and distract but do not cleanse. Celluloid crackles. Helicopters beat the air below the moon. Sirens howl. But what is beaten down, who quenched?

If you have made brilliant music at midnight, you may shuffle to the papershop at noon in your pyjamas. Neither your most extraordinary efforts nor your sloppiest will excite the street.

You may get on the turps all day—it's as valid a pastime as any. There is no right way here, no high road. The logic of the addict, the nut, the alky or the bored is as suasive as any other. If a healthy man elects to sit on his balcony twelve hours a day, or sleep away the afternoons in his bathtub, so be it. Anyway, he is alive—sometimes, that's enough. Disengagement is not rare, nor disemployment.

Death happens here so frequently and vigorously it flashes across the screen. We do not meditate on the significance of a single stabbing. Jealous de factos are not in short supply, nor thugs, nor careless drivers. Funeral parlours track in to the mortuary station.

Births too are commonplace: at the hospital around the corner, and in the houses where women strain to bring forth naturally. A scream or two does not matter. Up certain stairs brothels and abortionists serve their purposes. 'Gymnasium' has a flexible meaning.

It is a street of disclosure. Though each shopfront and curtained door hides secrets, things become known. The odd or nefarious event in the basement is broadcast almost as soon as it has occurred. Illegalities are noted but rarely acted upon. It is a street for getting away with things in public view. There are so many clowns you may cartwheel where you will, so many shoplifters it's worth a try, so many fools you may mount your soapbox, so many hucksters it's no crime to tout your dreams.

We throng like fairgoers, we preen like teenagers at a fancy dress, we hug our booty like kids at the Show, we paint our faces, we promenade our new clothes, we nibble fairyfloss and lick our lips. We savour the meritricious.

Flaneurs saunter in pairs.

We have no need of charities to remove our unwanted possessions. A moment in our street and they are gone. We learn to decorate with the cheap and disposable. 'You don't own me,' women tell the lovers who help them hammer up bars. Our newspapers circulate. We lend and cadge. We forebear. We are not wholly socialist, nor confessing capitalists. You must look out for yourself: that is the acquired wisdom we murmur to newcomers who flash their wallets or leave their bicycles unattended. Clutch your bag in your armpit close to your heart. Hold your baby.

We tolerate the anarchists amongst us, the doctrinaire cults, the bearded women, the fanatics, but we do not walk alongside them for long. We have seen too many come and go.

We do not search here for perfection. We take it as it comes. We make do. There is no retouched beauty here. The gamblers meet over the meatshop. The hairdresser is changing to a grog shop. The TAB is busier than the bank on pension day.

We giggle and curse in adversity. 'What the hell?' we shrug. Our multifarious gods ordain birth and death and, in between, this living on easy street.

At the first bus stop I skirt The Crazy. He's king of our street and he dresses in lordly fashion: every garment white, every day a fresh outfit. No-one can name his laundromat. The Crazy is Arabic, maybe—swarthy, anyway, with a shaven head and awesome stubble. He can be happily mischievous, pinching fruit like a kid, or he can be incomprehensibly profane. When 'The Widowed Isis' tried to take the king's picture for their record cover, he smashed their camera. They retreated to practise their saxs in the public toilets. We have smashing acoustics there, and all the sound effects.

At sunset the toilets are bolted, chained and padlocked.

In the Lebo restaurant, Johnny is helping his mother with lunch orders. He is such a fashion plate he loathes puffing chocolate onto the cappuccinos: the powder flies up into his lacquered hair and melts into sticky lumps.

Next door the rogues are flogging their furniture. They'll try anything on. One of them follows females at a too-close distance as they inspect the stacks of junk. The rogues' building is an old cinema with an ornate, crumbling facade. In high winds chunks of stone crash down onto the footpath. It is perhaps a ploy by the theological college which owns the premises to effect speedy conversions. One decade the college will bulldoze all its properties and erect a monument to words.

Artistes reside above the rogues, sweltering under a tin roof. One guy is a drummer with strapped wrists. He cultivates cactus, baby's breath and chain of hearts on the sill of his dormer window. When the rogues are standing below, watching the girl students pass, the drummer waters copiously. The communal toilet is down at the back of the yard and it's said the deluge is not always water. The drummer's neighbour convenes futurist symposia and maintains his acrimonious colloquium with the Department of Fine Arts. After dark he rings the campus with advertisements for meetings of Baudrillards Anonymous.

Beyond the vacant lot, an unshaven man sits in a tin shed full of green coppers and Kosi heaters missing their mica. He sells nothing and is content. He has no quarrel with the tax collectors. He is so ambitious to fail—he runs his hand so languidly over his chin—we fear he will expand his unbeautiful in-operation into the vacant lot.

Further along, the fruit shop men come and go, talking of Belize. They have prosperous paunches. After dark they tuck notes under the elasticised spangles of Mikah the bellydancer. 'Work it is no good,' they wink, offering thick coffee in tiny cups.

The dentist's building is spotless. Joan, his nurse, embroiders in her spare time. Her car has been broken into nineteen times to date, most recently by a junkie who'd borrowed a screwdriver from the body shop opposite. In her glovebox Joan has placed a square of linen embroidered 'Get stuffed'.

The Kota Kinabulu is so westernised its proprietor drives a Commodore, is divorced and barracks for the Bulldogs. At the Grand Final he chanted: 'Dragons, Dragons, poof, poof, poof. Doggies, Doggies, woof, woof, woof.'

Sometimes about here I bump into Ernie walking his young ewe, Sal, on a yard of rope. Sal's a skittish lass. She minces along on her clacketty hooves, skipping around telegraph poles and bunting at everyone she passes. Should you stop to admire Sal, tears well up in Ernie's eyes.

The bus stop outside the gay pub is where I first met the Paint Heir a year or two ago. He was a small, shabby fellow. In a quavering voice he told me he was heir to the local paint factory. The next time we met, he was wobbling along in women's court shoes. 'I'm changing,' he confided. He was pained but proud, like a teenage girl. The third time we met he was wearing women's stretch slacks. 'I'm getting hot flushes,' he whispered. 'Like power surges.' By trade the Paint Heir is a refrigeration mechanic.

Beyond the deli is the real estate agent who jubilates over attic potentials and wine-cellar futures. He has yet to locate a water-frontage, but he's keeping an eye on the stormwater canals.

At the bridge, where half a dozen roads collide above the railway lines, I usually spot the Penny Lady. She strides along, always in a hurry, with her arm extended—always the right arm—and a penny balanced on each finger. Around here, too, you may have to dodge the lady who sambas to the melody of a foam transistor and abuses the dummies in shop windows. She has grasped the essence of our street: there is a music in the air, if you will hear it, and a life in every body.

I stand at the bus stop on the bridge, opposite the adult cinema. A lad—brown, Maori perhaps—slouches up and drops his bag against a pole.

'Do you know where there's a shop?' he asks. There are dozens of shops in sight.

'What sort of shop?'

'One that sells condoms.'

'There's a pharmacy over there.' I point. The only other person at the bus stop, a middle-aged man, watches with a hint of a smile. The container trucks roar through the lights.

'A what?'

'A chemist.'

'Do chemists sell condoms?'

'Yes, I believe so.' I look away in polite discouragement.

'I asked in that one and they said they don't.' He is undeterrable in his simple fascination.

'Maybe you'll have to go to a bigger one.'

'Where's that?'

'A big one like Serafim's up in Darlinghurst.'

'What do you do with condoms?'

I look at him again. He is twelve at the most.

'Don't you know?'

'My mate knows.'

'Well, why don't you go and talk to him?' I fold my newspaper open at the Letters page. Opposite the letters is an article about a theatre director. I recognise the man in the photo. He is the one standing two metres away, watching me for a reaction.

'You've got a big write-up here,' I remark. On our street you may sneer or confront; hypocritical niceties are taboo.

'It's tripe.' His voice is surprisingly squeaky. 'Arrant nonsense.'

'That's no good.'

Have you noticed he is gripping a rolled newspaper in his right fist? Inside his white suit he is rehearsing a diatribe.

'As a matter of fact,' he announces, 'I'm on my way in to see the arts editor to lodge an impassioned complaint.'

I scan the article. Phrases pop out: *parochial regime*, *fascist aesthetics*.

The lad is restless. He kicks the metal pole, then balances on the gutter edge studying the cinema posters.

'Do you know there's a bondage and discipline place up the road?' I say it, I think, to titillate the boy. 'It's over Possum's Pancakes. Possum told me she stands at the back window whisking batter and watches these men in suits go up the fire stairs. She said they come down an hour later all red in the face.'

The lad turns around. 'What do they do?'

'Some men,' the theatre director states, 'like to be flagellated.'

'What's that?'

'Look it up.'

'Why aren't you at school?' I try not to sound too censorious.

'My mate told me where there's this place up in Enmore. I went and stood outside.'

'What did you see?' the theatre director enquires.

'The only thing that happened was a guy drove up in a red Fairlane and went in and came out with an envelope.'

'Money, do you reckon?'

'Have you ever been in one?'

'Not in Australia.' The theatre director glances at me. 'In Cairo. For research purposes.'

'Would it be all right if I went inside the Hub?'

The theatre director rubs the bridge of his nose. 'If it will quell your insatiable curiosity.' He smiles at last.

The lad dodges across between the stationary traffic and stands at the cinema doors.

'Isn't that the Cathedral School uniform?' I ask.

The theatre director assesses the boy. 'I went to Churchy in Brisbane,' he says, 'and that didn't stop me getting up to mischief.'

A 428 is approaching.

'Hey,' the theatre director calls. 'Bus'.

The lad scampers back. We wait until he has retrieved his bag and hopped up the stairs before we board behind him. All the seats are occupied. We stand in a row. I hang onto the back of a seat. The theatre director curls one hand around the rail above his head and holds the rolled paper in his other hand like a bayonet. The lad dumps his bag between his feet and tries to keep his balance without holding on. As we pass Possum's Pancakes, our eyes are not far below the upstairs window.

Getting out at Missenden Road I bump into my neighbour, Prue. Every autumn she goes out looking for the perfect pair of black pants. But perfection is never on sale.

The haircutting chamber is up a totally white flight of stairs: totally is the word here. I am amplified by metres of mirrors. It is a temple to everything our street, in its magnanimous tolerance, derides. The male stylists are laundry service white. Their female customers are encumbered by grey robes.

Waiting for a shampoo, I look along a row of upturned profiles: closed eyelids, flanging nostrils, parted red lips; air-brushed faces as laboriously sensual as a seventies poster.

I study the reflections of the women in the cutting chairs. They should look ugly in this white light with their wet hair slicked back off their foreheads. But they are uniformly radiant. They sit very straight, their pupils dilated. They are delighted and alarmed by the imminence of the ministrations.

The haircutter chats to me. He has checked the computer and can recite salient details. Last time he looked like Mr Spock; this time he mimics a bodgie. I compliment him on the length of his sideburns. Around me, women are simpering. Even when things are not turning out well, we dissemble, and pay up; then we rush home in flushing anguish to stand in front of the mirror or under the shower bewailing the disaster.

An hour passes. We low our thanks. We go confirmed in our youthdew beauty, a self-selecting herd indebted to our strawmen. Our scent is onanistic satisfaction.

At Social Security a sign reads: 'Everyone welcome to Larry Gelbard's Farewell.' The guy in the queue with me is quite cute in a sleazy kind of way.

'Imagine,' he remarks, 'if all the public turned up to Larry Gelbard's Farewell.'

'Let's try it,' I say.

Sometimes it is that easy.

The Time Del Got Hold of a Gun

You can see it coming, that's the worst part. And you can't stop it, you have to let it run its course: the crazy phone calls, the abuse, the threats, the police, the psych hospital, the commital. It's typical, the staff tell us. Poor girl. Poor child.

She could be such a beautiful girl. She's tall, with big bones and thick limbs and pale, dense skin and fair hair, that true blonde, and a round face with plump lips and buck teeth and eyelids with the fairest of lashes drooping over round blue eyes.

When she's pumped full of the doctors' drugs, she's like a great big doped out walking doll. Her legs stay straight, her soles graze the floor, and she moves with a serious, stately caution, one step at a time with her arms swinging, like one of those fat, solid dolls made of the early plastic. She's slow, creaky, vulnerable and magnificent.

In this area all the young ones wear black, but not Del. She's always in purple, very grubby purple. From a distance you see this great big creature coming, lumbering, swinging, staring ahead, proud and desperate, and she's like one of those bridesmaid dolls girls used to have. A toddler or a bridesmaid, or sometimes a princess progressing down an aisle in a gown and a train so heavy she can barely walk, looking straight ahead all the time at some heavy crown destined for her alone. You want to stretch out, and run your finger along the curves of her fleshy arms, and fall down and worship.

But when the terror takes over, she's a walking doll gone mad. She thrashes with those massive clubs of arms, and she boots with those mighty legs, and she glares fit to kill with those blue baby eyes. It's as if all the robots and cartoon strongmen in the kids' toyboxes have turned rabid, or a jack-in-the-box has punched you in the eye, or a top has spun out into the street to stand, whirling furiously, in the path of the traffic. You fear for her, poor child, and even more for your own children. One thump from that walloping right arm could knock a man for six.

Sometimes, suddenly, the violence goes. She blinks, twitches, topples sideways, quivers all over, and crashes face first—crashes so hard she bruises those beautiful limbs and splits open that infant head and her crown goes rolling away into the gutter.

Ah, Del, you are a heartbreaker.

The doctors, they say she's schizo or manic or something. They jab modecate into her bum. It works for a while, sure enough, but then she feels so sane she stops showing up for her injections, the dosage level goes out of whack, and then the whole crazy cycle begins all over again. The closer she leaps to sanity, the more likely it is she will skitter back into lunacy. Is that mad? Is that irrational? It seems to me it is the threat of permanent sanity which causes her to uproot herself, and toss herself back—deracinée—onto the compost heap.

Sometimes it has been funny. You have to laugh or you'd go crackers too. I remember once she went around calling herself a policewoman—dressed totally in purple, mind, so you can imagine the scene. She was trying to collect parking fines and abusing the trams for going on the road. Another time she spent every cent she had on fairy floss and set out to give a bag to every person in Fitzroy. Another day she wanted to book the Music Bowl for her own funeral. Then she told Ansett they had to fly her free to Sydney so she could sing in the Opera House. She's run up bills for thousands of dollars in Myer's, and played a squeeze box in the middle of Finders Street, and done a striptease outside the Art Gallery, and tried to steal a harp from George's. Merry havoc, I tell you.

Leave her to it, people tell us; she enjoys cocking a snoot. Sure enough she does, but at the same time she is letting loose with her tongue, upbraiding everybody who has been keeping an eye on her. When she spits the dummy, believe me, she sprays us all with saliva. Grudges, envies, criticisms—we've had them all, in the form of four a.m. phone calls and shouting in the street. What really galls is that she is shrieking out the truth. It may be a little skewed, a bit coloured, but you know darn well it is the truth about yourself and it pierces like a needle. She's a clever girl.

Soon enough, the violence follows. It has a way of driving out merriment and scattering tolerance. The four a.m. phone calls turn into death threats, compelling you to escort the children to school. Windows shatter, paint splatters, car doors crumple. She belts anyone who gets in her way. The walking doll has gone psycho with frustration at its own limitation of range. It is lashing out with its whopping plastic arms.

In this condition she moves fast. Those thick, straight limbs cease to be an impediment. She will grab a taxi, hop a tram, and in no time be on the other side of the city. Ambition thrusting ahead of her cunning unreason—those small nastinesses designed to bludgeon us into going on loving her—she goes for big targets. She bellows in banks and shouts at stockbrokers.

Soon enough, then, the police come running at her bidding. It is power, isn't it? They bundle her into a van and deliver her into Royal Park—another free ride through the city, another coronation. Ah, Del, you have reigned in splendour for a few weeks, you have flaunted your emperor's robes, and now you are back in those white hospital uniforms: clean, white, skimpy uniforms branded with the name of your palace, and they are piercing you.

We visit every day. We tiptoe in, peering around corners, seeking her out at her pleasure. We are the captives; she is still reigning, supine and wordless, in the magnificence of a needled repose. It is we who have been committed. We cannot ignore her. We must worship and pay our taxes. Fate gives them to you, these wayward child princesses. They are special from birth. You may try to rationalise away that royal imperfection, to substitute pity for fearful awe. You may say: there, but for the grace of God in whom I no longer believe. But are you kidding princess or God? And if you claim to be a humanist, you cannot walk away from a creature stripped to its humanity.

In Royal Park they try to reduce Del to one of the mob. They stab her with drugs. Her body swells. Her right arm twitches. She dribbles. Her breathing is stertorous. Her head lolls. She shuffles along corridors, reenacting her pageant.

When they are satisfied, they let her come home to her flat. Oh, foolish physicians. She outwits you every time. She circles right back to where she wants to be.

While the doctors' drugs are still discolouring her blood, Del looks unhappy enough to be sane—she shuffles like any poor worker. Her clothes are just as grubby as their's. We go back to setting an extra place for her and throwing her washing in with ours.

A sight for sore eyes, she is, down on Brunswick Street. 'Del's back,' people nod. And there she is at the tram stop, all those purple clothes tumbled on in a dreadful mishmash as if an idiot handmaiden had pulled them onto her while she was lying down. Your heart lurches: 'Look after yourself, Del,' we say. 'Yes, yes,' she says. 'Yes, yes!'

But you can see it coming, can't you? That is the sadness and the relief. That is the worst part and the best.

This latest episode began on the Friday night, at tea, when Philippa commented she hadn't seen Del since Wednesday in the chemist's and she had a premonition something was wrong. I said I'd walk down to the flats and check on her. The kids clamoured to come with me, but I limited it to Joey. He's the oldest—fourteen and springy. In an emergency he could grab a phone or push in a door without having to be told.

Del's door was propped open with a stool we'd given her, and I could hear her talking on the phone. She was ranting and accusing—something about Phar Lap's heart. Joey was all agog. He strained forward, bouncing on the spot like a boxer.

Del's shouting stopped suddenly in mid-sentence and she dumped the receiver with a clatter.

'Delma,' I called out. 'It's Brian. Can I come in?'

She came at me like a bull. Her face was terrible: all blotchy pink and puffy.

'Get out of here,' she bellowed, and went off into a mad tirade about me having wrecked her electric blanket.

'Get out,' she shouted, 'and take that little scum with you.'

I could feel Joey tensing, tightening his fists. I grabbed his forearm and pulled him back. Nodding and bobbing and apologising, I retreated. I was weak. I should have forced her to go to the hospital but I was scared for Joey and the kids at home.

'You should have let me belt her,' Joey complained, his voice all high-pitched and breaking.

Back home I made a round of Aktavites while Philly put the youngest two to bed. I was just about to switch on *Pot Black* when the phone rang. Joey answered. I recognised the gravelly, penetrating voice from the other side of the room. It was Irene Skurlnik, who lives in Del's block. Irene's a fantastic person. She's ninety per cent blind yet she copes marvelously on her own in her unit and goes out to work every day on a big switchboard. We'd given her our number in case she ever had any little emergency but she'd never rung before.

Joey waved at me to come over and listen. It was pandemonium at the other end: Irene's Pekinese yapping and someone bashing something and shouting and Irene yelling back. Apparently Del was thumping on Irene's door, claiming she was going to throttle the dog once and for all. Poor woman. Both of them, I mean.

Philippa's the pushy one at our place. 'I'll go down this time,' she said. 'Meanwhile, you'd better see if you can get onto the police.'

'Take the van,' I warned. It's not the area for a woman to go walking around alone after dark, even if she was taking Joey with her.

The younger boys were stirred up from the excitement of it all, as well as the prospect of their Kid's Klub outing the next day.

Jamie started throwing punches and trying to get me in a headlock. Jason, the ten-year-old, stuffed scrunched-up newspaper into his sleeves and strutted around playing a superhero. Justin dragged out the littlies' big pink panther and pretended to shoot it to bits with a machine gun and chop off its head with a plastic sword.

I was breaking up a wrestling match when Philly got back. Apparently Del had vanished.

One minute she'd been bashing on Irene's door so furiously she'd actually damaged the lock; the next she had marched off into the night, leaving her unit wide open and her shoulder bag on the stove. Luckily Irene's pretty level headed—she was brought up over a shop in Richmond. She was ready to barricade herself inside for the night and go to bed. Philly said she'd start driving around the streets. Del couldn't have got too far. Unless she'd hailed a taxi, in which case there'd be a flare-up as soon as she refused to pay. With any luck the cabbie would take her to the police station and it'd all be out of our hands for a few hours.

Philly cruised off with Joey sitting up grinning in the front seat. Once I'd got Jamie, Jason and Justin bathed and into their bunks, I phoned the police. I got onto a nice young chap, but I'm afraid I got a bit agitated trying to explain it all. I should have let Philippa ring. Anyway, he promised to tell the patrol cars to keep an eye out for Del, but that was as far as he'd go. I hung up feeling furious with myself for not having got something a bit more definite out of him.

I checked on the kids and then flopped onto the couch and opened Philly's *New Idea*. After about an hour she arrived back with Joey half-asleep against her shoulder. They'd spotted most of the local eccentrics and night people, and asked in all the coffee shops and milk bars, but with no success.

We bundled Joey into his bunk and, just before midnight, shut our bedroom door. Our door is the only one in the house with a working bolt. In some things we can be selfish.

'We should be lying here worrying,' I said.

There was no sleep-in for me next morning. I needed to be up at six, as usual, to get the four eldest ready for their bushwalk and then the two littlies ready for their pre-school trip to the animal farm. An extraordinary state of affairs, as any parent will have noted, to have all six of one's children off one's hands for an entire day. There is a lot to be said for these end-of-year special events, even if the expense is a killer. Let's be honest, with six boys you're grateful for any respite, and it's surprising—or not, I suppose—how few people will offer. They prefer to look at you sideways, as if it's entirely your fault for having six, as if you're irresponsible or a bit dopey or haven't got enough self-control. Though the same blokes, when they realise we've got all boys, will wink at me and say: 'Keep on trying, mate.'

Jason and Justin were already up when I opened our door. Justin told me he'd woken at four he was so excited. Jamie was still dead to the world with his baseball cap yanked down to his nose. I had to shake Joey awake.

We'd forgotten to pull their sandwiches out of the freezer, Joey had polished off the biscuits they were to take, and there was the usual scrambling to find sneakers, backpacks and cordial bottles. At half past seven Philly staggered out to croak a few last-minute warnings, and we saw them onto the Kid's Klub bus. They drove off looking bashful, refusing to wave in front of their mates. A couple of girls on the backseat looked to have their eyes on Joey.

Philippa lit a cigarette, got a bowl of Weetbix, and sat on the back step in her nightie staring at nothing. In the morning light, with the grass still dewy, you could see the little vertical lines around her lips, and the mascara smudges under her eyes, and the purple blotches in her legs. She looked so pale and wistful. 'You want to enjoy your day,' I told her. 'Go into town with Michelle. Do some window shopping.'

I wish you could see Philly. Not that I like the way she does herself up, but it keeps her young, it makes her happy. She's still in the sixties as you'll understand when you see her; the six kids and me haven't happened to her spirit or her body; she's still Del's age and bopping about on the lookout for a dream lover. It's all intact: the pancake makeup, the black eyeliner, the black curls at the outside corners of her eyes, the pencilled eyebrows, the false eyelashes, her hair blonded and teased and sprayed and pinned up in a beehive, her long witchy nails painted a pale, shiny pink. And her clothes, they're all originals: lurex tops and bermuda shorts and ski pants and mini skirts. Of course, there are crowsfeet under the white face-powder, and her tummy sticks out like a medicine ball and her nails break when she does the washing, but I tell her I love her whatever way she wants to be. She goes around singing all the old Cliff Richard songs and suddenly, in the middle of something, she'll do a funny little dance and smile as if she's just been introduced to the Beatles. Her shiny lilac lips will, for an instant, kiss the air.

The littlies interrupted our reverie. It was a marvel they had slept that long. I got them washed and fed and dressed. I tied on their sunhats and pinned on their handkerchiefs and strapped on their tiny backpacks and fumbled with buckles and wrote a note to the teacher and packed their lunches and changes of pants and, at last, dropped them off at the pre-school.

By this time Philippa was sufficiently awake to be back on Del's trail. She started in on a succession of phone calls: to the clinic, Del's counsellor, Del's psychiatrist's secretary, the hospital, the police, and Denise the GP.

I found my toolbox in the corner of the bedroom under a heap of sheets and headed down to see Irene. I was determined to fix her door before she called in a locksmith. You can't help feeling responsible.

It was a longer job than I'd anticipated. I had to do the rounds of the hardware stores to find the right lock, and then Irene insisted on making lunch for me. It was two o'clock before I got home.

Philly was sitting over a pot of tea with Michelle, her half-sister. Michelle's fifteen years younger than Philippa, and very pretty, and just lately she's moved in with a fellow and is trying to fall pregnant. She's a real chatterbox. She was going on and on about how a woman could miscarry if she caught some infection spread by cats. Word processors came into it somehow too. Philly was watching out of the corner of her eye as one of our cats stretched in its sleep on top of the video.

I felt peculiar that afternoon, really selfish. I wanted everything and everybody off the premises. I tossed the cat outside and said all the right things to Michelle and then I fished the change from the lock out of my pocket and dumped it in front of Philly.

'You've got two hours till the littlies,' I told her. 'Go to that place—what is it, Soda Sisters—and have the most fantastic lime spider you can get.' I know how Philippa loves to go out and sit in a milkbar with a juke-box and talk her heart out. She needs to do it, to let out all the strain. Though, I confess, I don't like imagining her describing all my little foibles.

Two-thirty on a November afternoon with a few dry leaves lingering and the pale sun slipping behind a cloud. Just enough time for me to have a bath, full to the brim, and let the water reheat before the boys came tumbling in needing showers and first aid. Of course a sparkie never gets around to installing a big enough hot-water service in his own house.

While the water ran I took the phone off the hook and put on some music. We were out of Radox. On an impulse, I tipped in some of Philippa's bath salts: gritty pink granules, like pink coffee, with a smell of chemical roses. At last I lay back and shut my eyes.

The door was slightly ajar because I'd been forgetting for weeks to fix the catch. One of the cats slipped in, jumped up onto the bathrim in one lovely smooth movement, and started parading all round the edge, only stopping to rub her face against the taps and lick my shoulder. I shut my eyes again and tried to doze. The hot-water tap was dripping onto my big toe. You can never keep up with all the practical things that need doing, let alone all the human needs.

The tape had run out. Half-an-hour without someone at the door or on the blower was unprecedented. I hoisted myself out of the lukewarm water. My leg muscles felt spindly and weak. There were towels everywhere—the children use two or three at a time, however much Philly shouts—and not one of them was properly dry. Philly keeps the clean towels in the top of our wardrobe to try to stop the kids getting out extra ones every day. I stepped into the kitchen. It was the first time I had ever walked naked through the house, possibly the first time I'd ever been alone in the house.

'Stop right where you are.'

It was Del's voice, with a crazy snarling edge to it. My first instinct was to grab a handful of tea-towels from the ring beside the sink.

'I said stop. Drop them.' Del was pointing a gun at me. Her face was red and fierce. Her right arm was swinging back and forth to a marching rhythm. But her left hand was gripping the gun still and tight, and I was pretty sure she was a left-hander.

'Del, don't be silly.' I was quiet and cautious.

'Shut up.'

'Del . . .' I was curling my hands around my crotch. It must have been a laughable sight: skinny me, scrawny, shivering, dripping wet in the middle of the kitchen, all knock-knees and goosebumps, and great big hulking Del, dressed completely in purple, pointing the gun at me and sneering like something out of a C-grade movie.

'Del . . .' I was so weak, a feeble excuse for a man.

'I came here to kill you Brian. You're a bad man.'

'No, Del . . .' I couldn't believe what was happening.

'Shut up.'

If I could only keep her talking, Philippa would come home. I prayed the children would not show up and be menaced too.

An argument seemed the way to go. 'Del...' I began.

I kept saying her name as if it were a magic word. The gun was shifting slightly. 'You know, Del ...'

'Shut up. You're a dirty man, Brian. And you're going to die for it. But first,' she looked down at my legs, 'you're going to do something for me.'

She jerked the gun like someone thumbing a lift—it was a gesture she must have seen on TV. I edged past her into the loungeroom. It was bizarre, something like this happening in our house in Gertrude Street on a beautiful afternoon with the cats curled up on the couch and the clock ticking.

Del jerked the gun again. 'Into the front bedroom.'

I walked like a chastised child down the hall. I didn't know what to say. I'm no good in confrontations. I couldn't picture myself overpowering this hulking madwoman while she held the gun so securely.

'Is the gun loaded?' I asked over my shoulder.

'Of course it is. Do you think I'm stupid? My father was a champion shooter.'

Every act had its own twisted logic. I stopped at the foot of our bed. Del followed me in and shot the bolt.

'Will you let me get a towel, Del?' Perhaps I could swing the wardrobe door across and knock the gun from her hand.

'Turn around.' I turned. She was pointing the gun at my chest. We were only a metre apart, inside that invisible barrier. The pores of her face were open and glistening with perspiration.

'You like big women don't you?'

'Please, Del.'

'You're going to make love to me, Brian. The way you do to Philippa. Undress me, Brian.'

Perhaps it was what I had to do. There was no other way of separating her from the gun. I spread my hands over her shoulders and pushed the purple cardigan down over her upper arms. She was a head taller than me. It seemed an obscenity.

We got her arms out of the cardigan. It wasn't easy, what with her right arm flailing about and her left hand clutching the gun. I felt like a nurse helping a patient. Del's breathing was the only sound in the room. It was loud, huffing, like a dog panting. I pictured Philly and Michelle laughing over their soda glasses, all my foibles exposed.

Del was pulling with her right hand at the zip which ran down the front of her pinafore. I decided to try humouring her.

Touching the zip edges, I said: 'That's a beautiful dress, Del. You like purple don't you?'

She brought her right hand up, closed it over mine, and transferred it to her breast. I tried to touch her without touching her—as difficult as seeing a pretty woman without coveting her. For an instant I thought of Michelle's slim body.

Del was huffing into my face. Her breath was foul. She probably hadn't eaten a healthy meal in days.

'Get on with it,' she snarled. 'Do what you do to Philippa.'

Only a couple of minutes had passed, yet the world seemed to be turning excruciatingly slowly. I was chilly and even, if it weren't for the gun, bored. Any minute I'd be able to disengage myself and hover, surveying this absurd scene. I'd float up near the ceiling rose, or swoop and circle round the light shade like a playful fairy.

The gun jabbed my arm. I pulled the zip down as far as it would go. Her hips looked too bulky for us to pull the pinafore down to the floor, so it would have to come off over her head.

'Pull it down.' She tapped the side of my forehead with the gun barrel. It was some sort of Luger, a nasty, grey thing. I looked past it into the baby blue eyes.

Bending my knees, I tried to roll the bodice down over Del's hips. The base of the zip was taking all the strain.

'Kneel down and pull harder. You're a stupid man.'

I knelt. Her hands met behind my head and pushed my face into her crotch. I smelt stale menstrual blood. The cold gunbarrel rested against my ear. We were perfectly still for a moment. Out in the street a car slowed, then picked up speed. Del huffed and pressed my face into her body.

I don't know which of us heard the tapping first. It came tap, tap, tap—up the front steps to the verandah. There were twenty seconds of silence, then a tentative knock on the glass, then a more confident knock on the wood.

'Shut up,' Del growled.

'Anyone home?' a woman called. The voice was loud, a voice used to calling to attract attention. Del recognised the voice too.

'It's that whinging Jewess.'

'Del—'

I pulled my face free. She shoved it back. She was breathing rapidly, trying to think.

'Stay right here, Brian. Don't move.'

Irene was thumping and calling again; she must have weathered a lot of knockbacks. Del pushed her hands through the pinafore armholes and struggled back into the bodice. Unbolting the door, she stepped out into the hall, holding the gun behind her left buttock. I heard her open the front door.

'Hello, Irene.' Her voice was so cordial, a parody of the society hostess. 'Come on in.'

'Delma. Well, I don't think . . .' Irene could not see the gun, of course, but she obviously didn't relish any more dealings with Del.

'Come on. You can trust me.' It was ingratiating, insinuating, the voice of a spruiker outside a horror show.

One slow, crouching step on the carpet and I could see out the bedroom door. Irene was still on the verandah, holding her thin white stick at an angle in front of her, her head cocked like a dog's trying to pick up clues to what was going on.

'Irene.' I hardly breathed it but it was enough, she heard me.

'What's wrong? Delma? Brian?' There was a grate in her voice. The modulated telephonist's tones had vanished.

'She's got a gun.'

'Shut up.' Del swung at my head. She missed and the barrel hit the wall. Still she didn't lose her grip.

'Don't be stupid, Delma.' Irene's voice was authoritative. 'If you want to bash someone, do it to me. I'm no earthly use to anyone. Brian's a good man—'

'Don't worry,' Del snarled. 'I'll kill you, all right. With pleasure. And your yapping little mongrel.' The venom was sickening.

'You can't shoot everyone, Del,' I began. Every minute we could delay, Philippa was getting closer. I longed to see her painted trollop's face. She would restore commonsense. A draught blew in off the street and I huddled my arms around my bald chest.

Irene's head shifted. She could hear something. Thirty seconds later Philippa pulled in to the kerb.

We stood still, perfectly still except for Del's twitching arm. Irene was listening intently, Del and I watching.

Michelle hopped down from the front passenger seat and turned to lock it. Philippa came round the bull bar carrying her cardigan and bag. They had not yet looked up at our little tableau. They might not see the gun, the danger, until it was too late. I opened my mouth to shout a warning. At the same instant Del raised the gun in a wildwest brandish.

'Stay back,' I shouted. I couldn't recognise my own voice, it was so hoarse and desperate.

Irene began slashing with her white stick, trying to lash Del's face and arms. Del staggered back, but she still had the gun securely in her hand. At that moment I could have rushed her from behind and pitched her down the steps. But Irene was in the way: she might have had her back broken. And, anyway, I could not bring myself to do it.

mirrors. His Jam collection was *sans pareil*. But his hosting skills were minimal—he entertained in coffee dens up checkerboard stairs and in pubs with Wurlitzers—and his wit was non-existent.

Pippa ruled herself out. She wasn't merely allergy-prone, she was hypersensitive to every substance known to woman. Cigar fumes would spread contagion through her dust-free retreat. And as for George, of course he wouldn't know how to begin to conduct a dinner party. He lived in unutterable Liverpudlian squalor with his girlfriend and her squalling child. The chip on his shoulder was so large he was barely tolerable even as a guest.

Felicity's flat in South Yarra was the popular choice. With her unerring nose for status quotients, she'd discovered a divine flat within two days of arriving in Melbourne and secured a long lease at a remarkably cheap rent. 'It's brilliant,' she bubbled. They called her Fizz. But when Noel, Felicity's boyfriend, announced he needed absolute quiet all that weekend for mixing his tapes of South Pacific percussion, Hugo's domain was nominated.

It had been inevitable all along.

Hugo was magnanimous. He would be honoured to have us all for dinner. We shuddered in anticipation.

When he wasn't being charming, Hugo was an irascible bully. One never knew what chance remark might spark an explosion. Nonetheless we wanted to see the inside of his house, a pretty Victorian terrace in Lygon Street. It was rumoured to be jam-packed with antiques and erotic curios collected on his forays into southeast Asia. Jeffery, Hugo's housekeeper/butler and general factotum, was a rare gem, unearthed in the Winston Churchill Museum in Brunei. His experience in concocting authentic Christmas dinners was suspect, but the magnitude of his other skills was not in doubt.

Responsibilities were soon divvied up. Hugo would provide the main edibles; Pippa would track down bonbons, the proper English ones; Dimity would assemble some unusual nibblies; and Felicity would do the decorations, ivy being plentiful around Toorak. Derek, who'd been reared on blackcurrant syrup and baby-cham, fancied himself a wine buff: he'd select the grog. George was delegated to help pay for and carry it—a role at which he took umbrage. Terry's sound system was commandeered for preparation of the festive music. Noel had offered his Gregorian chants, but the vote favoured comedy of the Pete and Dud variety and soppy oldies: *White Christmas*, natch, and a few of the brisker carols. Penelope would organise the games programme: charades headed the list. Patrick, who couldn't be relied on to contribute anything, was told to shave and be prepared to load the dishwasher. I was instructed to bring nothing but my delightful self. I took this as my cue to buy token presents for the tree: Fortnum and Mason preserves for the women, Twinings teas for the men, and a lethal-looking mango chutney for Jeffery.

'Superb,' Hugo pronounced over each progress report. 'We await the day.'

If you have been anticipating in Hugo a caricature—a monster of Falstaffian girth with a Rumpolian snozzle, elephantine moustaches and curious neo-colonial attire of the long-sock-and-sandal variety—I must disappoint you.

Hugo was lean and understated in appearance. True, the shaved scalp was the least bit suggestive of a pithhelmet, but it exerted a perverse attraction. Hugo's real power was disguised. You dismissed him at first glance, and then that mighty voice rolled out and you were enslaved. Hugo's father had been a bishop, and Hugo knew how to mesmerise with the poetry of speech. He knew how to lure, boost, flatter, beguile, and how to parody, and how to deflate and demolish. It was a fruity voice. He seduced you into fascination, then pounced. He knew how to bawl out a junior—you could hear him halfway down the firestairs—and how to debate with a superior. He could spout rubbish and get away with it. You needed to be very, very sure of your facts to defy Hugo.

What was he doing in Organization and Methods? Why was he applying his talents to analysing clerical procedures and suggesting departmental restructurings and consulting with the computer boffins he loved to despise? Should he not have been a barrister or actor, a detective or master criminal, a legendary orator or seducer? Perhaps. Was he not wasted playing office politics and brawling with computer nabobs whose language he refused to master? Why should he have employed his arts of blustering and cajoling merely to incite filing clerks to greater output? His temper tantrums were wasted on the beery section heads who vetoed his innovations the day after he decamped to head office. He could dominate restive staff so skilfully they agreed to try out every portion of his reorganisations, but within weeks things would be back to the usual bumbling and I would be trying to devise some fresh Special Project to keep Hugo out of the way.

I could not dispense with his services, you understand. He was still in too good an odour with The Man. But I was determined to get him in the long run. One day he would slip up, would take one liberty too many, and I would be justified.

His tragedy was that he was as anachronistic as his stopwatch.

He should have moved up or on years before. And now he was too fearful to budge. He sensed that no-one else would tolerate him. And so he had determined to fritter away his remaining working years in O and M. He had decided to stay put, to outlast me and every other new broom, to harass me, to terrify me, to undermine me. Having looked, and found everything trivial, he had dedicated himself to absurdist feuds and campaigns of attrition. He was on the skids, on the way out, whimpering and ranting into oblivion. He was still larger than life, but also smaller. I would get him before he got me.

'Cheers, Prunella.'

In the full knowledge that I detest nicknames, Hugo flourished his glass as I came down the hall. He was ensconsed in a massive camphorwood armchair, his legs up on an elephant footstool.

Felicity perched chummily on one arm of Hugo's chair, Pippa balanced on her tailbones on the other, and Derek stood proprietorially behind.

'We're all here,' reported Dimity.

'Except Patrick,' Penelope corrected.

'He'll show.' George was comfortably bleary already.

'Bring on the hors d'oeuvres,' Penelope instructed Dimity.

'We want nibblies. We want nibblies.' Young Terry set up a football chant.

Glacé fruits appeared. Then braised almonds, cashews, moist Californian prunes, pickled walnuts, even chestnuts. Dimity had surprised everyone.

'Where are the crisps?' young Terry complained.

'Shut your face.' George faked a punch.

The house was glorious in red, white and blue. There were tangles of streamers, big red Chinese lanterns, balloons, tinsel, a wispy Australian fir in a red pot, a Union Jack, and flowering poinsettias (miraculously discovered in a floral boutique by Felicity). Mistletoe dangled from the ceiling rose. Out in the courtyard the holly bushes supported strings of fairy lights.

'I can't wait till it's dark and we switch on all the flashing lights.' Hugo's eyes glinted with evil. 'Rolf will have apoplexy.'

Hugo and his neighbour had been enjoying a feud for years. Rolf played his Motown records till two a.m.: Hugo threw an egg in his window. Rolf's cat scratched up Jeffery's herbs: Hugo pitched his tea-leaves over the fence. Hugo sneered at Rolf's BMW: Rolf clogged his mailbox with supermarket adverts. Hugo played his funeral drums on Sunday morning: Rolf pushed a porn catalogue under his door. The fact that the combatants were a barrister and a Special Projects Consultant merely added to their gusto and inventiveness. Hugo's proudest moment to date had come when he'd had a portable toilet delivered to Rolf's door just as a notoriously pompous judge was leaving.

'Food,' young Terry was bawling. 'Food.' He found himself excessively amusing.

'No,' Pippa squeaked. 'We must wait for Patrick.' She smoothed down her pure wool kilt, flicked a peanut from her silk sleeve and rotated her hypo-allergenic sleepers. Any minute now she'd be ferreting in the fridge for a Claytons—alcohol inflamed her delicate white cheeks, making the fine red capillaries dance—and going upstairs to spray Evian water over her makeup.

'Patrick won't mind if we start.' George had no doubt skipped breakfast in anticipation.

'Yes,' Dimity affirmed from the kitchen door. 'Jeffery says we must start. The turkey's absolutely perfect.'

'No entrée?' Derek looked affronted.

Hugo seated himself at the head of the table. Derek secured the only other chair with armrests and positioned it mid-side, from where he could best conduct eye-to-eye combat with Hugo. Shambling over to claim the seat opposite Derek, George patted the seats either side of him and nodded to Felicity and Pippa, the youngest and slimmest of the women.

'I'm not afraid to enter the lion's den,' Penelope announced, occupying the chair between Hugo and Derek. Dimity returned in time from checking her tofu stir-fry to take the chair on Derek's other side. The stool at the kitchen end of the table was reserved for Jeffery.

Young Terry and I nodded to each other and took the two remaining seats below the salt, at Jeffery's end of the room. We were both happy to be distanced from Hugo's wisecracks. Patrick would have to squeeze in where he could—he was slippery enough.

'Sssh,' Felicity warned in a stage whisper.

'Da da!' Jeffery's forearms sagged under the weight of the silver dome. His biceps and wrist tendons strained.

'Let me help.' Derek spoke with a hint of patronage. His parents were old India hands.

'No, no.' Jeffery was defiant. He went to the gym every morning. Reverently he lowered the salver onto the heatmat in front of Hugo, who raised a long fork and carving knife.

'Would you like me to carve?' Derek enquired.

It was an excellent meal in the English style. After shop talk was banned, we conversed in clusters. At my end, Jeffery questioned me about US visas while Terry shovelled in his food. Felicity and Pippa leaned across in front of George to discuss Kensington fashions, while Derek told George a thing or two about football. At the far end, Penelope engaged Hugo in a hooting debate about the antics of a licentious earl, with whom both claimed to have spent a weekend.

'Look, you maniac.' Derek slammed the table in a semblance of joviality. 'Juventus will take it out, no worries.'

'Absolutely!' Felicity cried. 'Now let's talk about something interesting.'

'Like what?' Young Terry was plaintive. He had so much to confide about The Who.

'I know.' Dimity leaned forward. 'What were we all doing this time ten years ago?'

'Boring,' Penelope chorused, always ready to gainsay Dimity.

'No,' Pippa protested, 'it could be fascinating.' She detested Penelope's brassy, arch manner.

'OK.' Derek brandished a serving spoon. 'Two minutes to think up a censored version, and then we'll start with Jeffery.' It was a direct assault on Hugo's authority.

'Jeffery has to make the custard,' Hugo parried. 'I nominate George.'

'Come on,' Penelope prodded. She was determined to cut short Dimity's game.

'Ten years ago I was in the States,' George gabbled. 'In a ratshit old terrace on Avenue A. I was living off my savings'—Penelope raised her eyebrows—'and the occasional job: delivering handbills, you know, that sort of crap. July I can't remember,' he concluded. 'I was pretty out of it all that summer.'

'You must recall something entertaining from a whole year,' Dimity complained.

'Well, November I do remember. I got busted. On Guy Fawkes day.'

Derek whooped. 'So what's the inside of a New York penitentiary like?' Pippa waited, wide-eyed. She found George brutishly attractive, Derek debonair.

'Dunno. I got deported. Ended up in the Scrubs.'

'Bloody hell,' Derek breathed. 'Does The Man know?'

'Course not.'

'Mmmm.' Derek settled back smugly. He was a mere consultant, George—whose engineer's mind was his salvation—a senior consultant. Catching me watching him, he pretended to look abashed.

'Anti-clockwise now.' Penelope beat Dimity to the punch. 'Fizz?'

'I was in London,' Felicity began readily. 'Ooh,' she hugged herself. 'How I love London. It was so exciting. In July I'd just come up from Kent. I dropped out of varsity a month before my finals. I had a ball. Went to every party going. Met hordes of wonderful people.'

Young Terry was envious. 'What'd you do for money?'

'My darling old grannie had died and left me a thousand pounds. I spent the lot.' It was a fairy story.

'Then how did you get into consultancy without a shred of tertiary training?'

Consciousness of her Second Hons. weighed on Pippa's silken shoulders.

'Blackmail.' Felicity sparkled. 'I got friendly with an Australian fellow who was in McKinsey and Co. then and—well—he got me in as a typist clerk. I couldn't type to save my life. It was hilarious.'

'A good friend.' I spoke a touch too coldly.

Felicity shifted her glass. 'He was.'

Something made me look at Dimity. A faint horror infused her eyes.

'Your turn Terence,' she snapped. The game was turning up too much.

'Gawd, ten years ago I was still at school, wasn't I?'

'And did you always want to be in computers?' Hugo's sarcasm was palpable. Terry was the programmer attached to Hugo's latest project, in Inventory Control, and he had made a botch of it.

'Well, me Dad was a printer, see?' Terry began to explain.

'But you didn't ever go to a university.' Derek held out no hope for Terry.

'Polytechnic actually. I started off wanting to do art. Then me cousin—'

'A man of hidden talents,' Hugo pronounced. 'Now, we'll skip Jeffery—how's the hard sauce coming along Jeffery?' he winked as he bellowed. 'Which brings us to our esteemed lady chieftainess.' Hugo couldn't abide women in authority. Every Monday he railed against female ordination.

'I started out in journalism, as some of you know.' The clerical procedures writers detested my blue pencilling. 'But I got disillusioned with it. So, once I'd made it to the London bureau, I started doing the rounds of the banks and finance companies, thinking I'd get into a PR department—and it just happened from there.'

'I supposed you cried all the way to the bank,' George sneered. They were all obsessed with finding out my salary package. I suspected George had been the ring-leader of a foray into the Personnel files.

'A rapid rise,' Hugo's tone was arch. 'By my calculations you started out at the same time as Fizz and now you're deputy head of Consulting and young Fizzgig is still bashing a keyboard.'

'American know-how, sir. Plus a hell of a lot of after-hours study. Don't worry. I don't have any dim dark secrets.'

'Pure unadulterated talent.' Derek bestowed on me his most smarmy smile.

'Female talent,' Penelope amended.

'Dimdim's turn,' Pippa piped, her copper bracelets tinkling. George heaved forward and gazed into Dimity's sunless face. 'Were you always a vegetarian fanatic?'

'A vegan, yes, since the sixties.'

'Ah, ha.' George pounced. 'So you were one of those hippy radicals?'

Penelope spluttered. 'Can you imagine?' She could barely speak for laughing. 'Can you imagine our Dim...?'

'Yes.' Felicity took up the vision. 'Oh, yes. Dimity in Flower Power. Love beads. Caftans. Tight jeans.'

'Did you wear mini skirts?' Pippa giggled. 'And hot pants?'

'Ah, how time passes.' Derek sighed. 'Joe Cocker's virtually in a wheelchair. And our Dim's in tweeds.'

'And K's shoes.' Pippa couldn't resist.

'Ease off,' Hugo warned. Dimity's face was showing every one of its forty-five years.

'Come on,' George demanded. 'You started it, Miss Dimity. What were you doing ten years ago?'

'I'd just stepped off the plane. Wearing, as I recall, my Acquascutum raincoat and—'

'Was The Man here then?' Young Terry spoke on behalf of the younger brigade.

'Yes, the Board had invited him to join the firm the year before, when they finally realised the changeover from manual systems was inevitable. He found the place in a shambles'—she was directing her remarks at me now—'and he decided the first thing he needed was a good all-round systems analyst.'

'And our Dim answered the call,' Penelope supplied.

'Closely followed by *moi*.' Hugo was at his most magisterial.

He'd been asked initially to sort out the Factors Division. Derek had been hired a few months later as his assistant. The partnership was reputed to have lasted a mere two weeks. Rulers, Cafe Bar mugs, anything had served as ammunition at the height of hostilities.

Jeffery chose this moment to strut in, holding high a flaming plum pudding. He received a standing ovation. Hugo served, deciding the sizes of portions according to the current status of his feuds.

'Derek dear,' Pippa cooed. 'Where were *you* ten years ago?'

'I'd just got married.'

'She didn't ask what you were doing,' George spluttered.

'I can't imagine you married,' Penelope objected, questioning Derek's veracity even on this topic.

'I assure you I was, Penny dearest. The classic June wedding. Down in Zumerzet at Wells Cathedral.'

'Very pikkie-esque.' Felicity licked her lips. 'What did she wear?'

'White, you berk. Lashings of lace and fly netting and see-through . . . What do you call it?'

'Tulle.'

'That's it.'

'And orange blossoms?'

'I s'pose so. All I can remember is the moat and the swans and my feet freezing while we waited round for photos.'

'How long did it last?' Hugo was portentous.

'Eleven months. When I said we were coming out here, she ran home to Mummy.' He clicked his tongue against his teeth. 'She was so immature.'

'And you knew it all.'

'Come off it, Hugo. You're hardly a world expert on matrimony.'

'I came close once.' The entire company broke out into hoots of derision. 'Under extreme duress, I might add. You see, I was great pals with Lorna McAuley—'

'She writes detective stories,' Pippa squealed.

'Do you mind?' Hugo loathed being interrupted. 'As I was saying, Lorna and I decided to go through with the form of it, to keep His Lordship the bishop happy. Lorna had her own flat, of course. She'd have just had to show up with me at the odd drinkies session. But, fortunately, we both saw the light—a dawning horror . . .'

'And that was ten years ago?' Pippa interrupted once again.

'Good gracious no. Nearer thirty. I was an impressionable lad of twenty-five.' Hugo folded his hands, signifying a conclusion of sorts. 'Jeffery, coffee?'

Jeffery jumped up. Only a twitch of one eyelid betrayed resentment.

'Penelope.' Felicity's tone was ingratiating. 'What naughtinesses were you up to ten years ago?'

'None whatsoever, my child. I was engaged to a most respectable gentleman.'

'Who was this one?' Pippa almost groaned. Penelope had an alarming penchant for ageing gentlemen.

'Race Smithers, of the County Court.'

'Holy shit,' George roared. 'That bastard.'

Penelope maintained an expression of cold enquiry.

'You know what he did to my brother, don't you?' George expostulated.

'I'm not aware he ever laid eyes on your brother.'

'Put him away for two years. For something he never did. It was a conspiracy by the pigs.'

'Charming.' Terry believed George implicitly.

'It most assuredly does not sound like the man I knew.' Penelope was never one for sympathising.

'Soddin' bastard,' George muttered, refilling his glass.

'Pip?' It was Dimity's opportunity to take over as MC. Pippa blinked rapidly and shifted on her tailbones.

'She's blushing.' Derek pounced. 'She's got a guilty secret, for sure. Did I ever tell you, Pippin, you've got beautiful clavicles?' Pippa huddled her arms around her rib-cage and protested she was flushed from the coffee—at the office she drank only camomile tea.

'Ten years ago I was living in Lilian Street, Barnes,' she proceeded at last. 'I was freelancing in those days. Taking any tech writing job I could get. Half the time I was stuck with indexing.'

'Oh mercy,' Hugo roared. 'You weren't the brute who indexed, so-called, my Modern Workflow series?'

Two coincidences in one afternoon were more than enough. Pippa twitched her head from side to side while Hugo explained.

'It was some incompetent who lived out at Barnes. I distinctly remember, because I was so furious I was going to go out there and hurl the idiot over Hammersmith Bridge.'

'What was the problem?' My interest was professional.

'Invincible ignorance. Ineffable twaddle. Whoever perpetrated that index had never seen the inside of an office. It was the work of a moron.'

'I know nothing about it,' Pippa squawked.

'You're fortunate then.' Hugo had chosen to believe her for

the time being. Pippa's hand hovered over the hypo-allergenic chain on her breast.

'And now we're back to George.' Dimity smiled coyly. 'Do we want to go round again, people?'

'Shit no.' George spoke for us all. 'But, by God, when Patrick turns up we'll give him hell.' There was a roar of relieved laughter.

'Bring on the dancing girls,' Derek hollered.

'And some music.' Young Terry was suffering withdrawal symptoms.

'I propose a toast,' Hugo bellowed. 'A loyal toast. Jeffery, the glasses.'

Jeffery deposited a tinkling flute before each of us and Terry squeezed around filling from a magnum swathed in a vast damask napkin.

'Do you realise,' Derek announced, 'if Patrick was here there'd be eleven of us. And The Man makes twelve. We're a team, people. We've even got a twelfth man.'

'Or a jury,' Felicity sang. 'We could be a jury if somebody has committed a crime lately.'

Pippa glanced at George, who snarled back: 'I plead the statute of limitations.'

'Who's the hanging judge?' Derek gloated. 'Come on, who's the hanging judge?'

Dimity huffed in exasperation.

'Your trouble, Derek, is you're obsessed with physical diversions.' Hugo pointed a forefinger. 'If you raised your eyes ever so slightly above your gullet, you'd realise that what we are celebrating, at my expense, is a last supper.'

'But, but,' Pippa protested, 'there has to be thirteen for a last supper. Twelve apostles plus Jesus makes thirteen.'

'Yes,' Derek jeered. 'Pippip's right. Get out your teaspoons and count them.'

'No way,' Terry called from our end of the table. 'One went out, remember? Judas got on his bike.'

'Judas.' Felicity's eyes sparkled as she scanned each face.

'But why should this be a last supper?' Penelope demanded of Hugo.

'Intimations of mortality, my child. I fear this may be my last winter in O and M.' Pippa was looking aghast. 'Yes, my love'—Hugo reached across to pat Pippa's hand—'this is our last supper in Lygon Street.'

'Piffle,' Derek pronounced. 'Imitations of immortality is your trouble. Or our's, I should say.'

Hugo reared his head and looked down the table to me. His chest swelled as he took in air. Any second, I thought, he's going to start shouting like Lear. He's going to rail against the heavens and call down damnation on the lot of us.

Jeffery slipped to the back of Hugo's chair and twined his long, cool fingers across Hugo's shiny forehead.

Hugo expelled his breath and subsided.

'Derek,' he began in a tone of martyred patience. 'If I still believed in a deity, and if I considered you warranted the effort, I would vow to my god to take you apart limb from limb and . . .'

'Hugo,' Penelope complained, 'my Brut is losing its bubbles.'

'. . . take you apart and with the greatest pleasure . . .'

'Hugo,' Dimity enquired in her literal-minded way, 'if you don't believe in the supernatural, where are you getting these intimations from?'

'They're inflammations,' George told her. 'Piles, I'll bet you.'

'Or twinges of lumbago,' Derek vied. 'You should take Menthoids, oh great one, M–E–N . . . TH . . .'

Hugo was swelling again. His scalp was perspiring. 'You're trying me,' he growled. 'You're tempting my patience to . . .'

'Are you really,' Penelope pressed, 'trying to tell us something important?' She looked up to Jeffery for confirmation.

'The cold weather is not good for him.' Jeffery was bland as a hotel clerk.

'You could retire to Bali,' Pippa squealed. 'And I could come and— '

'But is he actually ill?' Penelope pursued her point while the others exchanged speculative glances.

If Hugo were truly ill, I would be free to get rid of him, but not with the flourish I had longed for; he would win, even to the last.

'Perhaps,' I essayed in my most diplomatically authoritative voice, 'Hugo would care to speak with me privately later.'

'What I have spoken,' Hugo declared in his Gough Whitlam manner, 'I have spoken.' He breathed out a great gust of tragedy, of grandeur and hubris and mortal smiting, and then closed his eyes below Jeffery's fingers.

Derek angled a quizzical eyebrow at Jeffery. Penelope made an 'it's not as bad as all that' face to Pippa.

'You lost me back at the last supper,' Felicity protested. 'Who's supposed to be Jesus?'

'Who else?' George grimaced and splashed his almost empty glass at Hugo's veined eyelids.

Penelope leaned forward to address the group. 'I move we

formally request Dimity to petition God on our behalf to put our poor pitiful Hugo out of his misery.'

Hugo's eyes shot open.

'Stone him,' Derek yelled. 'Rout him.'

Terry made a noise like a Red Indian warcry.

Hugo leaned forward to confront Penelope. 'Brute of a woman,' he spat.

'To Hugo,' I babbled, pushing back my chair. 'To an instantaneous recovery.'

'To a golden handshake, more like,' Dimity muttered.

'Drink with me, please,' I ordered as they straggled upright. 'To our host, Hugo. In recognition of...'

'Hugo,' George roared.

Felicity splashed her champagne at the ceiling and called out 'Wheee!'

'Well,' said Derek, 'that takes care of Jesus. And now, ladies and gentlemen, I give you God. Please remain upstanding and raise your elbows to—The Man.'

'The Man,' we chorused.

'The Big Man.'

'The Big Man.'

'The Bloody Big Man.'

'The Bloody Big Man.'

Dimity hurled her glass over her shoulder. As it shattered on the grate, she looked stunned at her audacity.

'Right.' Penelope clapped her hands. 'Charades.'

Once we'd warmed up, we did not so much act out syllables as impersonate characters. Felicity was a sultry Marilyn Monroe, Terry a gyrating rock musician. George told jokes about bishops and actresses. Pippa tried to be Piaf. Dimity appeared to be Margaret Rutherford playing Joan Baez. Penelope was Penelope Keith, or vice versa. Derek was Rudi Vallee and Tony Bennett. Jeffery was the entire chorus at *Les Girls*. Hugo, his dignity recovered and his voice box lubricated with a good port, was turning in a superb performance as Lady Bracknell when we became aware of someone standing in the hall framed by streamers.

'Evening all.' Patrick tapdanced in, executed a series of funny bows, bestowed a seraphic grin on us all, and grabbed for the sideboard.

'Quick, here's a chair.' Terry's few social skills had been nurtured in such situations. He shoved a Bentwood under Patrick.

'No, no, no. Want to party. Where's the party?'

'How unfortunate you left the front door open, Jeffery,' Hugo rumbled. 'I suppose we'd better give the man a drink. You missed the toasts, Patrick. We've already lauded our sponsors and benefactors. Would you care to propose a toast?'

Patrick giggled to himself, the glass wavering in his hand. The laugh turning to a whoop, he raised both arms in salute.

'The poor sod who owns the BMW. The poor mother fuckin' sod who owns the BMW out there.'

Fumes appeared to rise out of Hugo's brow. Jeffery rushed down the hall.

'Wonderful,' Felicity breathed, agloat, gazing from one face to the next.

'To Patrick.' George raised his glass with a ghoulish leer.

'To World War Three.' Penelope raised her's.

'To the end of Carlton as we know it.' Dimity was glowing.

'To mayhem,' Derek foamed. 'Drink, everyone. Bedlam has come again.' We drank, celebrating Hugo's catastrophe.

At the front door a hubbub had broken out. Jeffery's light, accented tones—pleading, conciliatory—were borne down by courtroom bombast.

'How bad is it?' Pippa whispered.

'Was just parking,' Patrick giggled. 'Just parking.'

Out the front, Jeffery scuttled inside and slammed the door. Rolf began pounding on the wood, roaring threats of due process, arrest, incarceration. Torture and hanging would be mild by comparison.

'You'd better go out there, Hugo,' Pippa pleaded.

'No.' Hugo was bellicose. 'No, I won't go crawling to that monster. If Patrick has sought sanctuary here, he shall be protected.'

The pounding stopped suddenly. There was an ominous silence.

'Quick Jeffery. The windows.'

It was too late. Rolf had his front garden hose to the sittingroom window and it was on full blast.

'Man the barricades,' Hugo bellowed.

'It's war,' Derek shouted. 'I'll take the top balcony.' He bounded up the stairs, followed by George.

Jeffery came running in from the courtyard towing a hose. He yelled to Terry to be ready to turn it on as soon as he had it aimed.

'Waters,' Hugo was commanding the ceiling. 'Rain down waters of forgetfulness.'

Outside there were howls of pain. I glimpsed Rolf falling back, pelted by potplants. Derek and George were keeping up a barrage from the balcony. Terry and Jeffery had the hose going now, with Hugo roaring encouragement. We women hovered, clutching cushions to protect ourselves.

'Come on you lot,' Hugo urged. 'The war's not won yet. He'll be back any tick with reinforcements.' And, indeed, new voices could be heard outside: neighbours questioning, demanding and abusing.

'Get them!' Hugo yelled. 'Get them. All these bloody plebs.'

'OK.' Penelope's eyes lit up. 'You asked for it. Come on ladies. Attack!'

We began grabbing small objects and lobbing them out the front door. Glasses, plates, cutlery, bottles, vases—all made wonderful missiles. Soon we had formed a process line and were assailing the enemy with speed and efficiency. Pippa and I scrabbled for missiles, Dimity passed them down the hall, and Felicity and Penelope hurled and ducked and shouted invective.

George had found a whip upstairs. He pounded down, flourishing it, and, taking up a position on the front steps, began lashing out at our assailants. Rolf led a fiery band of neighbours armed with shovels and rakes and garbage-bin lids. Luckily the front fence was a solid row of cast iron bayonets and no-one but Patrick had had the temerity to park directly out the front. Patrick's old Mazda Capella was now covered with dents and scratches and every window was shattered.

In the diningroom Patrick sat crosslegged on the table giggling. Fallen streamers and ivy wreathed his shoulders. Balloons drifted and exploded. The fir and poinsettias had long since been hurled out the door. As I watched, the mistletoe escaped from the ceiling rose and descended onto Patrick's head.

A siren was approaching along Lygon Street. I slipped out the back gate and strode away like a paged executive.

'Oooh.' A melodramatic groan heralded Hugo's entrance. It was ten a.m. Monday: starting time for the English contingent.

'A curse on all liquor,' Hugo moaned, dropping onto a typist's chair. 'Ooh. The end is nigh.' He clutched his brow and groaned gloriously.

'And a curse on all women. Why did I ever invite you?' He gestured flamboyantly and the chair rolled on its castors. 'Next thing you'll all be getting ordained.'

'And a curse on all barristers. Oh, my God, he's got us on every charge in the book.'

'Oh yes?' I prompted.

The Golden Temple

Jane's guitar is consuming her. It is a passion. She's at it every morning. She must do her four hours or she is angry and out of sorts. The guitar demands she come—barefooted, bareheaded—and bow over it to pay obeisance.

There is always a sequence of notes to be perfected and in her head Jane is constantly working on it. Imagining the fingering, she finds herself, at the most unfortunate public moments, playing soundless chords on whatever is closest to hand. She is constantly dreamy, listening for elusive bars.

She is a mediocre guitar player. She'll never be anything but a learner, she'll never play for an audience, except a few mates at a birthday party, but it eats her up. She will not answer the phone when she is practising. She has stopped reading newspapers and listening to the radio.

Jane has created a silent, methodical routine which prepares her to play. First, she washes: she lathers her face, checks her nails, and stands under the shower for five minutes with her eyes closed and face upturned, sluicing away apathy, looking with closed lids for an anointing from some muse. Then she dabs herself dry, pulls on a loose, yellow t-shirt and jeans, ties back her hair, and squeezes orange juice. At last, she approaches the back bedroom, where the guitar waits. She closes the door behind her and fiddles with the positions of the chair, the foot rest, the music stand, until each is pleasing. Finally, she breathes deeply and plays a note, a single, clear bell. She follows it with a beautiful graduating run of notes. Then she strokes the polished wood, adjusts the strings, and begins.

Too quickly it is eleven and she must stop. She starts work at the Tech at midday and goes through to nine p.m., when the last of the evening students scurries out. Jane is a conscientious teacher. She works right through without a break, merely grabbing a yoghurt or a sandwich if someone is going down to the canteen. There is always a pot of Darjeeling on her desk, beside a packet of B & H. When she gets home she flicks around the TV channels, downs a couple of scotches, and can't be bothered cooking a proper meal. She is intent on unwinding, preparing herself for sleep so she can rise early again to please her guitar.

Living so intensely, eating so little, Jane is thin and pale. Her breasts poke through her T-shirt like brussels sprouts. Her friends worry from a distance.

Jane's unit is creamy smooth. It has the feel of an ashram. The entry hall is carpeted in a pale plush which hushes and soothes. The ornaments on the walls are small and intriguing: embroideries, Russian icons, horsebrasses, sepia prints. A rosewood bookcase holds large-format volumes on exotic subjects: India under the Raj, the buildings of Leningrad, Biarritz, Turkish mosaics, Pompeii frescoes, the New Zealand coastline. Travelling, Jane has studied surface patterns. Like someone in a plane over the Australian desert, she has seen colours and lines, textures and contours, in extraordinary combinations. She has learned how to put together a silk prayer mat, a Chinese carpet, an English etching and an Eskimo soapstone to produce a harmony. Her rooms are to be rested in, peaceably; small discoveries announce themselves, marking each hour like a chime.

Outside Ipoh, Jane once told her sister, she found a cave. It had been a place of worship, a tiny Buddhist monastery. At one spot, deep into the hill, the limestone tapered up to a hole open to the sky. Here there was a mystery. An unearthly peace lingered, as if the gods had been drawn down through the hole, had been prevailed on to leave a benison of their tranquillity. The old fishpond was stagnant. The walls were brown and shiny wet like oilskins. The sky was royal blue. There was rubble underfoot and bats hanging in an alcove.

Jane's unit is on the fourth floor of the Connaught. From her balcony she looks across through the Hyde Park trees to the Pool of Remembrance. At the far end of the park is the office tower where her father spent two decades in a corner office.

Jane's kitchen is decorated with wood and bronze and brass: the colours of some sunset she has watched or some autumn forest she has crunched through. Her bathroom is quiet and rich, like thickened cream. There are porcelain fixtures, cool cream tiles, plush cream towels, and opaque, dimpled glass. It is opulent, fleshy as an Arp sculpture, a place to bathe at a leisurely pace, lathering on Pear's soap, and stroking oneself dry. Jane's bedroom is dominated by a puffy doona and four down pillows. Jane relaxes here, deliciously drowsy, looking through her travel books, preparing to sleep. On the wall are precise botanical prints of frangipani, gardenias, tropical fruits. Closing her eyes, Jane inhales their perfumes.

In the guitar's room, the furniture is simple, shapely Tasmanian blackwood, the walls are matt white, the suspended ceiling is a pattern of white acoustic tiles, the lighting is white and angled onto the music stand, and the floor is polished parquet. Every note can be heard. No sound is muffled or distorted. The ugly is rendered uglier and the mediocre remains so, while the rare moment of correctness hovers in the air, tingling, and then is gone, smashed, leaving only the tinkling of a blown lightbulb.

Jane's sister, Maisie, has a property, *Maravilka*, in northern New South Wales, out from Lismore. She grows peaches, mandarins and a few nectarines. Maisie's summers are unrelentingly busy. From October the trees are spotted with early-maturing peaches which must be picked and graded and packed and refrigerated and loaded onto the trucks which rumble in twice a week to take the fruit to markets in Sydney and Melbourne. The peaches closest to perfection fly off to Tokyo. Maisie directs operations. Picking begins early, before the sun; packing can go late into the evening. Every tree demands attention, every delicate fruit, and there are the casual workers to be managed as well. Hail, wind, electricity failures, rotting flesh—by the peak of the season Maisie's nightmares are unrelieved. By the end, she is emotionally exhausted.

Jane goes up then, trundling like Noddy in her old Mini, pressing the ludicrous little pedals with her bare, bony toes. The guitar, wrapped in the doona, commands the back seat.

Maisie's house is squat and cool, and empty of hubbub at last. When it was first built it looked cruel and raw, like an armoured tank grinding out of the hillside. Now the concrete blocks are whitewashed, the iron roof is forest green, geraniums and bougainvillea are spreading, and the hard angles appear to be crumbling.

Maisie sits out on her verandah, smoking, her kelpie at her feet. For a month she sits and knits and smokes and watches her trees. Her peach trees are resting now. Her mandarins are mustering strength for their turn.

Jane sits on Maisie's verandah, facing away from the trees, and plucks the strings of her guitar. In the mornings she works alone. Maisie stays inside cooking, or out the side washing, or takes her pony for a canter. In the afternoons the sisters go out in Maisie's ute exploring the moist green valleys. When the soft evening breeze comes, Maisie joins Jane on the verandah. She brings out her banjo and xylophone and they make fun: funky tunes and nonsense words invented on the spot. Jane begins to smile at herself. Maisie laughs at nothing. They share a joint, and giggle, and watch the trees darkening, their leaves merging.

Maisie cooks a meal then, something heavy on carbohydrates and butter and cream, and Jane eats the lot. Fruit is banned for Jane's entire stay, unless it be some mysterious tropical variety flown in from up north. Even Jane's orange juice is banned. Maisie gets up late and concocts huge American breakfasts and will not allow Jane to touch her guitar until she has reached the base of a stack of pancakes. In such ways they tend one another.

After dinner they sit in the loungeroom and listen to old tapes. Maisie brings out her tapestry. She is making covers for the seats of her dining chairs. She has been plodding along on the same picture—a ship under sail—for years. Jane reads, without plan, from the old hardbound books that were their father's and grandfather's.

'Listen,' she exclaims. 'This is John Gunther in 1936: *King Zog of Albania. This picturesque sub-monarch, ruler of the smallest country in Europe, is forty.* Isn't it a wonderful name, Zog? There've been two attempts on his life. He started two revolutions. He's playing off Yugoslavia and Italy. Isn't an Aussie lady married to the current King Zog? *Susan from Parkes becomes queen in exile* or some such thing?'

'Dunno.' Maisie inspects the back of her tapestry.

'Listen to this one,' Jane starts up a minute later. '*Boris of Bulgaria, gentle and retiring, now forty-one, is a doubter . . .*'

'And what's he been up to?'

'He's the worst-dressed king in Europe.'

'Surely not!'

'Listen to this, about Hitler.'

'Hmm.' Maisie is threading her needle, holding it up in the yellow lamplight.

'*Hitler, at forty-six, is not in first-rate physical condition . . . He takes no exercise.*'

'Smart man,' Maisie remarks.

'*Hitler cares nothing for books; nothing for clothes . . . nothing for friends; and nothing for food and drink . . . He is totally uninterested in women . . .*'

'Didn't he like music?' Maisie is almost pleading his case.

'*He is obsessed by Wagner . . . Hitler needs music like dope.*'

'He can't win,' Maisie laughs.

They lapse into silence. 'Tell me about someone pleasant,' Maisie prompts at last.

'One last thing about Adolf. *He had an Oedipus complex as big as a house.*'

Maisie bites off a wisp of wool. The sisters were brought up by their father. Their mother has not been in contact with them since the marriage breakup, when they were four and two. Jane can recall only the scent of perfume (she has identified it as Nina Ricci's *L'air du Temps*) and the feel of her socks being pulled up and her hair being plaited. She has kept her hair long. The sisters have broached the subject of tracking their mother down, but their father forbids it and as long as he is alive they will probably refrain.

These days their father is senile with Alzheimer's disease and lives in a nursing home in Lismore. Maisie—the baby, the favourite—visits him once a week when she goes into town for supplies. Sometimes he knows her, sometimes he points past her at a gunship or sub-turret, sometimes he smiles benignly and calls her Daph, the name he used for his young wife. Maisie wheels him out onto the verandah and keeps a lookout while he smokes the stinking cigar she has brought. Then they gobble marshmallows and sip from the flask in Maisie's shoulderbag and wink at one another conspiratorially. The sticky sweets play havoc with his false teeth. Maisie accepts his condition and contrives to invest her visits with small satisfactions, mute gestures of contempt at the system, the fate, which has brought him to this.

Jane visits, too, when she is up after the peaches. She leaves so distressed she stumbles into the park next door to cry and then broods all the way back to *Maravilka*. This is and is not the father she respected, the noble, clear-eyed man who knew about everything important.

'Leon Blum,' Jane is musing. '*A socialist exquisite*. Isn't that a marvellous phrase? *This elegant and fastidious man of letters, surrounded by beautiful books and a few delicately chosen objets-d'art, is the main counterweight in contemporary Europe to the blackshirts.*'

Maisie does not respond. Jane turns more pages.

'Ah! Mussolini.'

'Is he another forty-year-old besotted with his mother?'

'No. *No infantile fixations*, it says. He's—ah—fifty-three, and he's got five kids. And he lives on fruit! Listen to this: *He told a recent American interviewer, pointing to a basket of fruit on the table, "That is the secret of my continued health—fruit, fruit, fruit."*'

'There you go!' Maisie exclaims. 'A ready-made advertising campaign: "You too can be as healthy as Mussolini"' They laugh and make up silly slogans: Mussolini mandarins, Benito bananas, Fruit for fascism.

'Hey,' Jane cries in glee, reading on. 'There's a complex here after all. Stekel the Viennese psychoanalyst says he had a love-hate thing with his father.'

'I should have known,' Maisie laughs, slapping her thigh. They are in great spirits. They have been sipping brandy for the last two hours.

'What about Dollfuss?' Jane demands.

'What about Dollfuss?' Maisie echoes.

'He was only four foot eleven. Can you believe it? They were forever telling jokes about him.'

'I can imagine.' Maisie is short and strong-legged, with a big head. In cap, boots and red jacket she might pass for a gnome.

'*He broke his leg one day falling off a ladder*; *he had been picking a dandelion. The police discovered an attentat against his life*; *a mousetrap had been secreted in his bedroom . . . When agitated at night he either paced up and down under the bed or went skating on the frozen surface of his pot*. There's dozen of them.'

Maisie smiles discouragement.

'King Carol sounds fun.'

'King Carol?' Maisie responds on cue.

'King Carol of Rumania. He's got a mistress called Magda. *She is fortyish now, and getting fat . . . She is practically an ideal mistress . . . She is not frivolous . . . She is not avaricious . . . she is, according to all gossip, faithful to him, and this in a country monstrously licentious. She has no desire to marry Carol . . . Nor has she encumbered him with illegitimate children.*'

'Good grief,' Maisie mutters.

'Carol's forty-two like his cousin the Prince of Wales. *He is vain, stubborn, wilful . . .*'

'Sometimes,' Maisie announces turning her tapestry ninety degrees, 'I think the world is ruled by vain forty-year-old men.'

'Hang on. It gets better. *There is an ugly, jagged streak of maladjustment in his character, caused by jealousy of his mother.*'

'The father was a rotten sod too I suppose?'

'*Arid, flinty Ferdinand?* You bet.'

Jane skims on. Maisie makes a pot of chinese tea.

'Ataturk's even better,' Jane calls out. '*For his mother he had a typical love-hate obsession.*'

'Typical. For dictators you mean?'

'Apparently. *It is clear to the point of triteness that most of the great men of the world had remarkable mothers, and that the development of their son's Oedipus complex was of paramount importance*... dum de dum...'

'So where does that leave us?'

'We won't be great men.'

Maisie rolls her tapestry and puts it on the floor. 'That's about enough,' she judges, yawning.

'One more,' Jane insists. 'I have to see what it says about Stalin.' She flips through to the back of the book. Maisie stretches her legs out in front of her and rests her tea cup on her waistband, where it gives a pleasantly hot sensation.

'Miserably poor, as usual,' Jane précises. 'Sent off to a seminary... becomes a Marxist... in and out of jail...'

'His mother,' Maisie grumbles. 'Get to the point.'

'Don't rush me. This is great stuff. He likes opera and ballet, he smokes Edgeworth tobacco, he drinks brandy.'

'Ah.' Maisie grins and toasts him with the remains of her's. 'Come on,' she urges, after an interval. 'His father then.'

'I can't find that bit,' Jane declares and shuts the book.

One year the sisters go away to India together. Jane pays the fares: Maisie has had a poor season. They go in August, before the peaches. It is the perfect time for Kashmir. They stay on a houseboat and explore the valleys, then they head south, all the way down to Trivandrum. Maisie goes mad with the camera. Jane orders a rosewood dining setting. They eat like pigs and laugh at each other's foibles. Out towards the Rajasthan desert there is not a tree in sight. 'This is the way I like it,' Maisie exults. They do not open a book, buy a paper or listen to a single news broadcast. After about three weeks, Jane's craving for her guitar stops suddenly and she wonders why she has confirmed her booking back to Sydney. 'We shall return,' Maisie declares.

So another pattern is created. Each year the sisters spend a few weeks together at *Maravilka* after the peaches, and a few weeks together in India after the mandarins. Maisie comes to a standing arrangement with a Cowra couple who have lost their property and, with four teenage kids to get through school, are subsisting on odd jobs and unemployment benefits. They take care of the basics around *Maravilka* in return for their keep and a little tax-free money. The kids take off to the coast in the ute. In the nippy afternoons the husband services Maisie's farm machinery and the wife watches from the kitchen window as the jam simmers. In the quietness they discover new reserves of fortitude.

The sisters' father gave each a bequest when she turned thirty. It was to be put into property. Maisie's went towards her farm. Jane surprised everyone by buying not a spread of cheap income-producing properties but a single luxurious apartment. 'Always keep it in your own name,' her father begged, fearing that in a delirium of passion she might sign her possessions away and then, wronging spouses being what they are, forfeit the lot. He was no expert in family law but he had read a few novels.

Neither sister has shown any impulse to give away her property. Maisie, now thirty-nine, has had an arrangement with a Lismore man for five years. He is fiftyish and married to a housebound lady with a mysterious disease called lupus. He is a rep for a printer and he comes out to see Maisie on Fridays on his way home after the week's rounds. He's a fatherly bloke, enjoying nothing better than a beer and a smoke on Maisie's verandah. The bed part he's less comfortable with, but he feels obligated—she is a young woman, by his standards, and healthy, and it isn't right for her to be alone. Maisie does not enjoy the beery, perfunctory lovemaking too much either, but he has an easy soul. His visits simply happen and as they recur, week after week, she does not see much cause to spurn him. He is tactful enough to keep away when Jane is staying and in the harried weeks of picking. One day, Maisie expects, she will meet his wife. She imagines a charitable reception, a motherly cup of tea, a clasping of hands, even gratitude for a service rendered without fuss. Jane says the wife must be seething—no woman could be so saintly.

Jane's arrangement is not dissimilar. Sean is forty and divorced, his ex-wife is rearing the three kids, and he neglects to pay maintenance, for he is too busy being a teenager all over again, if he ever ceased. He is faithful only to his mates. They drink together every night and sail together every weekend. When he visits Jane it is often late at night, when he needs a place to crash. He has promised her nothing, given her little. Once in a while there'll be carnations and a splendid dinner, or he'll show up for a bit of domesticity: the soccer on tele and takeaways from the deli downstairs. Jane gets cranky with him and bans him for a month, as if he's an unruly student, but then she sighs and answers her buzzer again. He puts her contrariness down to hormones. He is a big, selfish, irresponsible baby, a cavalier oaf, but he's funny and charming when he's not soused.

On clear Sunday mornings, when birdsong can be heard between the traffic surges, Jane plays out the notes of joy and resilience. The bells of St Mary's ring—or seem to—and the bells of St Andrew's call back. One organ thunders, and its fellow rumbles in return.

One choir sings high, sweet harmonies and the other rises higher, even higher.

On such mornings Jane breaks her routine and, taking her guitar onto the balcony, plucks a happy descant for the birds.

She wonders where, at forty-one, her life is running. It has been like a coastal creek: narrow but full. At most stages it has been placid, but sometimes it has gurgled through stones and swished between confining banks and once or twice it has flooded, roaring out of control, rushing headlong, propelling logs and carcasses, cascading down rockfaces, overloaded with rain, destroying with an excess of what—in moderation—is good.

Jane will go on playing her guitar: of that there is no doubt. It is the live water in her life. Like a Yogi she has taken on a daily meditation, a lifetime's discipline.

She and Maisie will keep up their trips to India. She may even try new countries. This is how the working woman invites fate to overwhelm her. Maisie will stay on her farm: of that there is no doubt. She has unfitted herself for the city.

Intermittently, in comfortable moments on the verandah, Maisie suggests Jane move north. 'You could open a little coffee lounge in town,' she says cheerily, having a low estimation of Jane's capacity for outdoor labour.

'Too much like hard work,' Jane counters. She means her Tech hours are preferable because they leave her mornings free.

'You could open nights only, if you picked your spot.' Maisie is persistent. 'Practise all day, go swimming, get another gee gee.' Horses are a sore point since Jane's hack died of old age beside Maisie's dam; Jane had not ridden him in a decade.

'Practise,' Jane objects. 'I'm not *practising* for anything.'

'Well, playing then. I'm serious, Jano. You should get out of the big smoke for a while.'

'But I don't lead a terribly pressured existence. You know that. I just play my gee-tar and go to work. I know all the lessons off by heart.'

'Exactly. You're bored witless.'

'I'm not bored. I'm highly motivated—to play my guitar.' Jane's comic timing is out. She fails to elicit a laugh. 'You know, the rest of life seems to draw back when you're playing. The buildings, the traffic, everything looks tiny. People are like stupid little ants. I look out the window as I'm getting dressed for Tech and I think "Who cares?" Then, when I'm walking over, my mind's still caught up and I'm really vague. I try to walk on red lights, and I go into the wrong bank, and I walk right past people I know . . .'

'I thought music was supposed to open your eyes.' Maisie encourages Janc's rare passages of expansiveness.

'I suppose it does in the long run. But immediately after I've been playing I'm in a daze. I can't bear talking to anyone. If someone tries to make me talk, I'm really cranky. I get peeved at the slightest little problem. The other teachers know not to speak to me. They plonk me down with my pot of tea and say, "Don't open your mouth till you can be sociable." They all reckon I've only just got out of bed.'

'All right,' Maisie grumbles. 'But you want to do something.'

'What?' Jane asks. 'I've got pretty well everything people work for. I could do with a new car, I suppose—but so what?'

'There must be something else.'

'I should give away a lot more. When I look down Wentworth Avenue and see all the derelicts I think, "God, I'm lucky"...'

'You could give more, for sure, but it wouldn't make you happy.'

'It's not supposed to.'

'So—give away all you've got. Then what? Neither of us looks set to perpetuate the nuclear family.'

There is a minute of bitter, sweet silence.

'We've got to track down our mother,' Maisie says, looking out at her peach trees.

A car is coming up the drive. The kelpie rises and trots forward. 'Frank,' Maisie mutters. 'What's he doing here?' The dog yelps once, interrogating.

'You must be Jane.' The man holds out an uneasy palm. 'I'm sorry—' He is looking at Maisie, talking to Jane. 'I didn't see your car.'

'I put it in the shed.' Jane explains. 'The poor old thing's on its last legs. It needs a bit of mollycoddling.'

'Don't we all?' he concedes and rests his backside on the edge of the verandah.

'What can we do for you?'

Maisie has never spoken to him this way before. He angles his body towards them, resting his back against a post and putting one foot up on the verandah.

'Careful,' Jane cries. 'You're squashing the little wisteria.' Maisie has been trying for years to get one established.

'Whoa. Sorry.' He shifts on his tailbones. His shirt has caught on a bougainvillea trailer. He pulls and a small, three-cornered rip results. He twists to look at it.

'Damn. You girls wouldn't have a needle and thread handy?'

'Yep.' Maisie trots inside and, returning, hands him a can of

XXXX and a reel of white cotton with a needle protruding. Frank opens the can and drinks gratefully. He has been perspiring. His shirt back is damp. He takes his shirt off and shakes it into shape. His singlet back is clammy. There is the smell of sweat, a smell he does not find displeasing. He holds the shirt and thread out to Maisie. There is a second's hesitation.

'You must be pretty handy,' Jane challenges, 'having to look after all the housework.'

'I'm not bad,' he agrees, 'but I can't stand these fiddly jobs. I mean, I'm not very . . . what is it?'

'Dextrous,' Jane supplies.

'Exactly.' He is fondling the dog under the chin, looking for support.

'Well,' Maisie begins. They wait. 'Neither am I. The laundry'll do it for you, I'm sure.'

'Rightyho.' He drinks again, smacks his lips, smiles at Maisie, and adds, nodding his head, 'Good stuff.' He will always provide the orthodox.

Finally he goes. Maisie watches his car till it has left her gully.

'We're going to have to find our mother,' she remarks again. 'And shake off these bastards.'

Jane looks at her sister speculatively.

As soon as she gets back to Sydney, Jane tees up a personal loan and phones around for light-commercial brochures. She decides she wants a utility like Maisie's. With a good, tough, knockabout vehicle she will be more inclined to go up to see her father. Once she fits a canopy, the guitar will be able to ride in splendour. Her students hoot when she tells them and the insurance broker she phones for a quote assumes it to be her husband's purchase.

Jane spends all one Sunday afternoon in the Connaught basement polishing the Mini. The following Saturday she drives out west to a big red dealership. She stands beside a salesman's desk. Men walk past her. One answers the phone. 'Bloody quiet,' he complains. 'Not a punter in sight.' At the next place the advertised price is applicable to a single vehicle which was sold not an hour before. At the third dealership Jane test-drives a ute, settles on it, and they try to pull a switch. By this time it is mid-afternoon; Jane is tired and tears of outrage are pricking at the backs of her eyes. She finds a milkbar, orders a hamburger, slumps into the back booth, lights a cigarette and flicks through the proprietor's *Telegraph*. After a while she pulls out her diary and begins recording phone numbers from the classifieds.

That evening Jane dials the numbers. Only one advertiser is

home, and he lives down at Bundeena. Jane agrees to drive down the next day to see what he's offering.

It is a fine autumn day. Jane turns into the bush and winds down to the Audley Weir. An idyllic sight: the broad, still waterway, the row boats, the picnicking families, the gumtrees. And the weir: two fragile lanes, vulnerable, quickly covered by water when the river rises. Cars have been washed away by flash floods. People have died, floundering in this grey water in this idyllic place.

Climbing up from the river, the Mini labours. Jane studies the textures of the banksias, so gnarled and grotesque, bone-coloured. Blackboys spear up to a cobalt sky. She turns off for Bundeena and crosses a windy plateau. The plants are low, dense, small-leafed. Survivors. Topping a rise, she experiences a magic moment. On the horizon, across the haze of Port Hacking, appears a line of high buildings beside sandhills. It is surreal, a city rising out of the ocean, a birth of venus.

The road drops into the village. Slowing, Jane consults the directions she scribbled on a bit of paper, and then negotiates the skinny, hilly road leading to Jibbon Beach. She finds the fence and numbered gates. A dog is yapping and jumping as a stream from a hose plays over a ute.

'Yoohoo,' Jane calls, 'anyone home?' A man steps into view, waves, and turns off the tap. He is deeply tanned, his skin dry and lined around the eyes. He shushes the dog and holds out a stubby hand to shake Jane's bony porcelain fingers. The woman feels an instinctive trust, then reprimands herself. She has had a gutful of forty-year-olds selling licks and promises.

Jane inspects the ute, they talk, and she test-drives it around every available block. Max says he has a mate, Wal, who's a Mini fiend. Wal pops over in a gleaming Mini Cooper S and says yes immediately. In return, Jane agrees to take the ute, pending a NRMA inspection and the concurrence of the partner she has invented for the occasion. 'He'll like it for sure,' Max insists. 'It's been a great little unit.' He's selling, he has explained, because his scuba school is growing and he needs a bigger vehicle, a four-wheel drive, to cart around all the gear. Wal putters off home whistling; he has three Minis already.

'OK, then.' Max extends his hand. They shake and smile warily. It is two p.m. and muggy. 'You look like you could use a cold drink,' Max amends. Jane follows him down the concrete path to the door and waits while he washes his feet under the hose. The dog sniffs her legs. Max holds the screen door open. It is an old fibro place, bathroom-laundry-storeroom first, then a dim kitchen with a round table covered in papers.

Max takes a bottle from the fridge. 'Come through and take a look at the view while you're here.' His tone is casual. There is no overt reason for distrust, other than caution not to let a business adversary take the advantage while a deal is still to be finalised. Jane's father would not be accepting a mouthful of water, let alone imported mineral water, at this stage of proceedings.

She follows Max through the livingroom and along a hall to the front of the cottage. Glaring sunlight and the rumble of the ocean meet her at the door to the sunroom. The ocean is magnificent, a 180° panorama of waves meeting rocks, ocean meeting continent.

'The light—' Jane cries. 'And all that water.' She stands at the hopper windows staring, trying to take in all this splendour. It is impossible. Every breaking swell is different, every metre of sandstone. There are undulations, potholes, spiny ridges, a hundred shades of grey and white and cream and brown and gold and lichen. The water is constantly swirling and encroaching. Jane is turning her head from side to side like a child with too many delights to choose between. 'It's years,' she marvels, 'absolutely years, since I've been this close to something so superb.' Max is enjoying her rapture. He stays silent. Her eyes are stretched wide open.

'You should take up rock fishing,' he teases at last. 'Finish your drink and I'll take you outside.'

Jane follows Max out the laundry door and down a side path edged with nasturtiums and pigface. At the front of the house they step directly onto the rocks. Channels run right up to the house's foundations. When a swell breaks, sea water broils up the narrow channels and bubbles in potholes. Jane breathes in, again and again. 'Keep doing that,' Max instructs. 'It'll improve your lung function.'

'This lovely fresh salt air,' she enthuses. 'I'd forgotten what I was missing.'

Max is studying the cruisers moored off the beach to their south. At the far end of the beach are more rocks, and cliffs topped by low greenery.

'What's around that point?' Jane asks. She had always asked such questions; Maisie is more inclined to simply enjoy what she has secured. The obvious answer—more sand, more rocks—will not satisfy.

'A nudist beach,' Max answers with a dour grin.

'Oh!' Jane subsides.

'Actually, it's an interesting walk, all joking aside. I sometimes take scuba groups off that first point. It hasn't been spoiled by these lunatics with spearguns.' He nods at a fellow who is slapping across the rocks, ludicrous in flippers and pot belly.

'If you've got time,' he pushes on, 'I could take you down that way. It'd only take an hour or so.' Jane mentally surveys her clothing, her fitness level, her lessons for the next day.

Max reads her mind. 'Those shoes'll be fine. They've got a ripple sole, haven't they?'

'You've convinced me.'

'Whack your handbag inside. Bog Dog'll keep an eye on it. You'd be best to wear your sunnies. I've got another towelling hat—' He is walking and talking quickly, always one jump ahead of her. 'Slap a bit of this lotion on your neck. I'll go and check your car's off the road. The fuzz score a fortune in parking fines down here on weekends.'

In a minute they are off.

They scuffle through squeaking sand to the sea edge. I'd forgotten sand squeaks, Jane thinks—not in my mind, but in my senses. Max is walking briskly along the wet, compacted sand. Beer-bellied drinkers salute them from cruisers. Kids bob in the water around mooring lines. Toddlers scoop sand into buckets. Young parents dip naked infants' bottoms into the ripples. Young, single women sunbake in pairs, topless, on their backs, eyes half closed under costly sunglasses. Fit, tanned males jog and promenade. Pale women hug their knees under umbrellas.

It's easygoing over the rocks leading to the point. The water bubbles agreeably. Max talks about life under the surface. He is fascinated by an enormous stingray which frequents the reef off Jibbon. He fancies he will visit it every day and build up its trust until it will take yellow-tails from his hand. To Jane the notion is an absurdity, something grotesque out of science fiction.

Around the point, Jibbon is out of sight and it is just the two of them on the smooth, warm rocks between the headland and the sea. 'Up here,' Max directs. 'Here's the track.' They scramble up a 45° rise, slipping in grey, root-spiked sand, grabbing branches, to the top of the headland. Max leads in to a flat area of exposed sandstone.

'There,' he says. Jane can see nothing. He traces contours, incisions. Still she cannot see. 'Step back,' he orders. She crouches and tilts her head and pushes up her sunglasses. 'Stand up,' he orders. Suddenly, abruptly, she sees; the whole pattern reveals itself. There is a giant fish with a fin, and a kangaroo or wallaby, and a weird mammal, all bulbous body, with a flat head at one end and legs and genitals dangling at the other. Max points out indentations in the edge of the outcrop where the carvers sharpened their tools. He explains that, given the rate at which sandstone weathers, the carvings are only a few hundred years old.

'It's eerie,' Jane whispers. 'Can you imagine these guys carving away when suddenly they look up and there's Captain Cook sailing in?'

'Look, it's Cook,' Max jokes.

They walk on, playing with variations on the rhyme, following the scrubby edge of the headland. They stop to look down on an exquisite aquamarine cove. There are only two sunworshippers, and they are clothed.

Abruptly the vegetation stops and they are on bare rock at the top of cliffs, looking out over a shifting, roaring ocean. 'Race you to South America,' Max shouts. Jane has taken on a glazed, marvelling stare again.

'No wonder there were so many shipwrecks,' she calls back, awe deepening her voice.

'We can hop down and follow the rocks right round and go home over the top—all right?'

Not waiting for a reply, Max heads off to one side. A moment and he has disappeared below the line of the cliff edge. Jane follows, not letting herself contemplate what he intends. He is making his way down the cliff where it is least steep, scrambling down over boulders, shinnying down crevices.

'I'm not much good at this.' Jane's voice is tremulous.

'It's OK.'

Max climbs back up, holds out a hand, and helps her down the first funnel between two slabs of rock. She follows him then, skinning her hands, negotiating the boulders on her backside, testing each boulder before she commits her weight to it. At the bottom they are level with the ocean, but no longer equal to it. It splatters and rumbles.

'Let's go.'

Max turns south. The rocks are half wet, half dry. Jane tries to keep on the dry strip, close in to the cliffs. The rocks are covered with grey shellfish, tiny, sharp parasites which prickle through her soles. Max is carrying his thongs, unworried. He hops, jumps, skips, almost dances. He exults. He is unabashed, exhilarated.

Jane keeps her eyes averted from the ocean. She concentrates on finding a dry, stable path over the rock ledges. Every metre seems more difficult, fraught with holes and traps. Each step must be planned, not abandoned to the vagaries of instinct and chance.

The cliff to her right gives way to a jagged opening. Stooping she looks into a cave, big as a room, floored with rubble. She ducks and steps inside. 'When it's high tide,' Max observes from the opening, 'this is full of water. Completely full.'

Jane realises—as if for the first time—that the tide must come in. The ocean can extend its reach indefinitely; it is infinitely treacherous. The tide is, indeed, pushing in now. Each swell is more noisy and assertive. Each directs its malignant strength at Jane. She must keep going, or she will be overwhelmed. Max, for all his good humour, will not be able to save her if she cannot keep going. She is in a trap. She squints up at the cliff face. It is unclimbable. She looks around. More and more rocks, with waves breaking over them. No beach or headland or greenery—no sure end.

She is very afraid. The fear tangles her feet. She becomes unsteady. She stumbles, lurches, slips, catches at boulders. She is desperate to keep up with Max but embarrassed to cry out for reassurance. It is an endurance trial now, and she lacks the experience to be confident of finishing. She is reduced to a vulnerable body, porcelain bones unskilled in preserving themselves in the natural world. She knows how to fend for herself with her mind and words, but here words are worthless, and book-learning is denounced as self-indulgence. The mindless ocean will outwit her.

Max's pace seems to be sharpening.

'Aren't you worried?' Jane pleads to his ridged back. Her voice is squeaky as a gull's cry, as feeble and transient.

He looks around and winks. 'Nah. I know the tides 'round here. There's plenty of time.'

'It's coming in terribly fast.'

'Yeah, you're right. But there's not far to go.'

'What are these king tides you hear about?'

'Yeah, well, they hit sometimes. We get out the old sandbags and batten down the hatches.'

Jane has no reply.

Max stops. He has reached a spot where there is a head-high boulder ahead of him, on the far side of a chasm a metre wide. He watches the water. It rushes in, splashing up onto the boulder, then rushes back. All is still for a few seconds and then a new swell breaks and pours in. Jane draws in beside him, touching his elbow. They watch and assess. 'We'll have to be nippy,' Max comments, as green ocean splashes over their feet. He waits, braces himself, and leaps. His right foot lands on a knobbly bulge in the boulder, his fingers spread over the rock, his left foot scrabbles for traction.

The water roars in again. Max has made it to the top of the boulder. He turns and holds out both arms. Jane can see nothing but the crevasse, the slippery rocks, the waters conspiring to pull her under and whirl her out into the maelstrom. She can place no faith in her own capacity to jump. She is weak.

'Ready.' Max speaks like an army instructor. 'Jump. Now.'

Jane has hesitated too long. The water rushes in. The rock is shiny brown.

'Next time,' Max calls more gently, forgiving. 'Ready?'

She breathes in; her heart shudders, her legs tense. A flailing leap and she is spreadeagled against the boulder, panting and gasping, feet scrabbling to get a grip. Max has her around the shoulders. For an instant he topples forward and she fears she will pull them both in. The cold ocean rushes in, washing over her legs. Max hauls her up.

There is no time for words. Max leads on, faster than before. She is at his mercy. If he were not leading, she would panic. She would be overcome with terror. She would cringe against the cliff and wait for a tidal wave to overwhelm her, breakers to bash her against the sharp rocks, long slimy strips of seaweed to enmesh her.

'Look at this,' Max calls back. He has reached a quieter stretch. The rock platform is wider, and dry. The ocean is unaccountably mild. Max is squatting, looking into a pothole full of perfectly clear water.

'See the starfish.' He whispers, as if afraid he'll wake a baby. Watching him, she understands how he can love a stingray, and speculates how the stingray must feel.

They potter about the platform, calling to each other to look at odd shells and sea creatures. The rock is yellow, and layered and tilted like a stack of Maisie's pancakes. At the end of the platform they step onto a beach composed entirely of gritty grey-white shell fragments.

Max points. The cliff has broken down at last. It is a mere slope, a jumble of boulders. 'Easy,' Jane crows. 'I'll beat you up.' The prospect of escape elates her.

'Have a paddle first,' Max cautions. Jane realises it is very hot. The sky is uninterrupted blue, the sun gold, and she is red from sunburn, exertion and agitation. Max points to a spot where she can sit on a ledge and rest her legs in the shallows. She sits, and splashes her face and arms, and feels her breathing returning to its normal rate. 'I'm sorry,' she says in a flat voice. 'I was scared silly back there.'

In silence they scramble up through the boulders towards a line of greenery. Absurdly, it is a stretch of lawn—couch, recently mown. Jane laughs at her own terror. 'The natives have put out a welcome mat for us,' Max chuckles.

They trudge through wild grasses and tough, khaki plants, heading north, back towards Jibbon. Jane does not turn to farewell the ocean.

The low growth becomes shrubs, then saplings. Creepers and dense, prickly bushes encroach on the track. Jane jokes about huntsman spiders. Max is not so sure of himself in this terrain. The bush opens abruptly into a cleared patch with the remains of a cooking fire. Max laughs aloud with relief.

The track heads into a stand of tall trees. It is cool and moist and silent under the branches. They are in a fairystory hideaway, a magic cave.

'Did you know there are deer in the park?' Max's voice is hushed. 'I spotted a whole bunch of 'em late one afternoon.'

A whipbird cracks. They crunch over twigs. Another bird cries out, alarmed.

The bush thins. They are coming out. Jane recognises the southern end of Jibbon. The drinkers are still making rowdy fun on the cruisers. In an instant their presence will transform her from primitive adventurer to self-conscious promenader. Jane no longer cares. She tucks her dress hem into the bottom of her underpants, pulls off her shoes, and runs helter-skelter into the friendly water. No-one cares. She sluices herself all over, slopping water over her face until her hair is dripping. Max watches, amused, for a minute, then ambles, hands in pockets, up the beach. Jane runs on the firm, wet sand, sure-footed now, waving her shoes. She snatches at Max's dry elbow, overtakes him and runs on to wait, laughing and panting, on the rocks outside his house.

He directs her into the bathroom and hands in a towel and shavecoat. While she showers, he hangs her dress in the sunroom; it is sheer Indian cotton and will not take long to dry.

Jane slumps into an armchair in the dim, cool livingroom. In here, she can scarcely hear the ocean. It cannot menace her. She takes the plate of sandwiches Max has cut and eats the lot, not realising he meant to share them.

'So,' Max asks. 'When's this partner going to come down for a test-drive?'

Jane meets his eyes. 'We'll see. He's a pretty elusive character.'

Maisie phones on Sunday night after the movie. This is the sisters' custom.

'How've you been getting on with that business?'

'Which business?'

'You know—getting leads on Daph.'

They can no longer say 'our mother'. It must be 'Daph', their father's pet name, spoken in a coyly derisive way, as if she were a cartoon character.

'I've been too busy. Did I tell you I'm trying to get a ute like yours?' After spending all the previous Sunday afternoon rubbing duco and chrome and vinyl, she said nothing about it that night.

Maisie listens to the tale of the car: the Saturday encounters, in all their stark duplicity, and an abbreviated version of the Sunday negotiations. 'Okeedoke,' she clucks at the end. She sounds like a world-weary Consumer Affairs Investigator. Jane waits in vain for congratulations.

'Tell me,' Maisie tackles, 'why are you stalling doing anything about the other business?' 'You're the older sister,' Maisie used to say, 'you do it.'

'I know. I know. Look, I'm going about it in my own way. First I've got to get my own house in order, get a reliable car...'

'Then?'

'How's the old man?'

'A lot less cranky now the weather's cooling off.'

'You're doing a marvellous job, little sister.'

'All right—see what you can do this week. Please. I mean it.'

'Sure. As soon as I get my new brrmm brrmm.'

The following Sunday Jane takes her Mini and bank cheque and rego documents down to Jibbon. Wal and Max have a little celebration lunch ready: king prawns, crab, lettuce, bread rolls and beer. After they have eaten, Jane stands at the gates watching Wal drive away in her Mini. For the moment she is forlorn—friends of twelve years' loyalty are not readily waved off.

Max seeks to cheer. 'You'll have to come down and see the old girl when Wal's tarted her up.'

Jane turns aside, toward the house.

'Cuppa tea time, eh?' He speaks as if he understands loss.

'Want to sit out in the sunroom?' he calls from the kitchen.

'No.' Jane sits resolutely in the livingroom. Even in here she can hear the power boats.

'So,' Max says, settling into his reclining chair, 'why are we both unattached?'

'You're hardly subtle, sir, but go on.'

'I'm interested, seriously.'

'You tell me then.'

'I'm divorced.' Jane waits for him to continue. 'We split up four years ago. She was a real go-ahead lady. I couldn't keep up with her.' Jane is silent still. 'She had this incredible intensity. She was all the time changing. Pushing ahead, you know? After a while she was bored to tears with me.'

'You left.'

'No, she left.'

'How long ago was that?'

'Four years.'

'I'm sorry. You said it before.'

'The first two years were hell on wheels, I can tell you. Then I snapped out of it and decided to get stuck into the diving.'

'And—voila—a happy ending?'

'Well, if you call obsession happy, things are looking good.'

Jane nods her understanding. 'Well, how come you haven't been working these two Sundays?'

'I had to cancel a course. Technical difficulties.'

You couldn't get enough starters?'

He looks surprised.

'It happens at the Tech too,' Jane explains.

'Leaves you feeling a bit inadequate,' Max takes up again.

'Sure'.

'Wal tells me I need something else.'

'A woman, I suppose.'

'Yeah.' He studies the coffee table. 'I meet a few girls through the courses. Funny relationship, though, when they're twenty metres under and you're up top holding the line.

'What's Wal do with himself?'

'He's a mapmaker. Draws up those street directories.'

'He seems a good bloke.'

'Not much in the brains department, our Wally, but he's painstaking.'

Jane sees the contour lines, the cul-de-sacs, the whorls like fingerprints, a shifting psychedelic design which renders the land negotiable but not the ocean.

'So, what's *your* obsession?' Max pours her another cup of tea, obliging her to answer. 'You're a pretty intense type, aren't you?'

Jane had thought she radiated serenity.

'My guitar. I die a thousand deaths if I can't play it every day.'

'It's funny you say my *guitar*, not *music*.'

'Well, score one point.'

A new pattern is mapped out. Throughout the winter Jane drives down to Jibbon very early each Sunday, the guitar riding on a foam mattress under its canopy. Jane occupies Max's sunroom and plays away the rest of the morning, wooing the ocean to teach her new sounds, to wash away remembrance. If Max is teaching, she does not see him until late afternoon. If he's at home, he keeps out of her way before lunch: washing sheets and towels, cleaning his four-wheel-drive or giving Bog Dog a flea rinse. After lunch they go out on Wal's boat, or swim if it's mild enough, or walk. By unspoken consent they never go around the rocks below the cliffs. Jane has been tested sufficiently. In this environment she is the weaker vessel.

In the August Jane and Maisie go, again, to India. In Amritsar, outside the Golden Temple, Maisie asks: 'What are we going to do about our mother?'

'What is our mother doing about us?' Jane responds.

In India's equivocating wisdom there is no answer. Their mother must be seventy now, an elderly woman. Surely sentiment will propel her to them.

'What have you done about Frank?' Jane asks at Devprayag, where two rivers run into each other to form the Ganges.

'His wife had to be put into a nursing home. He started turning up every second night. I had to tell him to shove off.'

'You should have done it months ago, when you said you would.'

Maisie does not respond. 'Who's this, then?' Jane asks, watching Maisie address a postcard.

'Howard. My latest gentleman caller.'

'What's his problem?' Jane does not mean to sound harsh, but a younger sister is a ready target for protective scolding.

'He's a perfectionist, I suppose you'd call him.'

'An obsessive–compulsive,' Jane translates. 'What's he do?'

'Oh, he doesn't work. Chiefly because he can't ever finish anything to his complete and utter satisfaction.'

'That's a good excuse.'

'Everything has to be just right. He won't buy a newspaper if it's got a creased corner. He spends hours in the newsagent's, he told me, going through all the stacks.'

'In vain, I suppose.'

'Yeah, he goes away with nothing.'

'What's he doing about it?'

'Nothing. Except talking. He garbles on incessantly.'

'What about?'

'Half the time it's the most marvellous gossip. He knows the entire district. The rest of the time it's about his traumatic upbringing, for which he blames his father.'

'Huh. We should lend him John Gunther.' Maisie looks

blank. 'You remember. Benito bananas. Dictators with dominating mothers.'

'Oh yeah.'

'How often do you see him?'

'He shows up every few weeks, whenever the mood strikes him.'

'How can you stand it?'

It is a rhetorical question. Poor old Maisie. It is evident she could love him.

'It's just occurred to me,' Jane announces as she addresses an envelope. 'You'd get on well with Max's friend Wal.'

'No matchmaking, kiddo.'

'Don't worry, you'll never meet him if you won't come down to stay with me. But I'm sure you'd understand each other. You go about things the same way.'

'I'd come down if it weren't for the old man.'

'I know.'

As summer approaches, Jane's pattern changes. Sean's intercession is not required. She now drives down to Jibbon on Friday night and does not get back to the city until eleven a.m. Monday. She is not unhappy to spend the weeknights alone at the Connaught, for she stays at Jibbon on Max's terms. She has not sought to alter him or his house. Inevitably both are changing, but comfortably, in a natural response a woman's presence. There have been no flare-ups. It is the sort of still loose connection where, if too much static develops, one party will simply detach themselves. They are both too wearied to want wholesale reformation of temperament. Jane will accept a certain amount of trickery. Max will tolerate reserve, the refusal to divulge what matters most. Both conserve a measure of energy for their obsessions, which prevail unaltered. These obsessions have demanded accommodation; the new pattern has had to be sketched in around them. Jane disdains the female who abandons a vocation to reassure a male, who takes on male-hunting and male-securing as her obsession.

Then, one blustery April night, in one of those instants of determination which fill the mind at three a.m. and are forgotten at eight, Maisie renews her resolve to find her mother. It will mean a trip to Sydney.

She waits for an exceptionally lucid moment in her father, feeds him a swig of Courvoisier, and extracts her mother's last known address. It is the same as the one they have always known. It must be the starting point.

Maisie proceeds methodically now: she secures the services of the Cowra farmsitters for a fortnight, has her ute serviced, buys a dress, mails Howard a meticulously printed note, contacts suppliers and visits the bank.

'I'm going away for a little while,' she tells the neighbours. She cannot stop miming the refrain, 'I may not return.'

Maisie times her arrival at the Connaught for ten p.m. Tuesday. She presses the security buzzer.

'Come on up, little sister.' Jane fusses around arranging parking (she has borrowed an absent resident's unused space for the fortnight), setting out supper and clearing hanging space.

'Calm down,' Maisie complains. 'I'm not royalty. Anyway, you can't have been home long yourself. Don't you lecture till nine?'

'Oh, didn't I tell you?' Jane looks innocent. 'This is the May break. I'll be able to come out hunting with you.'

Maisie had envisaged a sole triumph. She would locate her sweet, mellow mother, stir the old dear's latent affection, and then with due solemnity introduce her elder sister.

'Oh, well,' Maisie smacks her palms together. 'Last known address: Kangaroo Street, Manly. Nine a.m. tomorrow.'

'I can't start till eleven. I have to do my guitar.'

Maisie spends the morning with an open phonebook. There is, of course, no Daphne Muriel Lamerton listed at the Manly address.

'There's not much point in going to Manly then, is there?' Jane interrupts, pleased with her power to deflate. 'But—' seeing Jane's face, 'we might as well.'

Maisie phones twenty other Lamertons and that evening over supper the sisters plan a campaign: Births, Deaths and Marriages, the Red Cross tracing service, interstate phone books, old people's homes, and advertisements.

By Thursday night the tussling between the sisters is disturbing the unit's calm. Jane retreats to her bathroom and stands under the shower, combing conditioner through her hair. Maisie bends over her phonebook and note pad. Jane pads into the bedroom and slips on a fine Swiss cotton nightgown. She plumps her pillows and takes down a new picture book she has been saving for a stressed occasion. Then she opens the door, says 'I'm going to Jibbon as usual tomorrow night. Sleep well,' and closes the door gently. Maisie is sleeping on the sofa; the guitar's room may not be invaded.

Jane returns the following Monday chatty and light-hearted. Maisie has been working all weekend, methodically following up leads. Jane joins in with a rush of enthusiasm, but she is a liability. She needs to be told what to do, so she will not retrace Maisie's steps, but she is not pliable enough to take direction from a younger sister. On Tuesday Jane finds things to do back at Tech. On Thursday night she asks: 'Why don't you come down to Jibbon? Enjoy your last few days.' Maisie acquiesces.

Wal likes Maisie at once. At the RSL he jokes and exaggerates and buys her drinks. She matches him middy for middy. Next morning he tells himself not to be a loon. Jane has already appropriated his best mate. He was never a fan of *Seven Brides for Seven Brothers*. Maisie tells him she will head home to *Maravilka* on Tuesday.

A message is waiting on Jane's answering machine back at the Connaught. The director of the Anglican Nursing Home at Gordon has a patient called Daphne Muriel Haines, also known as Daphne Lamerton.

Maisie phones at once. The old lady is said to be frail, a wee bit senile, and she cannot take too much excitement, however her son is not averse to her meeting the two ladies. Would they care to visit for morning tea at ten the next morning? Matron will be delighted to make her private sittingroom available.

'Her son.' It has never once occurred to the sisters that their mother has betrayed them by giving birth to more—dearer—children. The simplest, most obvious, natural possibility—but in their egocentricity they have thought themselves the only ones. They have believed she has been avoiding them out of guilt and grief, even malignity, but not because she has had other loved ones. One son—how many more? One lover—how many followed?

'We'd better leave about nine,' Maisie muses, wondering whether her dress will be good enough.

'I can't.'

'What do you mean?'

'I have to do my guitar. Change it to afternoon tea.'

'Jane, this is your own mother! We've been looking for her for thirty-seven years.'

'Then another few hours won't hurt.'

'I can't believe you. You're . . . you've got no heart!'

'I'm sorry. But my music is the greatest thing in my life. I owe it that much loyalty.'

'You drop it readily enough when we go to India.'

'It hurts every hour I'm away, believe me. It hurts like an amputated arm.'

'But—'

'No, Maisie. Phone back.'

'Look, *I* was going to leave tomorrow morning. My farm matters just as much to me. And so does Dad. But there's no question I'll go now.'

'I won't go in the morning. That's that.'

'Do you want me to go without you?'

'No. Oh, no. We'll go together. I'm sure the afternoon will be O.K.'

They cross a stone-flagged terrace, open a white door and look into a sittingroom with drawn curtains. A lumpy woman fills a wheelchair. A man sits primly at her elbow, leaning forward, hissing to her. 'Who are these people?' she asks, blinking at the light. Jane pulls the door shut. Maisie kneels and looks into the pink eyes. Jane sits and plucks limp fingers. The woman has no idea who they are. The son stands in front of a tapestry of a Spanish galleon and watches.

A nurse aide serves tea in Country Roses cups on a silverplate tray. 'Where's my biscuit?' the old woman quavers. She always has one arrowroot, the son tells the aide.

'I brought you something,' Maisie croons, opening her shoulder-bag. The smell of peppermint has lingered with her for thirty-seven years. She draws out a packet of Extra Strong Peppermints and holds one to her mother's lips.

After a nurse has wheeled the old woman away, they stand with the son on the terrace. Jane twists her hair in her fingers.

'There's no doubt, of course?' Maisie ventures.

'No. I have all the papers. Birth Certificate and so forth.'

'Are there more children?'

'No.'

'I'll be glad to get back to Jibbon,' Jane thinks. 'It's cleaner.'

The pieces have all come together now. The pattern, once revealed, is not entirely satisfactory. They will think about it on winter nights and, plucking at the pieces, imagine other outcomes.

The Hoary Frost of Heaven

Delivering the keynote address at a crusade in Hobart one July, Leonard Faulkner chided the Tasmanians for the freezing weather they had turned on for him. Whose bright idea was it, anyway, to make the earth's climate so various? Well, God's of course. My God, Leonard confided, owns whole treasure houses full of snow and hail. Ice is born of Him. He spreads the clouds and throws around the lightning. There is thunder in His pavilion. Rain has no father but Him. It is He who spreads out the sky like a molten mirror. Even the frost—the hoary frost of heaven—who has given it birth?

As he moved on to declaiming Job's response, Leonard became aware of a young woman watching him intently. He was used to female adulation and welcomed it on these occasions as a spur to a comic performance; it was, however, the older males in the audience to whom he played. A callow youth kept glancing over his shoulder at the young woman. The limitations of his intentions were written on his smooth forehead. Leonard felt a twinge below his heart. He cringed like Job and then, straightening up, read God's part in a hectoring voice: *Where were you when I laid the foundation of the earth? . . . Have you comprehended the breadth of the earth? Tell it, if you know it all.*

The youth lacked the perspicacity to look rebuked. He rubbed at a pimple with his index finger while the young woman regarded Leonard with crooked eyes. Leonard stared back with the late-night bravado of the lone male driver compelled to honk at the lone female pedestrian.

At supper, Leonard contrived to speak to the young woman, whose name was Nerida, and obtain the name of her employer.

The following day he phoned her at work and, at eleven p.m., after the evening's meeting, they drove south out of the city in Leonard's hired car. Past Taroona, Nerida pointed out the Shot Tower and attempted to explain how it had been used. She had a self-conscious little laugh. At Snug, Leonard asked if she were warm enough and she assured him the heating was great, much better than in her mother's car. At Kettering, Leonard pulled over and they sat looking out across a black channel to an unseen island. Unnerved by the absence of talk, the girl began to describe Bruny's attractions: Captain Cook's landing place, Cloudy Bay, the lighthouse, the Missionary Hills. Hot air blasted their ankles. Outside it was frosty and extraordinarily still. They wound down their windows and snorted the fierce midnight air. The cold stung their eyes. The girl's nervous, anticipatory blinking made a toy of thought.

'I want the best for you,' Leonard said. 'You want to ask for more out of life than a small-town lout.' The girl looked up and across at him, submitting to whatever he ordained.

Leonard had not intended to let her slip between his fingers. As he drove back, he told himself she was less mature than he had at first fancied. Her wordlessness confirmed it. I was a father in God to her, his serpent told him. He cut the engine as he turned into her family's cul-de-sac and coasted into the driveway. The house was utterly quiet and secretive, the lawn frosted over. The young woman smiled at Leonard in relief and apology and scampered inside.

Leonard Faulkner's first wife, Joyce, survived in a shoebox in the bottom of the wardrobe. She had reduced herself, like a genie, to a bundle of photos, letters, documents, and radiologists' receipts. When he needed her, Leonard conjured her out in miniature and held her in his cupped hands before his audience. 'Behold,' his attitude said, 'suffering. Behold my years of devotion.' He made his trial seem exceptionally difficult, his devastation more painful than the average. One day, at the behest of his fans, he would author a book about it. His second wife, Merle, who had been his secretary through all those years, would man the word processor whilst he dictated.

In addition to his wives, Leonard had a son and a sister. The son, now twenty, had left home and was rarely referred to in public. The sister, Valerie, lived down the road in Zillmere, opposite a poultry farm. It was Leonard and Merle's practice, after calling at the farm for a tray of brown, smelly eggs, to drop in on Valerie. They never stayed for long, however. Leonard could not abide the young ones' caterwauling, and Merle recoiled from the pity and disparagement with which Valerie regarded her.

Valerie's existence was ruled by the unreason of her hormones. Unable to give birth, she had become obsessed with having babies around her. Every room was occupied by a couple of squirming bundles and their accoutrements. She minded as many infants as the Council would permit and then more. She was unscrupulous in getting hold of them. Working women, immature teenage mothers, deserted fathers, the sick, the idle—all were sources, and she pursued her quarries without compunction.

Her husband was cowed into acquiescence. He crept in late from work, ate, watched TV and crept into bed. Fumbling and reticent, he reached for his wife and she spurned him. He had failed through no insufficiency of his own as a procreator.

It was a place devoted to feeding, excretion, ablutions and babytalk. Anyone might bring their vile body here and feel accepted. Hunger, thirst, colic pain, squalling, infantile jealousy, sniffles, giggles, sleepiness, juvenile infatuation—all were encompassed. The body sat on the throne. There was always some visitor at the kitchen table. It was a place for helping hands. The only reciprocation asked was a demonstration of love. The babies were to be cuddled.

Leonard had fathered his Believers' League at forty-five. Its birth was the culmination of a steady grappling rise through the ranks coupled with what he now described as 'a bit of a thrash' with a past dignitary. He had created for himself an open brief, a roving ministry. He kept in good with the boards and committees, he was *au fait* with the gossip, he knew which head was about to roll. He had appropriated for himself the position of informed adviser, the man of the world whose beat was out there in the marketplace. He had a realistic estimation of the limitations of his entrepreneurial freedom and, knowing the quarters from which resentment was most prone to emanate, had secured the banishment of several critics. He accepted only a small retainer from his denomination, insisting that, if his Foundation were truly of the Lord, it would be self-supporting. He was zealous in distributing reports and audited balance sheets. He appreciated the virtues of both autonomy and official sanction. His renown as a motivator had spread, and he was frequently invited overseas. He had spoken in La Paz, Lautoka and Lausanne, Keswick, Kenya and Karachi.

He was an advocate, as appropriate, of both the fundamentals and progress. He popped up at unlikely gatherings, secular and religious. Tables were held for him. On home territory he nipped from group to group, Merle driving steadily through the night while he consulted his portable card index. There was a phone on the van's dashboard, a typewriter in the back and a change of shirt rocking against the side window. Merle would not accompany Leonard outside Queensland, having a superstitious dread that her elderly mother would expire while she was absent. She was content to stay at home in Boondall, attending to the office, the literature and tape distribution and the juggling of Leonard's appointments.

Leonard worked hard on his lectures, the portion of his activity most often scrutinised by the powerful. He laboured to splice his footage into a seamless moving picture. One sales pitch merged into the next. His pauses were as precisely placed as sprocket holes.

Figures, however, had a habit of escaping his control. His enthusiasm was such that the estimated attendance at a rally rose by a thousand with each retelling. Conversely, his salary dropped by a thousand with each low-voiced confiding of a supporter.

Leonard's overt calculation was regarded by some with winks of recognition and disdain, yet no-one moved against him. It was grudgingly agreed his style must be endured rather than cramped. There must be the presumption of innocence. Certainly it was hoped the Big Boys would clip his wings, or he would leap so high he'd come a nasty cropper, but no-one would aim the first stone directly at his breast. Women excused him; men acknowledged themselves out-manoeuvered. 'Caio, caio,' he'd call cheerily to his detractors. 'I've got to hit the cane!'

In his person Leonard flaunted the tougher expanses while protecting the smaller, more intricate mechanisms. Thus his shins—great scarred, ridged columns of bone packed with marrow—were exposed by the too short legs of his trousers, yet his ankles were shawled in woollen work socks and his toes relaxed between steel caps and one-inch soles. His freckled forearms were bared by short-sleeved shirts worn with suit jackets too short all over, yet his watchface was cupped under a brown leather shell. His thick neck, bullish shoulders and broad, flat hands were all on exhibit, along with that characteristically Australian cube of the lower face, yet his low forehead, hairy eyebrows and narrowed eyelids protected his eyes so thoroughly that he looked like a blind man, his eyes closed into two useless lines of gluey secretion. His lips stayed so close, and he spoke in such a rapid slur, that teeth, gums, and tongue were all kept secret. The ears protruded, yet riffles of fine hair guarded their entrances. So, too, with the nose and nostrils. His bald patch was evident, and he made no vain attempt to rule lines of hair over his scalp's blank paper, yet a hat was always within reach to shade the brainbox. Within his loose trousers the genitals were covered yet unencumbered, free to flop about with an animal's unselfconscious peacockery.

On the platform Leonard was a country man on speed. He affected a zany, hail-fellow-well-met stupidity. He slapped his brow with an open palm and called himself a nutcase for forgetting someone's name. He hurled cowpats at hecklers. He rapped his knuckles, kicked himself up the backside, belted himself soundly, and told his missus off. Children loved it: he was a one-man Punch and Judy. Animals cringed.

With all the rapid fire patter and rowdy jocularity, he conveyed a genuineness. Audiences knew he really did believe in the old-fashioned values—which were, after all, *true*. In slaying the ten thousand, he convinced. A figure of ridicule, of tomfoolery, a buffoon, a horror, a reactionary tyrant, a self-educated yobbo, but, at heart, a true lover of the Bibles which he waved between his broad, flat fingers and thumped against his temple and offered at super-duper discount rates. Audiences detected in him something he did not expose, or even hinted he ever possessed: a soft centre. Thus, he ploughed the fields of evangelist, humanitarian, mystic, and—as the social sciences took over—facilitator.

In his talks Leonard anticipated and rebuffed criticism by reminding everybody he had been engaged in full-time Christian work for twenty-five years. Raising one leg so his genitals bulged and his shin was angled like a can-can girl's, he would shake his steel-capped boot and growl: 'Size thirteen. Want to walk a mile or two in these, sonny?'

Each new trend enjoyed a spell in Leonard's theological cosmos. He could refer to movies and too-popular bands and produce at will a touch of feminism for the ladies, a wink to the fellows, an armgrip for a handicapped seeker, or a visible squeeze of a coloured brother's fist.

As a sports fan, Leonard frequently used game-playing analogies: surfing breaks, golfing holes-in-one. He even encompassed netball and ponyclub pennants, though he could not rid himself of the suspicion that the salvation of a twelve-year-old girl was a diminutive victory. He watched TV sports coverage whenever he was free and sat up for post-midnight satellite telecasts. A stateside contact sent him videos of the gridiron and major ball games. Even tenpin-bowling stirred him.

On Sunday nights a radio talk-show was broadcast under Leonard's name. Leonard was too frequently out of the country to host it regularly or to write his newspaper column—but his producer was a stoic woman skilled in finding upbeat guests, and his reporters and contributors were eager to impress. Every few weeks listeners had the treat of a live hook-up to some foreign city where Leonard was privileged to be enjoying God's challenges.

At his crusades, Leonard delighted in splitting the multitude into clusters as a chef breaks a cauliflower into flowerlets. 'Remember, ladies,' he'd call out, 'each of you is a beautiful flower.' 'As my wife Merle will tell you,' he'd boom at the men, 'I like my cauliflower with a nice big dollop of white sauce, and today I'm going to give you fellows a bit of sauce.' Another day he'd give them curry. He pranced between groups, bantering, blustering, touching, drawing out warmth. He was like a fierce conductor who once in a while needs to stretch his muscles in the orchestra pit. Neither men nor women resisted him.

Recovering his energy at home, Leonard slept heavily and ate well, preferring fatty foods: spring lamb, brisket bones, pork, spare ribs, avocados, peanut butter, and cream in his morning coffee. Every few months his system told him a fast was needed. His fasting was meant to be a secret, but, as with all his activities of a quasi-devotional nature, it invariably became known. One supporter had him supping on honied water for forty days.

Leonard attained his fifty-second birthday in Auckland, where he was speaking at a Bible college summer school on the topic of Fundamentals Reexamined. A female student produced a cake at morning tea and, with hurrahs, Leonard was confirmed threefold as a jolly good fellow. The lecture hall was not air-conditioned and by early afternoon everyone was sweating and yawning. The more liberal women students wore loose T-shirts or singlets which exposed moist, hairy armpits and the round outer hemispheres of their breasts. Perspiration channelled down their thin chests. The traditional women wore sundresses; in the heat their shoulders slumped and their bra and petticoat straps slithered down. They set up a rhythmic chorus, alternating jerking up their straps and fanning their faces with concertinaed handouts. The men sprawled back with their elbows extended to allow the air to circulate around their armpits. Periodically they wiped their foreheads with open palms, unconsciously mimicking Leonard. Eyes rolled toward the ceiling, intestines chugged.

One woman bothered Leonard. She persisted in wearing a loose jacket over her T-shirt, as if hiding a tatoo or parodying his attachment to his suit coat. At afternoon tea he approached her. She was leaning against a vending machine sipping black tea out of a styrene cup and looking up at him from under a brow lowered like a nervous cow's. There was a knowingness about her, admixed with a chronic lack of certainty. Leonard spoke quietly, aspirating his *h*s, puffing out small clouds of authority. For the remainder of his time in Auckland they met clandestinely in air-conditioned hotel bars.

On each occasion Ashley wore insipid clothes, affecting an inoffensive sloppiness compounded of untailored jackets with pockets into which she could plunge her forearms, faded khaki or blue denim skirts and pants, bare legs, and flat sandals. She wore no makeup although her face was without contrasts, her eyes, eyebrows, eyelashes, cheeks and lips all skimmed milk pale. She wore no jewellery, not even a watch, she did not colour her hair, although it was greying, and she did not smell of scent, nor lotions, although her skin was dry.

This commendable absence of vainglory puzzled and provoked Leonard. He waited for an opportunity to look into her drawstring denim shoulderbag. It contained, he found, a romantic novel with an elderly woman's name written in an elderly hand across the top of the title page, a purse with too little in it to rattle, a diary interleaved with bills, a couple of tissues and a bottle of B12 tablets.

An enthusiast friend had prevailed on Ashley to attend the summer school. The Aussie guest speaker, she had said, was a political neanderthal but not a complete emotional retard. Owing the woman several debts of gratitude, Ashley had accepted a prepaid registration form. Her wistful manner regularly emboldened such enthusiasts, as well as the inquisitive and unscrupulous. In the lecture hall Ashley was put off by Leonard's abrasive delivery, but beside the vending machine she submitted to his approach. She was a fatalist.

Ashley's mother had been through three marriages and still collected pictures of Errol Flynn. In her turn, Ashley had had no husbands but a succession of ungenerous lovers. She was a bit defeatist, she admitted to herself, a bit inclined to attract losers, a bit prone to fall for whatever man came along. Yet, she insisted, she still hoped for the best and looked for the hidden good. She did not protect herself. She lingered waiting to see what would happen.

Her life was predicated on dependence. Her actions were programmed. She moved, without shifting, from man to man. One treated her bad—she cried on the shoulder of the next. She was always waiting, this innocent victim, for a male to present a cheque. The first glimmer of a man's attention would set off a spiralling fantasy. Her head was lined with little-girl presumptions; she would surrender her dignity before the meanest exemplar of the male. She would wait for a man to come along, waiting a little aloof from female competition, and—fuck me—one always did.

All these years of congress had produced just one child, a boy, now sixteen, called Scott. The boy's father was an islander with bulldozer good looks and a surfeit of gold jewellery. Ashley had been warned, but had stuck with him, stubborn in attesting to her own defeat. Scott was born with the difficulty which seemed to be Ashley's lot in whatever she drifted into. He was a square infant and Ashley had to be slashed open to permit his passage and then stitched together again in a verisimilitude of innocence. For several years afterwards she was anaemic and had to depend on her mother's help in caring for her son.

Ashley's pale face induced Leonard to drop his guard. He described aloud for the first time the ambivalence of his feelings for Merle. As he spoke, he felt more and more sorry for himself. He became convinced that, while he had apparently been living a life overflowing with purpose, hard work, manly companionship and marital consolation, his special endowments had actually elevated him to a condition of eremitic seclusion and self-denial.

Within a week Leonard and Ashley were echoing each other, completing each other's sentences, referring smilingly to little contretemps at previous meetings, and devising a private code. After all, their age difference was not so great. They touched with the red flesh exposed by their bitten fingernails.

Restored to Boondall, Leonard retired in the breezy evenings to his study to write a new set of lectures. After an interval of two weeks, he sent an Interflora bouquet. Then, emboldened by the certainty that Ashley could not afford to return his calls, he phoned. In July Leonard set off for an international hoe-down of itinerant evangelists. From Lagos he sent Merle a swag of tapes and transcripts, his radio producer an enthusiastic account of African revivalism, and Ashley a sealed League envelope. There were further despatches from the Ivory Coast, Tanzania and Botswana. A detour via Auckland was out of the question, Leonard assured Ashley when he phoned from the Cape. The phone went dead in his hand.

Greeting her husband after their five-week separation, Merle was unnerved by Leonard's eyes. They held the surprise, discomfiture and concentration of a snake readying itself to shed its skin. 'You're out of sorts,' she told him, bussing his chin. 'You've had too much funny food while you've been away.'

The following afternoon Leonard did an unaccustomed thing: he went alone to visit his sister. Sitting at Valerie's table watching her preparing bottles of formula, he told her about the African children—poor skinny little runts—and the wonderful work of the orphanages. She coddled him in her milky warmth.

In September Leonard began suffering sharp new twinges below his heart. When gallstones were diagnosed, he tried to visualise the little granular stones jiggling about inside him. He submitted to the operation. They sliced around his midriff and pincered out the little coloured balls. Then they sewed him up with ragged stitches. For months it hurt to belly laugh. He walked gingerly, one hand hovering between his heart and his gut, the other on Merle's shoulder.

In November Leonard flew to Palm Springs to address a businessmen's breakfast. Swallowing the last of the linksausages, he rose to speak. 'I want to congratulate you,' he boomed, 'on your glorious weather. I love the fall. You know, I'm positive it was an American who said life was one great ballgame and this earth one great ballpark. I want to put it to you that our time on this earth is one long game of gridiron. I know you all love gridiron.'

His audience cheered. 'Think about it,' Leonard said. 'One tryout after another.' The waitress at the kitchen door smiled.

Spit and Polish

Once you've been dealing with us for a couple of years, you'll notice the girls don't last. Simone replaces Francoise, Helene follows Justine, Paula supplants Ilsa. They're always sassy girls of nineteen or twenty. They've been to charm academies, they call themselves Executive Assistants and they sound magnificent on the phone, as superior as the people who take plane bookings. They're attracted by the fashionable product, which means the glossies are doing their job.

JB will hire a new girl in March or September, when the air is stirring, urging change. He never advertises: he hears of prospects at the yacht club or at 'The Oaks'. She taps in on heels at nine-thirty, pert with repartee. He's lethargic, sloe-eyed. He offers her a Moccona and apologises for not being fully with it: he's been up all night on the phone to some designer in Italy, or he had to make an appearance at the opening of a new club. He lights a cigarette and the girl, who, I am to learn, loathes smoke in her eyes, says: 'Go ahead, it doesn't bother me.' He wears dry-cleaned jeans with blue and white boatie moccasins. His chest hair curls so cutely over the neckline of his ironed sweatshirt that the girl longs to insinuate a finger. His adam's apple moves beneath the tanned throatskin. His eyes are sharpened by sunglass frames with optical lenses: classic Rayban if he's feeling cool, Toledo or Staccato if he wants to be cheeky. Spectacles suit his face, and he knows it. When he needs to shift a slow range or some novelty frames, he will model them for the buyers, who never fail to smile at his banter. After all, one or two of a fun line never hurt a boutique, did it? But of course you're not interested in that kind of plastic junk.

JB moves slowly with the new girl. He's as smooth as creme

brulée. A confidential smile, a quiet word, a grateful nod. The girl is not an amateur; she reciprocates, but JB conducts the proceedings. It is he who signs the pay cheques.

JB watches the girl enhancing her appearance, confirming her attractions. He remarks on her new hairstyle, not necessarily favourably—he doesn't need to crawl—and from then things flourish. At Easter, when the air smells green as apples and the mornings are russet and gold, they are off to Leura. October brings weekends at Palm Beach.

In the office the girl is high with efficient verve. You must have noticed. She trills over the phone. She couldn't be more obliging. She works back: JB and she alone on the fourth floor, among the shelves and cartons, with the late afternoon sun rosy outside. JB's apartment is just one floor above. The night is young. It's a cinch, isn't it? I sing to myself as I walk home. I swing my arms, and bounce on the balls of my feet. I feel free and unencumbered. I shower and change and ready myself for my own responsibilities.

Summer brings a week at Noosa or Mollymook. Winter means skiing. And then, subtly at first, the joy seeps away. When the girl is preoccupied on the phone, and your back orders drop out of the computer, you may presume things are on the skids. When she's distant, embittered, unhelpful, she is leaving early for interviews. It is almost March again, or September, and rearrangement is imminent.

I cannot feel aggreived for these girls. JB has a candid, plausible face. They're fools for hoping for anything more. He speaks with solicitude when he takes the orders between girls.

Me he leaves alone. I've been with him through four years and eight girls. I know my job backwards—all the stock, all the clients—and I don't make mistakes. I work so quickly and automatically my mind is free to wander. I'm as busy as a spider spinning daydreams. I stay because JB pays well, it's clean and straight-forward, and I can get out of the place by four-thirty. Perhaps I despise him. I know he's suspicious of me. He wonders why I stay. I look too good for it. I'm quick-witted, thin, agile and fast. I have floppy black hair and darting black eyes in the style of Sylvia Beach. I am also Aboriginal. Did you realise such a person packs your orders? I'll bet you didn't. I'm not pure, if that makes it any easier. There is an overlay of white, a few brush strokes.

I know how to elicit evasive-eyed courtesy, unctious compliments, twitchy do-gooder chatter and amorphous guilt. JB fears I am anti-capitalist. He doesn't know me. Once I asked—to stir him—why I couldn't be the guy out on the road. He said no, as I'd hoped. He wants a thick-set, blonde type out there, Cranbrook perhaps, articulating with white toothpaste teeth. I'm his back-room boy.

Did you realise I work for old men too? They pay big bucks for services rendered. I'm quick and clean. Don't worry—I shall not contaminate your orders with this second impediment.

The old men show me off. We eat at the newest restaurants, dropping bon mots and wrangling about art and privilege. Oh, how they bitch. They get jealous of each other and accuse the rent boys of necrophilia. They ask me what I want out of life. I say: 'To please you. To be your wallpaper.' Should I let it slip I'm going away, they whine and up the ante. They offer me gifts, my choice, anything that'll entrap me. I choose furniture: Deco of course, and nice fifties things in blondewood. My flat is superb. Everything in it is fragrant with polish. I won't let the old men come to me there.

My clients are my friends for as long as they last. They call me an embryonic artist and fancy they're boosting a protégé. I produce nothing. They know it and tut-tut. I tell them I shall sit in the Bauhaus Museum and compose poetry. The old men pay for me to linger in auction rooms and galleries. I am training my eye. That is possible, as you would concede. Month by month I'm improving, and I can always onsell my mistakes. In Berlin I will see what I love in context. I should have no trouble supporting myself there. You have to stay in a place long enough to see how to put things together. I read early Isherwood.

My windows look onto buildings, flats, bedrooms. At night I see charcoal figures moving in black ink shadows.

I live at the top of St Neot Avenue in a block called *Grantham*. Its bricks are the colour of cut liver. Its white pillars speak of Culture, its opaque glass panes of Home.

The flats at the front watch a curving white P & O liner swoop out into Wylde Street. The flats on the topside look down on HMAS *Kuttabul*. At the back my flat looks across asphalt into modern lego units. Beyond the units, Oak Lane leads to old buildings with glorious names: *Stanford Hall*, *Green Gables*, *Elysee*. *Elysee*! Water views, naturally.

In the morning I walk over to Surry Hills. I walk out of one life into another. They are separated by Oxford Street, my faultline.

Setting out for JB I pass a row of ugly, human, middle-aged buildings: *St Neots*, *Trent Bridge*, *Allambie*, *The Lachlan*, *Craigleith*, *Park View*. At the bottom of the avenue I bounce down a flight of steps into the pigtail end of Grantham Street. To my right, *Kaloola*, to my left, *Wirringulla*. Someone here cultivates pansies: purple and gold and black, the colour of a splendid currency. From the walkway round to Victoria Street, I glance across at the Opera House peaks and the Bridge. To my right is a carpark roof, all concrete turrets and periscopes; to my left, two terrace houses dated 1900. I like auspicious dates.

Around the curve a choice waits for me. I may leave Victoria Street immediately, belting down the McElhone Stairs, or stay on it till the Butler Stairs. I stay on Victoria when I feel like moving amongst grand old houses, but this means I must pass *Melton*.

An age ago, before I found my place in *Grantham*, I rented a room in *Melton*. My life was as seedy then as the peeling paint, as rough as the yellow stucco. Up the road is *Arthur's*, where I met my first old man. Arthur presided as we negotiated. At the top of the Butler Stairs is a plaque to a dead activist: that was all before my time.

If I go immediately down the McElhone Stairs, I must confront the present. There are two flights of thirty-eight steps—I always count as I bounce down—then one of thity-six. Some modern tidier's paving has upset an older symmetry. In Brougham Street, I dodge Commonwealth Z cars. Hordern Stairs issue out of the backside of a new monolith. The sandstone cliff-face is civilised with seepage stains and sewer pipes. A lamp post grows out of litter and rubble, cactus and weeds. I can never resist stopping to look up, through Rowena Place, at the brick arches holding up the backrooms of the Victoria Street mansions. Any second, plumed horses whipped by warriors in chariots may gallop out.

It is time now to leave Brougham Street, down the stairs with no name. The men who dotted the sandstone with pick marks must have had a name for them. Old women sweep the pavement. In holiday times kids skip in the street.

Down into Dowling Street, past the Revolving Battery, and into the fag end of Cathedral Street. The Eastern Suburbs railway skims over roofs like the underbelly of a low-flying jet. I climb up towards William Street, Forbes Street rising steadily, residential becoming commercial. Sometimes I see an entrepreneur. Corfu Street diverts the victims to St Vincent de Paul.

On William Street the footpath is too narrow to prevent the lost tourists and crazies brushing against you. Cars roar out of tunnels. I cross at the lights—it's safest.

The stairs between the ABC building and the car rental place are always slippery with amber glass pellets. I nick through St Peters Lane into Bourke Street and begin the ascent to Oxford Street.

If I'm ahead of time, I detour down Stanley Street: *Reggio's* opens at ten to eight and his cafe latté is wonderful. Refreshed, I stride uphill. In Crown Street I am pushing against the traffic. Yesterday afternoon's newspapers gust against my legs. The tiny houses cringe. Old men poke their heads out and yank them in again, assaulted by noise and force. Here only the details are piquant. One morning a girl in a pink leotard opened a door holding a hundred-dollar note and another girl inside called out her order: Diet Pepsi and a toasted cheese sandwich.

On Oxford Street the fashionable cafes are shut. At the bus stops, people with camouflaged haircuts smooth down their office clothes and hope no-one recognises them. I step down off the catwalk, onto the ground of the employed.

Crown Street takes me into Surry Hills, past the leather shop and Value Funerals and the poultry shop lofting the sign 'Killed on Premises'.

In Campbell Street, I pass the CIB. The plain-clothes D's glance at me. They've seen me somewhere, after dark. I hum and swing my sandwich bag and look clean. I've seen them too. I am a nightfly, a moth circling a globe.

I flick my hair back off my forehead, sway my bum, toss my *Gitane* into the gutter, kick a drink can, stoop to tickle a cat. I feel on top of the world. The car fumes rise. The mist disperses. The sun waterpaints stripes between the buildings. The plane trees rustle. The cabs swoop down Foveaux Street. The deros lean on their outposts. The Mission bus cruises. Hungarians squeeze their cars into lanes. Vietnamese go in to sewing machines on concrete floors. Parking police saunter. Delivery vans squeal into U-turns. Milk-bars dole out yellow mugs of coffee. Stock boys bite rubbery vanilla slices. I have spring fever when it isn't even spring.

I always arrive in a good mood and JB loves me for it. He's quiet and slow. He watches me smiling and tossing cartons aside and greeting his girl with my newest endearment. While I eat my sandwich I check the exchange rates. If the Bristow cartoon is good, I add it to my noticeboard. My favourites are the ones where he's hankering for his holiday at *Funboys sur la Plage*.

My windows look back over to Oxford Street. I detest Darlinghurst. I hate balding thirty-five-year-olds in gym shorts. My old men hate sport. They despise all Australian pastimes: Leagues clubs and Tooheys pubs and public beaches. They are, however, friendly with some of the thirty-five-year-olds—the art directors and Labor lawyers who come to Sunday lunch and talk about Italy and compassion. I look brooding and pass the wine. I'm a little bushfly hanging about at a barbeque. Sometimes they make passes, thinking they can acquire the old men's reputation through me. One tucked a couple of hundred-dollar bills into my sleeve as a down-payment. I opened a new account with them. I didn't flicker an eyelash.

The thirty-five-year-olds write me into their scripts and defence addresses. They create bit parts for precocious, romantic savages, but I slither out, quick as an eel in a muddy creek. They don't know what words to put in my mouth. I don't exist, I tell them. Go back to Darlo. With luck, you'll graduate to Paddington; with help to Darling Point. I'm happy being me. I like to look at myself. I love to stand in front of the big round mirror I rescued from the old Ashfield Cinema. On hot nights I open the windows and lean out, staring into the lego bedrooms. I swallow the night air until I am intoxicated, as giddy as a baby on a swing. Then I fall back onto the sofa, posing like a young, smug Capote. That's me. Four years in *Grantham*, four years with JB, eight, ten, a dozen old men. Some of the old men didn't last long. They knew when it was time to go back to polishing their blind old daschhunds.

But JB and I have gone the distance. Five days a week for four years. He doesn't realise it, but I know him as well as his best mate (who doesn't exist). I know what he eats, what he drinks and when he goes to the shithouse. Strolling with JB, a girl may ask—a throwaway line—why he keeps me on. Surely I'm a little, well, slippery. He may agree I'm sly but he has no evidence. I'm a fast worker, and—that defence when all else fails—punctual. I'll admit I haven't been so impeccable in other company. When one old man tipped his drink down my fifty-dollars pants, I told him they cost a hundred and fifty and he wrote me a cheque at once. Things like that. I'm quick on the uptake. I could live off the streets. But I have my flat, and my collection, and my savings, and I'm clean with the cops. A little longer and I'll get my passport.

I am what I can make of myself. Sometimes I think I'm only as good as my next old man, but fortunately they are getting classier.

I was reared by a superfluity of mothers and uncles. My blood mother was born nor' nor' west of Utopia. When she was sixteen, she came across to Sydney and found a live-in job in Rose Bay. Her employer, Miss Abbott, had grown up on the land in the Central West with maids called Annie and Lizzie, and she still liked to have a cleaning girl about the place. On her second free day, my mother met a German merchant seaman at Circular Quay. She scarcely understood she was pregnant until it was showing, and Miss Abbott had little option but to keep her on. So I was brought up in what Miss Abbott calls comfortable circumstances—dressed at David Jones, and sent to Scots to acquire a bit of polish.

My mother's boyfriends, the uncles, are a hazier memory. Just one uncle remains distinct. He was a Finn, a pathetic, drunken migrant worker. Foolishly, my mother let him stay at *Melrose* while Miss Abbott was away in Hobart. I was about eleven at the time.

This Finn came into my room long after midnight, roaring drunk, and pulled the sheets off me. He was waving a great pair of garden shears and he would have used them. I'm sure he would have used them. I screamed and my mother rushed in and dragged him back at the last second.

As far back as I can remember, my mother has always been thin, like me, and elegantly dressed, courtesy of Miss Abbott. She wears pleated silk and carries a bunch of keys and looks after confidential tasks such as the banking. She is adept at fending off the charity collectors—'We already gave,' she says—and the investment consultants and the security grille salesmen. She has absorbed all of Miss Abbott's little rituals and snobberies. Miss Abbott says true gentlefolk are always civil and good manners are a proof of consideration and what gauche young people need is the polish imparted by a good schooling.

JB is a Pole with all the sheen money can buy, but his brand of commercial shine is not what Miss Abbott admires. 'Trade', she sniffs. She is eighty now: imagine a daffy old bird with opera glases and a fox stole and a ruched bodice and an Edwardian brooch and long pins stabbing her bun and white circles of ancient deodorant in her armpits and a neck reeking of Chantilly and a beaded purse and gloves. A silly old dame, all tail-feathers and commotion, a cassowary in the firing line. That is why my mother stays.

I don't visit Miss Abbott or my mother often. They paid for my flat on condition I stopped going with old men. Miss Abbott would have liked to add a second proviso—that I stop working for this vulgar Pole. Of course Miss Abbott does not care for me calling my employer 'JB'. Perhaps you don't either. His surname is, as you know, Bayscho, and he usually goes by the first name of Jim, but his actual first names are Marek Stefan.

Who cares? Rose Bay is my past. Surry Hills is my present. I love it. I drop coins in the buskers' guitar cases, wave aside the winos without offending them, step over the drunks without interrupting their dreams, feed my crusts to the pigeons. I know the graffiti sprayers, the poster pasters, the garbage bin rummagers, the Bob Dylans with their harmonicas. I have watched car breakers, smash and grab artists, junkie muggers, torches. I know the name of every corner pub. I've seen the old shops go. *Val Anglim's Pet Shop*—do you remember it? I've seen the businesses go broke and burn out. I know the GPs, the barbers, the newsagents. I know the old Indo-Chinese woman who shouts abuse and pulls a knife. I know the crutches man with his elephant legs and bare feet wrapped in rags. I know the Gaelic Club, the railway recreation hall, the junkies who shoot up outside the Quakers' hall.

I've only ever been invited up to JB's penthouse for Christmas Eve drinks. We knock off at three and go up and sink into the pastel leather sofas and shuffle our soles on the zebra rugs. JB asks what we're doing after Christmas. The Cranbrook rep tells us he'll be out on the water watching the start of the Sydney-Hobart yacht race. The girl says she'll be having a family Christmas and then—she glances at JB—going away for a few days with a friend. I say I'll be staying in Potts Point.

'But it's foul in the city in summer,' they protest. The blistering concrete and melting bitumen; those awful hot winds and the glaring brickwork; the offices all empty and dead, and the taxis cruising, and all that rubbish left over from New Year's Eve.

I think of the evenings. In the warm stillness I wander down near Elizabeth Bay House, or catch the bus out to Bronte. Later I throw open my windows and let the air circulate while I oil my furniture. My nightingales are the shouts of the suburban fools hitting the Cross.

I am my Christmas present to myself. I spend the day with my mother and Miss Abbott; the evening alone, half-listening to showtunes and flicking through art books. On Boxing Day I go to the beach. Obelisk is best—it's exclusive and far away. The next night I return to the demands of my current old man. He has missed me. He's querulous and hung-over. I am clean and rested. Fresh—ready to be killed again on his premises. He presses an envelope into my hand.

Next Christmas I shall go to Berlin. I'll be twenty-three then. JB won't want to let me go, but he'll act blasé.

My mothers will not try to stop me either. They know there is a time for mixing the shellac with your spirits, taking up the finest badger brush, and applying one taut layer of varnish, and then another.

Life, it looks to me, is an accretion of these layers. You add jobs, old men, cities, nights, and each new layer enhances the lustre. That is how I see it without glasses; maybe you older guys see differently through your bifocals.

With each new layer I am smothering the plywood and tacks, and moving glowing toward my benefactors' hearths. The sheen of your person transports you, and so long as you go on duly, dully gleaming, without a shadow of dust or smear of fingerprints, they will insure you as one of their exhibits.

My mother knows this, and JB. They also know you cannot complete the deliverance. You cannot step out of the exhibit case and become one of them. You are still plywood bound tight with layers of shellac. Struggle too fiercely and the layers will crack. You must glide through life's reception rooms. Don't scrape against rough edges—cosset yourself. Keep thin and agile. Laugh at their dessicated humour, soak up the spiritous liqueurs they pour for you, stand, pose, reek of polish, assist their guests to admire their far-sighted patronage in finding you and doing you up.

You will have, then, a life of comfortable circumstance. You may even be shipped to the far side of the empire and paraded in a cage of notoriety. Don't worry; when you grow bored, you can always doodle on your banknotes. And when you are old and blind, they'll care for you—they have their decencies. They'll smooth in unguents to stop your skin drying and fading.

Let them, I say. Let them burnish you.

Next Christmas I shall step from the plane into icy air and walk through the pristine snow, past stone buildings and the silhouettes of trees, to the Bauhaus Museum. My life will sing like a poem.

Tonic for Two

Ever since his employer had introduced compulsory retirement for fifty-five year olds, Ted Buchanan had remained fifty-three.

He was a jaunty little fellow with a stumpy body and exceptionally short legs. He moved with a snappy strut, swinging his arms like a dwarf. His hair was coarse, wavy and still predominantly the colour of a peanut. His eyebrows and nostril hairs bristled black. His skin was pink beneath a spatter of brown freckles, his eyes amber. He wore a short-brimmed hat, a cardigan, a white shirt, a football-club tie sent out by a great-nephew, button-on braces, trews of that changeable blue-grey which is called tonic, and scrupulously shined laceups.

'Ted's a tough old bugger,' younger men commented. Every day for thirty years he had cycled into the city until, when he was fifty, an impudent taxi driver had flung open a door, deliberately pitching him onto the roadway. None the less, at Hogmanay he could still kick up his kilt with the best of them. He was a corker wee fellow, a real ripper.

The womenfolk of Ted Buchanan's youth had appreciated his debonair courtesies and the alacrity with which he raised his hat. Modern women found him irritating.

His approach to any task was a combination of good cheer, capability and persistence. He liked marching, baton-twirling, bagpipes and brass bands. His sentimental streak came out when he recited the old rhymes his mother had taught him. *Miss Polly had a Dolly* was a favourite, along with one about a dolly which was lost in the woods and trampled by cows but eventually, happily, restored.

The city's retirement villages and nursing homes were Ted Buchanan's club circuit. He was a natural entertainer and always eager to deliver one of his recitation—*gratis*, of course, though he did not turn down travelling expenses and a scone or three. Every Saturday and Sunday afternoon he could be spotted on stage exulting in *Archie and Mehitabel*, *The Sentimental Bloke*, *The Man from Snowy River* and *Hiawatha*. He told long jokes, too, chuckling at his own humour but growing quickly impatient with others' flippancies. His favourite put-down was *My eye and Betty Martin*, his strongest adjective *blithering*, his strongest oaths *Gadzooks* and *Hells bells*. He was expert at putting the kybosh on any deletion mooted by the silly old duffers who organised the afternoon entertainments.

A Presbyterian from birth, Ted had reluctantly stayed on when his local church turned Uniting. The new name alone was enough to raise his hackles. As traditions were gradually abandoned, he grew more and more vituperative in their defence. At Parish Council he gave the compromisers merry hell. As treasurer he held the floor, confident his grievances were being fully and faithfully recorded by his sister, Elspeth, who had been minutes secretary for nineteen years. They were a formidable team and rarely knew the ignominy of defeat.

Elspeth Buchanan was thin and firm and fit, always a strider, never a dawdler. She had cycled and played tennis. She had a long reach and a steady grip. Since her fiancé, to whom she had been plighted for seven years, had succumbed to tuberculosis, she had devoted herself to her brother's welfare and to the church—and were the two not intimately intertwined?

Nineteen years as a backstop: nineteen years of observing fluffed catches, wild swings, loopy deliveries and complete misses by the men who played the game. They had refined Elspeth's sense of the ridiculous. Everywhere she looked she could see things which made her chuckle.

A good clean prank by the church's teenagers would set Elspeth laughing till tears ran down her powdered cheeks. One Christmas concert she permitted herself to be persuaded to take to the stage and promptly entertained everyone for an hour with jokes, stories, impersonations, and improvisations on the old Beale. The performace became an annual event, an indulgence.

During the year Elspeth refused all encouragements to perform, for she felt disturbed by the worldiness of her humorous gifts. Why should the doughty Lord have equipped such a one to prance about like a dog dancing on its hindlegs?

She took, however, to exercising her gifts daily, at home, *sotto voce*. Pacing the hall she would tell a string of comic anecdotes, throwing in impressions and sound effects, grabbing tea-towels and tea-cosies for props, and supplying all the voices and the audience's guffaws. Ted she played as a battery-operated bantam rooster, the martinet of the fowl yard, or as a snappy terrier with a ruffle of plastic bucket around his neck to prevent him gnawing at his rear end.

Elspeth would have made a roaring flapper had she been born a few years earlier. Perhaps conscious of having been thwarted of something, she had always dressed in the style of the twenties. She wore her pepper-and-salt hair in a bob with kiss curls, dabbed her cheeks with rouge, and favoured a cloche hat, long cardigan, pleated skirt, lisle stockings and button-strapped shoes with cuban heels. Teenagers marvelled at her.

She shopped shrewdly and ran an economical house. Everything was in decent order. The darning was always up-to-date. During the day she organised discussion circles and handicraft bees for the elderly folk her brother contacted on his circuit. The younger women on her committees quailed at her vigour. Half-a-day's work could be completed most satisfactorily, she assured them, before nine o'clock. She visited, phoned, invited, wrote notes, delivered meals, and bullied with calculated, high-speed kindnesses. In her presence the freest pulled themselves into line. Few detected the twinkle in the amber.

By night, Elspeth allowed Ted to rule the roost. He was the nominal bosscocky. Providing everything on the domestic scene was to his liking, good humour prevailed: he perched straight legged on his rocker in front of the TV, talking back to the politicians and deploring the farcical plots of the soapies. But should his evening's routine be in any way disordered, he was snappy as a thwarted terrier. He would gnaw on a complaint till Elspeth rectified the matter. It was the male prerogative, he said, to instil forethought. His sister played the feebleminded femme as far as was required to permit him the periodic outlet of a hearty burst of choler. He was best managed by stealth. Her respect had been tempered long ago by knowledge.

When Elspeth Buchanan was fifty-four, God felled her in her tracks. She pitched down the front steps and broke her hip. The first operation was a failure. Elspeth was sure she could feel the metal pin gouging into her flesh.

She lay on pressure sores in the ancient orthopaedic ward of a teaching hospital, amid two long rows of grey women on silver morgue trolleys with hoists and pulleys suspended above them like mystic triangles. All night the old ones whimpered and snorted, cried out and wet their beds. At last, in the torchy light before daybreak, the ritual washing would begin.

Ted Buchanan, fit as a fiddle, had always said public treatment was good enough for his kith and kin.

If Miss Buchanan was ever going to crack, the younger church people said, it was now. They named her years of abnegation as wilful negligence in personal development and hinted that this calamity was punishment from a God who demanded full and proper self-actualisation. Older folk detected the hand of the devil, who was wont to chuck a bluey when a servant was doing too much good work.

Trust and obey, Elspeth hummed. Faith, she thought, has soaked all the way through me, like custard through cake; but the analogy lost its usefulness when she imagined the crumbling, soggy cake. Faith, she thought, is as omnipresent as calcium in bones; but calcium had a traitorous habit of seeping away unnoticed, even in the most impeccable woman, leaving her brittle as a stick. Under Ted's influence, Elspeth had never cared for artificial supplements.

The second operation was declared a success and Elspeth was released into the care of her brother. She had imagined a homecoming reception replete with bagpipes and kettledrums, but there was no-one but Ted to two-step beside her, and the house seemed cramped and dingy. She had grown inured to clatter and to expanses of lemony disinfected linoleum.

Ted was a bumptious nursemaid. He insisted on a regimen of warm milk and walking. Visitors and phone calls were rationed.

In hospital Elspeth had missed her daily Royal Command performance. When she had stifled giggles at private amusements, the staff had looked at her as if she were senile. Now she filled the long days by going through all her routines. Abandoning circumspection, she talked out loud, clapping, gesticulating and cackling with delight. She was as preoccupied with fantasy and secret jokes and songs and magic words as a pre-schooler. She played with a child's concentration and then fell back exhausted.

After the high of such a day-long performance, the late afternoon was a let-down. The younger church folk were occupied with their own families or jobs, the older folk were preparing for their early evening meals, the better TV shows were yet to come, and there was nothing but politics and traffic reports on the wireless. The day drooped and greyed into putty. The air chilled. A fresh pot of tea was insufficient comfort. Elspeth wanted to moan out into the gloom. She remembered her fiancé: the cold night air they had made him sleep in, her helplessness. She too was no longer indomitable. Old age stooped to tuck a grey blanket around her slim, unloved hips.

Ted Buchanan declared there was no problem. Was God's arm shortened? Well, neither was Elspeth's leg. She'd be right as rain, whatever that meant. But when visitors came, Elspeth saw it in their eyes: they were startled by the difference. Something had gone out of her. She'd been winded, permanently. She asserted she was not bitter; God had been unfailingly merciful. And—she smiled a secretive smile—she still had all her faculties.

In the old people's homes Elspeth's groups had survived without her, flourished in some cases. And at the church there had not been a six-month hiatus in engagements, marriages or births. The parish minutes had been more than adequately handled by a young beauty therapist.

Elspeth became so bored she took to looking through the thickest volumes in the house: the phonebooks, Arthur Mee's Encyclopaedia and the Family Bible. Resorting then to the dictionary, she lingered over the music of her Scots heritage. Among the worlds beginning with *Sc*, she discovered a new, worrying language of doubts and portents. *Scissile*, she read: *capable of being cut.* And *Scissel*: *metal scraps left after blanks have been cut out. Sciosophy*: *the shadow of wisdom*; *a system of what claims to be knowledge but is without basis in ascertained fact.* It got worse with *Se*. *Se-baptist* she said out loud: *one who baptises himself*.

Lifting away the heavy book and closing her eyes, she tried to think out a prayer. The words and tune of a hymn came to her: *I vow to thee, my country*. Planets whirled above her as she sat propped amongst the pillows. The whole firmament of certainty spun about her. Bits fell like satellite refuse, tumbling over and over. *I vow to thee*, her mind recited. Across the back of her eyes she saw the scraps which were left after her mother had cut biscuits from a round of pastry. It is the just fate of these useless trimmings, some curved, some angular, to be discarded. The canny may rework them into gingerbread men, but the pastry goes rubbery and the results are not palatable. Only soap scraps had, in Elspeth's experience, been worth hoarding.

When she tried to converse with her visitors, Elspeth discovered that the anaesthesia had weakened her memory. With a terrible cunning, men's drugs had wafted her into a black, singing universe; promising to obviate pain, they had shattered her reason. She could no longer recall everything perfectly, no longer make connections. Faces and names were as jumbled as a drawer full of gloves.

She fell back, in her private world, on ancient comedy routines and the saucy songs her father had sung.

Elspeth Buchanan came back to church on a walking stick. Ted strutted before her, proud as punch. She was his handiwork. Elspeth sat in the back pew, where there was space for her gammy leg, and bowed her head. The church whirled and tilted and jangled like a rotating ride at a funfair. She mumbled to the planets: *I vow to the . . . the love that never falters.* During the service they prayed aloud for her, thanking God for her restoration; she who had been laid aside for a time by a cruel joke of nature was now safe in the family of God. *And there's another country*, she thought; I am spinning towards it.

After the service Ted crowed at the gate. 'Isn't she a bonnie lassie?' he demanded of each well-wisher. 'My gal Sal. She's the boogie-woogie bugle girl of company B.'

When Elspeth was able to be left, as he put it, Ted Buchanan resumed his entertainment circuit. The enforced hibernation had sparked a new vigour. When, at the beginning of spring, an overnight bushwalk for the church's teenagers was proposed, he insisted he would come along. Qualms relating to his fitness and the possible killjoy effects of his company were brushed aside. He had always been a great promoter of outdoor pursuits for youth.

All the way out across the plain Ted instructed the boys in the virtues of hiking: moral development and self-sufficiency. The outdoor life was a fine preparation for marriage, employment and citizenship. The boys were mystified but sufficiently excited not to puzzle for too long. The girls, apprehensive, sat across the back seat of the minibus and talked about pretty male singers.

The leader, a geography teacher, set a fast pace down into a valley. The boys jumped and called, unworried as yet by the loads on their backs. The leader's offsider, a domestic science teacher, herded the girls along in the rear. Outnumbered, they were determined to act out a stereotype in self-defence. Ted scrambled down between the two groups.

The descent completed in less than an hour, the youngsters dumped their packs and waded, splashing and teasing, into a round blue pond. The water was fearfully cold. The geography teacher explained to those who would listen that the pond had been a water source, once, for the steam trains which hauled up the Blue Mountains. The domestic science teacher called out the programme for the remainder of the day: set up camp, cook a barbecue, sing around the campfire, and *behave, please.* Ted confided he had prepared a Robbie Burns recitation.

The rowdier boys clamoured to climb and explore. They had barely stretched their muscles yet. The geography teacher agreed to take them all further into the bush for the hour or two till sunset. The domestic science teacher said she had better stay with the girls, who, regarding themselves as more sophisticated, had formed a huddle on the sand. One had brought a cassette player, a second a stack of *Dolly* magazines, a third a bottle of black nail enamel. Each had three or four changes of clothes in her backpack.

Ted Buchanan felt constrained to accompany the boys.

The party set off at a fast bat. The geography teacher had only a vague idea where the leading boys were heading. He envisaged scrambling around the valley slopes and dropping back down to the pond from a new angle.

The sun was low, shafting through the leaves. Crows passed overhead cawing. The bush looked ragged, its floor littered with grey organic debris. Back at the camp, the womenfolk would have the homefires burning. They would be bending their heads together, gently examining wildflowers and giggling over girlish trivia.

The route was getting steeper. They were climbing, pushing into the mountains, zig-zagging up to a ridge. For the valley around the pond was not a symmetrical basin; it was a long fissure running into the mountains between spurs of rock. The geography teacher must surely realise this, Ted thought, yet he let the boys keep going. They were willing climbers.

Ted's breath grew short and snuffly, as if he were hurrying to some climax. Each step demanded concentration.

The boys did not look back. Yodels and cooees indicated the first of them had reached the top. Ted put his head down and ploughed on. A final exertion of effort and he was there.

For a minute he was dizzy. His head spun, he blacked out and died a tiny death.

The boys did not notice. Ted lowered his backside onto a rock. The world was a black carousel, the boys' voices an infuriating fair-ground tinkle. The geography teacher was pointing out fire-trials. It seemed they were on a peak with valleys all around them. A couple of boys were asking each other rude riddles.

'OK, Ted?' the geography teacher encouraged.

'A bit weary on it,' Ted conceded.

'We'll go back the easy way,' the teacher soothed.

'Straight down,' he added, winking, as the boys set up a chorus of complaint.

Already they were off again. Ted stumbled behind them.

They traversed the ridge and began to scramble downhill, racing one another, yahooing and pretending to be mountain brumbies. At the base their mistake was apparent. They had dropped into a dead-end, a culvert.

They would have to climb out again and find the correct route back to the pond. The teacher looked chastened. The bolder boys jeered.

Ted look a deep breath. A fear crept into him.

The boys were climbing again. They were quiet and intent. The teacher waited for Ted to rise from his crouching, resting position. Inhaling slowly and deeply, Ted began to climb. The teacher kept pace at first, but gradually, temptation overcoming him, he pulled ahead.

Ted laboured upward. His only purpose now was to keep going. It was a two-in-one gradient. Halfway up, the teacher called a halt. Ted heaved himself up level with the feet of the waiting boys, wheezing out a witticism they failed to understand. Immediately the boys set off again, flaunting their buttocks. They were insensate, merciless.

Ted scrabbled on up, slipping and grabbing. He was close to despair. He had to keep going. There was no-one to help him. He began to pant. Into his eyes rose the water of self-pity and desperation. The task was beyond him.

He was breathing erratically now, sweating out a cold, slimy film, clutching at thin branches, reeling with dizziness. A gust of music buffeted him. It was sad, strong, Scandinavian music. He could not put a name to it, but he knew there were words. Elspeth would know them.

A fir tree blocked Ted Buchanan's ascent. He grabbed at the trunk. The music came back and with it a name—*Finlandia*—and words: *I rest on Him, my shield and my defender*; *I rest on Him, and in His strength I go. The Mighty God, the Everlasting Father, the Prince of Peace, throughout eternity*. The music swept on. Drums resounded. Ted Buchanan clung to the tree, pressing his eyelids against the bark, gouging the flesh of the trunk with his fingernails. He saw black. The earth whirled.

'Elspeth,' he whimpered and began to sob.

The teacher and a couple of the bigger boys hoisted Ted up the remainder of the slope, hobbled with him along the ridge, and finally half-carried him down to the pond. It was almost dark. The girls had put up the tents and gathered kindling for a fire. They greeted the boys with remonstrance and high spirits. The domestic science teacher bundled Ted into a sleeping-bag and held hot tea to his mouth. Ted could say nothing. Tears rolled down his cheeks.

The geography teacher stood over him, legs apart, arms dangling out from his side, shrugging, deflecting reponsibility, like a man watching a woman weep.

Once they had offered Ted food and settled him into a tent, they gathered around the fire telling jokes. The boys skited. The girls prompted, enquired and exclaimed, 'Oh yes, I'll bet' at the grosser exaggerations. Every now and then a head would poke through the tent flap and a mouth would ask if Mr Buchanan was all right. No-one missed the Robbie Burns recitation.

Curling into a foetal position, Ted shut his eyes and tried to click his ears shut also. The ground was heavy and compact with damp. He had never felt anything so cold. The chill penetrated through his thigh, hip and shoulder, seeping right into the bone. He would die of cold, his mind told him. He had no means of getting warm. He was still fully dressed and had been given the only down sleeping-bag, but it was not enough. There was no-one to chafe him into warmth. Eventually, to the noise of whispering boys swapping tents, Ted went to sleep. About four a.m. he woke shivering. He stretched out, feeling for another face, longing for consolation. But he was alone in his tent. Snivelling, he huddled down into the sleeping-bag, hooking the hood completely over his head and pulling the cord till it cut into his throat over the adam's apple.

When Ted woke again, at about seven, he crawled to the ten flap. It was a misty morning, with sunlight as thin and pale as streaky egg-white and a kookaburra cackling. Two boys were up already. They crouched, splashing their faces at the edge of the round blue pond, which still wore its night time blanket of glistening mica. The boys were wearing only tracksuit pants and jogging shoes. Their backbones, shoulder blades and ribs, their bands of muscle, the dimples at the small of their backs, were all shadowed.

Ted eased out of his tent. One boy turned.

'Morning, Mr Buchanan,' he called in a taught, insincere manner.

'How do you feel?' his friend added.

'Like a Tooheys,' Ted retorted, pleased with his presence of mind.

He shuffled around to the far side of the pool, knelt, broke the silver film with one hand, and sluiced his face. The water was so shockingly cold it momentarily blinded him. He leaned forward and doused his head, not caring that he was soaking his collar and shoulders. He splashed again and again, toppling forward like a blind Narcissus. He gulped mouthfuls of water. He could not think.

Girls came running. They pressed towels around Ted Buchanan's head and pulled him away from the pond. Sobs of self-pity shook him, and he tried to struggle free. But they overwhelmed him, sat him down on a rucksack, held a thermos of lukewarm tea to his lips, and looked for matches to light a fire. Tears streaked his face. He gulped down ignominious, hiccuping sobs.

One by one the girls crouched beside Ted Buchanan and told him he'd be OK. He looked aside. The fir tree music swept away their chatter in a welter of melancholy. He was still cold to the bone. The surface of his skin was moist and chilly, like that of a thawing chicken; deeper in, his flesh was iced solid.

On Ted Buchanan's account, the geography teacher cancelled the remainder of his plans and led the party up out of the valley. Ted had to be propelled upward with a boy on each side gripping his arms. He went with a towel draped over his head, choosing to be blinkered, steered by the elbow like a blind man. At one point six of them had to hoist him up over their heads and then lower him down a rockface. He did not protest or pause to look back. He looked down, at the rocks and the grey Australian dirt and his own dusty boots.

The church bus was waiting. While the engine warmed, they settled Ted across the back seat. Then they drove him down out of the mountains, over the river, across the plain, and in along the freeway.

The teachers bundled Ted into Elspeth's custody with a clamour of self-excusing explanations. She took him to her with a funny little smile and they hugged, pressing into each other, breathing, brother and sister in God's cold world.

An Early Release

The Eggbox sat on a sloping rectangle which only the Department of Main Roads could have coveted, and fortunately the Labor Council had prevailed on the DMR to cede its claim.

Behind, parallel to the western alignment, ran a light goods freight line. At the shoulder of the track, chunks of blue metal broke away and tumbled downhill, under a canopy of serpent-toothed leaves and beady black berries, into the stormwater canal.

Before, to the east, and golden yellow in the street directory, lay a major secondary road. All day semi-trailers grumbled across country from the docks to the factories and warehouses that had pushed south and west in pursuit of cheaper land.

To the north were the Great Western Highway's six lanes of fuming acceleration, to the south the diesel and electric locomotives of the Great Western Railway Line. Trucks and trains cooperated to fill the noisome air with tiny particles as black as the nightshade berries. Coagulating with the dust, this fallout bestowed on every surface a toffee coating.

Into the air—air rendered visible by the miracles of science—rose power poles and neon advertising hoardings. And above them, aircraft cut flightpaths through the haze.

Over the years the Eggbox had settled into the slope. Rust stains streaked its cement blocks and a crack zigzagged across the northern wall. While the building's shape and colour had no doubt suggested its name, there lingered the psychic odour of battery hens, the sound of the flapping of clipped wings, and the bushy, sweet, clovery scent of imagined freedom.

At lunchtime there was nothing to do. Those without cars played five hundred in the tearoom on the ground floor. Those with cars drove to the Marketown shops. After work, prospects for the carless male improved. Just one station away, in the Oxford Tavern, a bevy of topless maids celebrated the rituals of the happy hour.

The new editor, Clyde, puzzled everyone. On his first day he worked—or, at least, read—right through the lunchbell. Urged to take a break, he snapped on his bicycle clips and pedalled off, whistling, to explore the sidestreets.

The Indo-Chinese, he observed, were the most noticeable residents. When they were inside they left their thongs at the door, under the little red altar attached to the wall. Outside, they turned neglected rockeries into vegetable gardens. Old women in pyjamas squatted on driveways, old men spat. The new editor waved to them, but they were suspicious.

At afternoon tea, Julie the receptionist wobbled all the way up the hall with a cup and saucer, only to find the new editor making his own brew with a funny little dripfilter. To add insult to injury, he tried to sell her a packet of beans which he declared to have been imported direct from the plantation workers' hands and to be as pure and wholesome as any drug could be said to be.

At five o'clock the new editor was still reading. Swinging their briefcases on their fingers, the Managers polkaed one by one to his door and enquired: 'Haven't you got a home to go to?' The new editor replied that he got his best thinking done between six and eight, when the phones stopped jangling.

This habit did not, in the Managers' opinion, compensate for Clyde's lateness in the mornings, which turned out to be chronic. They suspected he stayed back to make free international phone calls. The Accountant went so far as to advise the General Manager a meter should be placed on the new editor's phone, just in case. The GM compromised by having the receptionist close off all lines at night except for one of the three which purred all day on his desk top. It was a polite fiction that the GM stayed late to take overseas calls. He took them in comfort at home—that was why he needed a telephone allowance.

The new editor didn't mind taking his calls at the GM's desk. While he talked he scanned the letters and notes in the drawers and in-tray. He tried the filing cabinets, looking for a pen, but they were locked. He regularly took calls from his parents in Auckland and his sometime girlfriend, Merryn, in Tokyo. A couple of authors who were living overseas phoned in too, chasing royalty cheques. The new editor was proud of his self discipline in limiting his outgoing calls to local numbers.

The ground floor of the Eggbox comprised a loading bay and compactuses full of stock. Pickers (female) trudged around on the concrete, pulling out books imported from Europe and the States. Packers (male) stood on mats at metal tables, transforming books, wadding, brown paper and tape into mysteriously satisfying packages.

The Business Manager, Old Joe, sat in a glass cubicle smoking and dealing with customs agents, couriers, suppliers and the delivery truck-driver who arrived every afternoon at three. He'd been doing it for twenty years in the service of the cause, for eighteen without a job title. His staff were universally acclaimed as meatheads, incapable of seeing the larger picture. Left to their own devices they would never have had the orders ready by three.

At the top of the stairs were the Ladies' and Gentlemen's rooms, enjoying a northerly aspect, and the reception counter. The new editor did not like having to pass Julie the receptionist every time he went to the Gents. She told him he was funny. Her Brad had a good haircut and a tan. The new editor wore a foreign uniform: button-down shirt (Brooks Brothers, he told her), Fair-isle vest, corduroy trousers (even in summer), Oxblood brogues and spectacles. He looked like Woody Allen distraught in the Californian sun.

Julie wore crease-free polycotton uniforms. She renewed her nail enamel daily, changing it finger by finger between calls. She flitted about on high-heeled sandals exposing her coloured toenails and flapping message slips between tacky fingertips. Her blonded bob was so neat you could see the comb tracks. Her underarms were impeccable. The new editor supposed she waxed her pubic hair.

First along the western side of the hall were the accounts clerks: an arthritic woman called Gwen and two younger women who strained Gwen's patience by arriving late (on alternate days, seemingly) complaining of modern delays—car servicing appointments, swimming pool maintenance men, and fertility clinic check-ins.

Opposite them, in a sound-proofed room, a woman sat all day at a data input terminal. Actually there were two women. They did six hours each, covering the daylight hours from six to six. They swapped hours and shifts as it suited them, and no-one was ever too sure which of them was tapping away behind the door. Since they were both Chinese, the new editor was not certain which was which anyway. Lee Ling and Poh Chuen, he recited as he cycled.

The Accountant, Alf McGarity, occupied the office next to the computer room. He had aspired to be GM but had been rolled when he had gone away on Long Service Leave. He had received the bad news in the hotel at Banff. His wife was terrified he'd take a turn, he went so pale and quivery. His rage was still contained. He was serving out his last three years, bypassing the computer and monopolising the GM's secretary with volleys of correspondence which could have been better despatched by phone or form letter.

Next along from Alf was the Marketing Manager, a good bloke, Mick. In the early years of expansion he'd been Sales Rep, Sales Manager, Order Clerk, Customer Relations—the lot in one thin, freckled ockerism. He was nobody's fool. He relaxed now with his credenza and dictaphone. Through the woodgrain partition he listened to Lorraine—the secretary he shared with Sales—reciting in sing-song mock courtesy: 'No, I'm sorry, Mr Jellicoe is in conference right now.'

Lorraine was an organizer with no free time to marry. She was stocky as a three-door filing cabinet. Recently she had sold her unit around the corner because the Vietnamese had been worrying her mum: their cooking smells alone, not to mention their other habits. She was rebuying further west, not far from Mick. 'Good for train strikes,' she beamed, thumping the stapler.

Opposite Alf's office was Loco, the Sales Manager. He was out most of the time, so did not mind having one of the western rooms, which were chilly in the mornings and sweltering by mid-afternoon. Loco was a wildcard: he had an ex-wife and teenagers back in Yorkshire, a new girlfriend and baby girl in Fairfield. He softened up clients by showing them photos of the baby. Her colic smile declared: 'I'm not offloading you with something you can't move.'

The room next to Loco's was reserved for the Sales force, Ray and Roy. The appeared on Fridays to boast of the week's feats, line up appointments, collect their pay and compare petrol prices.

Next along from Sales and opposite Lorraine was Sylvia, the GM's secretary. She was continuously tied up with typing for the GM and Alf. No-one had had an uninterrupted conversation with her in years. The new editor was told to send his work out to a manuscript typist called Christine. She typed at home, syllable by syllable, whilst entertaining her sister's toddler. She produced so many literals her pages looked like the effusions of a Joycean autodidact.

The new editor's office was next to Sylvia and opposite the GM. He had been installed in this exclusive preserve not because of status but because he was presumed to require a quiet area away from the flow of visitors. This was fair enough—but the GM's voice was as a thousand visitors. It boomed across the hall and reverberated through the boardroom which occupied the southern end of the Eggbox.

The new editor soon knew the GM's end of every murky deal. He shut his door and moved his desk but could still hear more than enough. He began to record the GM's ideological breeches in a notebook which he kept in the bottom drawer where the previous incumbent had left her tampons.

The GM thought the new editor an odd fish. Nonetheless his credentials sounded good when announced at trade fairs, and he was willing to work for the award rate while carrying all the responsibilities of a Manager and getting none of the kudos or perks. It was a nice set-up. How long it would last the GM could not predict. It had been eighteen months with the previous one.

The unworldly have their purpose, the GM had decided. You merely had to ignore their bicycle helmets and dotty enthusiasms. They were usually unmarried and scruffy. Unless suitably spruced up and kept away from the grog, they could not be trusted at Board meetings and Sales presentations. They could not keep to the point. They found their raison d'être in bizarre causes. They scattered their offices with broadsheets. They gave out pamphlets. They wrote letters to newspapers and companies and the wrong politicians. They sticky-beaked into balance sheets and share holdings. You could not even have a cup of tea in peace without them wanting you to contemplate the deprivations of the Tamils. They were at once one jump ahead of you and a couple behind.

The GM lived uncontentiously at Denistone in a privatised community of middle-managers and right-wing Laborites and second-generation Bible-belters. He wore uncreasable viscose suits from his shop at Eastwood. 'It's all in my wife's name,' he had assured the Board, who were warily impressed. The GM drove to work in an Alfa leased by the shop and invested his car allowance. No-one on the Board chose to argue so long as he did not angle for a profit share. Power was a tax-free emolument.

The GM had begun life speaking a Calabrian steel-town patois. Now, if he wasn't sure of a word or fact, he turned up the volume and switched on the lights in his black eyes. He had an instict for hyperbole. He was devoted to building up the Sales team and Distribution network. The Publishing arm—which was terminally unprofitable, given the size and mentality of the market, but close to the Board's heart—was to be carried at least cost.

The GM had replaced the partition between his office and the Boardroom with folding doors. These he always left open.

For his first six months the new editor tasted authority with the tip of his tongue. It tingled like sherbet. He flew to Melbourne to a book fair; he went by train to Canberra to a conference; he phoned Perth. He rejected a couple of manuscripts a day. He pushed on with the projects which his predecessor had left at page-proof stage. He brooded over what next to publish. There was no written policy.

'Whatever will sell,' Mick advised.

'Play safe,' Loco cautioned.

'Something with a strong cover,' the Reps begged.

'Commission a story from a big name,' the GM suggested, hopeful of an overnight hit. 'But don't neglect our regulars.' For the regulars had mates on the Board.

'What is our rationale?' the new editor asked. We are an arm of the Labor movement, he was told. We don't put out radical stuff. We have our established ambit. Look at our backlist.

Down in the warehouse the pickers did not open the books they tossed into their trolleys. The new editor did not know any unionists or party members who read these books. People he cornered at co-op meetings derided the titles he mentioned. Libraries buy us, he was told, and colleges, and specialist bookshops, and education officers, and there's always the mail-order trade. We get rid of them one way or another.

'But do you change society?' he wailed.

'That's not our brief,' Mick sighed.

'So it's pure profit. For who?'

'According to our constitution we're not a profit-making organisation. Otherwise we'd pay taxes.'

'But the distribution business runs at a profit.'

'And it all goes back into the movement.'

'So what's the point?'

'The point is for you to turn out a dozen books a year on approved issues. Without upsetting the apple-cart. Without incurring losses. And without talking bloody politics all the time.'

The new editor dreamed of going for the popular market. Meanwhile he read Phd theses, ethical rambles from retired clergy, reform manifestoes from fanatics, polemical faction from feminists, unfunny memoirs by retired senators, ballads by old-time union men. The decent writers preferred to go with glossy publishers who had tie-ups with papers which would publish extracts. The new editor fielded visits from eighty-year-old metal workers and cancerous poets and shouting Stalinists.

He was responsible to no-one but the GM, who was inordinately chummy. On wet nights the GM offered the new editor a lift home. Once he invited the new editor to a barbecue and introduced his diet-streaked wife and nubile daughters. He tolerated the new editor's questions and demands as those of a feverish child calling for lemonade.

'Just do the job,' Loco said flatly.

The new editor sat in his compartment of the Eggbox and downed the Cafe Bar murk the receptionist delivered. He drafted letters to the Board exposing Management's lack of commitment to fundamentals. Pragmatism dictated the Board would side with the GM and his team. And who was to say it was not the new editor who lacked fervour? Strip away his causes, his idiosyncrasies, his need of a dollar, and did you have one of the true faithful? He was as lukewarm as the rest.

The new editor was coming up to eight months at the Eggbox. He had set himself a two-year deadline. Once he'd achieved something—books with his name in the Author's Note—he'd go back to Macquarie Uni and finish his Master's. He was tempted to get back into it now, in office time. He began to make freer use of the photocopier and stationery. The Accountant watched.

One November morning, before the new editor and Mick and Loco had arrived, Alf went in to see the GM.

'The half-yearly figures,' he said. 'We're way over budget.'

'In what areas?'

'The computer's eating money.'

'I'm relaxed about that, Alf. We knew there'd be big capital costs, and running-in costs, and the Board okayed the outlay.'

'The salesmen's expenses are getting out of hand.'

'They've penetrated an entire new State this year, Alf, and we've never had so many Christmas orders. We'd be cutting our own throats if we clipped their wings.'

'Mick's way over his promotional budget.'

'Mick's a good bloke. We have to tread carefully.'

'Then there's Publishing.'

'Where we've got one bloke doing the lot. And he's hanging on by the skin of his teeth.'

'We're facing a whopping printing bill from Singapore in the first half of next year. All these books he's been tying up the loose ends on—they're all overdue to go off to the printers—I've been stalling him for weeks now— '

'Yes, he's looking to a multiple release about May next year, with Mick tying in a big print campaign. His first wham-bang spectacular.'

'But Publishing hasn't got the cash flow to print six or eight books in one hit. Why aren't they being staggered, one every couple of months? Or at least spread the payments...'

'I've told him I want one a month. He's been slogging to get this lot out of the way before Christmas so he could start on the new manuscripts we've okayed. He's figuring on a one-a-month release from July onwards, he says.'

'I tell you, Tony, Publishing hasn't got the money to put up for all this.'

'He doesn't know that.'

'He's got to know. We can't go borrowing from Distribution to print books that'll sit on the shelves from now to kingdom come.'

'We could.'

'The Board expressly vetoed it when I put the idea to them. When that long-haired editor...'

'The Board have a soft spot for Publishing.'

'Not if it's twenty-five thousand down the gurgler they don't.'

'That much?'

'We could risk putting out the dough for the May releases provided I knew there was nothing coming along for a clear six months after that. It'd give us time to recoup a bit of the outlay.'

'That'd mean...'

'Yes.'

'Leave it with me Alf. Meanwhile get me some hard figures on how much fat we've got to cut.'

The GM was in the habit of meeting with Bill, the Chairman of the Board, once a month. They held their breakfast conference, as the GM referred to it, in the Chairman's backyard at Eastlakes. They'd sit drinking tea and watching Bill's kelpie pacing around the fence. They'd talk golf until Bill's wife Marcia took the washing up inside, then the GM would broach his latest plans.

At their November meeting Bill began reminiscing about the Whitlam dismissal.

'I have a dismissal of my own in mind,' the GM ventured, pleased with his adroit use of the language.

Bill ruffled the dog's neck and murmured encouragement.

'This new editor is a troublemaker.'

'Uh-huh.'

'I had in mind giving him the pip after the Board dinner. If that's all right with you?'

'I've never met the man.'

'Perhaps you should.'

'You want the Board to be involved?'

'It's not necessary. If you watch him at the meeting you'll see what I'm getting at. He's a malcontent.'

'Let's see how he performs then. I don't want to be seen to ditch a bloke I've never met.'

'Our last Board meeting of the year is always a bit of a knees-up,' the GM told the new editor the next day. 'Each of you Department Heads is invited to make a presentation. Then we all go to dinner at the Chinese in Concord Road.'

'Wear a tie,' he added at the door, 'and keep to the bloody point.'

They presented themselves—Old Joe, Alf, Mick, Loco and the new editor—for inspection at six p.m. It was a hot evening. The air conditioner in the new editor's office had not been repaired, although he had asked Alf twice, and he had been close to passing out as the western sun hit the concrete and galvanised iron. He had been slogging since eight that morning to get all the manuscripts photocopied and ready for Singapore. The GM had driven home to shower and change into a wool-silk mix suit and YSL tie. The others had pulled on jackets and combed their sweaty hair. Julie had inspected each one as he passed to the Gents for a last-minute tinkle. She was staying back to welcome the Board members and hand around drinks. She wore new iridiscent nail varnish.

The Board Chairman was always a Labor Council nominee, a diplomat with authority to crush extremists, a head counter and kicker. But the Deputy Chairman was traditionally given more latitude. He could be a bit of a stirrer, provided he did not also have supporters. The position was currently held by an inner-city leftie who published a free newspaper and was reputed to understand the practical tribulations of small business. The new editor's attempts to effect an alliance with him had been cold-shouldered, but he hung onto his belief that the Deputy had influenced his employment. Newspaper schedules must give rise to choler and aloofness, the new editor had decided; it was the least distressing conclusion.

The remainder of the Board consisted of a Catholic priest, for probity, a Labor branch president, for democracy, a woman, for intuition, three retired union men, and four businessmen who had kept on side with the unions. The businessmen were ranked according to the size of their companies' profits.

They all stood holding drinks in the reception foyer, edging closer to the air conditioning units. The new editor talked to one of the businessmen, an importer called Barney Ko, about protectionism. Mr Ko deplored Australia's tariffs and quotas; the new editor described the hibiscus-shaded sweatshops he had glimpsed on a cycling trip through Indonesia. When the GM, circulating and booming, kicked his anklebone, he excused himself and went to the Gents. At the wash basins he found himself beside Bill.

'How are you getting on with us?' the Chairman enquired, inspecting his moustache in the mirror.

'It's very challenging,' the new editor replied, turning on a tap too hard, splashing the Chairman's suit, 'but I need clearer goals.'

'They'll come.' The Chairman ripped off a length of paper towel, rubbed at his suit, leaving a speckle of white, and pushed out the swing door. The new editor cleaned his nails methodically under the running water.

Collecting glasses, Julie asked the gentlemen to join the Chairman in the Boardroom. The GM held the door wide and patted each back as it passed in. The new editor was the last in, equal last with Old Joe. Most of the Board members were still standing and bending, fussing over settling the lone woman in the seat of their choice and arranging themselves in an advantageous pattern based on hierarchy and planned participation. Old Joe backed out and returned pulling a couple of clerks' chairs. 'Three more,' the GM instructed.

At last all were seated: the Chairman at the head, with his back to the street windows and the chugging aircon unit; the Deputy to his right; the GM to his left; the businessmen facing each other; then the priest and woman and branch president facing the oldtimers; and, in a semicircle at the far end of the table, nudging and edging on their castors, the five Managers.

'I'm delighted,' the GM boomed, 'to be winding up the year on such a positive note. Our Distribution operation is showing very healthy profits. I expect the mid-year figures, which Alf here will be preparing straight after Christmas'—Alf inclined his head, to jibes about no rest for the wicked—'will show a substantial increase overall. Messrs Jellicoe and Locanto will be telling you more about that. Our import side is running very smoothly, thanks to our good friend Joe. And there are some promising prospects for exporting our own products to south east Asia...'

The GM went on for ten minutes, producing sheets of interim figures typed flawlessly by Sylvia. 'A wonderful worker, Sylvia', Alf observed. 'And a good sort,' one oldtimer winked. The men chuckled. Most knew her only as a formidably efficient voice—she kept typing when she answered the phone.

'Tony can pick 'em,' the Deputy applauded. He had once made a pass at the GM's wife. The lone woman studied the priest's red neck, where it folded down over his dog collar.

Alf, Mick, Loco, Old Joe—they gave their little speeches in that order. The GM listened attentively, adding riders. The Board stirred. The lone woman went out to the kitchen and came back with a jug of tap water and glasses. It was heading for eight o'clock and stomachs were rumbling.

'Last but not least,' the GM announced, 'our new editor, Clyde, who's given us all a most challenging year.' His black eyes shone.

'Ah well,' thought the new editor, 'as well for a sheep as a lamb.'

'I had planned,' he began, pressing a pencil tip into the table, 'to summarise the projects I've seen through to the printing stage this year. And to foreshadow next year's publications. But,' he raised his chin in the GM's direction, 'there will be no worthwhile projects unless we have policies. Publishing is the poor relation of Distribution...' He was making no impact. They had heard it all before.

'We don't stand for true Labor ideals any more.' He jabbed the pencil into a knothole. The Deputy was studying his face.

The phone on the GM's desk chirruped. The businessmen's hands lifted in a reflex response.

'It could be for me,' the new editor said. 'One of my authors is in Geneva.'

'I hope he isn't in the habit of reversing the charges,' the Deputy growled.

The GM stretched towards his desk. His fingers dislodged the receiver, which fell to the carpet.

'Harro,' shrieked a girl's voice. 'Harro, Cryde. Is that Cryde? This is your rittle Tokyo Rose cawing.' The dreadful pidgin Japanese echoed around the room. Everyone was silent, listening. The girl shrieked out her witticisms.

'Too much saki,' Barney Ko observed at last. The new editor tumbled off his rolling chair and grabbed the received.

'Merryn,' he ordered. 'Merryn. It's not convenient for me to talk now. Merryn, I'm serious. I'm hanging up now— '

'I'm sorry.' He wiped his forehead. 'A silly friend. Christmas. I'm sorry.'

'Your die is cast,' the Deputy thought, rolling a pen across his patch of table.

'Let's move on to dinner,' the GM said, folding his papers.

The Chairman cleared his throat. 'Would anybody like to move we accept those reports?'

Next morning the new editor came in earlier than usual. He could hear the GM on the phone. 'Yes, yes, Bill... This morning. My opinion too... One month's is enough... No, no handouts... OK Bill.'

A few minutes later the GM came into the new editor's office without knocking. He sat in the visitor's chair, legs wide apart, and scratched his crotch.

'The Chairman wants your resignation, old boy. Pronto.'

'You're sacking me.'

'No, I'm not. The Chairman thinks it's best if you resign.'

'Why? What have I done wrong?'

'The Chairman thinks you'd be happier somewhere else.'

'Why didn't you stand up for me?'

'I did. It was me who hired you, remember? My reputation was at stake.'

'Then who rolled me?'

'Nobody, Clyde. I keep telling you, nobody. Can't you see reason?'

They wrangled on and on. Their voices carried down the hall to the women. Ideals, pay, job title, lack of support staff—Clyde plied his complaints. Naiveté, the GM countered, immaturity, inconsistency, discontent, bad influence on staff, failure to turn out enough product, not one new thing in print in nine months.

It was approaching midday and another scorcher. The new editor's head ached—he had drunk more than was wise at the Board's dinner. He stood up.

'I'm going out for a breather.'

The GM noted the time, then walked up to the Accountant's office.

'Clyde is resigning,' he told Alf. 'Cut off his pay as from today. He's going to finish off those page proofs at home. When he brings them back in, we'll settle.'

At Marketown, the new editor rang a solicitor friend. 'I want the max,' he ranted. 'Damages, the lot.'

'A small matter,' the GM boomed to the company's solicitor. 'A disruptive influence... refusing to go quietly... termination.'

When he came back from his cycle trip, the new editor found Sylvia packing the papers on his desk.

'The boss says you're going to work from home.'

The new editor slammed into the GM's office. Their voices

bounced down the corridor. Loco shut his door. Mick opened his and told Lorraine to give the typewriter a rest. The air conditioners buzzed, the computer hummed.

Loco gave the new editor a lift home with his bike on the roof-rack and all the manuscripts and reference books in cartons on the backseat. The new editor had taken a more than adequate supply of stationery, as well as samples of all the hardbacks in the warehouse, though he knew he would never care to open them and would hate looking at them on his shelves.

The new editor worked out his time at home. He felt a loyalty to his authors. And—where the GM had not got to them first—they responded: warmly at best, diplomatically at least. The GM phoned daily, at varying hours. The only days he did not ring were the Christmas and New Year public holidays.

The new editor's money was almost exhausted by January. He emptied his Building Society account to keep the rent up to date and gave his family IOU's in place of Christmas presents. Friends, among them Merryn, received the foot-and-mouth painters' cards which had been sent to him unsolicited. To cap it all, his bicycle was stolen on New Year's Eve.

On the fifteenth of January, a hot, still Friday, the new editor caught the train west and, bending under a backpack of papers and folders, trudged beside the railway lines to the Eggbox. Inside, the computer hummed, the air conditioners churned hot air, dust danced in shafts of sunlight. Downstairs, Old Joe picked and packed. At the top of the stairs, Julie buffed her nails. The GM was in Alf's office bending over the midyear spreadsheets. Further down the corridor Sylvia was typing. The new editor stood at the accountant's door.

'I've come to drop back these papers.' He spoke in a voice as dreary as the air. 'And to pick up my pay.'

'We won't be long,' the GM said, still bending with his backside towards the new editor. 'Meanwhile there's a bit of paperwork to be cleaned up in your old room.'

The air conditioning was still out of action. The desk was dusty. Both chairs had been poached. The new editor borrowed Lorraine's chair and began working through a heap of unanswered correspondence and unchecked proofs. When the heat threatened to overcome him, he took the papers into the Boardroom and sat at the head of the table with the cold air playing over his back.

By three-thirty he had finished. He sat, then, and waited. At four he went down to the warehouse and borrowed something to read. At five-past-five the GM came to the door of the Boardroom and indicated with a thumb for the new editor to follow him.

'Alf's got your cheque,' he said over his shoulder, 'but first you've got to sign a release.'

The new editor looked up into the GM's black eyes.

'Got someone else lined up?' he asked.

'Possibilities.' The GM was cheerily confidential. 'One chap of very high calibre.'

'Will you set him up too?'

'The same employment terms apply. The job hasn't changed.'

'I'll tell my friends.'

Rising from signing, the new editor rubbed his aching neck and wriggled his pack onto his shoulders. He walked out past the GM.

At the top of the stairs he said, 'See you later, Julie.'

'Good luck,' she cooed.

'Give my best to Brad.'

'You too.'

The new editor steeped out into the hot westerly wind and, whistling through his teeth, headed for the station.

Half way up the slope he clicked his fingers, exclaimed 'Damn!', and turned around.

Alf was just getting into his car. The new editor realised he was blushing and the realisation made him go redder. He followed Alf's damp shirt back and shiny seat upstairs and accepted a sealed envelope. Flushing and twitching, he fled out past Julie again and down the stairs.

On the train he eased his pack onto the floor, opened the envelope, studied the cheque, and did a quick count on his fingers.

'The bastards,' he whispered, and tears filled his eyes. 'The bastards.'

Gidget in a Parka

To get to where I grew up, you must turn off the highway at the first lights after the Shoalhaven bridge. Turn left, mind, not right. (I am assuming you are coming from Sydney). The road, you will find, is at first broad and pleasingly surfaced, but it soon narrows. And, while your map may show it as straight, it in fact slummocks along like an old drunk.

You may wonder where you are heading. With the river now out of sight, lying low beyond a green swathe, you may not realise it is determining your route, washing you out to the ocean. Nor, unless you stop the car and trespass across a few paddocks to the bank, will you see a shapely little oval of land basking in the middle of the stream. This is Pig Island. If you have your binoculars, you may spot a porcine lorelei sunning her pink belly and enticing rowboats to strand themselves in the mud.

Keep going, now. The road stretches before you. The sky is peacock blue.

Speed is relaxing. The air rushes past you. The colours blur. Hit the brakes, quickly.

You have stopped, ladies and gentlemen, at a most interesting waterway. Stopped a little abruptly, admittedly. Stopped dead in your tracks, indeed. Now, this strip of water may look to you like a boring creek. But the cringing land on the other side is that oddest of inventions, a manmade island. It is called Comerong, it is shaped vaguely like a tuba, or a bong, yes, and it spans the mouth of the river, taunting Scylla to dip a toe in Charybdis and blocking your view of the ocean. It is a spoilsport and a tease. The creek, by the way, is actually another manmade phenomenon, a canal—I will not bore you with its history—and to get across it you will need to trust that oddest of conveyances, the punt.

Of course, I must remind you, there is no need to cross the canal. Consult your map again. As you can see, you have overshot the turnoff.

Around we go. Please be careful not to get bogged as you execute your three-point-turn, and have a little regard for people's gateposts.

On the way back it may be as well to pay some attention to the landscape.

I can tell you that from the air these riverflats look like a Mondrian laid out to dry on a bowling green. The red squares are coral trees, the pink gardens, the yellow sheds, the white silos and the grey tanks. Between run black fences. As you dogleg around the squares and rectangles, you will see the colours are not pure. That pink cottage garden is really a pointillist medley of white pickets and paperdaisies, red roses, orange pelargoniums and yellow citrus, all on a ground of squelchy lawn and black, bubbling soil. That bowling green, too, on which the Mondrian rests: it is flecked. Someone has spattered it with cows. Each cow is a beautiful sleek design of black and white. Each one is as individual as a snowflake. And each one is accompanied by its own picky little white handmaiden. Did you notice?

Perhaps you were distracted by the joggle of villages. They are named Terara and Numbaa, and I'm sure you have them confused already. Last century they were self-important towns with all the appurtenances of law and order. Purblind Canutes, they commanded the floodwaters to stay back. But in '70, and '74, and again and again, the river rose, flushing men and their works out of the antheaps they had constructed with such temerity. Purple mountains watched as the intruders retreated upstream to Nowra. Blackbutts watched too, not entirely inhospitably, and the black bowls of treeferns, and black rocks ebony shiny with clean running water.

Now I've lost you. Go back along the road until you see a sign saying Jindy Andy Lane. On second thoughts, look out for a turnoff on your left: the sign may well be missing. Follow the lane for three kilometres. Yes, city slicker, it is a lane. Only urban lanes are short. Country lanes are narrow channels, and they are as long as they are long.

By now you should have realised you are heading at right angles to that treacherous, pigidle river. If the paddocks become too dull, crane your neck and look up. Sunglasses may help. There are pelicans in this part of the world, and pairs of black swans, and, craft imitating nature, aeroplanes.

Not far now. Jindy Andy Lane, our quaint byway, has come to

its end. You have reached the true road out to the true beaches.

Turn left—it *is* always left, isn't it?—and drive another three kilometres. The house where I grew up is over there, towards the swamp. But what I really brought you here to see is the hall on the corner.

The Pyree Literary Institute is a wooden temple painted scarlet, or roan, or burgundy, or rust red, depending on the bias of your eye and the height of the sun. Above its doors a plaque—painted, to guess from the lettering style, in the thirties—states *AD1894*. *AD* of course, lest any of you archaeologists and artists mistake our hall for the crowning achievement of a classical civilization. *AD*, too, because the Pyree Literary Institute, stands still, and always, for the grandeur of the past extrapolated into the future.

At sunset the hall glows red, a fire for the swamp dwellers, a beacon for seafarers, a physician's sign for a dying age. At dawn, as the mist clears and the kookaburras laugh, the cowdung steams and the calves stumble, the damp, smelly veil of agriculture lifts and the Shoalhaven is taken bridal into the kingdom of the spirit.

It is time for you to imbibe this pungent, humid air and, trusting to the currents, launch out. Follow the white, effervescing, crushed aspirin beaches out to the heads. Look at the patterns in the tesselated pavements. Count the ramshorn shells. Swoop down to stroke a flannel flower. The merest touch to the rope sets the bell reverberating.

Hail! cry the bull ants. Can you hear them? *Hail!* roars the mud. *Hail!* the watertank beats out. *Hail!* the tin roofs resound. *Pyree*, they sing. *Pyre*, *pyre*, *pyre*, *Pyree*. The flames of a brushfire tongue a sapling. The undergrowth must be burnt out before a new age can begin. *Py-ree*, the native bees exult.

Down by the river the grass is quiet. Too lush and sodden to join our chorus, it murmurs underfoot. Whole paddocks grumble. The cows caress the grass with their thick lips and, anointing it with their piss, draw it into the communion. *All hail!* nature cries.

But, while you are caught up in your rhapsody, I have slipped away. At the far extremity of that cringing manmade island, I am launching myself toward another island, an island weighted down by a million columns sunk into the bedrock. *America*, I vow.

Beside the subway booth where I queue to buy bus tokens stands a fat black woman. She notes how many tokens are requested and how much money is tendered and she pitches her spiel accordingly. 'Can you spare a dime, sir?... A dollar, m'am?' I don't know if it is public observation, guilt pangs or admiration which drives each of us to hand over our change. She is possessed of a mind as fast as a calculator in a body shiny with health. I figure she'd be raking in a hundred an hour. Perhaps there is a little white pimp around the corner.

On the grid my hotel is between Hells Kitchen and Times Square. Next door is a bathhouse. Farther up the cinemas are flashing out pleas and assertions: *Make Me Wet*, *Black Chicks Do It Better*. Across the road are two little black cubes: an actors' chapel and an unlit theatre.

My business in New York—the gift fair at the Javits Center—requires only a few days, but I have decided to stay on for a couple of weeks. There is no need to hurry back: I've at last broken in an excellent shop manager, and my husband is away in Asia. Had I cared to contact them, a number of my husband's business associates would have entertained me in their homes upstate, along the Hudson, but I intend to remain anonymous on Manhattan. I do not anticipate feeling lonely or unduly alarmed. I am by now accustomed to the hazards of big cities.

Sunday morning: I open the window to the roar of hundreds of motorbikes. As TV cameras pan across the snowy street, men in black leather with bulbous helmets swarm into ranks and pyramids. Girls in red leather miniskirts pose across handlebars. From ten floors above, they are bull ants skittering across an ice-rink. *Leader of the Pack* is to open on Wednesday. It will close on Saturday night as rain washes over the sidewalk and hookers cringe back into doorways and the damning reviews hit.

Monday: Stepping into the elevator, I confront a man holding a Jack Russell terrier to his chest. 'Oh, what a cute little fellow,' I babble, forgetting caution. The dog permits me to joggle his paw. I have not touched another mammal's body for a fortnight. I learn the dog bears a name as long as his jaunty body, Jubilee Prince Dartington, and his owner, Morton W. Clarke, is in town for the Westminster dog show. The Hispanic hotel staff have turned a blind eye to their four-legged guest: they are used to Washingtonians' oddities. Mort's other entrants are correctly benched in the basement at Madison Square Garden. As Mort holds the doors open at my floor, I wish them both luck.

Wind chill is taking the temperature to thirty below. By day I have been confined to the galleries and museums. At one place I have, in exchange for a dry, warm hour, sat through a multi-screen slideshow on the privations of the early traders.

Tuesday night: As I lie alone in my shit-brown hotel room watching the grand final judging of the dog show, self-pity envelopes me like a smelly blanket. On the screen a balding man in a tuxedo watches perspiring bachelors and lurex women with muscular calves lead half a dozen animals round and round. On my kingsized bed I huddle under a jacquard spread eating chocolate-chip cookies.

I have received one phone call from my husband. He is staying in his usual hotel, the Regal Meridian, and seeing the usual developers. For light relief he has been out on a run with the Hash House Harriers. He has also, I guess from his reticence, renewed acquaintance with the systems analyst he met last time. He has described this woman to me as a tenacious hard worker, the type either of us would be delighted to employ. I suspect she is on the make, looking for a sponsor to help her get out. How little one sees at first acquaintance through the cultural lattice-work, I once remarked to my husband. He retorted she would get whatever she wanted without his help.

Wednesday: Mort has sent a message via Reception: he is about to walk Dart in Central Park if I care to come along. The sun is out, the wind has died down and the snow is white as a gull. It will be an opportunity for some photos.

We slosh along muddy tracks between traffic and snow banks. This is not the winter wonderland I have seen in movies. I force myself to enumerate the park's attractions for people confined on this rapacious floating hotel. The same attractions, I figure, which lead Londoners to rush out onto a sodden heath with makeshift toboggans the minute the first snowflakes tickle their noses: attractions of the imagination.

Dart scampers about, hockdeep in powdery snow. Mort shapes snowballs and shies them at treetrunks. Emboldened, he tosses one underarm at me. His grin is goofy, like that of the retiring type who is inevitably dragged up onto the stage of the theatre-restaurant to cringe at the banter of an underwired hostess in fishnet stockings. Celebrities seem to look down on us from gigantic screens and hoardings, patrons of this flickering city, muses of romance. Compelled by the memory of all those surf and ski movies, I hurl a handful of snow at Mort. He retaliates. We cavort as if a *gentil organisateur* stands at our backs. He is as unsophisticated as the boys I grew up with. A girl from the Shoalhaven and a boy from Washington. For the moment I am Gidget in a parka.

Mort tells me he worked as a wardsman to put himself

through college. After graduating, he joined the government. He says he is a clerk but is evasive about his duties and department. Persistent questioning leads to the admission by silence that he works for the equivalent of our ASIO. His duties are no more than marginally nefarious. He does not tap phonelines. Sedition and subversion are not his direct responsibility. He is a salaried cipher, as I am a providore of luxury inessentials, both loyal operatives in a system beyond us.

Thursday: Daily for a week, Mort and I have gone about together, with Dart our proxy offspring. Mort is movie-mad. He insists on seeing every new release, and then all the old ones at the art cinemas. Inbetween sessions we ferret through cult shops for additions to his collection of stills, recordings, posters and badges. When he pushes up his sleeves, I see tattoos of the movie studios' logos. Once Mort pushes the MGM logo under Dart's nose and dares him to growl back.

I have kept on asking Mort when he is due back at work, and he has retaliated by asking me the same question.

He is badly besotted with me, I fear. But he is immature, I do not respect him, I could never seriously countenance an alliance with him. The poor guy is lonely. Then, again, he is a spy. Perhaps he has been assigned to pry into my husband's business connections. Ridiculous. I have seen far too many American movies lately. But where does one begin to distinguish dissembling from infatuation, and self-delusion from actuality? Why should I bother? It is time to clear out.

Friday evening: Another phone call from my husband. Regarding the Chinese lass he has been trying to help: matters have become complicated. She is infatuated with him and he has had to let her down gently.

Mort tells me his parents would approve of me. I dress modestly—in this cold, who would not?—and I observe the proprieties. There are no portents of an unleashed spirit.

Saturday: This evening over dinner Mort hints at an engagement. I tell him I am agreeably married. He bridles.

Sunday: I check out of the *Ambassador* early in the morning. Taxis are cruising. Fast food purveyors are pushing up their roller doors. Hustlers are leaning against ticket booths chatting to women whose spike heels stab the litter.

Mort, Dart and I take a final promenade along 49th. Mort lugs my suitcase and bags of samples. I hold Dart's leash and let him tow me from one exciting stench to the next. At Grand Central I catch the express bus to JFK.

The road passes acres of tombstones, legions of toppled men and women confined under snow and slush with grey slabs of stone weighing down their heads. I have forgotten you have to pass this to get out of New York.

All hail to the living and the dead. All hail to the spirit of the Pyree Literary Institute. It is time again to ready ourselves for flight. Down around the headstones the earth is sodden. It sucks on the homeless. Acres grumble. Winds buffet the ice.

I look back—along the freeway, over the bridge—to that fabled, manmade island. To those pigidle lorelei. *Australia*, I sigh.

He was infatuated with me, I shall tell my husband, but I bowed out gracefully. It is easier to come home, provided you know where home is.

What Happened up There?

'And now,' the priest lifts his hands, 'we'll share the sign of peace.'

We're expected to shake the hands of our neighbours and say, 'Peace be with you,' or 'Good to see you,' or somesuch. I'm always put out by this interruption to the flow of confession, forgiveness, petition, preparation. I turn unwillingly to my left.

There's a young bloke directly beside me. He's taller than me. I usually keep my head down at Mass, so I've seen a lot of his cuffs and joggers, but only a hazy outline above the knees. I look up into an embarrassed, nervous face.

I raise my hand to reassure him. His hands are hovering at waist level. There are no fingers. No fingers on either hand, just one hooked thumb. I take both his hands higher up, around the wrists and squeeze them momentarily.

'Peace be with you,' he says.

'And you,' I respond.

Later I queue behind him to take the Host. The priest hesitates before placing the wafer on the cupped palms. A quiver goes through the young man's shoulders. He raises his hands quickly to his mouth, throws back his head and gulps.

At the end I don't want to talk to anyone. I nod at the altar and stride out to my car.

Next day the lunchtime trade is hectic—they all seem to come out to the bank and shops on a Monday these days—but we're empty mid-afternoon. I'm changing tablecloths when a young guy comes to the door.

'You open?'

'Sure.' I wave him to the table I've just reset.

He flops down, dumps his back pack, elbows off his jacket, and begins to pull off his gloves. They're fingerless gloves. I look up and recognise the face: my neighbour from Mass.

'What can I get you?'

'Pot of tea, please.'

He gets a magazine from the rack: *Interview* with Clint Eastwood on the cover. I listen to him turning the pages. Sometimes he has to have two stabs at turning a page, crumpling it in his palm. 2SER is playing old punk tracks. He doesn't strike me as an aggro type. I switch to 2DAY.

I carry over the teapot, milk jug and cup and saucer and lower them in front of him, checking a tendency to cringing reverence.

I wait. He may need help with pouring. 'OK?'

He nods. He's pouring OK, but wincing. The aluminium teapot is scalding and he has to steady it between his palms and use his thumb to guide the spout. He should have left on his gloves.

I finish changing the tables. He sips, rolling the cup between his palms.

'Didn't I see you last night, at St Joseph's?' I speak cautiously. He has a plain, pleasant face, but you never know.

'Umm.' He looks surprised, studies my face for the first time. 'Yeah, that's right.'

'I haven't noticed you there before.'

'No. I'm just up here for a few days.'

'Where from?'

'Tassie. Strachan.' That explains the pack and heavy duffle coat.

'It's beautiful country down there.'

'Sure is.'

'You always lived down there?'

'No, I moved down about, oh, six years ago.'

'To work?' A faux pas. He'd be hard put to get a job.

'To train. I was doing a lot of climbing. Precipitous Bluff, all that. These days I help organise raft trips down the Franklin.'

There's no way he could hang on. He must wave them off from the base camp.

'Must be a bit tricky for you when you hit the rapids,' I say.

The young guy looks up at me deadpan.

'What are you doing in Sydney?' It's none of my business, but people usually want to tell you.

'Looking up some old mates.'

'Great.'

'And, ah, seeing a guy at the hospital.'

'Yeah? Someone fall off the raft?' It's a joke, a joke. He's so po-faced.

'No. He's a microsurgeon. He can't do anything to help me'—he looks down—'but he wanted to take a look at me, show me to some students.'

'So, you're a guinea pig?'

'Yeah.' He laughs at last.

'Another pot of tea?' 'On the house' is implied.

'Thanks.' He must be filling in time till an appointment. I still want to ask. He's such an earnest young man, inherently good.

I carry the teapot over. I now have the upper hand, so to speak.

'Would it help if I poured?'

'Please.' He is gracious in defeat. 'Have a cup yourself.' Country manners.

I fetch another cup.

'What happened?'

'You had to ask, didn't you?'

'Fraid so.'

'People can't help themselves. I get a lot of fun watching them work up to it.'

'You've got a sardonic sense of humour.'

'You've got to.'

'Well?'

The lad has his head cocked listening to the radio. It's the tailend of a commercial for an expedition to South America. He's incurably adventurous, it seems.

'OK,' the radio voice exults, 'You want a brochure, write to Australian Himalayan Expeditions, GPO Box blah, blah, blah . . .'

'I suppose you'd like to climb Mount Everest,' I tease, and then stop, cursing myself.

'I have,' he says.

So humbly it hurts.

'How high did you get?'

'The top. Fifty metres from the top.'

I look into his eyes. They are opaque, milky blue as mountain lakes. He does not blink.

'My God.' I'm almost whispering. 'And here I am sitting beside you. You look so ordinary and you can do a thing like that.' Touch the feet of the gods.

'It's not hard, in a way.'

'A bloody bushwalk in the Blue Mountains scares the shit out of me.'

'It's different. It's all to do with your mind, how you see things.'

'What did you see? Besides the snow and ice?'

'Footprints.'

'One of those whatchamaycallits? A yeti.'

'No. Imaginary footprints. The giants who once walked the earth.'

Perhaps he's a little touched. But he's definitely not one of the local loonies.

'You sure you're for real?'

He holds out his fingerless palms. 'I'm for real.'

'So—what happened up there?'

'There were five of us going for it. Simon was in the lead, then Clark and Tom, and Warwick and me. We'd told the Sherpas to stay back, further down . . . My crampon broke. It was as simple as that.'

'So you were left dangling?' I picture the classic cartoon of two blokes dangling out over the street, with the bottom one bawling 'Stop laughing, this is serious.'

'There was no-one to help. The others had kept going.'

'You're kidding!'

'No. They called back, "You OK?" I think that's what they said, but with the wind and sleet and the headgear you couldn't be sure. "It's all right," I yelled back at them. "Keep going." They'd have kept going on up anyway. I had to concentrate on saving myself.'

'And that meant?'

'Yeah. I took off my gloves.'

'Knowing your fingers'd snap-freeze?'

'It was that or fall.'

'Couldn't you yell for the others to come back?'

'They had to get to the top. We were so close.'

'That mattered more than your fingers?'

'You don't see it that way up there.'

'But you do now, surely?'

'Sometimes I'm bitter now. But not so much about my hands. More about not getting to the top.'

'And you haven't got anybody to blame?'

'Except myself.'

'And them. They could have hauled you up.'

'No. You don't know what it's like up there.'

'You're a hero nonetheless.'

'No way. The papers all made a distinction. They said Simon and Clark and Tom and Warwick made it. Simon'd always be put first because he was the leader, and the spokesman. And then, they'd say, there was poor old Halfwit Hodge who got stuck fifty metres from the top.'

'That'd make you feel great.' He studies the tea-bag label. 'Did they have to carry you down?'

'In the hardest parts.'

'How do you feel about each other now?'

'We don't have much to say to one another. It was different up there. Weird things happen.'

'You were pretty close?'

'We were like brothers, the one blood. But at the same time we were competing. You take the world with you.'

A Milkman in the Green Room

In *tutina mertis dubia*, the soprano agonised, *fluctuant contraria lascivus amore et pudicitia.*

O Fortuna, the chorus roared. *O Fortuna.*

The Green Room was a hubbub of newspaper faces on bodies unexpectedly slight and truncated. Influential men twitched their buttocks. Women side-stepped on flimsy heels.

From her armchair Sherrie watched Geoff elbowing toward the bar. A minute later the throng fell silent and parted to allow Wafik to pass through. Annabel clomped close behind, her palm on Wafik's shoulder-pad.

Eyes flickered over their triumphal progress. Then glasses were lifted in insolent salute and ash flicked and eyebrows fractionally elevated. Only a few people—uniformed choir members—wore expressions of unequivocal admiration, and it was they who stepped forward to tap at Wafik's arms and gabble their congratulations. Power seemed to go out from him. His face shone like melted butter.

'Wafik,' Sherrie hailed, heaving to her feet. She had scuffed off her shoes, and the carpet was sodden and gritty under her soles.

'You were terrific,' she assured Wafik. His long black eyelashes curled.

'So were my raw materials,' he conceded, victory engendering gallantry. 'The choir was most responsive.'

'Except for that bit, you know—' Annabel hummed a passage where the altos had come in too quickly.

'I just thought it was all terrific,' Sherrie interrupted, sinking down. 'No-one minds the odd mistake.'

An elderly man with crumpled cheeks was listening. Wafik moved his feet farther apart and rocked back on his heels.

Geoff reappeared grinning like a great dane and gripping three glasses round their cold, slippery waists. 'Sorry, Wal, I wasn't expecting you to join us so soon.' From his joviality Sherrie guessed he'd had a quick snifter at the bar. He handed Annabel her G and T and lowered the other two drinks into Sherrie's hands.

'What'll it be?'

'I've earned a brandy,' Wafik declared.

'A double, at least,' Annabel barracked.

'Napoleon, of course,' Sherrie said.

Geoff retreated. Sherrie put his glass on the floor, then fished the iceblock out of hers and dabbed it against her cheeks. Annabel held her drink to Wafik's lips.

Wafik studied Sherrie for a moment and felt moved to a reprimand. 'You shouldn't be drinking in your condition.'

'I only do it for the ice.'

'Bacardi.' He sighed. 'And you realise there's caffeine in the Coke?'

Sherrie arranged the hem of her dress over her knees and stroked it.

'You're looking absolutely lovely tonight, Sherrie.' Annabel blurted out her endorsements as unsubtly as her criticisms. 'I now know what they mean when they say pregnant ladies look radiant.'

'That's brides, isn't it?'

'One and the same, more often than not.' It was the sort of thing Sherrie would have expected Geoff to say, not Wafik.

'Cynic.' Annabel smacked Wafik's wrist.

'Am I allowed,' Sherrie asked Wafik, 'to say Annabel's looking lovely tonight?' Revived by her drink, she felt provocative. 'The soprano's pretty too,' she added.

Annabel leaned forward to share a confidence. Sherrie could see down the front of her fuschia blouse to the cleft of solid white breasts. Annabel whispered, 'She lives with an actor, so-called, who's in one of those doctors-and-nurses soapies. I keep imagining them at home. You know, she's in the bathroom practising her trills, and he's in front of this floor-length mirror saying: "Oh God, how I love you... God, you're beautiful... I'm afraid I've got some bad news..."'

Annabel had such a good ear she could have gone on all night. Once given the floor, she was an exceptional mimic and raconteur, a dogmatic orator, a mover of motions, a law-maker, unbrookable in her self-certainty.

Sherrie and Annabel had met in nine a.m. Psychology I,

sitting side by side through a series of deadening closed-circuit TV lectures. 'Dendrons', one used to hiss whenever the other nodded off. Sherrie had learned what most men seemed to pick immediately: Annabel's heavy eyelids, dense black hair and camellia flesh hid no depths of mystery and sensibility. She was utterly unforgiving of deception and weakness, except in Wafik.

Sherrie studied the soprano's firm bottom as a hand patted it. 'What's her name again?' She and Geoff had economised by not buying a programme.

'Solvig,' Wafik supplied.

'Solvig,' Sherrie echoed. 'Sounds like some sort of solvent. Or a disinfectant. *Solyptol*, that's it.'

Wafik's expression made her stop.

'And the boyfriend's Garry something,' Annabel butted in. 'Apparently the choir people call him Garry Glitter. He always wears a leather jacket with a bird on the back, all done in sequins. It must have taken months for some poor creature in Hong Kong to sew then on. It's a—what is it, Gobram?' Annabel always addressed Wafik by his surname. 'A Phoenix, that's it. Shaking its tail-feathers at his bum, which isn't all that bad, incidentally—'

'Anna,' Wafik cautioned. 'They're coming this way.'

Sherrie twisted around to get a better look. 'God, she's skinny. Or is that just me feeling like an elephant?'

'Baby elephant,' Annabel amended.

'Solly,' Wafik was mouthing. 'Come and say hallo.'

Groups of men split to let the soprano pass. Her breasts were tiny and unsupported.

Wafik raised the soprano's hand and kissed her red fingernails, then they hugged with celebratory laughter. Annabel caressed Wafik's sleeve. Then, 'H–e–r–e–'s Garry,' she bellowed, like a quiz show voice-over.

Garry had that cheeky jockey charm which is buoyed by flattering experiences and the possession of more than one female. Watching him, Sherrie concluded he was not unlike a young he-goat: eager, scrambling, rogueish, with a perfect white coat and curving blonde horns and a sporty tuft of tail and a comical beard and clacking hoofs. One minute he was gobbling the geraniums, laughing with yellow eyes, the next he had scampered away leaving nothing but a scatter of black pellets.

Annabel motioned Sherrie to stand up and join in. Sherrie shook her head. As soon as Geoff returned, they would make their farewells and leave them to it. His beer was flat and warm.

Solvig and Wafik were screaming over some witticism, as people do at first nights distinguished by acid champagne, orange juice and derivative entertainment, when Geoff reappeared. He dumped a brandy balloon and half a dozen packets of corn chips on the nearest table, then yawned and wriggled his shoulder-blades.

'It's a bloody scrum over there,' he grumbled, not unhappy. 'How are you going?' He rubbed Sherrie's neck.

'All right. A bit tired.'

Geoff peered at Solvig and raised an eyebow. Sherrie nodded.

This time Annabel was determined to include them. 'Sherrie and Geoff,' she announced, 'meet Solvig and Garry, ah.' She had almost said the wrong thing. Geoff gripped Garry's hand. Then, recalling the brandy, he retrieved it and presented it to Wafik.

'My little bit,' he said. 'Tribute' was what he meant, or merely 'contribution'.

'Your health, sir,' Wafik responded. Sherrie beamed up at Solvig and said, 'You've got a wonderful voice,' not daring to specify notes.

'Can I fetch you two a drink?' Geoff had cast himself as water-boy. They ordered as if used to such gestures. Annabel held out her empty glass with a grin. Sherrie nodded down at hers. For a second they despised their benefactor.

Garry, Solvig and Wafik bent forward exchanging shop-talk. Annabel was ostracised.

'Bel,' Sherrie cooed. Annabel jumped, as if disturbed in an illicit act. 'I brought something for you.' Sherrie had pushed the little package into the base of her handbag and the tissue paper was rumpled. 'It's a belated engagement present, just for you.'

Sherrie pointed out the minute stitching, the handmade lace, the rotting silk, the embroidered swans with necks entwined. 'It would have been part of a trousseau,' she guessed. 'I thought you could have it for your "something old".' As Annabel was spreading the silk over Sherrie's knee, Geoff interrupted them with a tray of drinks.

Distribution of the drinks effected a change of positions and obligations. Garry stood beside Geoff with his back to the plate-glass, feet astride, resting his beer against his belt buckle. Behind, a concrete flight of stairs swooped down the curve of a tiled sail to stop, hovering, in mid-air, a metaphysical joke.

'What do you do for a crust?' Garry asked.

'I'm a milk vendor,' said Geoff. Normally he'd have said: 'I've got a milk run.'

'And your wife? Oops, I can see what she does.' Garry nodded down at Sherrie.

Sherrie wondered how he knew she was Geoff's wife. Her fingers were so swollen she had had to take off her rings.

'Her sister's holding the fort,' Geoff explained. 'They've got a shop. Sell colonial furniture and old linen and lace. Woman's stuff.' His New Zealand accent was so obvious.

'So you'll be the one giving the kid the early feeds before the milk run? You've got a lucky lady.'

'She doesn't complain,' Geoff said.

A tall man was approaching, a man so attenuated one longed for the punchline and found it in his slip-on shoes. As he propelled the soprano away to meet somebody, Garry's eyes followed. Wafik and Annabel exchanged a knowing wink.

Geoff and Garry resumed their dialogue this time fronting the plate glass as if it were a urinal. Wafik began kneading his neck.

'Let's move on,' Annabel responded. 'I'm dying for something to eat.' No-one had touched the corn chips.

'I wanna dance,' Wafik objected, striking a pose.

'How about the Basement? It's always good value.' Sherrie had not been there since she married. 'OK, honey?' She tapped Geoff's hip pocket, the one squared out by his wallet.

'Huh?' Geoff had been talking Rugby Union. 'Talking Rugby with a bloody actor,' he would say later, as if it had all been a bad party.

'Were going on to the Basement,' Sherrie told Garry. 'Would you like to join us?'

'Oh. Oh, no thanks.' 'A bloody milkman in the Green Room,' he'd say later. 'We've got a long drive home,' he began explaining to Wafik as they turned towards the corner where Solvig was looking up into the tall man's face. 'We're out at Lane Cove.'

'As far out as us,' Geoff sympathised.

'Well, I'm a definite starter,' Sherrie insisted. 'This could be my last night out in a long time.'

Annabel picked up their handbags and jackets, and Geoff hoisted Sherrie to her feet.

'Don't you have to be up early?' Annabel was offering Geoff an escape route.

'No milk on Sundays. OK, girlie?' He took Sherrie's elbow, giving her his cooperation.

Wafik was already down outside the shop. 'Come on,' he yelled. 'The parking station shuts in half an hour.'

Annabel consulted her watch. 'An hour,' she said. 'Don't hurry.'

Sherrie felt weak at the prospect of the jolting bus, the trudge up the stairs, the irritable cruising to find a parking space in some lane, and then the trek back to the Basement.

'Look,' Annabel instructed the men, 'you two fix up the car

business. Sherrie and I'll walk up slowly and grab a table.'

A bus rumbled. Without argument, the men ran for it. Annabel stumped after Wafik and squeezed Sherrie's gift into the breastpocket of his tails. Then Wafik ran back to Annabel to retrieve his wallet and keycase from her handbag.

Sherrie refused Annabel's offer of a taxi and they began their walk. The air was cold and cylindrical in their nostrils. The illuminated sky was the bleached uncolour of a wilted hydrangea. Sherrie tried to calculate how much Geoff had left in his wallet. Halfway around to Circular Quay she stopped beside a telegraph pole to rest. Annabel took a noisy breath. For the last five minutes she had been preparing to say something significant.

'I'm sorry,' she burst out.

Sherrie tried to cock one eyebrow as Wafik did.

'I couldn't tell you earlier. Wafik and I are putting off the engagement. He's moving out.'

All Sherrie could think of was the handkerchief. 'Oh Bel,' she mumbled and pulled her friend against her stomach.

They plodded on. 'What's been happening?' Sherrie asked. They were under the station and a train wheezed above them.

'Wafik's still really keen for us to get married. It's always been his idea. But I'm not happy about it. He's still so . . .'

Sherrie nodded sufficiently for Annabel to see she agreed but not so vigorously she would offend.

At the Basement couples waiting for tables filled the stairs.

'We'll have to go somewhere else.' Annabel was adamant. 'Wafik won't hang round in a queue.'

They meandered a few metres and leaned against parking signposts. Sherrie stood on one foot, then the other, easing the weight.

'He's going to have to grow up quickly if he's moving out,' she remarked.

'Yes.' Annabel smiled her indulgence.

'He's found a flat a block from his father's house. He says he's going to tell people it's his rehearsal space. It's not a bad idea, really—he can have private pupils there, and nick round for a bash on his father's baby grand. Only—'

Wafik had dreamed up an elegant explanation, Sherrie thought. It was plausible, partially true and open ended—thoroughly in character.

'Its really funny.' Annabel was smiling again, forgiving a fractious infant. 'You know I've been going out to the new house, painting and cleaning and all that.' She had at last sold her unit near the Opera Centre in Surry Hills and bought a house replete with borers and wandering jew. 'Anyway, a few of the local shopkeepers turn out to be Egyptians, and there's a big Coptic church up the road in Sydenham. But do you think Wafik can bring himself to so much as nod to them? His father says they're all peasants.'

'His father should be grateful he's chummed up with a nice SCEGGS gel then.'

'Gawd no.' Annabel imitated a woman swooning. 'Only the purest little jewel of the Mediterranean will do for his son. With a certificate of celibacy, preferably.'

Wafik's father was a piano importer. Sherrie spread her hips against a car bonnet, eased off her shoes, and slipped away into a bit of a reverie.

'Annabel,' she enquired after a while, 'you wouldn't be pregnant?'

'Oh, no. Oh, God no. Oh, heaven forbid!'

'I was told to beware of Greeks protesting too much,' Sherrie said.

Annabel raised one palm. The men were approaching, strolling side by side. Wafik must have changed his tails in the car, for he was wearing an Italian cardigan with padded shoulders. Geoff had rolled back his sleeves. One cuff flapped as he gestured.

'What were you two gossiping about?' Annabel cried, stepping forward to kiss Wafik.

'It looked like Geoff was demonstrating his underarm bowling technique. Or a new conducting method, perhaps, sweetheart?'

'It *was* cricket, actually.' Wafik appeared surprised by Sherrie's deductive powers.

She played along. '*You*? Talking cricket!'

'I'm desperate for the smallest crumb of knowledge. I have to coach it next term.'

Wafik taught music and art at a public school, not Greater but thankfully Selective.

'I've told him,' Annabel told Sherrie, to stick to batons, not bats.' The predictable mad-dog cracks ensued.

Geoff interrupted. 'They're chocka here, I gather?'

'The Regent's just across the road,' Annabel essayed.

Wafik sniffed. 'Supper club,' he said, po-faced. 'Where, no doubt, all they serve is Bacardi.' He looked at Sherrie.

'The Inter-Cont, then,' Annabel decided. 'My shout. We'll toast Wafik's—'

'Genius,' Sherrie pounced.

'Umpiring,' Wafik grimaced.

'And the baby,' Annabel hurried on. 'We have to wet its head.'

'And the engagement.' Geoff's blithe remark bounced off the others' silence.

'Right. Well,' Annabel clapped her hands.

Sherrie could have met Wafik's eyes. It was only fair play to indicate she knew—but she concentrated on squeezing her swollen feet back into her shoes.

Geoff led the way, though he wasn't sure which street they were heading for, and Annabel drew in beside Wafik, her fingers sinking into the folds of his cardigan, hiding her sapphire ring. She had planned a complementary wedding dress, midnight blue, in the calf-length, broad-shouldered style her mother had worn for her going-away dress. It had sounded dangerously close to her usual dowdy outfits, and Sherrie had been trying to think of tactful suggestions to make the effect more flattering. One idea was the silk handkerchief impaled by a silver brooch above the left breast, as was the fashion for a while in their mothers' heyday.

Now Sherrie lumbered behind, a dreary matron of honour.

'What're you doing tomorrow?' Geoff asked Wafik as they sat down at last on the thirty-first floor.

'Today,' Sherrie chided. Next thing he'd be inviting Wafik to the footie.

'We're supposed to be going to Freedom Furniture,' Annabel said, rubbing the pad of her ring finger on the marble table top. 'Wafik wants to buy a bed.'

'Ah ha,' Geoff sang.

Neither of them would say anything. Like two kids fooling around with bubble gum, they pulled a little way apart, the pink gum stretched like a muscle, but then they sprang back together, entangled in salivary strands.

'And you've bought a house, I hear,' Geoff enquired of Annabel. 'What suburb's it in?'

He was learning their Sydney ways.

'Tempe.'

'Eh? Tempe Tip and all that? You finance company people can borrow a bloody fortune for next to nothing. Why didn't you go for a classy spot?'

'A pair of semis, my friend, for a tenth what you'd pay in the eastern suburbs. What do you think?'

'But you don't have to live in them.'

'Precisely my argument.' Wafik looked surprised at himself for agreeing out loud.

'It's not a bad area, really,' Annabel protested. 'It's only cheap because of the airport.'

'And the highway,' Wafik listed. 'And the railway. And the bus depot. And the loud-mouthed peasants.'

'What about the Cooks River?' Annabel stabbed her forefinger against the edge of the marble. 'We're directly above the river.'

'Sludge,' Wafik informed Geoff.

'I look across to a beautiful old white mansion.' Annabel was warming to her oratory. 'It's like a Greek temple.'

'Only it's owned by the Catholic Church,' Wafik pointed out.

'So? And there's a park.'

'Great for walking the cat.'

'Ooh, you!' Annabel punched Wafik's arm.

'I know all about Tempe,' Sherrie plunged.

'Spare us, please,' Wafik groaned.

'I've been trying to trace Geoff's family tree and it turns out his father's people come out here to Sydney first and then—'

'That figures,' Wafik interrupted, running his eyes up and down Geoff's untidy shirt as if checking for the arrows. To pin a New Zealander as both a crim and a peasant was an undeniable pleasure.

'The Valley of Tempe,' Sherrie instructed the marble, 'was sacred to Apollo. It had a temple,' she nodded to Annabel, 'and it was extraordinarily beautiful.'

Wafik jumped to his feet, flexed his biceps and struck a pose. 'The Apollo of the Tiber . . .' Sherrie raised her eyebrows in admiration. 'And now, the Apollo of Tenea . . . What about the Apollo Belvedere? Or, last but not least'—he threw a straight-armed punch at Geoff's head—'Apollo knocks out the Centaur.'

'Hang on,' Sherrie objected. 'Apollo was supposed to take a special interest in the peace-loving peasants, shepherds especially.'

Wafik subsided into a limp shepherd lad fingering a Pan pipe. Geoff bleated.

'Did you know America's got a Tempe?' Sherrie asked?

'It would have to, wouldn't it?' Annabel chuckled.

'It's just outside Phoenix.'

'Phoenix Arizona?'

'Yup. It sounds boring as all get out.'

'The perfect place to despatch that bloody Glitter character,' Geoff observed. Sometimes he took in more than Sherrie gave him credit for.

'I want to hear about my Tempe,' Annabel pleaded, whilst Wafik capered around the table piping to the amused on-lookers.

What magic is there, except to the misty-eyed family historian, in describing a creek edged by old houses and smelly rural pursuits? Or extolling a canal which bears the emissions of industry down to the sea?

'It's a dirty little story,' Sherrie told Annabel. 'Perhaps I'll just tell you about Tempe House. I started off imagining Geoff's forebears swanning about there.' She hadn't really. 'You know, water music and peacocks and sundials and rustling silk. A real temple to the arts, where you could come and drink great draughts of laurel water.'

'Sounds like the Opera House,' Geoff crowed. Something had gone to his head.

'Drink that river water and it'll kill you,' Wafik assured Geoff.

'Once upon a time,' Sherrie said, 'it was a glorious place. Bulrushes and birds and willows. The boiling-down works was one of the earliest offenders. Do you know what they used to do? Once they'd boiled down the carcasses and got the tallow, they'd tip the leftovers into Wolli Creek.' Wafik pretended to look horrified. 'And then there was the pig farm, and a tannery, and wool scouring, and the Primitive Methodist Church. And do you know what the nuns used Tempe House for?'

'What?' Wafik sank down onto a chair, hanging on Sherrie's words, ribaldry shaping his lips into a fleshy leer.

'A laundry.'

'Well, then,' cried Wafik, throwing up his hands at an opportunity lost, 'it's a very clean little story, isn't it?'

'I'd imagined myself,' Annabel mused, 'sitting on my verandah—when I'd built it—looking at the river and seeing water-babies splashing about.'

Geoff and Wafik glanced at her and shook their heads.

'There is an ice-cream factory,' Sherrie smiled.

Geoff studied Wafik. 'So Tempe's not good enough for you, eh? You expect the lady to buy you a house in Vaucluse or somebloodywhere?'

'Geoff,' Sherrie chided.

'She might have consulted me.' Wafik was petulant.

'Surely—' Sherrie glanced at Annabel, whose face was perspiring.

'I am not a little boy, you know,' Wafik told Annabel. 'Next you won't allow me to go out conducting unless I've got half-a-dozen clean handkerchiefs in my pocket.'

'That'd spoil the line of your tails,' Sherrie chirped.

Annabel lent her elbow on the table, put her face into her

cupped palm, and sighed. Sitting up, she pulled a man's handkerchief out of her handbag and wiped it across her brow. Then she looked Wafik in the eye.

'I am not,' she said loudly, 'and have never intended to be—'

'Calm down,' Wafik snapped. 'We don't want to stage a domestic here.' Putting his hand into his cardigan pocket, he produced a small cream wad and pressed it into Annabel's palm. For a moment Sherrie took it for a tissue which had gone through the washing machine, but as Annabel shook it out she recognised the silk handkerchief. Annabel spread it on the marble and straightened each rolled hem. Then she took off her engagement ring and placed it precisely at the centre of the square.

Raising her chin, she resumed her address. 'If you want to carry on it this—' She paused. Geoff was rearranging his chair as if settling back to enjoy the soapies he watched every weekday after lunch.

'Go ahead,' he ordained, and signalled to the waiter.

'I can't believe it!' Annabel fumed. Geoff folded his arms across his chest and smiled fulsomely.

'Love,' he said. 'You two don't know the first thing about it. But go ahead, please.'

A tall man came striding in past the waiters. In the elevated, carpeted quietness his slip-on shoes squeaked. Behind him trotted the soprano and Garry Glitter.

Wafik raised his hand to call them over. But they passed, hurrying, without acknowledgement.

'Up you too,' Annabel snorted and raised to her lips the limp left hand of her boy conductor.

The Chop

When the fowls began squawking in alarm, I ran to the kitchen window, fearing a fox might have sneaked into their yard.

Elgin was flogging the pig: lashing my beautiful, pudgy, pink girl across the shoulders and flanks, bashing the stick down onto her spine, slashing the side of her face.

I screeched. It was a ghastly, sickening noise. I didn't know I had such a sound in me. It was like the terrible scream torn out of a woman as she is giving birth.

I ran outside. Piggie was down on her side, puffing out little screams of pain, and Elgin was still hitting her. I flung myself down, shielding Piggie's head and shoulders. The next blow came angling down across my neck. I gasped. Elgin staggered back, panting, his left hand pressing over his heart. I turned my face away, kissing the pig's shoulder. She was struggling to get back onto her feet. I held her down still and listened to her breathing till Elgin had walked away.

As the pig scrambled to her feet, I heard the front door shut and then the car revving. I sat on the ground in the late afternoon sun and watched Piggie limp into her pen and slurp from her water trough. She had probably done nothing worse than snuffle in Elgin's vegie patch. For that he had thrashed a creature of pre-moral beauty, vilified a state of grace.

There were awful welts cutting through her fine hair, marking her sides, but she did not appear to be hurt internally. I waited and watched as gradually her vigour returned. After half-an-hour I went inside, collected the burnable rubbish and brought it out to the incinerator.

Elgin and I have been married twenty-five years. I am forty-three and he is fifty.

Elgin's heart went bad when he was thirty-eight. Thirty-five, more like, but he wouldn't see a doctor till he was undeniably breathless and exhausted. We were in South Africa then, in Durban. Elgin's work with a big mining machinery firm meant he had to travel out to the mines every few weeks. Poor Elgin: he hated the outdoors, unless it was an English country garden. His eyes were too sensitive for the sun.

He loathed too the competitiveness, the pushy younger men, the back-stabbing and the huge amounts of money. One look at his soft, folded white face and you knew he should have been in something gentler. His relaxation was the comfortable life: an eiderdown and a lie-in, a hot toddy and a nice pork chop. He should have admitted it, not fought against it. I should have made him. But I loved the income.

I've always been a wee bit extravagant. That's what attracted Elgin in the first place. He adored my flighty ways. He called me his scatty Cyn. I was always on for an outing. I loved the bright lights.

We both grew up in villages outside Weston-super-Mare. At eighteen Elgin went up to London to begin his first job: junior junior with a mining firm. But he still came home every weekend to his parents. The minute I was old enough, we got married. It was the early fifties and the austerity thing had passed. I was able to have a beautiful ivory frock with yards and yards of crepe. I had twenty-four pairs of shoes then, and a dozen little cocktail hats, and six or eight pairs of gloves. I had a tiny waist and good legs. Elgin liked me to wear a big bow at my waist. He adored me. I didn't think what he'd be like at forty-five, what he might turn himself into.

I discovered soon enough that he was irritable. He wanted things done properly, and when they weren't he got impatient. He'd cover his annoyance, hide it under his bland softness. His face was wide like a mask, with round cheeks and little eyes and full lips. I had the gentlest, kindest man in the world, except that inside he was tense. His lovely, gentlemanly, courteous ways covered up a habit of judging. He could not find a way of living both sides of himself at once, even with me.

Elgin did not realise how quickly and how much he came to rely on me. I looked at things more lightheartedly. I could pull him back, with a laugh and a cuddle, from despondency and fretting and going over and over some hurt. My silly old Elgin. He wouldn't hurt a fly, we used to say. Though actually he did hurt people with his expectations. He didn't intend to, but he wanted so much.

When the children came along, he expected perfectly clean, impeccably mannered little darlings to show off his own high standards. But we were out in Durban by then and I was having a ball and our house-girls did for us well enough. They loved the children. Serious Shane: so pensive; big and rolypoly like his father; good-intentioned; high-minded; always wanting to do the right, decent thing. He worried so, even at five or six, about the poor blacks. And silly laughing little Melinda, blonde and fine-boned, always skipping about and playing pranks. A real girly little girl. Elgin worshipped her. Shane he expected more of.

Some dreadful fights began when Shane was fourteen or fifteen. Elgin demanded the very best school marks, perfect attendance and a spotless uniform. Shane was supposed to be in the football team—we were in Melbourne by then—and the tennis and the debating. Poor lad, he could never do well enough to please Elgin. He used to cry sometimes. I'd stroke his shoulder and say again and again I loved him—my big, flabby, serious lad. He was utterly unattractive to the girls, while Melinda—well, you can imagine. She was a minx. We had every boy for miles around turning up on the doorstep.

Elgin worried so, but he couldn't bring himself to caution Melinda. Instead he'd grouch at me, demanding I control her. I'd beg him to have a word with her, but he couldn't. He'd go to pieces when he looked at her giggly little kitten's face. He didn't dare touch her. When she was larking around on the tennis court with her girlfriends, he'd stay inside. He always said the sun hurt his eyes. In her company he was like a teenager: too reserved or over-eager. Rough and tumble games were out of the question with both children. They would have toppled over into something else.

By then Elgin's heart was playing up well and truly. He got exhausted, his face went grey, his lips white. He'd flop onto the bed, so heavy, so desperately tired. We had to keep a flask of whisky beside the bed. There were tablets to take, naturally, and they'd do tests, but all they were ever really doing was observing his heart's action at one instant and giving it a name. We let the race of doctors do this to us, we defer before their self-aggrandisement, for there is nothing better on offer; no-one else will look into our hearts. The doctors chastise about diet and exercise. But that is nothing. Where would they begin could they *really* see the workings of men's hearts?

Elgin grew fed up with the specialists and their condescension. He'd call them 'sir' whilst he seethed with anger. 'My prospects?' he'd ask them. 'It's these blooming tablets for the rest of my days, or—?' He could never finish his sentences.

He returned to eating whatever he liked. Fortunately he had never smoked. When he caught Shane trying a cigarette, he roared at the boy. But when Melinda and her girlfriends took it up, he said nothing. Shane was furious at the inequity.

Elgin's firm became a bit dicey, so we took a gamble and moved to Sydney. Elgin said he wanted this one to be his last job: ten years and he'd retire. He still had to travel a lot: up to the Northern Territory, down to Tasmania. I couldn't believe his pictures of those stripped hills at Queenstown.

The Sydney cardiologists were more go-ahead. They recommended a bypass. They sawed his breastbone open. My husband. My soft husband hacked open like a lump of white meat: like a beautiful animal sawed apart in an abattoir.

We survived. Elgin went back to work a lot perkier. But, underneath he was sombre and unconvinced; I could feel his heart pumping with a dogged sadness. He had tiptoed right up and touched death. I knew, despite what they said, that I wouldn't have him too many more years. I began to get books out of the library: biographies, astrology. I read in secret. I could not understand what I was reading, but words stayed with me. I wanted to know what would happen and no-one could tell me.

The children were nearing the end of their schooling. Shane wanted to do the full six years of high school, Melinda would be lucky to last four. I began to think of getting a job, though I didn't dare say anything to Elgin. All my life I had been playing the organ at home: first an old pedal job, then the electronic Suzuki Elgin bought me one birthday. I had always been the entertainer at Elgin's business gatherings. Sensing an opportunity for employment, I soft-talked Elgin into getting me a top-of-the-range model and settled into a routine of regular lessons and practice. It was a real release at the times Elgin got cranky and unreasonable—and they were more and more frequent.

Shane began his working life behind the counter at the Motor Registry. He was so patient. I felt proud and a little sad for my boy. He'd come home irritated and upset by the stupidity of the people he had to help and the jibes from the other men. The long-sock brigade, I called them. He worked too hard for their liking. Red in the face, hiding his tears of frustration, he'd stomp around in the kitchen and then slam into my car and take off, far too fast. Other afternoons he'd go out jogging: big, flabby, white, grumpy Shane slogging round and round the backstreets. When he got home he'd smoke and watch stupid, childish videos.

Melinda dropped out before her School Certificate and started as an apprentice hairdresser. She spent her first pay-packet on clothes, then said she wanted to move into a flat with a girlfriend. Shane was still cosy at home, despite the bickering. Elgin complained it would take a bomb to shift him.

The bomb came. It came all right. Elgin was retrenched. At forty-eight. Night-night and thanks for all you've done. Perhaps it was a blessing in disguise, but of course he didn't see it that way. He was humiliated and vengeful. I had never seen his face so white, the folds so pronounced.

Elgin still went out every morning at eight-fifteen, to line up interviews. In truth there were not many interviews. He was too old and his ill-health showed on his face. He was too slow, too tight, too polite. He hunched, holding himself in, protecting his heart, conserving his energy. He was afraid and alone. Melinda began running round with a dreadfully rough Army lad, while Shane turned depressed and withdrawn. I had my hands full.

Elgin had always loved the country around Wingham—it's so soft and green—and the town, with its square, and the ancient forest which reminded us both of a hometown we had not yet found together. I persuaded him a few days' holiday up there could not ruin our budget and we toddled off in my little car. There was no more company car, nothing deductible. It was an older, sadder honeymoon. We were back on our own.

As soon as we got back to Sydney, Elgin put our house on the market. No discussion, no consultation—he had decided. It sold, my lovely blonde brick home and, while Shane went out looking for a flat, Elgin and I drove north to find a cottage on a bit of land. A Tudor cottage, we joked, in an English country garden full of flowers. We sang out the names of the flowers: delphinium, phlox, liliums, lupins, foxglove, tuberose, iris, meadowsweet, columbine. We vied with each other to name all the perennials we would grow.

In no time at all we found a cottage within our means: full brick and tile, all mod cons, minimum maintenance. It sat at the centre of four hectares of land. Australian land, of course—saplings, fallen twigs and bark, dry stubble, a trickle of a creek, rocks, tiny native blossoms, spiders, ants and wasps.

Elgin had it all worked out. We'd grow all our own vegies and have a milch cow and fowls and a pig to fatten for Christmas. And apple trees, I said, for the apple sauce. And cloves, if we could find out how to make them.

The exertion of digging the first garden plot put Elgin in bed for a week. For the first time I raised the possibility of my teaching music. Elgin looked at the wall but did not say no. So I hot-footed it into town, found the vicar, volunteered to play at the church whenever they needed a stand-in, and put up little handwritten signs in the shops advertising organ lessons.

We were dipping into capital already. Elgin insisted he had to have all sorts of weird and wonderful gadgets and machines for his farming. And I have always liked my comforts. I had furnished our little cottage very comfortably and stocked the freezer. My phone calls to Shane and Melinda did not come cheap either.

Melinda had moved in with a chap who was far too old for her—a policeman—and Shane was practically living at the local club, taking all his meals there and wasting his time drinking with an inferior sort of fellow. Sometimes, I confess, I wished Elgin would take himself into town—to the club, the pub, anything. He had let all his social contacts go and was wholly dependent on me. And, consequently, it was me he took all his worries out on. He was terribly troubled over Melinda, first blaming himself then me, and his farming efforts were being shot to pieces by rabbits and birds and bugs and our own ignorance. The neighbours, I heard on the grapevine, gave us two years at the most.

In the evenings Elgin sat near the oil heater listening to the BBC on shortwave and I knitted for Shane and turned over in my mind a dozen money-making schemes which would not hurt my dear man's pride.

The rages grew worse. They became unpredictable and violent. One afternoon, when I was about to go out to give a home lesson, Elgin struck me across the cheek. We were both stunned. He stood there shaking, holding his hand, looking at it. I cowered for a moment; then, as I looked at my poor, shaking husband, I rebounded. I put my arms around his chest and called him my own darling sausage and settled him on the couch and soothed him.

To hit a woman: that is forgivable in my book. A woman is a woman, after all, and tempting. But to hit an animal—to see Elgin whipping my poor, sweet, devoted piggie. It broke my heart. He had stepped out of forgivable territory, he had crossed a creek into rough bush. Elgin was no longer himself. He was fifty and dying. He had chosen to take my love with him. I lit the incinerator and went inside and opened the freezer.

I would cook Elgin a nice pork chop with all the trimmings. I would put on a pretty dress, open a bottle of red wine, and lay the table with wildflowers and candles. After we'd eaten we would put on an old-time record and dance cheek-to-cheek in front of the oil heater. Then, side by side—hips bumping, arms around each other's waists—we would lead one another into the bedroom. I would undress my man and pull the eiderdown up around his shoulders. He would lie there, so grateful, squeezing my hand and smiling his thanks. I would look into his soft, small eyes. He would close his eyelids and settle his head into the pillow and breathe out gently. It would happen that way, one evening.

Bristol Cream

Clive is not a photogenic man. He succeeds in merging with the background when you attempt to photograph him. What you find on your film after staying with him is a mere ghost, and as years pass the ghost fades to a blur of white hair and grey contours while the facial expression, non-commital to begin with, vanishes altogether. He has escaped you, just as you have escaped him.

Within his domain, Clive enters a room as he fades from a photograph: imperceptibly, on rubber soles. It is as if he passes right through doors. Whenever Clive enters or leaves a room, everyone hushes. It is, after all, his house they are occupying. His self-effacement commands attention.

Clive will permit anyone to stay. He is both conspicuously and inconspicuously kind. He never asks for payment and pooh-poohs gifts, but it would be rank ingratitude not to thank him tangibly and sincerely. Freeloaders, however crass, sense this and scuttle on. There are no thrills in stillness, however sizeable the hotel bill being avoided. It is like lodging free at a monastery: one either obeys the brother in charge, keeps one's mouth shut about petty discomforts, and bows the head to the Holy Father, or gets out. It would be unthinkable to leave with the silverplate, even a handtowel.

Clive's house—number 26—is never locked. There is always someone inside: someone sleeping off jet-lag, someone brewing tea, someone writing home. There is the semblance of perfect freedom. Every room is open to every guest. Doors are there for purposes of modesty and noise reduction, not exclusion. Even the bathroom door cannot be locked. The bath is not to be hogged, one understands. If someone knocks and calls 'I'm sorry, I'll come back later,' the occupant must shift.

Food in the pantry is not individually owned. If you see a wedge of tasty cheddar you may eat it; but then there will be none left for Clive and you will feel obligated to buy a replacement slab twice as big. Thus the catering sorts itself out. Some guests try to contribute excessively; the stingy seek to avoid contributing; but gentle communal pressure works to even and equalise.

Cleaning, too, is achieved not by regimentation but collusion and compromise. With so many passing through, each feels a duty to dust something. Dirty tea-towels vanish down to the launderette, the carpet sweeper is whipped around, crumbs are wiped away, the sittingroom is readied for new guests, new conversations.

Clive leaves each morning at eight-thirty. He tiptoes through the house, bestowing on any he encounters a courteous good morning. For nine hours his guests are free citizens. At five-thirty he slips in on rippling soles. A meal is underway in the kitchen, someone is setting the table, someone pours a sherry (Bristol Cream, Clive has mutely made known, is his choice). There is warmth and protection and laughter over the day's mishaps. Clive's guests have been out exploring the city he loves, and he—a wise, indulgent father—can comment on their discoveries and errors. He has a shelf of guidebooks and tube maps.

Clive does not lend money and it is doubtful if anyone has ever touched him for a loan, no matter how severe the temporary shortage. Indeed, the traffic is all in the other direction. Clive attracts coinage as surely as the Trevi Fountain. He owns the house, his guests pay for food and day-to-day bills, and he is employed in a senior position, so he should not be skint. Yet he looks as poor and humble as St Francis. He'd be in sandals year-round if the climate were milder. And so he attracts contributions: anonymous cheques in the mail, envelopes pushed under his door or hidden in his jacket pocket. No one calls on him to report what he does with this money. Seeing no proof of usage—no new electricals or bed linen—the donors surmise he gives most of it away.

Clive's only recurrent expense of an indulgent nature is his summer holiday on Santorini and here, again, he is willing to share. While his companions pay their own way, they let him organise the programme. They feel the whole time in Clive's debt. He is giving them this glowing experience, scooping out of his beneficience. They are people who would not venture if he did n invite them. They enjoy touring and staying within the invisible shelter he affords.

Clive feels at home amid the ancient, rocky peace of the island. Guests fancy that, in his company, they will engage with a mystical higher culture. They swim and sunbathe and eat salads and arrive home feeling so invigorated they are convinced they have. 'Perhaps,' their host murmurs, 'you have indeed.' Each must find his own way.

Some guests at 26 are simple or crazy or desperate for respite. They stay as long as they need. Only one has met with violence whilst a guest and his disaster occurred when he ventured out of Clive's surveillance range and stepped out of a train between stations. His ghost, which lingers in the back bedroom, carries no message for later guests. They can feel compassion for a sad case who hurled himself out of a train (his history has gained in drama over the years), but what more? Clive seems to expect more.

Spiral stairs revolve down from the back door to a bedsitting room in the basement. This is Clive's retreat. He calls it his priesthole. No guest has slept here. The host whiles away his evenings with music and videos of old movies. Guests call out a warning before they trot down the stairs. They sit with Clive, drink his sherry, listen to his Frank Ifield tapes, and converse softly. It is expected that each guest will climb down to exchange greetings before he or she retires. A cup of good mocha coffee on a tray is all the tribute required. Clive rarely goes to sleep before one or two a.m.; he likes to know each guest is safely settled for the night.

The priesthole is decorated to remind Clive of Santorini. It has white-washed walls, natural brown wood, and blue decorative touches: glazed pottery, tiles, Mediterranean scenes. Gifts of other colours are banished upstairs. It is one man's cell, his shelter from the shifting sands of callers. The room looks onto the back garden at ground level. In summer, there is a constant pageant: buds bloom, sparrows splash in the bird bath, frogs mate, butterflies swoop. The blinds are never drawn.

Upstairs, the middle bedroom—the darkest one—is where short-term visitors sleep. There are two single beds stacked with spare mattresses. The front bedroom is larger, lighter, handsomely proportioned. Here the exceptional may be expected. A baby has been born, a woman has died, a child has pulled out of a severe fever, honeymooners have quarreled in whispers, homesick young backpackers have cried, bashed wives have rested, discoveries of direction have been made or consolidated.

Advice is never profferred unasked. Clive is a monument to

tact. He deploys tacit commentary and active moderation to convey judgement. In the light of his apparent tolerance, others realise their shortcomings.

Clive defines his own weaknesses as those of omission. Guests sometimes gripe about him, but never under his roof. They may debate his behaviour hotly, but briefly, on a tube station or a bus. Once back in their own territories, Clive's guests are reluctant to comment or even recall. They choose tact. Their host's generosity requires it.

Clive does not change perceptibly from year to year. He is past hazardous journeys and reorganizations. His visitors provide sufficient variety and are kept sufficiently powerless to obviate any pressure for internal reassessment.

Clive is a fan of the royal family, believing they set a good example. Once a year he is modestly delighted to receive HRH the Patron of his pet charity as his guest at a fund-raising dinner. At the conclusion of the evening, he thanks her for attending. He speaks in a low, careful voice, pronouncing his vowels in a satisfactorily rounded manner. Almost all traces of his Melbourne upbringing have been expunged.

Clive deplores the Australian accent, the vulgarity, the exuberant, immoderate frankness of a dingo-fenced civilisation. But his friends—his guests—are almost all Australians. He still cannot deny this part of himself. He practises magnanimity. He pities, welcomes, subtly deplores, but always accommodates. At Christmas, especially, they arrive from Heathrow daily. 'We can't possibly squeeze another one in,' the installed guests moan. But Clive opens his door, suitcases are jostled in, and the displaced, shamed out of their selfishness, resolve to make the newcomers doubly welcome and shift onto the floor to free the beds. Frequently, amongst the ordinariness of changing sheets and pillowcases, they discover they have made room for an angel.

Guests are not creative—and rarely procreative—under this roof. It is no Charm School. The guests' freedom is not a licence to outrage or experiment. They may read, or play the piano, or write, or sketch, within the established modes. The unknown animal is not to be lured home, for fear of rabies. The domesticated, the inoculated is preferred. The great English authors, the treasures of the National Portrait Gallery, the classic ballet repertoire—these joys are to be savoured. Not venerated, but appreciated. Philistines are set to learn respect, to absorb quietening, enculturing influences. They are led, as it were, to sit beside the fountain in the courtyard of the Frick Museum, or to wander the narrow streets Salzburg. Emulation is the key.

Current politics do not obtrude. 'All that' is left behind at the charity's stone facade and spiked iron railing. 'Sufficient unto the day,' Clive rumbles and changes the subject. He does not care to speculate about the reasons why his charity—a Victorian innovation—continues to exist: either the immediate social causes of distress or the more elusive existential reasons. He is implacable in the face of mass need. His reticence on this score has infuriated more than one young guest. They must content themselves by telling each other his silence indicates wisdom of the world's ways; and he is, of course, not slow to succour.

Clive has never married nor fathered children. As an advocate of eugenics he is secretly repelled by his pet charity's prolific 'clients'. On the rare occasions Clive has studied a female guest of suitable age, intellect and appearance his expression has been misinterpreted. More often he has assured his young guests they are his putative offspring. His good deeds, they infer, will live on in them. They resolve to do their best by him.

Clive will remain a bachelor. Occasionally a female guest becomes infatuated with him, but it is an enthusiasm nurtured in her own head. Clive is never seen to encourage it; he keeps at a precise, practised distance. Occasionally he is attracted toward a guest, but he elects not to topple into disturbance. For better or worse, he murmurs, he has chosen his austerity. Guests refrain from teasing or upbraiding: it is a singularity, continence, chastity, celibacy, call it what one will, commanding grudging respect, not pity. He approaches old age with serenity. Should he need a nurse, he has plenty of favours to call in. He will fade away politely, without raucous demands, to the music of Ifield.

Clive remains the still, all-seeing eye at the centre of the cyclone. Some find the calm intensely boring, or irritating. Others are unnerved by the scrutiny: small, cherished idiosyncrasies become unconscionable wrongs. Whatever their reaction, they learn something about themselves and are grateful, chastened and resentful. They leave when it all becomes too much. Speaking of gratitude they feel shamefully relieved, like refugees from a nunnery.

It is recounted, among certain rebel guests, that Clive once had a mistress. She was possessed of a title and a chauffeur and a ... plummy voice (although no one can be found who heard the ... the Daimler). When it broke up, Clive built his retreat ... rest of the house over to whomsoever chose to ... guest under such circumstances is an equivocal

Caitlin next door is also said to have played a romantic part in Clive's past. She and he, it is claimed, bought 26 jointly, before a falling out drove Cait next door. Clive avoids Caitlin. Not actively—he would not nick across the street, or duck back in the front door, to escape nodding to her—but passively, by staying within proven schedules. He intimates to all new arrivals that reserve is recommended, lest an excess of chummy neighbourliness lead to dissension. Nonetheless a few guests—attracted by Cait's ebullient manner—contrive to find their way into her unclean kitchen for a drink while Clive is at work.

Caitlin will talk on any subject except Clive; lured in that direction, she winks largely and says he does not like being gossiped about, which is true.

Caitlin has not lacked gentlemen callers. It would be an act of kindness if she moved away. However she does not care, apparently, to submit to Clive's unspoken commands. Every night Caitlin's cat strolls the fence and jumps in the window of the priesthole. Clive slyly overfeeds her with the double cream he inveigles guests into supplying with his coffee.

There are a thousand confidences concealed in the bosom of Caitlin's diaphanous Indian caftan. Late at night, after their gigs, musicians come to her house.

She is a knob of garlic, bulbous and lumpy, her wispy hair peroxided a dirty blonde, her white flesh tinged with the grey of the indoors, her pungency barely concealed. She overwhelms with her strength, and the novice, gulping on too much, baulks and gags.

Her face is a pretty panel between two slabs of cheek, a garden glimpsed through a slot in a wall. The cheeks have the same effect as a nun's headgear. Hiding half the face, they irradiate the little which is revealed, turning plain eyes and nostrils and lips into features of sparkling beauty.

Her house has its own smell, as every residence does. More than one visitor has fancied it is not the odour of cooking, cat, dust and cigarettes, but of garlic secreted by warm flesh and absorbed by the veil of talcum powder she applies to mop up her perspiration.

One November a ruddy fellow in his early thirties arrives to stay at number 26. His name is Athol, he's a friend of a friend of a previous guest, and he's in Britain to do a term of psychiatry at St Thomas's. It is soon established, over a Bristol Cream, that Athol was, like Clive, reared in a conservative family. Both men claim to have discarded their religious faith and political affiliations but not their moral fastidiousness.

Clive's brotherly warmth towards Athol cools a few evenings later when it emerges that the guest has recently divorced. Clive abhors divorce: vows are vows are vows, whether civil or religious. Athol pleads extenuating circumstances.

His bride, Gail, was a good girl, rather like his mother in manner. That was his mistake. She had no imagination and distrusted learning. She wanted, simply, to have her babies and be wife to a humble, dedicated healer. She was besotted with the notion of serving the needs of the innocent, wholesome body.

She gave herself to him on a platter. She conceived promptly and the baby arrived in Hong Kong, where Athol was doing a stint at a community psychiatric centre. Citing the fearful pollution and congestion Gail stayed indoors with her baby. Seeing disturbed people all day, closeted in a rented flat in his leisure time, Athol began to think he too was going potty. The docile wife and cooing infant girl were not enough. He began to seek mental stimulation where he could find it: drinking with colleagues, taking excursions over the border. He felt guilty and torn in two. The second baby was born fifteen months later in Melbourne, Gail having flushed away the pills he'd prescribed—a tiny boy, soon revealing the symptoms of autism. Gail's unmindful seclusion was now a lifelong certainty.

At the hospital Athol talked regularly to a stocky nursing sister. She confided her relief at the death of her gambling husband. The two, unlikely allies, began a romance which consisted chiefly of talking. The interludes afterwards in the nurse's bed were surprisingly passionate. Gail smelt unfaithfulness in Athol's dirty shirts. When she and the children failed to return from a holiday with her parents, Athol filed for divorce. The week after the decree was finalised, he flew out for London. The stocky nurse gave him a leather bookmark inscribed *Mizpah*.

Clive is bothered by this tale. The dutiful wife is blameless, theoretically. How can he sympathise with the feckless husband? Positions are adopted. Clive sustains a dour reserve. Athol works night shifts and keeps out of Clive's way. He slips one-quarter of his salary under the door of the priesthole; three-quarters (minus a few pounds' pocket money) goes to Gail. This self-imposed penury condemns Athol to a frugal winter. Entertainment must be found in free concerts, at work, and in listening to the younger guests recount their expeditions.

One morning, coming off night shift, Athol meets Caitlin retrieving her garbage bin. Seeing his overcoated weariness, she invites him in for breakfast. As she brews strong mocha and offers coffee crystals and cream, Athol begins to talk. It is always his downfall.

Caitlin explains, unsolicited, that she does not go out to work. She lives off the earnings from her occasional work as a club singer, plus alimony and regular contributions from an anonymous benefactor. The benefactor, she winks, lives not all that far away.

'Ah,' Athol smiles, wondering what wrongdoing Clive is doing penance for.

'I had an abortion,' Caitlin supplies.

'I had an affair,' Athol parries, rubbing his beard, 'with an old sister with whiskers.' Cait laughs indulgently.

They become discreet lovers. Clive locks Caitlin's cat inside to prevent her returning home. His guests, tiring of cleaning up messes in corners, buy her a litter tray.

Late one March evening, Athol knocks at the door of the priesthole, elbows in with two cups of coffee on a tray, and asks whether they may talk. Clive turns down the volume on *Girl of the Golden West*.

'I'm planning to get married again.'

Clive watches a wagon train cross a prairie.

Athol elaborates. His term finishes at Easter and he wants to take Cait back to Melbourne, where they'll have a big wedding breakfast with all his friends. (He hopes his old school and med school mates will remember him.) He feels immensely honoured that a woman of Caitlin's experience and, well, succulence, should agree to become his wife.

'I trust you aren't planning to live next door?' Clive remarks, calculating whether he could afford to buy the place.

'No, no, Melbourne.'

Before they go, Athol says, they would like to have the actual wedding here, in London, with the people who have brought them together. A civil ceremony, in—if Clive would not mind—the front room of 26. It is such a handsome room, almost Georgian, and they sincerely desire Clive's blessing.

They cannot expect children, of course. Athol is hurrying now, saying too much, thrown by Clive's silence. Perhaps they will take in foster kids, or he may take over the care of his son—he feels responsible, even more now than before.

'Let me think about it.' Clive turns up the volume and Athol backs out to a paen of praise for California.

A sealed letter in longhand slides under Athol's door:

I cannot actively condone divorce, any more than infidelity or abortion. Therefore, you will understand, I could not make my home available as you request. Nor would I feel comfortable with my conscience if I attended the ceremony. I do not wish to appear uncharitable. I may be wrong, but I am too old to change my beliefs.

In November Caitlin and Athol marry in Melbourne. In time Clive receives, via a new arrival, a photograph, a copy of the ceremony (the vows are cautiously worded and self-justificatory), a netting bag of sugared almonds, and a slice of fruitcake with a thick overcoat of marzipan and a glaze of royal icing.

Clive tosses the marzipan out into his burgeoning garden and then eats the cake slowly, savouring its aroma. It complements his Bristol Cream. As he lifts the last crumbs with the pad of his finger, the cat kneads his thigh with her claws.

Victor Nee Counts His Blessings

'Finish these will you, Knee,' Beatrice instructed, thudding out of the kitchen to catch the phone.

Victor Nee had not offered to help prepare their meal. Taking up a bean, he sliced off the top and pulled away the string. Then he turned the bean, sliced off the other end and pulled free the opposing string. He was not in the habit of cooking, for there were three or four good Vietnamese takeaways near his house.

If Bee bought snow peas instead of insisting on growing these runty things, Victor Nee thought, I wouldn't have to be doing this. He never called his hostess Bee to her face, although he knew she enjoyed puns and disrespectful nicknames. Every November she sent Christmas cards to all her past students, even the Applied Science people who had sat through her course with closed notepads to secure their Humanities credit points. This year the card's illustration had shown a huge, grinning watchdog licking his chops after making mincemeat of Santa's reindeer. Out of his jaws issued the words: 'Oh deer'.

After three beans Victor Nee was bored. He tried to listen to Beatrice's conversation, but it was a splutter of Germanic sounds and he wondered whether her choice of a foreign tongue was a rebuke to his incorrigible nosiness. Not wishing to pursue this line of enquiry, he began to examine the kitchen.

From Monday to Friday Victor Nee was custodian of the records of an Asian bank. His job required an admirable blend of his personal obsessions. He was not a professional archivist, nor a statistician, but something inbetween, a paid hoarder. His awe of figures and words was so profound he was unwilling to throw out the meanest exemplar. A column of numbers seemed to Victor Nee worthy in its own right. Scanning it, one could not help but be ennobled. To count and calculate was in Victor's experience to be calmed and elevated. He drew apart into numbers and documents as into a secure, virtuous haven. His pulse slowed, his brain relaxed, and he breathed deeply. He revered the algebraic sentence as another man values exercise or music.

Victor Nee's house did not contain a working stove. The kitchen, like every other room, was occupied by middens of paper. Finance newspapers, journals, prospectuses, cuttings, receipts and brochures towered to the light bulbs. There were unused calendars and used stamps, unopened diaries for the past decade, and, amongst it all, in chronological strata, Beatrice's Christmas cards, still in their envelopes.

Victor Nee did not invite people home. When he felt lonely, he would call unannounced on a neighbour or shopkeeper or acquaintance from his university days. He would sit and listen to whatever his host cared to reveal, hoarding the words for later analysis. Sometimes he questioned on matters of diet, family, income or investments. Should a reluctant host turn the monologue to some uncongenial subject, as a last resort, short of asking Victor Nee to leave, Victor would go on sitting, recording, until it suited him to depart, and then he would be gone in an instant, without a thank you.

He was able, having set his mind to record certain sounds or scan certain figures, to let his eyes and imagination wander. As a consequence, he appeared to be always slightly off, fractionally out of synch. He regularly missed the point of jokes and stories, came in a second too late on choruses, and misunderstood witticisms. Falling between two cultures, he floundered in each.

Victor Nee was not a fluent speaker of English, Hokkien or Mandarin. The sounds he made with his voicebox were to him of negligible importance, the twitter of a canary. He preferred the silence of his fishes.

There were papers on top of Beatrice's microwave. Easing back his chair, Victor Nee crossed the floor, sliding on his leather soles, as stealthy as a martial arts expert poising to strike. In one outstretched hand he held a bean, in the other the knife.

Victor Nee rose on his toes and skimmed the top page of the papers. A paragraph in italics read:

I was feeding my baby (breast f.) when I sensed someone outside the window. The curtains are lace and they were pulled together. A prowler couldn't see in unless he stood right up close and looked through the little holes. I was too scared to scream out. I could not see the person but I was certain his eyes were looking at me through the holes. He had black eyes.

Lisa, No. 37

Victor Nee had black eyes, of course, and black hair. His hair was thinning and his face was screwed into a worried expression, as if a washerwoman had taken his head and twisted it in her hands. The inner sides of his fingers bore rows of straight little cuts and scars, the stigmata of someone who was constantly handling reams of paper.

Earlier, sitting on the floor in Beatrice's lounge room, Victor Nee had studied the label tagged to the corner of the Persian rug. When Beatrice had gone out to make tea, he had twisted his neck to read the manufacturer's plate on the underside of the coffee table. Shifting, at Beatrice's insistence, onto the sofa, he had read the labels sewn into the cushion seams. Passing the laundry he had noticed the compounded words and chemical formulae on the gardening and cleaning products. Dodging the exuberant lunges of Beatrice's dog as he negotiated the stepping stones to the toilet, he had wondered that such a foolish creature, which had never interpreted a spreadsheet in its life, could appear so happy. He might have acknowledged a *nostalgie de la boue* had such a phrase figured in his calculus.

Back inside, washing his hands in the bathroom, Victor Nee had peeked at the prescription bottles in the cupboard behind the mirror and noted an unopened packet of contraceptive pills with an expiry date.

'Yeah, well, as I say, I'll call in next week.' Switching to Australian, Beatrice was winding up her conversation. Victor Nee could not resist reading one last paragraph:

Comment: two similar incidents reported last week in Union Street. Women describe a young male of short, stocky build, possibly Aboriginal. Does not seem to be a thief, as he has been within inches of VCRs etc. Presumably voyeur.

With her customary vehemence, Beatrice dumped the phone in its cradle. Victor Nee jumped back from the microwave. Colliding with the fridge, he dislodged a train of magnetic hippos and papers fluttered onto the lino tiles. Squatting, he retrieved an electricity bill and a child's texta drawing of a pinheaded, clubfooted woman observed from ground level. Victor Nee was squatting, deciphering a yellow and white Bankcard statement when Beatrice came through the door. He looked up past the thick columns of her jeans to her square jaw and saracen earrings.

'Caught you,' Beatrice boomed.

'Sorry,' Victor Nee simpered. 'I was just—ah—' He gestured from the fridge to the table, where the beanstrings made an artistic litter on the laminex.

'Well,' Beatrice said easily, ignoring his preposterous explanation, 'you're making a right old fist of it. You should cook more often.' She had schooled herself in forebearance.

'Get up,' she ordered, 'walk over there, sit down, and drink your Cinzano.' Having insisted Victor Nee stay to dinner, and presented him with a fishtank she had found abandoned in the lane, she intended to do the job thoroughly.

Victor Nee watched as Beatrice finished stringing the beans—so quickly, considering the thickness of her fingers—and put them with the other vegetables into a segmented plastic plate resembling a dog's feeding dish.

Leaning against the bench beside the microwave, Beatrice instigated a conversation.

'This *Neighbourhood Watch* thing's goodo. Have you got it in Marrickville?'

'I don't think so,' Victor Nee lied. He did not care to participate in government-sanctioned spying.

'Take a gander at this.' Beatrice tossed across the typed, stapled printout pages from the top of the microwave. Victor Nee reread the top page and then observed, as it if were a new thought: 'Woman shouldn't live alone.'

'Women,' Beatrice corrected automatically. He persisted in getting plurals and tenses wrong.

'Have you had any problem?' Victor Nee pressed.

Beatrice was too much on top of life to countenance any. 'No way, Hosé,' she crowed. Her Bankcard statement, Victor recalled, disclosed an available credit of $2,932 and her parents would have left her plenty of money.

'Have I shown you my plans?' Beatrice was scooping down an offwhite roll from the top of the broom cupboard. Victor Nee had been wondering what this paper would reveal. He studied the drawing from all angles with a degree of interest gratifying to them both. He even examined the scale gauge and made rough measurements with his scarred pointer finger. Finally, he allowed the sheets to recurl themselves and placed the roll to one side, handling it gently, as if it were an antique parchment.

'Well, what do you think?' Beatrice pressed.

'It's good to bring the toilet inside.'

'Actually it's never greatly bothered me having an al fresco loo. What's wrong with a bit of rustic charm?'

'I bet the prowler likes it.' Victor Nee's tone was somewhere between a chortle and a reprimand. 'I bet the prowler likes watching you going out there in your pyjamas.'

'How do you know I wear pyjamas?'

'You always wear trousers.'

'True.' Beatrice pushed back her fringe. 'I'll tell you what, this prowler must be desperate for thrills. Who cares, anyway? He can't hurt me. Dougall always follows me down to the lav and sits outside. The poor little guy'd have to fight him off first.'

Dougall was large, as befitted a six-foot mistress, and prone to mount anything in sight.

'Dougall,' Victor Nee mused.

'Do you know what, yesterday he knocked over three garbage bins outside the flats and then wrapped himself around the gas meter lady. I told him: '"Look hound, if you get any further out of hand I'll have to do something very nasty to you."'

'You must get him done,' Victor Nee lectured, trying to mimic Beatrice's minatory tone. It was not often he had just cause to rebuke her.

'Bah, humbug! You sound like the Cat Protection Society. Bloody loonies creeping around with shears.'

Victor Nee's expression was still dissatisfied. 'Aren't you worried at all?'

'What about? Feel that, my boy.' Beatrice pushed up her T-shirt sleeve to display a creditable bicep. Weight training was another of her disciplines.

The microwave dinged, Beatrice served, and they tossed back the last of their drinks. Beatrice ate with gusto. Victor Nee tried to keep up, but he found European food heavy-going and the alcohol had made him uncoordinated. A mountainous pork knuckle waited his pleasure.

'Don't you ever cook Asian style?' he asked.

'No.' Beatrice was holding her knuckle with both fists and gnawing.

Victor Nee pulled the architect's drawings across the table, partially unrolled them, and reexamined the bathroom plans. His elbow nudged his fork and it bounced onto the diagram of the sewer line.

'Better put those away,' Beatrice cautioned.

Victor Nee confronted the knuckle for a second time.

'Quicksticks,' Beatrice cheered him along. 'Dougall's slavering for the bones.'

Victor Nee chewed until his jaw ached. Still Beatrice would

not relent. She merely sat watching him like a teacher supervising an insubordinate child on detention. She could have been holding a switch.

The meat seemed tight with adrenalin. Victor Nee lowered his fork and asked 'Are you doing any new research?' He hoped Beatrice would pull out some sheets of statistics and permit him to relax.

Beatrice described, in her usual lucid, positive way, a six-year scheme for measuring reading acquisition in refugee children. Victor Nee harboured an immovable contempt for such enterprises. Behind his spectacles his eyes wandered.

He was counting the canisters when Beatrice leant across and thumped her fist down on the table right under his nose. The knuckle and fork rattled on his plate. 'Am I really that boring?' she demanded.

Victor Nee rolled his eyes to the ceiling for inspiration. Hundreds of fly specks waited to be counted.

'You're right again, Victor Kneebone. I am bloody boring. And browned off. And fed up to the back teeth. And sick to death of work, and bodgie statistics.' She waved her arms so vigorously Victor Nee ducked.

'I keep trying to inject a bit of excitement.' She seized the plans and raised them like a cane.

'New car.' She whacked the table.

'Renovations.' Another whack. Victor Nee winced at the dent in the roll.

'Tennis.' She served an imaginary ball.

'Golf.' She swung her paper club, pretended to miss, and threw the roll across the room.

'It's all *blah*. What am I supposed to do, Victor Nee? Tell me.'

Victor Nee had never heard of a respectable lecturer beating a table.

'You need a friend, is it?' he hazarded.

'Too right I do.' Beatrice pitched a clean knife onto the sink. 'Bugger all that fish and bicycle crap. I'm recanting.'

'Fish?' Victor Nee was puzzled.

'I'll tell you what, I've got the bed for it. I found it over on Parramatta Road at that Eytie place.' She was already pounding up the stairs, surmounting them two at a time, her calf muscles bulging.

It was not quite etiquette in Victor Nee's book to enter the bedroom of a lady and a teacher. But curiosity and obedience outweighed decorum. The bed must have some merit, beside its undoubtedly large cost and dimensions, to warrant Beatrice's glee.

She was not devious or avaricious. She could sleep on a horsehair mattress and wake up hearty. The story of the princess and the pea was not in her curriculum.

'Da da!' Beatrice was posing, arms akimbo, beside a space-age rocket-launching platform. The bedhead was a jumbo jet's flight panel. Victor Nee giggled.

'Lie down.' Victor Nee obeyed. He lay flat on his back. Realising he was too bowlegged to keep his knees touching, he crossed one ankle over the other and folded his hands below his belt buckle.

Beatrice hit a knob and the radio roared. Then she slid another knob and the reading lights flashed. A button set an alarm clock braying. A dial started the whole contraption pulsating. Finally, snorting out loud at Victor Nee's bamboozled face, Beatrice pressed a square and the mattress shot up to a 45° angle. Victor Nee yelped and scrambled off.

'Look at you,' Beatrice hooted.

Dizzy and humiliated, Victor Nee was gripping the door frame.

'Relax,' she soothed, and switched off the noise. Down at the back door, Dougall was barking.

'Look, here's something you *will* like.' Gesturing Victor Nee into a rocking chair, Beatrice began pulling books off shelves. Victor Nee leant back in the chair. It plunged, and his short legs shot up in the air.

'Here.' Beatrice was lobbing books across the carpet. They were all reissues of forgotten novels by women. The chair rebounded and Victor Nee crouched forward with his feet secured to the floor. *Self Control*, Victor Nee read out. *Bond of Wedlock. Female Quixote*. Beatrice could not resist a dissertation on the alternative pronunciations of *quixote*. Then, sprawling across the foot of her bed, she watched Victor Nee examine the ISBN numbers and publication dates.

The french doors onto the balcony stood open. A southerly buster had been predicted and the first stirrings were in the air. The scent of gardenia and jasmine wafted in.

Yawning, stretching, turning over onto her back and locking her fingers under her head, Beatrice broke the silence.

'Did I tell you I've been looking at a weekender up in the Blue Mountains? Coralie's trying to talk me into going halves in it.' Beatrice had an abundance of capable chums.

'Two houses.' Victor Nee chided. 'And no man to put out the garbage.'

'Are you offering?' Beatrice tipped up her chin and studied him upside down.

'Oh no no no no no no no.'

'That's fortunate, because you're a foot too short.'

Heaving up her legs and supporting her hips with her hands, Beatrice cycled the air.

'Knee and Bee,' she chanted. 'Will you marry me? Knee and Bee. Will you marry me?' She could not be drunk. Victor Nee had counted just one Cinzano.

Letting her legs flop, Beatrice sighed luxuriously. 'Females are fools, aren't they? Read me a story, Victor.'

Victor Nee flicked through a few pages before shrugging his inability to find anything digestible. The curtains ballooned into the room.

'Ah, dear.' Beatrice sighed and rolled up into a sitting position. 'Madness, madness.' She planted her feet on the carpet, her calves a foot apart. 'You notice,' she said, 'the kids always get ratty when it's windy.'

Victor Nee turned a page. The doors rattled. Beatrice freed them from the hooks holding them open, subdued an armful of curtaining, closed the doors, and turned the key in the lock. Turning, she was seized by an inspiration.

'Music,' she cried. 'That's what we need. Music, maestro.'

She pounded downstairs. Victor Nee was uncertain whether she intended to return. Deciding it would be safest to beat a retreat from the bedroom before she put on anything sentimental, he bent to collect the books and fit them into their slots. Then, thinking better of it, he left them as they were and went out onto the landing.

Rollicking square dance music filled the kitchen.

'Yeehaw,' Beatrice yelled. 'Come on down.' Victor Nee advanced to the bottom step.

Beatrice skipped around the table, clapping above her head and laughing raucously. Dougall scrabbled at the screen door, yapping to be let in to join the hilarity.

'Come on.' Beatrice jerked Victor Nee off the step and spun him around. He stumbled and blundered into the fridge. For the second time, the bills and drawings fluttered onto the linoleum.

'Outside,' Beatrice cried. Linking her arm through Victor Nee's, she jostled him out the back door. Dougall leapt at them, rearing, barking, prancing. His plumed tail waved like a pennant.

'Dance,' Beatrice roared, and whirled Victor Nee around the rotary hoist.

'Heel and toe, heel and toe,' she sang, 'grab your partner, round we go.' Every time Victor Nee stumbled, Beatrice dragged him on. At last the tape stopped in the middle of a jig. Reeling with giddiness, Victor Nee clung to the clothes hoist. The dog pranced around him, a slobbering, galumphing adolescent.

'The prowler,' Victor Nee panted. 'That black guy. Aren't you worried?'

'Hey, prowler,' Beatrice bellowed. 'Come on out. It's a corroboree.'

Victor Nee tightened his grip on the hoist. At the bottom of the garden the toilet door creaked. Dougall growled deep in his throat and took one straight-legged, bristling step forward.

'A tomcat,' Victor Nee divined.

'Something nasty in the potting shed,' Beatrice amended. Raising her voice she called: 'Come out, you scurvy knave.'

The shape of a male approached out of the shadows. Beatrice reached for Dougall's collar.

'Having a good time?' The voice was uneducated. Beatrice and her colleagues had a label for it.

'We sure are.' Beatrice's accent was now a parody of a redneck's. 'What bout you, fella? What can we do for you in this neck of the woods?'

'I had to use your toilet.'

'Fine, brother, fine. We all know what it's like to get caught short, don't we Victor? Now I suppose you want to wash your hands?'

'I could use a drink of water.'

'Better still, you may have a port.' Beatrice had abandoned her redneck voice. 'Provided you ask politely.'

'How do you mean?'

'Red stuff. Wine. Grog.'

'I thought you meant a suitcase, like.'

'You must be from north of the border. Banana bender.'

'That's right.'

'Come inside then, before you freeze to death.'

The wind was now strong enough to stir the rotary hoist, and the youth was wearing stubbie shorts, a singlet and thongs. There was no indication of an offensive weapon.

Still restraining Dougall, Beatrice motioned the youth to unclip the screen door and go inside. A fresh gust made the hoist spin. The wires rattled and sang. Victor Nee hugged himself, fingering the goosebumps under the arms of his T-shirt.

In the kitchen the youth was sitting with his chair back at ninety degrees to the table and his dirty feet extending into the centre of the room. Beatrice replaced the plans on top of the broom cupboard and the *Neighbourhood Watch* bulletin face down on top of the microwave. Then she secured the bills and drawings to the fridge door, shifted the used plates into the sink, and tossed the two knuckle bones out to Dougall.

'Get inside,' she muttered to Victor Nee. He was standing in the doorway, poised to flee or send in the dog as need be.

'There you go.' Beatrice plonked a beer can in front of the youth. He pulled the ring and drank for a long second.

Victor Nee shut the screen door and sat down.

'*You'd* better stick to soft drink,' Beatrice told him, taking a can of ginger ale out of the fridge.

'In America,' said Victor Nee, 'port is woman's drink. They take it with soda.'

The youth was staring at the used plates.

'I'm ready for supper,' Beatrice announced. 'Do you eat toasted sandwiches?'

She cooked a stack. The youth chewed off hunks, shaking his head, impatient as a famished animal. Beatrice matched him sandwich for sandwich. Resting, then, they assessed one another.

Beatrice stood up. 'Ale, sir?'

'Sorry?'

'Beer?'

'Yeah, OK.' Twisting toward Victor Nee, the youth asked: 'Got a smoke?'

'Kneebone doesn't indulge,' Beatrice mocked. 'He'd rather burn ten-dollar notes.'

'Waste of paper,' Victor Nee confirmed.

'Besides—' Beatrice rapped the table, 'this is a healthy household.'

'What about that stuff?' The youth jabbed the decanter.

'You're gorgeous,' Beatrice spluttered. 'We're got the same sense of humour. What's your name?'

They talked, teasing and wrangling. The youth had only a rudimentary general knowledge but he was a fast learner. Victor Nee laboured to keep up with their repartee. Growing bored, he went out to the laundry for mosquito repellent, and then went out a second time, to the lavatory.

When he came back in the second time, he found Beatrice harping on a familiar theme. 'Troy,' she lectured, 'you should read more. Even comics would help.'

The youth's silence was an explanation.

'I'll teach you,' Beatrice proposed.

'Nah.'

'Go on. It's easy as falling off a log.'

'Nah.'

'Why not?'

'You're too bossy.'

'Strike a light.' Beatrice slapped her forehead in frustration. 'Look, Vicboy'll help you. You couldn't be scared of him, could you?'

The two males studied each other, calculating.

'One condition, mind.' Beatrice was undeterrable. 'You both stop skulking about snooping through other people's windows.'

The youth jumped up, twitching, ready to run.

'You,' Beatrice said to Victor Nee, 'know what I'm talking about. While as for you, young man, the whole neighbourhood knows about it.' She rose, stepped around him and took the bulletin off the microwave. 'They reported it, the ladies you perved on.'

The youth tightened his fists. Then, reaching some sort of resolve, he sat down and said: 'I was looking for me brother.'

'Your brother isn't a twenty-year-old breastfeeding her baby.'

'Well, I dunno, do I?'

'What do you mean?'

'I said, didn't I? I'm looking for me brother.'

'Then why don't you go to the proper authorities?'

The youth snorted.

'He probably had to move on,' Beatrice explained. 'All the houses are being bought up and renovated. They may have got a Housing Commission flat.'

'He's still around here.' The youth was obdurate. 'You wouldn't know anyways. He's real light.'

Outside, a discordant clatter set in. Victor Nee jumped as if a gun had gone off.

'You're twitchy tonight,' Beatrice teased. 'Got a guilty conscience? Don't worry, it's only Dougall playing soccer with the garbage bin.'

Victor Nee stood at the window and watched the dog rolling the bin over the stepping stones to the hoist; the great nincompoop's tongue hung out, dripping, and his face was delirious with enjoyment.

'I better go,' Victor Nee said. He did not fancy helping pick up the scattered garbage.

'That's all right.' Beatrice was willing, once again, to forebear. 'You can give Troy a lift home.'

'I'm stopping with me cousins in Redfern,' the youth volunteered, 'but they're most likely out someplace.'

As Victor Nee's mind rehearsed a statement of regret, Beatrice slapped her palms together and said: 'Rightyho. Victor will drive you up there. And, don't forget: *reading*. Make a date for Vic to start teaching you. He's good at sums too.' Another minute and she would be ordering them both to thank her for feeding them.

Victor Nee unlocked the passenger's side of his Gemini and the youth got in and slammed the door. Victor Nee was starting the engine when Beatrice rapped on his window. 'Fishtank,' she mouthed. Victor Nee got out. He left the engine running—the battery was low and he had been economising by not replacing it.

Beatrice and Victor Nee were goosestepping along the side passage, gripping the slippery tank between them, when they heard the Gemini revving.

'Shit,' Victor Nee exclaimed and dropped his end of the tank. A couple of glass panels cracked with a report like a popgun's. Beatrice and Dougall hurdled the tank and followed him out into the front yard.

The Gemini was already half way along the road, weaving at speed, heading against the One Way signs.

'He'll kill himself,' Beatrice cried. 'Stop, you bugger.' She pounded out into the road and, with Dougall leaping at her side and barking in exultation, ran after the car. There was a squeal as the youth rounded the corner in third. Victor Nee began to run too, gulping and snivelling as he went.

From the corner, Beatrice watched the car career up Munni Street and swerve right into the butt of Gowrie.

'Now we've got him,' she said to herself, and sprinted up the slope.

The young fool had careered into a council roadblock. He reversed, revved, and tried to swing the vehicle round in a single spin. But the Germini stalled. The youth hit the ignition. The motor faltered into action, then died. At the driver's door, Dougall reared up, scratching at the window.

'Got you!' Beatrice hollered. Sweeping aside the dog, she hauled open the door and dragged the youth out onto his feet. He fought her custody, kneeing and punching without reservation, but she was twice his size and unafraid. When the youth did momentarily escape her grasp, Dougall seized an arm in his slobbering jaws.

Within a couple of minutes the youth was subdued and panting in the gutter.

'That was a bloody stupid thing to do,' Beatrice remonstrated. Victor Nee detected a degree of humour, even admiration, in her tone, and it rankled. Stepping forward, he began to examine his car as meticulously as was possible given the single streetlight. Pausing at the driver's door he took his keys out of the ignition.

Beatrice opened the passenger's door and told the youth to get in and do up his seatbelt. He obeyed.

Victor Nee looked at Beatrice incredulously. 'Do it,' her eyes snapped. He stepped back, considering the youth's stocky strength and his own feeble biceps.

'You'll be right,' Beatrice said.

'That's what Australians always say.'

'*She'll* be right, stupid.'

Victor Nee capitulated. 'Thank you for dinner.' He sounded like a television English lesson for migrants. 'Goodnight doggy.' Dougall lashed his tail, bashing the fender.

Victor Nee restarted his car, hauled on the wheel, eased forward and, as the engine picked up, moved away.

Beatrice was shouting again. 'Fishtank,' he was sure she was yelling, but he pretended not to hear. He would call back in the new year, one lonely January evening. By then Beatrice would have replaced the cracked glass.

Victor Nee crawled up the highway through Newtown. Saturday night gangs of boys ran out, dodging the traffic, throwing insults and feining punches. Beside Victor Nee the youth sat sulking.

As they passed under the university footbridge, Victor Nee panicked. 'Where are we going?'

'Redfern. Like I told you.'

'Which street, I mean.'

'Hugo.'

'I remember I saw something about some fellow who lived there.'

'Koori?'

'Aussie.'

'Bullshit. There aren't any whites in Hugo Street.'

'He owned a house. No, I've got it. He owned a whole row of houses. Got them really cheap. We lent him the money.'

'That'd be right.'

At last, with the youth yielding last-minute grunts of direction, they turned into Hugo. The street was in darkness, every streetlight smashed. Victor Nee's frail headlights shone on a litter of glass pellets, bricks and garbage. He crept forward.

A gaggle of children spilled out of a little playground onto the bitumen. They were scuffling, shrieking and passing something amongst themselves. They were all girls. Arrested by the headlights, they scattered and moved towards the car. One raised her hand in an obscene gesture. Another pitched a handful of gravel at the windscreen. Victor Nee braked to a halt. The youth rolled down his window, put out his head and snarled at the girls to get out of the way. They jeered in return.

'Don't,' Victor Nee pleaded.

The children had surrounded the car now and were kicking the tyres and beating on the panels.

'Stop them, can't you?' Victor Nee whimpered. A hail of stones rattled on the back window.

The youth pushed open his door. The interior light came on, illuminating Victor Nee's contorted face. Outside, the girls were a mocking horde of shadows.

'Who's the Chinaman?' one crowed.

'Yeah,' another laughed, 'who's the Chinaman, bananaface?'

'Chinaman,' the others chorused. 'Bananaface. Chinese cunt.'

The youth got out and slammed the door behind him. The girls jostled and backed away. His fists were opening and closing.

'Get going,' the youth commanded over his shoulder.

Victor Nee stretched across to wind up the window. His sole slipped off the clutch and he stalled.

Sitdown Strike

At six-thirty one spring morning, Jack Brocklehurst was walking across the backyard to feed the chooks when he came over dizzy. He grabbed at the hibiscus and then must have passed out for, when he came to, he was sprawled on the ground. His breathing was shallow and his sight blurred. The grass blade brushing his eye looked like a sword and the stalks of the self-sown heartsease were thick as tree trunks. The earth was wet.

Jack brought his free hand up to his face and saw red smears on his fingertips and the pad of his palm. He moved his chin and saw—in peculiar perspective—long dribbly trails on the inner legs of his trousers.

After an uncountable length of time, Phyllis came to the back door calling Jack to breakfast. She gasped and ran and tumbled and gripped his shoulders and shivered and tried to raise him. Grunting and stumbling, they made it inside. Phyllis staggered with Jack into the bathroom. He tried to sit on the edge of the toilet bowl but he was so weak and dazed he toppled backwards. Phyllis lumbered him down onto the floor, where he lay in the coma position, hands loose on the tiles, eyeballs close to the silver drain grating. The backside of his grey drill trousers was sopping with darkening blood.

The ambulance crew were unperturbed. They cruised through side streets, stopping to collect an elderly gent scheduled for an X-ray. Jack tried to speak but his tongue seemed swollen. Suspiciously pale fluid tricked down a tube into a bandage on his arm. He closed his eyelids and concentrated on the jolting.

At six-thirty p.m. a bed was freed and an orderly wheeled Jack out of Casualty, across a driveway, into a lift, out into a corridor with a sign saying Colorectal, and into Ward 16. Phyllis followed their little procession like a pallbearer working to regulations.

At seven Jack croaked at Phyllis to go home and get some rest. He had not shaved before the collapse and his cheeks were now white with stubble. His eyes were bloodshot. Through the floor-length windows he watched a tangerine sunset fade to a thin yellow and grey dusk.

A snappy woman came around pulling down the holland blinds with a pole. Jack turned his head and sniffled with self-pity. The view across the ward was not soothing. The lights seared. Jack closed his eyes against the clashing.

About eight a workmate poked his grinning dial around the corner, dumped a packet of Iced Vovos on the stainless steel bedside cabinet and made a crack about Jack's intravenous pint of lager.

Every hour that night a nurse jingled over to check Jack's tubes. A light glared over the door and the clatter in the pan room was amplified in the stillness. Old men snored and snorted. One fellow kept trying to cough up phlegm. Another lit a surreptitious cigarette.

After eight days of transfusions, examinations, enforced inactivity in girlish elastic stockings, two deaths, and harrowing screams from the Burns Unit down the corridor, Jack was opened up. He was lucky: only the upper part of the bowel was excised and he did not require a colostomy.

For five days afterwards, the ordeal was so dreadful Jack concluded death would have been preferable to treatment. He could not recall ever having signed a consent form. His one diversion was directing malignant glares at the staff who catalogued his tortures. When he was finally allowed up, he shuffled across the disinfectant floor gripping his belly, just as he had watched the others do.

In the TV lounge the returned men were re-winning the war. Jack had stayed at home in a protected industry. Pre-empting a rebuff, he told them he had been too young to volunteer. 'So was I,' said the jaundiced fellow from Coffs, 'but I put my age up, didn't I?' Jack retrieved a used newspaper and decided to have a go at the crosswords and teasers. He had always liked the puzzle where you had to change one word into another in the fewest possible number of moves, but now he could not complete a single one. He could not hold the pen steady, and his brain would not work. He could not reason. Letters were merely squiggles on a page; singularly and collectively they had no meaning.

When Phyllis came, they spoke of practical details such as the foods Jack could no longer digest. When a nephew on Phyllis's side visited, Jack told him without preliminaries to get a bowel cancer check-up. The young man grimaced. 'Don't blame me, then,' Jack growled. He would have liked to have been able to blame his own father, but he had never known the man, and the surgical registrar would not put a figure on the proportion of cases where heredity was the culprit.

When Jack was released, he did not present cards and chocolates to the nurses, whose female chatter and skylarking he would not miss. Nor did he compose a special little speech for the quacks. He gave the credit for his survival to his own boarish fortitude, and to his wife. He could not have gone home to an empty house.

Phyllis's nieces and nephews had decorated the livingroom with balloons. Their mirth was unseemly. They had prepared a trestle of food, none of which Jack could stomach, and had invited in the Korean neighbours.

Phyllis patted Jack's arm where the drip had gone in and scanned his face with a tender, soggy concern. His dour expression was not unfamiliar, but it had acquired a mordant shading. In two weeks he had not smiled voluntarily, except out of feigning politeness when nurses and diggers had approached him. Now as he shaved in front of the old bevelled, spotted mirror in the laundry, where the light through the louvres disclosed every bristle and hollow, he smiled like a skull and said with relish: 'Jack the Reaper strikes again.'

Day after day Jack sat in the backyard. At first he could not concentrate on anything. It was all he could manage to flick through his stamp albums. Phyllis blamed the anaesthetic. After a fortnight he began fiddling with a Rubik's Cube and graduated to Mr Wisdom's Whopper Crosswords.

Phyllis told Jack to put on his hat. He ignored her. 'You'll get headaches,' she pleaded. 'You should protect your scalp.'

Jack let the chooks out of their pen and watched them pecking amongst the dandelions. Pretty moths flitted around the cabbages. The broccoli sprouted tall, seedy shoots. The snake beans withered. The melons poked tiny, clenched fists out of the dirt but did not emerge any further. The Koreans watched the garden's deterioration through a gap in the palings. Jack told Phyllis the soil needed to lie fallow for a few months. He loved his garden, second only to his wife.

The wisecracking workmate came calling a couple of times a week. He brought stubbies of KB, messages (of increasing sparsity), and jokes and trick questions. When conversation fizzled, they would sit in silence in the late afternoon sun, the workmate swigging at an increasing pace.

Jack had exhausted his accumulated sick leave and holidays and was now into his long service leave allowance. 'You're lucky you're not a Jap,' the workmate encouraged. 'Only eight days holiday up there, fair dinkum.'

The buffalo grass was now ankle-high. Jack took to shifting his rocking chair hourly so he flattened different patches. Bees occupied the clover, and crickets sang amongst the couch. Down near the chookyard, the barnyard grass was half a metre tall, and inside the yard a clump of groundsel had taken root in the droppings.

Since Phyllis did not drive, Jack's car had not been used in three months. The battery was probably flat, and the concrete floor of the carport had soaked up an oil leak. The schoolteacher nephew who had refused to undergo a bowel investigation had, to placate Jack, promised to put the car in for a service. But instead he had taken off to Indonesia for his Christmas holidays. His postcards showed volcanoes overgrown by green jungle.

January was hot and humid. The buffalo grass flourished. It was now knee-high and rippling like a lake. Stinkwort straggled around the back steps, and a big nightshade with black berries was silhouetted against the fence. Jack made terse work of Phyllis's plea to call in a gardener. No-one except the Koreans could see what was happening to the backyard. The front garden was small and fully paved and Phyllis was able to slip out to weed the potted azaleas on the porch whilst Jack was in the bathroom.

Apart from Jack's physical lassitude and the pernickety, suspicious attitude he had adopted to Phyllis's cooking, the casual visitor confined to the sittingroom would not have picked he had had major surgery. He was healthfully tanned, lean and mentally alert. He pounced on errors of addition and pronunciation. He recited odd facts he had heard on the radio. He tested people with tongue twisters. When the neighbours' children came in, he told each one a joke. It was as if he needed to cleanse himself of his jocular workmate's garrulous deposits. When one boy wanted to see the operation scar, Jack told him a weird story about turkey gizzards and quizzed him on the plural of 'appendix'.

In February Phyllis's Uncle Charlie arrived unannounced to sit amid the chickweed patch which Jack was occupied in flattening. Uncle Charlie was an old-time unionman, a retired timbergetter still active as a numbersman, a healthy, gutsy old bastard going on eighty. Keeping one eye on the laurel, he spoke of men who had been paradigms of reformation, men who had, after surviving sawmill and felling accidents, taken a fresh look at their lives and resolved to conduct themselves differently in the bonus years granted to them.

'Look,' Jack said, 'I got over it because I wanted to. I make my own decisions.'

'Are you saying you decided to get sick?'

The old bloke was always on for an argument. He was a master heckler.

Phyllis was approaching with a tray. Her uncle jumped up to take it from her. He offered her his chair. She demurred. He insisted on lugging out a third chair. She fussed, fetched extra hot water, and finally sat down. The chickweed tickled through her stockings.

'I was saying,' resumed Phyllis's uncle, maintaining his advantage, 'that Jack has been preserved for some purpose.'

'Pickled,' Jack said.

'Jack,' Phyllis cautioned.

'Tell me,' said Jack, 'why does the Big Bloke allow suffering?' Recalling the gastric juices sucked out through his nostril, he sought only the uncle's discomfiture.

The uncle had attended the bedsides of many good unionmen, and he was not lost for a reply. He rambled on about nature's cycles, dieback and regeneration, clearing and culling. Phyllis arranged her feet side by side on the squashed white flowers and studied her toecaps. While Jack was in the operating theatre she had asked directions to the hospital chapel.

Suddenly the uncle began making moves to leave. It was as if he had recalled a vital meeting for which he had to fix the numbers. 'I'll put in a good word for you,' he said.

Jack hunched and looked at a clump of shivery grass. A few cold drops of modesty trickled down his forehead.

'Thank you, Uncle Charlie,' Phyllis said in the tone of a good little girl.

After she had seen her uncle off, Phyllis returned to carry in the tray. 'He could at least have offered to scythe those weeds,' she said in an aggrieved manner.

'I have acquired,' Jack spoke into the hot afternoon air, 'a profound love of the bees and crickets. How could I deprive them of their home, mow them down in cold blood? How could I hack off the heartsease? Slash open the cocoons of infant spiders? Grind ants into the dirt? Poison the happy weeds? Mutilate the droptail lizards?'

It was as though his guts had softened. Depletion had made him squeamish.

'Well, I'm not going to do it,' Phyllis shouted at the back of his tanned scalp. 'I've done enough of your dirty work.' It was the first time she had referred to the weeks of nursing, the washings and dressings. A stench blocked her nostrils.

Neither of them slept well that night. Jack woke at four-thirty, as he had ever since his hospital stint, and lay thinking malicious thoughts about Phyllis and his jocular workmate.

At the beginning of autumn, Jack's leave expired. The personnel manager came out to ask whether Jack wished to submit his resignation or apply for early retirement. The production side, he remarked in passing, was suffering as a result of Taiwanese imports and a hundred process workers had been laid off with half a day's notice. Jack observed that he had begun with the company when he was sixteen and had now clocked up forty-five years. The personnel fellow stared at a clutch of little green pouches nodding at the top of slender stems. 'Quaking grass,' Jack said. 'Blowfly grass.' Management too could be squeamish.

Jack requested a month's leave on half-pay. He must consult his surgeon, he said, and you couldn't get an appointment at the drop of a hat. A premature return might, he hinted, result in a compo claim. He had always stuck by his union.

The surgeon examined Jack with a long scopic instrument.

'Doesn't this job give you the shits?' Jack enquired, trying for his workmate's irreverent tone.

'You can get used to anything,' the man replied.

As he dressed, Jack attempted another joke: 'You could say you're more interested in the ends than the means, eh?'

'Yes,' the surgeon said, without signifying agreement.

The surgeon's report declared Jack free of regrowths and fit to work. Complaining of pernicious weariness, Jack obtained a referral to a physician. The physician put it down to stress and recommended walking, resumption of light duties, a pastime such as gardening, and a diet free of tomato seeds. Jack pressured Phyllis into phoning the personnel manager with the ultimatum that her husband had been forbidden to return unless the duties were exceptionally light. 'The bastard's angling to be pensioned off,' the manager complained to his secretary.

In April Phyllis resorted to using a home-delivery laundry service because she could no longer haul her washing trolley through the tangled grass to the clothesline. However thoroughly Jack flattened a path with his rocker, the army of weeds sprang back up. Beside the paling fence there were ugly great things a yard high.

On Anzac Day Uncle Charlie called in for a drink. Afterwards

Phyllis escorted him out to the car and returned with a stack of letters, envelopes and computer-printed address tags, a finger stall and a sponge in a little glass dish. 'You don't mind helping Charlie out, do you Jack?' she said. Jack freed a redwood bench from its canopy of kikuyu runners and arranged the papers symmetrically. A perusal of the letters told him he was helping further a powerplay designed to defeat certain non-aligned election candidates.

When the uncle came to collect, Jack quoted him the clerical officers' award rate. The uncle blanched, reared his head, flared his nostrils, regarded Jack's unyielding face, and wrote a cheque for half the amount.

'Exit my new career,' Jack told Phyllis.

Jack returned to his seat in the backyard. The weeds were flourishing. Tendrils brushed his forehead. The earth was moist and seething with worms.

'How high,' Jack asked a leech, 'can grass grow? If I sit here long enough, will it stop at a certain pre-determined height? Or will it swarm all over the house?'

Get Back, Jo Jo

In the middle of an extraordinarily long, fierce storm, David Drevikovsky's dog Jo Jo raised his paw in supplication. 'Oh, Jo Jo,' David sighed, but there was no alternative.

Water pounded on the tin roof, sloshed through downpipes and holes in the guttering, and cascaded down walls. Wind gusts shook the windows. Thunder rumbled. It was as if the ocean had invaded the sky and the air through which people struggled had become a thrashing shark tank. David could not remember such torrential rain since the cyclonic January rains of his childhood. He had not been able to see out the windows for hours. He knew if he switched on the seven o'clock news it would be nothing but flash floods, blackouts, record downpours, boys lost in stormwater channels, rescuers overwhelmed in creeks, and infants swept from their parents' arms.

Jo Jo had not been outside since eleven, when David had gone for milk. He was getting desperate, but David had been ignoring the signs.

'OK, Jo Jo,' David said, toeing off his Kung Fu shoes.

'You're a creature of habit,' he scolded, stretching on the clammy socks he had worn outside that morning. Jo Jo scrabbled deliriously at David's head as he bent to pull on his riding boots.

'Down, damn you,' David roared. The dog ran to the door, scratched on it, and ran back, his long nails clicking on the lino. David took down the leash from its bent nail and crouched to clip it to Jo Jo's collar. The dog began leaping, twisting and snorting.

'Down,' David ordered, 'or you won't be going anywhere.' Quivering, the dog sank onto his haunches just long enough for the leash to be snapped on, then shot upwards, cannoning into David's chin. It was their nightly routine.

David found his keys behind a paint can and lifted his greatcoat off the open cupboard door where he had been airing it. The coat was still damp from the morning's outing and sodden around the shoulder pads, cuffs and hem. It was so heavy it had to be shrugged on.

Opening the door, David said: 'OK, Jo Jo. Let's go.'

The dog pitched down the first flight of stairs, his leash bouncing on each tread. David jerked the door closed and shook it to check both locks had engaged. The dog waited grinning on the landing, his skinny tail lashing.

The storm was even louder.

There were rulers of light under doors, and Alberta Hunter on one turntable; but no-one was stupid enough to be hanging about in the stairwell in this weather. A couple of light bulbs had blown and black pools filled corners: they might have been pools of water or blood. There had been a stabbing, once, on these stairs. And an overdose. There had also been an arson attempt using newspapers sprinkled with petrol. The police had spoken of drunken louts but the collective suspected emissaries of the owner, who wanted to evict his arty-farty tenants, gut the building and implant a shopping centre.

The wind was bashing so hard against the front door that David had to press his shoulder to the wood to get out. A blast of wind-driven rain splattered his face.

'Rightyo, Jo Jo,' he said, turning south into the gale, 'you asked for it.' The dog cringed against the brick wall.

'Come on.' David stubbed Jo Jo's hindquarters with his toecap. He loved the dog immeasurably.

This was David and Jo Jo's second period of occupation of the warehouse. The first was remembered by long-term residents for the originality of David's affectations. He had outshone the most outrageous artiste.

His nails were buffed then, his moustache was waxed, his eyebrows were combed, and his straight, collar-length hair was dyed black, parted high on the crown and induced to flop over his right eye. To read, he had drawn out a monocle on a gold chain; to write, a fountain pen; to check the hour, a fob watch. He was dandified in three-piece suits when everyone else was in jeans, and on gala occasions he had added gloves, cravat and top hat. In inclement weather he had stood unfazed beneath a cape.

He had spent whole Saturdays promenading. He had lounged,

loafed, posed and drifted with exquisite elegance. He had acquired a frail whippet, named her Nana, and paraded her on a pink silk cord. Ambling beside his charge, his free hand in his fob pocket, he had whistled or recited scraps of Yevtushenko. After the whippet was stolen, he had acquired an amiable Borzoi, as tall and thin as himself, named him Jo Jo, short for Emperor Joseph the Second, and fitted him out with a red collar and leash. Whenever Jo Jo had accelerated in pursuit of a cat—a not uncommon event—David was pitched off balance. Picking himself up off his knees and straightening his accessories, he would resume—with the aid of a peck of snuff—his dandy's dignity.

David had always claimed Russian and Hapsburg ancestry, although his parents and grandparents were known to live only three or four suburbs away. He had confided he was descended in a direct line from the secret alliance of Joseph II with Catherine II of Russia. On feast days, he had impersonated an array of military officers and aristocrats and driven everybody on his floor mad with brass band marches, Gluck, Mozart, and the 1812 Overture. His passions were—then and now—war histories, war games and war movies. He was intrigued too by the interstices between official wars: the coups and incursions and cold wars. The Kennedy dynasty so fascinated him that he ordered each new biography and assessment as soon as he heard of it. One of his favourite possessions was a plate, *circa* 1962, decorated with a transfer of JFK. He admired women who resembled Jackie Kennedy and was delighted by pillbox hats. He liked, also, nineteenth-century clothing; in particular, goatskin shoes exercised his imagination.

David had been employed during his first term of residence by the Department of Veterans' Affairs. Always an early riser, he had reached the office at seven-thirty and built up his flexitime hours reading old files and making spider-leg notations with a propelling pencil. The only other regular early starter had been a programmer named Rhoda. One Friday Rhoda had invited David to dinner, served up Veal Stroganoff, potatoes with sour cream, and Strawberries Romanoff, opened a third bottle of wine, put the cat out, and pressed her guest onto the sofa. The following day she had taken David to meet her mother. He had been subdued with the simplest of campaigns.

Marriage had diluted David's pleasures. He had foresaken his suits and packed away his monocle, fountain pen, fob watch and snuff box. Jo Jo had adapted to the garden and reached a truce with Rhoda's cat. The peace of pragmatism had prevailed.

After completing her part-time degree, Rhoda had decided to slot in a baby. Instructing David in a forthright manner throughout the conception, gestation and birth, she had produced it. Oscar had been weaned early and Rhoda had returned to Veterans' Affairs. David had resigned to care for the infant.

Rhoda had washed-up and baby-sat on the night David went out to his war games group. When her next increment had come through, she had increased David's housekeeping money. At the Department, she was then working closely with the boss of her section on the changeover to a Macintosh system. She had begun getting home late every work evening except David's war games night, and David had ceased keeping a meal hot for her.

David had turned the house into a battlefield of skulking guerillas—fleas, dust, mould—and wholesome offensive troops. As he cleaned he dramatised for Oscar all the great battles from the Pelopponesian wars to Long Tan. The child had laughed aloud as he waved his plastic gun. 'Shoot Mummy,' David used to urge. 'That's right, point your wifle at her.'

Striding along with the stroller, David had talked equally to the child, the dog and himself, declaring his opinion on all the watersheds of history. Jolting his chin, flicking back the Hitlerian forelock he had allowed to regrow, he had assessed the Bay of Pigs, Entebbe, Afghanistan. Often his walks had led to the university library, where, Jo Jo tied up outside, he read until Oscar grew impossibly restive. At home he had ceased to tell his wife about his explorations and campaigns, as she had ceased to try to explain her own, and they spoke through the child.

One morning Rhoda had announced she intended living with her boss and that, this being her house, David would have to move out. The rout was thus accomplished without the firing of a single shot. It had been agreed that David would continue to take most of the responsibility for the child, since Rhoda's work load could not be expected to diminish, and she in return had undertaken to support the two of them.

Instinct had led David back to the warehouse. An unpopular printmaker had been ousted and David, Oscar and Jo Jo had tied up in their safe harbour. 'Welcome back to the phalanstery', David had said to himself. One week in four now Oscar went to his mother.

Lately rations had been short. Rhoda, under pressure from her lover, had cut the allowance back to an amount barely sufficient for the child's food, clothes and pre-school fees. David had been living on bread, mandarins (which were in season), beer, milky tea and Lebanese rolls. Jo Jo had been confined to Good-Os and water. Once a week David ingratiated himself with the Argies at the truckstop cafe by buying half a barbequed chicken and requesting the leftover bones in their language. '*Huesos*,' he would mouth, gesturing with his painty hands, '*huesos*, please, with plenty of *carne*. . .' If no bones were forthcoming he had to eat his chicken out on the warehouse stairs with the dog locked inside, or it would have been wrenched from his grasp.

Earlier in the year a war games adversary who called himself Killer Kowalski had come up with a money-making proposition. Killer was the mastermind of a garage industry turning out plaster figurines: grotesque representations of Dracula, Godzilla, Frankenstein's monster, Marilyn Monroe, skulls, pigs in police helmets, monkeys, frogs and characters from Dungeons and Dragons. David had agreed to spend every fourth week, when he was free of Oscar, painting Killer's figurines and, on the Sunday, selling them at Rockdale Markets. On Monday, Killer would arrive with a ute-load of ghastly white statues. All week David would paint and lacquer. On Sunday morning at eight-thirty Killer would collect David and his retinue, deposit them in the Rockdale carpark, and go to the club.

The market customers were men and women accustomed to bargaining: Vietnamese, Turks, Arabs and Slavs. It was exhausting trying to keep an eye on all the figures, prevent theft and deliberate damage, extract correct payments, secrete the takings and answer insistent questioners. It was not the career for a boulevardier. Still, unexpected alliances were forged with other beleaguered stall-holders, and, in the flat intervals, David could leave his table in the care of Jo Jo and his neighbours and take a brisk tour of the carpark.

Over the months he had picked up a few nice Kennedy volumes, a trunkful of lead soldiers, a tortoiseshell comb, an ivory penknife, a fob chain, a silk bowtie, and a bit of scrimshaw. The warehouse had nodded in appreciation. Young Oscar's attire, until then strictly utilitarian, began to take on a rakish air. He sported a Cub cap one day, a wildwest scarf the next. To top it all, a dog-loving stallholder knitted Jo Jo a red coat which tied under his belly with pompoms.

Lowering his forehead and pushing his fingers under his pocket flaps, David barged south into the wind. Jo Jo followed unwillingly, teetering at a slant, cringing, his ears back. The leash trailed between them.

Cars ploughed through the water in the kerbside lane, throwing up waves which splattered David's calves and sluiced across the pavement, merging with the water flushing out of downpipes and spilling from gutters. Signs dripped. Awnings rattled. Doors slammed. Rubbish cans and advertising signs cartwheeled. Hoardings creaked. The rain was now scatty, now torrential. A couple of college girls came running to the pizza shop, clutching billowing garbage bags over their heads and shrieking.

Everything which was not wet and black was gold: the headlights, the streetlights, the takeaway neons. Interiors glowed through misted windows like steaming woks of stir-fried corn. At its centre the road was so slick that tyres were reflected as hemispheres. The pavement, where it was not awash, was glimmering as the yellow lights caught the thousands of tiny conglomerate chips in the tar. Each chip shone like a diamond. Together they shone in dazing op-art patterns, like the outpourings of fire crackers.

At Georgina Street, Jo Jo turned unbidden and they went down into the blackness of dripping trees. The phone boxes had been vandalised again: broken glass shimmered on the pavement. Tripping over a tree root, David cursed. Jo Jo stopped at the corner where street met park. He sniffed around the communal rubbish skip, raised his leg, and crunched a chicken bone. David unclipped the dog's leash and urged him to have a run.

Above them the Moreton Bay figtrees groaned. David wondered whether he had turned off the radiator. It was a part of his evening routine to switch off everything electrical before he went out. Since he had only one powerpoint—overloaded with double adaptors—this was a task easily achieved. The harder he now tried to visualise himself turning off the radiator, the less certain he became. The newspaper under his wet sandshoes would be getting hotter and drier; its edges would be curling. Worse still, the paints and thinners on the window sill—the explosion would take the roof off. Everything would go up. And come down. A monstrous hail of white limbs and heads: Marilyns, Draculas, pigs, monkeys. The building owner would bless David for his subversive genius.

'Ah, well,' David said, and stamped his boots. So much water had entered the riding boots through the split seams that he felt he was sploshing barefoot in a mud puddle. His socks were sodden and the excess water circulated, squelching and bubbling as he moved his toes. Still, the desire to hurry home had left him. There were no soft towels to dry his toes, no fine talcs, no hairdryer, no laundry.

'Come on, Jo Jo,' David bellowed. 'Do your business.'

The dog raised his muzzle, looked offended, and resumed sniffing the discoloured grass around a lightpole.

'Jesus,' David complained, but he knew the dog needed to

walk a fair distance before he could relieve himself. Summoning Jo Jo, David reattached the leash and began to walk along the high side of the park, raising his chin and going forward with an influx of determination. He had nothing but his son, his dog, and a talent for eccentricity so mediocre it no longer raised eyebrows.

A grand row of three-storey terraces looked down on the park as if it were their private domain. The owners were so conceited in their comfort they had not even bothered to weld bars across their bay windows and etched-glass door panels. On fine nights, when the curtains were looped back, David had studied the reception rooms on the ground floors. Of the higher rooms he could see only the upper walls and light fittings. One bedroom had a chandelier, the second an Arthur Boyd, the third a native shield, and the fourth a pillar serving no apparent structural purpose. In front of TVs and on downy beds, the residents basked in their artificial sunlight.

David turned left, then left again, into the lane behind the grand terrace. Scenting cats, Jo Jo trotted forward into the gloom. The high brick wall behind the houses gave protection from the worst of the gale. Letting Jo Jo's leash go and stretching up on the balls of his feet, David peered into the first backyard. He saw cobblestones, cumquats in tubs and French doors. The second yard was a dog's breakfast of old bricks, window frames and heaps of sand. In the third yard David could make out only a clothesline and a table and chairs. In the kitchen a woman of about fifty-five was beating something in a china bowl with a rotary beater. After a minute, she stopped to rest, touching her chest above the heart with the flat of her right hand. The fourth yard was so dark it cried out for surreptitious entry. Near the wall grew an old tree which David recognised as a loquat. His grandparents had one in their garden, and his grandmother served the fruit, stewed, with rice custard. At its centre the loquat fruit had a round slippery stone.

'Let's go,' David whispered. He walked gingerly, careful not to let the metal tips of his soles clatter against the roadway. At the corner he slowed Jo Jo by grasping him around the haunches. Then he picked up the leash, which had developed the sliminess of drenched leather, and steered Jo Jo down Fitzroy Street, the park's northern border. The storm propelled them with a flurry of wind-driven rain.

David was acquainted with a couple of the people in the houses he was now passing. His favourite was a no-nonsense lady who hobbled with her old blind bitch, Sooky, every evening in the twilight. She had addressed David several times on the subjects of mange and canker. A few doors further down was an elderly gentleman who appeared to live alone. David had often seen him coming home about six-thirty in his overcoat and hat. Closed venetians blocked his windows.

At the base of the park, David swung left into a wide, trafficked street. There were no more protective trees, and the southerly gale whipped his coat.

He held Jo Jo on a short leash, for cats often sheltered under parked cars in this stretch and once one of them, startled by Jo Jo, had run out under a van. David had not been able to leave Jo Jo and Oscar unattended in order to retrieve the cat's body from the road. Scolding Jo Jo, and hauling Oscar by the upper arm, he had begun knocking on doors, searching for the cat's owner. The people in this row of semis were all Laotion or Cambodian. They had shied back from the dog and denied knowledge of any cat. When David had looked back the cat was a smeared mess.

Past the semis, Jo Jo stopped at the entrance to a narrow easement which ran uphill between two fences to a cul-de-sac. He always insisted on scampering up this uninviting passage in search of cats. Tonight the raked concrete was acting as a funnel: water was pouring down through it. David let the leash go and the dog splattered ahead, hopping on his skinny legs from side to side of the river. David followed, straddling the flood. The passage was unlit and wet ivy caught at his shoulder; he had to rely on the tinkling of Jo Jo's name tag to know the path was clear ahead.

Bounding out into the cul-de-sac, Jo Jo undertook an inspection tour of gateposts. David waited, impatient now, and cold. Fallen leaves had washed together in heaps in the gutters, and the wind had brought down scores of twigs. There were lights on in most of the cottages but not a soul in sight.

Suddenly all the lights went out. It was so fast and easy, effected without a sound in a fraction of a second. David stood transfixed. He imagined the people indoors: panicking, groping to touch each other, children crying out and adults wondering where they had put the torch. Still there was no sound but wind and dripping water. He looked around for Jo Jo and spotted a pair of shiny cataracts approaching on clicking claws.

A door opened and a couple stood silhouetted in the frame. 'Must be powerlines down,' the man speculated. They left their door open, the women expressing the hope this would let a bit of light in, and withdrew to look for the tapers which the man said he had put away somewhere for relighting the gas water heater. A fresh gust blew the door shut and one of the panes shattered.

'Fools,' David said. He picked up Jo Jo's leash and moved to the other side of the road, where he stood behind a tree trunk until the woman had finished exclaiming over the breakage.

Leaving the cul-de-sac, David headed west up Queen Street. This leg completed his usual evening circuit. On summer evenings he always paused to chat to the old-timers. There were two chaps with a foxie (called Muscat in salute to their favourite tipple) and, opposite, a very old woman with swollen, mottled legs. Once Jo Jo had slipped into her front garden and she had lumbered out, slashing with her walking stick and bawling. Tonight man and dog passed her picket fence unchallenged.

Half way up the hill was a deep hole, a car wide, fenced off with Main Roads barriers. Muddied water lapped at the rim and spilled down the roadway. If one dropped something in, it would be lost for a long time.

Jo Jo began pulling. There were often cats ahead, crouched around the side door of the Indonesian restaurant amidst the prawn shells and split garbage bags. The restaurant's lavatory was always leaking out onto the footpath, and the stench was sickening. While Jo Jo snuffled, David held his breath and studied the townhouses behind the restaurant. Most nights the residents left their blinds up while they sat slack-kneed in armchairs watching blue TV screens. David never protested if Jo Jo hopped up onto their lawn to investigate a cat odour or do his business. Tonight the windows were dark and the TVs disabled.

Jo Jo was at last squatting, a comically fringed boomerang. The wind, which had eased, began to bluster.

'Hurry up,' David told the dog, disguising his satisfaction. The animal's eyes bulged as he strained to obey. David settled his back against the side wall of the restaurant and tried to straighten his spine. He wriggled his shoulderblades against the graffiti and posters. Opposite, on the corner, was a chemist's shop with a flat above it. Once, waiting like this, David had looked up and seen a man standing motionless behind a curtain looking down. A spasm of fear had passed between them.

Jo Jo had finished now. Positioning himself a metre from his efforts, he gave a triumphant, derisory backward scratch at the mud.

David picked up Jo Jo's leash and walked up Queen Street to the highway, which ran along the ridge top. If he turned left, he would be back inside the warehouse in two minutes. Standing at the kerb edge he studied the barred windows of the women's residential college on the far side of the highway. Gutter water swirled up around his boots and a passing truck sprayed him from waist to knees.

Under the greatcoat, dampness was penetrating David's bib-and-brace overalls and rollneck sweater. His overall legs flapped, clammy against his skin. Shivering and folding his arms around his chest, he fancied himself succumbing to pneumonia and lying helpless in his room. Perhaps Rhoda would come to him. She would pat the sweat on his forehead with a folded man's handkerchief. She would care for Oscar, but who would walk Jo Jo? The poor fellow would swell up and explode.

Some uncivilised mob, David had been told at the markets, had the habit of sticking a vacuum cleaner nozzle or tyre pump into a goat and pumping till the creature exploded; the blood signified a betrothed girl's virginity.

'Fools,' David said, looking at the college windows. The women would be huddled in the TV lounge. A simple natural calamity reduced them to useless stupidity. Youth, beauty and wealth were of no avail when the waters swirled over one's head. A chain of hands might haul someone free from a torrent, but could they be relied upon? The storm, like war, brought out selfless bravery and conniving selfishness in equal proportion. It beat equally on the heads of the just and unjust.

David Drevikovsky stood on the ridge top, at the corner of Queen Street and the highway, with the wind lashing his greatcoat and the rain beating against his cheek. He turned his back on the southerly wind and looked north. The central business district was blacked out, its skyscrapers like black tombstones against a charred sky. Lightning skittered down to the Centrepoint summit. There could not be a soul left alive in such a battlefield.

'Fools,' David pronounced. 'City of fools.'

Perhaps he should retrace his path, knocking on doors and seeing how the old people were faring? He could tap, first, at the window of the old woman with the walking stick. Then the pair with the foxie. Then the gentleman in the hat. Then the old girl with her blind old Sooky. And finally—an unlikely prospect—at the grand etched door above the park he would enquire into the wellbeing of the lady with the rotary beater. She would shrink back in distaste from such a drenched, shabby caller. Or, perhaps, she would be grateful for any company on a night when the wind thrashed the trees and she was too afraid to go to bed and surrender her vigilance.

Thunder rolled across the city like a tank over corrugations. A weapon, David thought. A weapon: in case the old woman lashed at him in sleepy confusion with her walking stick; in case the businessman took him for a robber and waved a pistol. Jo Jo leading the way, he went back down Queen Street, into the cul-de-sac, down the passage, along Wilson Street, up Fitzroy, and across the top of the park to the rubbish skip. There were shorter routes back to the skip, but it seemed important to go back as he had come, and Jo Jo was of the same mind.

Groping into the rubbish, David's hand encountered mushy papers and slippery plastic bags but nothing solid. A large glass bottle would serve the purpose, but he could not feel one. There were a couple of fallen branches, but they were unwieldy and looked as if they would snap when brought down briskly on anything.

Remembering the backyard full of building materials, David went around behind the grand terrace. The brick wall could be scaled easily enough, although, in his heavy coat and slippery boots, he would need all the strength in his shoulders. Telling Jo Jo to stay, David hauled himself up to the top and scrabbled to throw one leg over. The other leg following, he toppled forward, tumbling headlong into a heap of rubble. Swearing and sucking at his skinned palms, he clambered to his feet and began feeling about for a weapon. The house was still dark, yet it was impossible to be sure it was empty. Who could afford to leave a mansion empty while it was renovated? Who would leave such a possession unattended on a night like this?

David weighed a length of four-by-two in his palm. A splinter snagged his skin. He could not risk tossing the wood over the fence: the clatter would be too great. Stretching up, he rested the timber on top of the wall and then scrambled up beside it. This time he kept his balance and, pulling his legs up and over, sat for a minute on top of the wall like Humpty Dumpty. His fringe dripped. Water ran down his nose and dripped from the tip.

Swiping back his hair, David jumped. His leather soles hit the bitumen and skidded. His legs went from under him and he sat down heavily on a brick. Jo Jo licked his face. David nursed his left hand, which he had instinctively put out to save himself. It felt sprained and bruised. Still no-one came out to investigate. The beat of rain on roofs, the roaring in the downpipes, was shielding him. Easing up onto his feet and rubbing his haunches, David reached up with his right hand for the chunk of four-by-two.

Jo Jo beside him, amiable as always, and the four-by-two comfortable in his right hand, David walked around to the front of the houses. It took a moment's concentration to be sure which one was the woman's.

David pushed open the iron gate, walked up a slippery tessellated path, and climbed the steps to the verandah. Slim castiron pillars rose to the first-floor balcony. While David peered in the bay window, Jo Jo sniffed at a ventilation grate.

David stood still, listening to his own breathing. It was the first time in forty-five minutes he had been under cover. He realised he was sweaty and flushed. His clothes felt steamy and he longed to pull off the outer layers. Remembering the four-by-two must be concealed, he slipped it down the front of his overalls and pulled his coat closed at the neck. Then he tested to be sure the timber could be easily pulled out. His left hand was still weak and he had to practise four or five times before he was confident he could produce the timber with any alacrity. Whispering to Jo Jo, he knotted the leash around the closest pillar. Then, licking his lips, he stepped onto the coir mat and knocked on the glass. After a moment's wait, he noticed a buzzer to his left. It was not too late to withdraw. He pressed the buzzer for a full two seconds, counting 'one and two and one and two'. There was a typed name above the buzzer but he could not read it. Jo Jo raised a paw and David whispered: 'Sshh. Soon.'

Steps were approaching: a shortish woman in high heels. Would a fifty-five-year-old woman, at home alone, working in the kitchen, wear high heels? A certain class of woman, yes, and a certain moderate height of heel. David imagined petite goatskin ankleboots tapping down the hall.

'Who is it?' Her hand rattled the security chain.

'A neighbour,' David supplied. His voice sounded strange to him, like a brief burst of artillery fire. 'From up the road,' he added.

The door gave inward. The woman was a hazy shape. Behind her the hall was lit by a candle on a side table, a serviceable candle of the type once stored in every pantry. David was conscious he too was a black silhouette against the grey drizzle. His right hand rested in a napoleonic attitude across the top of the four-by-two.

Jo Jo strained forward to sniff at the woman's toecaps. She moved to acknowledge the dog, but drew her fingers back from his wet forehead.

'Back, Jo Jo,' David growled.

'He can smell my Tammy,' the woman surmised. Of course such a lady would have a little companion dog. Any minute it would scurry down the hall, yapping with fury, alarming every neighbour for a kilometre.

'Back,' David growled again.

A blast of wind made the woman's knife pleats billow. David shuddered. His fingers grasped the four-by-two and he drew in his shoulders and upper arms. The woman gripped the door, bolstering it against the gale. She wore a dark ring, most likely amethyst.

'Well—' The storm whipped away David's words before he could frame them. 'I'll—ah—let you get back to your cooking.'

'My dear young man'—the woman's voice was sharp—'you can't cook in a blackout.'

Berating himself for his slip, David crouched to unknot Jo Jo's leash. As he bent, the four-by-two toppled forward, bumping his chin. Shrugging, he tried to shake it back down into his overalls. Jo Jo's exuberant lunge along the verandah allowed him to swing his back to the woman and twitch the timber further out of sight.

'Good evening,' the woman said. Any further remark—any thanks for his claimed concern, or caution against getting too wet—would have struck a false note.

'Good night,' David said over his shoulder as the lock engaged. He paused, listening for the woman to reconnect the safety chain. She did not. Her high heels moved down the hall. She seemed to pause. David wondered whether the storm had put all the phones out of service.

'OK, Jo Jo,' David said, and started down the steps. But Jo Jo propped on the edge of the verandah.

'Come on.' David jerked the leash. 'I know it's wet.'

But Jo Jo looked up into David's eyes and raised his paw in supplication.

Locus standi

These are chosen people disrobing and stepping down into this pool.

Perhaps, to the elders' eyes, Susannah glowed with the same inner light as she prepared to bathe.

We who are honoured to wait upon the chosen ones must serve with decorum and tact. As we usher them to the steps, we must be sure their pearly white limbs are unfettered. We must know, too, when to halt. The chosen ones must be loosed to take that final step at their own pace.

We may creep close to watch. We may hold these white fingers till the last moment: but limply, not clutching. We may look into the pool and trail a fingertip in the eddies.

But then we must slip away. As the chosen ones have vanished, so their attendants must go also, unrecorded. We have merely done a sort of duty, obeyed an authority. Our questions will not be answered.

Risk is present in such service: few volunteer to be handmaidens. Think of Nebuchadnezzar's furnace, superheated seven times, and the crack army men, obeying orders, pitching the three heretics into the pool of fire. It was the army men whose flesh was dissolved by the flames—while the stubborn, meek heretics strolled unbound with their angel, and came up out of that pool without a scorch, and were promoted in the province of Babylon.

Here, in Kings Cross, I attend the chosen ones as they step—swathed in beauty—down into the pool, into the blue flames. I have noticed each chosen one turns for a final look at what he or she is relinquishing, at all the world's joy and insufficiency. Gazing, these chosen ones look right past me, to the boychild who always stands at my shoulder. Relief softens their muscles. They know then it will not be annihilation, merely an easing into another texture of life. I let go their fingers and they step forward alone and I draw back my emptied, tingling hand.

I am bound to enact rituals. I am compelled to obey a routine. So long as I serve the chosen ones with modesty and love, my golden, wafting boy is with me, keeping me balanced, steadying me against that dizzy, swirling pool, holding me at the brink.

I have to keep going. Every day I have to earn my parents' forgiveness. It was me, you must understand, who found my little brother. I went in to his cot to wake him and he was perfectly still, his flat, round, white face turned up and his woolly yellow hair like angels' breath.

Twice, three times suitors have glimpsed my boy's face and have run. I was angry each time, humiliated and frustrated. I remonstrated with my boy. 'Cool it,' he replied. And, indeed, each time I realised, later, that he had acted for my good. None of those suitors would have been right for me. If they were flummoxed by my boy, how would they have appreciated my first duty to my dying ones?

Even to get up in the morning now I must have a plan: a written-down routine, a list in my secret code. I must first pray seven times for strength. Then I must wash: it is very important to go out clean. Then I must brush my hair for one hundred strokes. Then I must walk to the coffee lounge.

I cannot eat at the flat because I cannot keep food there. I cannot keep food there because I cannot control myself. I—the great dietician, the great nutritionist—am too weak to stop myself opening every can in the cupboard and dredging every packet. I must keep a diary of everything I eat, every cent I spend. I must tally every kilojoule, just as I tell my patients to.

Two blocks along my sunny, seedy street and I am at St Vincent's Hospital. I must work. I would love to give it away, to relinquish the demands, to be a simple waitress in the coffee lounge, serving the living, but I must labour to impersonate a professional. Somebody said we can forgive our parents anything if they are proud of us.

The nursing nuns are very kind and patient. They must be patient, for with me any task takes an eternity. I must think about it, pray about it, write away to experts. A ward round can take all day if I want to *really* talk to my patients. A piece of research can take a year.

I get through the days, I get through them somehow. I do not stop to eat. I do not relax. I work. I dither. I flap in circles like a chook with its head chopped off.

No patient has ever complained about me. Why should they, when I lavish attention on them so? I want each failing one to have a full and proper dying, to go in company, in dignity. I cannot take a repetition of what happened to my boy.

I radiate, they say, a hard-won peace. My face is shiny and round and yellow gold, like a ball of amber. My surface is smooth and close-grained. A sticky warm resin holds together all the sharp little fragments of which I am composed.

People see only the surface, the glowing amber, the lustrous pearl. They do not know what I know: that I am stinking grey ambergris in the guts of a whale; that I am the unopenable oyster shell; that I move across the floor of an ocean.

Every day I must entangle my life in the drifting, tingling tentacles of people who will die. Die soon, I mean. I ask their permission to keep their photos on my notice-board at home. For each one I choose a special mantra or poem. Then I set the sounds to a little melody and croon them. Each chosen one is a beautiful object in heaven's sight: a shell, a pearl, a coral, a starfish. I have a picture, a verse, a little story for each one. My mind works that way: it is how I describe and explain difficult things to myself. Yet I cannot find the tune to sing my own life. All I have are the codes in which I secrete my living.

I cannot hear my own melody or see my own texture half as clearly as I can know my special ones. They grow whiter and whiter as they take in death. I prescribe sweet, fortified fluids but it is nothing. They are already in another body: the white, pearly orb which grows inside the grey shell. I soothe and hum, lullabying these people gently into death.

The children are the worst. Thank God I do not see the dead children. Every evening I sing their songs, I sing the *kindertotenlieden*.

After work I visit the hospice. I am compelled to seek out the ones further advanced in their dying, to accept what they have to offer. They are a special order, like madmen, and old people, and children. They think differently: big things no longer matter, only little things.

These fey ones are always complaining about the food they're given. I listen to hours of virulent complaint. Then, suddenly, the complainer will run out of steam, turn his head away, relax his long, bare, white arms, and shrug.

'Who cares?' he'll say, 'It doesn't matter any more.'

The young men, the AIDS men, are the saddest. It is too early for such a humiliation, and they are so often spurned. I must be the substitute. The food I proffer, the little delicacies—that is only the tiniest part of it. People outside don't have an inkling. The shell is very precious at its centre. A filmy benediction rests upon the chosen ones.

At eight o'clock I go to the hospital cafeteria. I eat simple, sweet, soft foods, junkets which slip down and are easily digested.

And then I walk home along my street. The sun has vanished by then, but the cement and sandstone retain its warmth. Along The Wall, that wailing wall of streaked sandstone, boys wait for pick-ups. Outside the Jewish building, too, they wait, flagrant, shameless in their need.

I push the varnished wooden doors of my building, and unlock the inner door, and cross the cream and green foyer, and climb the stairs composed of granite chips. I never use the lift: it is a cage.

At nine o'clock I change into a housegown to clean the flat. I use two buckets, a mop, sponges and disinfectant. As I sluice the water over the tiles, I lullaby my chosen ones into sleep.

And then it is time for my final ritual: the taking off of the clothing, the face washing, the removal of the contact lenses, the teeth cleaning, all the elements of stripping and cleansing, the reduction to a body naked before heaven, flesh composed of singing atoms and the melody of prayers.

At last I stand in my nightgown before my window, at the top of my building, to brush my hair. As I stroke the brush down from the crown of my head, I breathe a prayer.

In bed I lie on my back and listen to the night music of the Cross: the laughing, smashing glass, the heehawing, screaming sirens. My brother shows me his face and says, 'Sleep tight'.

My building is a tower of coops inhabited by whimsical old birds who cluck to themselves and peck on ceilings and chatter with shadows in the foyer. It is one of the last surviving company-title buildings, and its proud, cantankerous nesters are the last of their feather in the Cross.

These old folk are so lonely. On the weekends I sit in their dim, dusty, stinking rooms and dip my lips into their sweet sherry. As they talk, I see they are addressing my golden boy behind my shoulder. Sometimes I flick my head around, for I suspect he is smirking, but he always ducks out of view. Such twitches do not bother the old-timers—their wrists judder as they pour another sherry—but in sharper company I must pretend to be flipping my veil of hair off my cheek.

So far we have lost only one of our company. Miss Lily Levine was my neighbour on the top floor, and the last of the displaced maidens.

I first met Miss Levine on the stairs. She was toiling up with a paper bag of pharmaceuticals—mineral agarol and cod liver oil. I took the bag from her hands and we were friends.

I hoped from Miss Levine's appearance that her rooms would be immaculate, but they were putrid. It was the servant problem, of course.

She showed me her heirloom jewellery and told me about her grand old family, and the barouche and the violinist and the masked balls and the host of suitors. Each time I called on her it was the same treasures, the same stories.

Miss Levine had a nephew, Darcy, whom she entertained each Friday evening. It was not long before Miss Levine effected an introduction on the landing as I was coming in from the hospice.

Darcy seemed to me a little edgy and unmannerly, almost furtive. His clothes were new but unmatched. His leather shoes were rubbing his heels. He put his hand in his pocket, pulled out a scrunched fifty-dollar note, examined it, and slipped it back. He looked away from me, at the stairwell, the lift cage, the windows, the skylight, as if he were checking for points of ingress, or egress, and assessing their resistance. I decided he had been out of society for some time, in the bush perhaps.

'My nephew has been away travelling,' Miss Levine told me. 'All around Europe. A grand tour.'

He has gone again now. *Gone missing*, a phrase Miss Levine would not have countenanced.

During the day I am occupied enough not to think of him. And for the nights I have devised a special incantation to exorcise him, a soft, sweet song which I croon over and over to the starlight. But still, on bad nights, when the sirens are gaining on one another down in the street, he sneaks into my room and jostles aside my brother and I remember.

The mad thing—the thing nobody knows but Darcy and me—is that it was a joining never consummated. I am the crypto-maiden of Kings Cross.

When Miss Levine's prognosis was undeniable, Darcy moved in with her. I held the security door open while he lugged in cartons of paperbacks. The ones on top were fantasies. On their covers bosomy maidens in wisps of pelt stood astride misty peaks while unicorns reared beside crystal pools.

As the weeks progressed, I saw the other books. Darcy was buying them by mail-order from a mob in Philadelphia who called themselves the lunatic fringe of the libertarian movement. I can recall some of the titles: *Methods of Disguise*, *The Right to be Greedy*, *Basement Nukes*, *How to Start Your Own Country*, and *How to Kill*.

Darcy would sit crosslegged on the felted grey carpet with these fanatic books all around him and his face numinous, lit by a vision he could not articulate. He had a prescription for the world: an anti-order of anarchy. He did not work, you see, and drew dole cheques in several names.

'I've outwitted the fiscal field,' he would gloat. 'I've withdrawn from their fucking system. Listen. One word. *Vonu*: "Invulnerability to coercion through withdrawal from society." The aim, my sweet, is to vanish.'

His skin was thick and pliable and scented. He would tan easily, if he ever went outdoors, and heal without a scar.

As Miss Levine deteriorated, her manners and modesty tided away. She became bony and bristly. She grumbled and nagged.

Darcy bore it mildly. He seemed to have made a vow to himself to remain for however long was necessary. He was not required anywhere else.

My routine altered to accommodate Miss Levine and Darcy. Each evening, after the hospice, I would sit on the end of Miss Levine's bed, my hand cupping her toes, and listen to her complaints. Then, when I enquired into the progress of her pointless therapies, she would haul up her nightgown and push down her swamee bloomers and jab the radiographer's guidelines on her crepey white belly.

Then Darcy and I would talk. I always had a lot to tell him—there is so much to learn from each chosen one.

And then I would tiptoe to Miss Levine's door to whisper 'goodnight', and she would quaver: 'I cannot sleep for the pain. Darcy, come here. Bring me a tablet.' And I would touch Darcy on the lips and squeeze out.

So it was for a year. They lived together, bickering and tending to one another, the symbiotic squabbling of an aged parent and a retarded adult child.

Darcy had a long-sighted, squinting patience, as if he were focusing on an island a long distance away across shiny water. I thought it was his utopian ideal which invested him with such preternatural calm. I thought it was the grandeur of his plan which made him babble with fervour or stumble over the simplest syntax. It took me months to realise what he meant when he dismissed my knocking with a mumbled excuse about Lily needing an early night. It took me months to hear him saying: 'Go away. I'm tripping.'

One Monday morning Miss Levine stepped down into the pool. She stepped down into the dark water whilst I slept on the other side of the wall. Stepped down with only Darcy to steady her arm. Stepped down with her protests muted. Stepped down with her nightgown tangled around her pearly white limbs and the blue radiographer's cross glowing in that twilight between night and sunrise.

The men in uniform were grunting as they jostled the stretcher through the concertina lift doors. The cage went creaking and clanging down and I was left alone on the landing.

'Darcy,' I called, and pushed Miss Levine's door. It was not locked.

The sittingroom was empty, the carpet a grey pool. In Miss Levine's bedroom all the drawers were hanging open and the jewellery box was upside down on the coverlet. In Darcy's bedroom the bookcases were empty, their shelves stepped with echelons of dust. *Vonu.* He had vanished. *Vonu.* He had seen my little brother peering over my shoulder.

I could not bear to sit with my dying ones that day, that week. The nuns came to me and we talked and prayed. At night my little brother showed his flat, round, white face to me. 'It had to happen,' he whispered. 'You knew it could not last. All things must pass away, beautiful girl. Think of the chosen ones. They need you. They are waiting for you to guide them into the pool.'

'Why?' I snorted.

'What else do you have?' he crooned. 'What else, fair maiden, are you fit to do in Kings Cross?'

The Plaited Ring

Ferreting under a market stall in Clignancourt one blustery afternoon, a woman grabbed the corner of an old frame which would do nicely for one of her linocuts. Someone on the other side of the table was pulling the opposite edge. She hung on, clenching her fingers around the gilded wood. Her opponent kept pulling, harder than she. Fearing the glass would crack, she looked up and found herself staring across into a coarse-grained Australian face. Mara Torv got her frame; Imants Richter carried away the military print inside.

Mara and Imants had known each other since they were schoolkids in Adelaide. They were both from Latvian families and the community is so small all the Latvians keep falling over each other and intermarrying and generally going quite gaga—as if they weren't paranoid enough already, seeing KGB men round every corner.

They were both now thirty-three and for two decades had been alternately pursuing and eluding one another with increasing degrees of subtlety and circumspection.

Imants' immediate quarry in Paris was an early Antarctic voyager, Dumont d'Urville. He argued one must know the facts of the early incursions if one was to fairly evaluate the current territorial claims. Look at the Soviets, for instance, basing their claim so precariously on Bellingshausen. Mara replied the bellicose disputes would persist whatever Imants dredged up; no study of the Czars' tablemanners would dislodge the bear from the captive nations.

Mara was tantalised by the closeness of Latvia but dared not apply for a visa. There had been too many years of cryptic letters and aunts' stories. She had been contenting herself—and filling in her weekends—searching second-hand shops and flea markets for Latvian books and decorating her room with Latvian graphics, folk art both simple in its clarity and sophisticated in its elaborations.

The union of the left hand was to last only six months: marriage was assumed. They toyed with the idea of a tiny, private ceremony in the chapel at Notre Dame—Mara sang in the choir there, and Imants was always demanding she tell him why the place should not be reconverted to a Temple of Reason.

Giving in to duty, they settled on a family do back in Adelaide. Not that all the family were enthusiastic. Mara's aunts spread a contagion of doubt.

Mara's mob were true, patriotic Latvians: emigrés. Imants' grandfather, Janis, had been a merchant seaman who jumped ship in Fremantle and married an Irish maidservant. Mara's family advocated the correct political line. Imants' people were shifty: sometimes apolitical, sometimes suspiciously left-leaning, sometimes rapidly right-wing, all queen and country (though which country they weren't sure). Always they were strident and opinionated. They alarmed Mara's family, who wished to draw no attention to themselves.

Imants was potential trouble. His pronouncements on modern history were not always what the ordinary man wanted to hear and would surely attract the notice of church and state, while his work with a military academy must place him under the eye of KGB informants.

In the wedding photos, Mara was twisting her ring, which was made to a traditional plaited design, round and round on her finger. They lived at first in a flat in Yarralumla. The former occupant had been a Tass correspondent and there were unaccountable marks on the skirting boards.

Imants taught and wrote, as before. Mara taught at the French school and read the drafts which tumbled from Imants' word-processor. After Mara fell pregnant they bought a house at Ainslie: an old cottage (now demolished) opposite a park filled with tall gums and carolling magpies. The baby arrived—in Mara's tidy, unobtrusive way—between books.

Mara smiled at Imants' banter and cooked for the long, clarety dinners he hosted. It was said she cooked traditional French food as well as anyone in Canberra. Imants tolerated Mara's pernickitiness. They squabbled around the supermarket like any other couple.

During Ziggy's infancy, Imants limited his overseas research to brief forays. A backlog of matters requiring investigation of primary sources accumulated. Imants began arranging a six-month sabbatical in Brussels, timed to end just before Ziggy began school. The explorer Adrien de Gerlache was his latest *amour*. Mara felt disgruntled at having her teaching career interrupted once again, but she was accustomed to playing second fiddle. On the positive side, she always felt at ease in Europe, whereas in Canberra she felt dowdy. And in Europe Ziggy could hear real French.

Ziggy already spoke Latvian at home with Mara. Imants, who spoke no Latvian on principle, taught Ziggy rude words in half-a-dozen European languages to toughen him up for the trip abroad. When Imants threatened to enrol his son in an under-five rugby team, Ziggy hid his big, round, brainy head in his mother's skirt and Mara scolded Imants until he pretended to weep for mercy. Between themselves, Imants and Mara seemed to be getting along all right. Perhaps not so well as their colleagues had hoped after such an attenuated, wary courtship. There was a hum in the air, like a circling blowfly; mutual exasperation was incompletely disguised.

Sorting the winter clothes they would need in Brussels, Mara watched through the sliding glass doors as Imants and Ziggy built a barbeque area. Dressed in a towelling hat and Yakka trousers, his tubby body smeared with grime, Imants sweated over the pavers, trying to arrange them symmetrically in Ziggy's old sand pit. He was no good with figures, other than war casualties, and his measurements were way out. Swigging from a bottle of claret and humming bursts of *Paris in Springtime*, he fumed his way through arrangement after arrangement. The winter sun was hot and flies stung his legs. Ziggy helped by dragging pavers over to the pit and letting them topple. Some cracked and chipped. One hit Imants' ankle bone. As the sand was flattened and covered, Ziggy's Australian infancy came to an end.

The woman Imants was seeing was an Indonesian: beautiful, doe-eyed, shiny, with a soft roll of flesh around her waist; semi-literate, not yet twenty and already with two children. At first Imants had claimed—feebly—he was interviewing refugees, getting on the oral history bandwagon. Finally, worn down by Mara's small, probing questions, he had admitted he was seeing one woman only. She had entered Holland as a twelve-year-old parentless, illegal immigrant, already probably selling herself, and found her way via Amsterdam to the luxury hotel trade of Brussels. Mara was convinced the woman was infected with every tropical and venereal disease known to science and would not let Imants touch her. He went to Dewi—as she called herself—all the same.

Mara went out walking around Schaerbeek. Every avenue carried a name. Imants knew a little about most of the names—Anatole France, Jean Jaurès, Georges Rodenback, Eeckhout, Giraud, Severin—and deplored Mara's lack of curiosity. 'They're all dead,' she expostulated. In whichever direction she walked, skeletons pursued her. The roads were not straight, but curved back on themselves like Canberra's. One crescent inevitably swooped into another with an even longer name. Great men crossed swords and negotiated treaties. There were just three resting places where relief could be found from this conspiracy of achievement: in Princesse Elisabeth Place, in St-Famille, and in Square Riga. Sitting at the edge of Square Riga, Mara wrote letters in Latvian recounting Ziggy's good health and Imants' research progress. Then she turned back, through the swooping avenues, past buildings and buildings, to their apartment in Av. M. Maeterlinck.

Imants pulled a few volumes of Maeterlinck from the shelves of the academic whose apartment they were renting. He skimmed through *The Blue Bird*, summarising the story out loud for Ziggy, and shuffled through the others. 'Stuff and nonsense,' he declared. 'When did the birds and bees ever demonstrate intelligence?'

Walking, Mara discovered her limits, the borders beyond which it was difficult to wander with a young child. To the north there were the railway lines and canal, to the west a major road, the Boulevard Lambermont, to the east the Cimetière de Bruxelles, and to the south a hospital, a sports complex and another cemetery. 'I'm closed in by the quick and the dead,' she told Imants.

'You can't trudge around the one quarter for six months,' he protested and continued urging short expeditions, to Ghent and Bruges.

'I shall be studying lives,' Mara said.

'Come off it,' Imants growled. 'You need something practical.' The flat was too small to clean with any sense of victory. There was no barren land to seed, no grape vine to watch. In the hospital foyer Mara picked up a pamphlet listing phone counselling services; the English-language line operated on Tuesdays and Thursdays. No doubt the hospital could absorb a volunteer visitor, and churches always had niches for willing givers. But nothing enthused her. She envied Imants his preoccupation. However ridiculous his quarries, he was always excited by the chase. Every mundane detail of every expedition waited to be rediscovered. Salt beef and muskets revolved around the Pole. 'Does it really matter?' Mara longed to ask, and did sometimes, when she could not hold down her impatience; but she could not cut away his purpose from under him.

Winter set in, ferociously, in December. It was self-inflicted torture to go out into the stinging sleet. Mara played board games with Ziggy and helped him with his melodica. There were no interests of her own she wanted to pursue here. She had lost the desire to polish her French, she knew little German, and Flemish and Walloon were merely words. Shopping and Mass were as much as she chose to attempt. She bought pre-cooked delicatessen foods and ate them with her hands. Increasingly frequently she went through a couple of bottles during the day. 'Imagine,' she said to Ziggy, 'we're marooned in a hut at the South Pole.'

Imants urged Mara to find a nursery school for Ziggy, but she turned irrationally protective and shouted at him. He arranged for the old lady across the hall to mind the boy, but Mara did not use the opportunity to go out. She sat sipping and staring at the gas fire. She had read nothing since shortly after they arrived, except for a children's encyclopaedic history which Ziggy had pulled out of a bottom shelf, and it cut off in 1961 with Benelux and the Congo's independence. Ziggy entertained himself pulling books out and examining them upsidedown. He was clamouring to understand, but Mara would teach him nothing but counting.

On Christmas Eve Mara cooked a grand, ceremonial meal and they were happy. On Christmas Day Mara cried. Imants talked to Ziggy about his old, old Latvian aunts and uncles in far north Queensland—emigrés who, ludicrous as it sounded, had been dispatched direct from the boat to cut cane with their white fingers. He talked about beaches so warm you could pull off all your clothes and run down into the waves. On Boxing Day Imants took Ziggy walking around the soggy perimeter of the field of Waterloo. When they saw a poodle Ziggy grabbed at his father's paunch. 'Keep away Pappa,' he implored. 'That dog might bite.'

'No lions here,' Imants reassured him, 'only puppy dogs.'

On New Year's Eve Mara sat up waiting for Imants. She had determined to plead, coolly and sympathetically, for him to return with her to Canberra at once. She waited, and waited, and pulled out a bottle of *Dewar's* from under Ziggy's toy cupboard. Imants arrived at two a.m., tipsy and satiated, warm with bonhomie, clasping a magnum of champagne; he intended to share a sentimental toast with his patient little wife.

He found Mara ugly drunk. It was the first time he had had to admit what was happening to her. Recriminations tumbled out, as fast as sheets from his printer. Imants flushed the remains of the

Dewar's down the bidet. Mara pitched the champagne out the window. It exploded against the alley wall.

When morning came, Mara began cleaning. She spent the entire day cleaning the apartment meticulously, and then went down into the alley and picked every fragment of glass out of the snow.

Imants wrote his research was going well. He expected to close it off, on schedule, in late January and fly home as booked on the Australia Day weekend, in time for Ziggy to start at the French school.

Ziggy chattered about going home to his slobbery cocker spaniel. He hugged his koala bear continually and tried to climb into his mother's lap. Mara was erratic with him. She would screech at him and then gulp black tea and grimace: 'I shouldn't have done that.'

The family had to be out of the apartment by the twenty-first. They would camp in some *pensione*, Imants said, for the week till they flew out.

As the twenty-first approached, Imants continued to go to the archives each day and to Dewi most evenings. He waited for Mara to start the packing but Mara was listless. She didn't answer when Imants asked whether the flight bookings had been checked. Ziggy hammered at her thighs, demanding attention.

The morning of the twenty-first brought the inevitable blow-up. Imants harangued. Mara shouted and then cried. Ziggy clung to Imants' legs and wailed.

No *pensione* had been booked. Mara stood at the kitchen window elaborately ignoring Imants' reprimands. Ziggy whined and pulled at her skirt. She spoke sharply to him in Latvian, then stroked his cheek.

'Pull yourself together,' Imants growled. 'You've got a child to look after.'

'Two,' she sneered.

The remainder of the day was a dirge of sorting and packing. Much of what they had accumulated was not worth shipping home. In happier times Mara would have loved selling it off at a market. Imants loaded it into a cab and dumped it on the doorstep of St-Famille. Ziggy snivelled for his abandoned toys, but only a fraction could be carried onto the plane and no-one had organised sea freight. Imants' books and precious photocopies filled the suitcases.

Mara stood by, indifferent. At four p.m., as evening closed in, Imants heaved the suitcases into a cab, bundled in Mara and Ziggy and directed the driver to a hotel where Dewi had once alleviated his ennui. Leaving Mara and Ziggy in their room he returned to the apartment to finish cleaning.

The hotel room was locked. Imants thumped and called. A hiccupping sob escaped under the door. Returning with a porter, Imants gained entry. Ziggy lay on the floor. He had been crying so long he was reduced to dry retching. The luggage was where Imants had heaped it. Only Mara was missing—along with her shoulder bag and hooded overcoat and galoshes and perhaps one or two items of clothing and underwear (on that point Imants could not be sure).

Imants went about his search like a military operation. He walked every metre of Schaerbeek. One crescent saw him frantic, the next furious. The hospital knew nothing; the police would not act if she had voluntarily absented herself; shopkeepers tried to be helpful; the station attendants shrugged. Imants' bookish pastiche of the language aggravated the people he implored. Trailing and carrying Ziggy, he fanned out through parks, squares, shops, galleries and the grander hotels. He had postponed the plane bookings, putting them forward a week, and written to the Adelaide folk giving the amended date and a white lie. Doubtless the aunts' antennae were already quivering. Too soon a platoon of uncles would be airlifted in. They would assume Mara had been abducted by the KGB.

'Foul play?' Imants echoed the polite consular man. 'Suicide?' 'The Florentine disease?' Imants could make the possible sound laughable. He spoke of military flare-ups in a similar tone.

Depression, Imants assured the man, was the most likely explanation.

Amnesia, a breakdown, an overdose, an alcohol clinic. It had to be conceded she had been hitting the bottle. Imants began the round of hospitals, clinics and refuges. Going through Mara's suitcase a second time, he found the phone counselling leaflet and tried the number.

The bank disclosed M. Richter had taken one-third of the amount left in their account, precisely down to the last BF.

A fellow behind a bar suggested derisively she must have gone on the game. Imants came back hoarse from his enquiries and entreaties.

Her passport was not in the suitcase. By the end of the week, the obvious had to be admitted: Mara was not in Brussels.

Amsterdam, perhaps. Or—Imants attempted a joke—Riga? Paris, his subconscious replied.

Imants spent that evening with Dewi. In the early hours he left her, collected Ziggy from the hotel room, and flew to Paris. He was too tired to search systematically. He let his feet direct him and, mysteriously, they conveyed him to places Mara had known: certain shops, the American Hospital, her old room, the flea market.

In the evening Imants tramped to Notre Dame. Mara was there in her old seat in the choirstall. They touched hands, and smiled as Ziggy chattered.

'If you've had enough of Europe,' Imants said, 'the last boat leaves next week.'

He had promised the university press a first draft by his fortieth birthday and he could see no reason to let them down.

Angels Descending

Bernard Krautz's angel hovered above the gas heater. He was a solidly built, androgynous teenager with long hair, bare feet and girded breasts. He wore a satin caftan embroidered with gold at the neck, a gilt tiara, and a pink stole which drifted around his shoulders as if wafted by a breeze.

The angel's two young charges had gambolled to the edge of a precipice, where the boy was reaching into the void to capture a butterfly. The girl, hampered by her brother's self-steadying grip on her arm, was bending to pick bluebells.

As children, Bernard Krautz and his sister Audrey had known every inch of Annandale and Leichhardt: the open land, the stables, the canals and creeks, the cliffs, the little factories making lollies and leathergoods, the pigeon houses, the tenements, the corner stores and verandah posts. Their favourite pastime was balancing on the rocks where Johnstones Creek ran into Blackwattle Bay and competing at throwing sticks far out into the water. On Saturday afternoons they visited their father's hat factory in Moore Street. It was spooky with antiquity. Wooden stairs creaked up, past cedar-framed pictures of their grandfather and great-grandfather and an ornamented rollcall of the employees who had served in the Great War, to the benches where the felt was steamed like a pudding over upturned basins. The children would fool around, trying on soliders' slouch hats while their father finished off the week's bookwork, and then they would all walk home, hand in hand, with the sun setting behind them.

The Krautz family's house was one of an Edwardian row which balanced along the edge of a sandstone cliff, peering through rosy, bubbly casement windows across a timberyard to the bay.

The air was always fresh and gusty, or so it seemed up so high, and the steep streets were made for billycarts.

In 1959, when she was thirty, Audrey married a taxi-driver of Japanese descent, a man laughably squat and fat, like a wrestler, his huge head ornamented with round spectacles and a ludicrously thin beard. People expected him to speak in comical sing-song pidgin, but at the wedding he gave his name—Stanley—in a loud voice with the twang of a home-made banjo. Stan and Audrey rented a cottage one suburb to the west and instituted a routine of visiting Mr and Mrs Krautz and Bernard every Sunday morning. None of the family went to Mass any longer and the visit took the form of a responsorial psalm to be run through in grudging fashion.

In 1963 Mr Krautz had an incapacitating heart attack. Bernard having shown no interest in any vocation other than primary school teaching, it fell to Audrey to save the hat business. Mr Krautz helped as much as he could until his death in 1967, when ownership passed equally to Audrey and Bernard. Audrey continued to manage the factory, and Stan gave up his taxi to go into it full-time with her. Hat-wearing was on the downswing, however, and imports on the up. With the loss of Mr Krautz's acumen the enterprise floundered. In 1969 the factory shut down, Stan returned to driving, and Audrey walked home into the setting sun. She was by now too old to have children and, although she had not wanted them, blamed her father for eating up her fertile years.

Bernard continued to teach at St Brendan's and to live, meekly, with his mother. He felt, although he could not justify it, a hostility toward his sister. On Sundays he assailed her for the collapse of the factory, the lingering debts, the local shaking of heads and wagging of fingers, the betrayal of their father, and the diminishing health of their mother. When Mrs Krautz had her first stroke, in 1971, Bernard determined to take upon himself the total care and cherishing of his mother. Audrey was henceforth repudiated by both mother and son.

The older she grew, the more stridently Mrs Krautz deplored Audrey's choice of husband and failure to preserve the factory's prosperity. To her neighbours she lauded Bernard's devoted ministry to her needs, although to his face she was more often testy and unreasonable. Resigning from St Brendan's, Bernard tended to his mother's demands in a calm spirit. He was like a man who, having survived his first heart attack, has sorted out his affairs and can anticipate his second with equanimity. In 1975 Mrs Krautz died, and Bernard's juvenescence began.

Through the winter evenings Bernard had sat with his mother in front of the gas heater watching TV. Now, in the summer evenings of his solitude, he sat in the same position with the rosy windows open, the TV off and the heater covered by a scalloped throwover. Occasionally the siren of a ship or the tooting of a horn came in with the dusty breeze. The house had always been in Mrs Krautz's name and she had left it to Bernard in recompense for his devotion. To Audrey she had left her paste jewellery and a lump sum which—with galloping inflation—was of negligible value. These bequests had deepened the rift between brother and sister and the two had not spoken since the finalisation of the will.

Searching his mind and old magazines for an occupation his mother would approve, Bernard chanced upon cake decoration. He enrolled in classes, untroubled by the fact that he was the only male student—he felt most at ease in the company of women. At home he practised for hours at a stretch, delighted by his ability to fashion replicas of the finest lace and the most perfect flowers and butterflies. His guardian angel, far from deserting him, was inspiring him with creativity. He felt he might still have it in him to reach out and at least stroke the living butterfly which had so far eluded him.

A small frustration shortly presented itself: Bernard had no-one besides the neighbours to whom he could present his decorated cakes. One neighbour—an elderly seamstress who could not possibly consume the masterpieces with which he kept on endowing her—suggested he advertise for customers. A notice in the paper-shop window brought Bernard's first order, for a ruby wedding anniversary. Bernard's hands shook as he delivered his masterpiece. The recipients, pleased by his modest charges, invited him to the party.

Thus a congenial routine emerged. During the week Bernard baked cakes in the mornings, before the day grew too hot, and iced in the afternoons, and on the weekends he joined in his clients' festivities. He loved his work. He poured into it the raw sugar of unrequited emotions and teased out a picture hat of flounced lace and netting and full-blown roses.

Given his choice Bernard would have always created traditional decorations, but some customers specified cheeky designs requiring not only a bold spirit but unexplored levels of artifice. Bernard worked on these in a state of neutrality: the shaping of a fondant breast or bottom stirred no nameable response.

Invitations to family gatherings were soon plentiful—there seemed no end to people's magnanimity. It was still an old-fashioned suburb and, once word had spread, people's kindness and tact manifested themselves. Bernard enjoyed the christenings and birthdays and weddings with a grateful decorum. He conversed with the old folk, bounced a tot or two, inclined his head modestly whilst the cake was photographed and cut, and left at a discreet hour, walking home through quiet backstreets. He always felt a sadness as he left, knowing his work of love had been cut up and consumed.

At one of these parties, Bernard was cornered by an insistent divorcee named Verna. He was shocked, over the following weeks, to find acquaintance changing to regular meetings and from thence to a betrothal. Verna booked a church, restaurant and Sunshine Coast holiday. It remained solely for Bernard to decorate his own celebratory cake. Too familiar with acquiescence to halt the momentum, he found himself married.

A ceremony, however, was insufficient to kickstart Bernard's libido. Verna retaliated with vituperation. Unequal friendship deteriorated quickly into enmity. Verna went out every day to the Ashfield RSL. Bernard tried to decorate his cakes, but he was stifled by resentment and a quaking fear of the woman's tongue. She, having seen his weak-spirited compliance for cowardice, was constantly on the attack. She was at heart unhappy and vindictive, and found in Bernard an easy victim. He became obsessed, constantly quailing at her voice. Having lived a mild life which provoked wrath solely by its inoffensive nature, he had never known this sort of anguish. Verna found out in him and named failings he had never associated with himself. His health suffered. He was assaulted from within by palpitations and feared he would, like his father, succumb to a heart attack. He had headaches, too, and a tic above one eye. The service of his mother had been a dignified responsibility; of this woman, it was slavery.

One placid Saturday night in January, the month which brought the fewest orders and invitations, Bernard meditated on the fact that in two days' time it would be the second anniversary of his mother's death. He decided there was no-one on earth who could ever love him as his mother had, and concluded he must delete himself from the roll of life. He knew he must make his departure look like an accident or illness. The family reputation must not be further sullied.

Leaving the house unlocked, its windows open to the breeze which played around two half-finished cakes on their foil-covered boards, Bernard made his way around the timberyard to the edge of the bay. It was unlit down here. Behind him rose wiremesh fences and stacks of stripped timber, pale as green flesh in the darkness. In front of him, across the water, were the moving yellow lights of traffic, and the hulls of moored vessels.

It required but a step into the black water. Bernard was a weak swimmer, and dogs were said to have been taken here by sharks—a single splash and the dog was whisked under.

Bernard stepped off the rocks. But he did not plunge under. A solid promontory, a submerged concrete jetty, led out into the bay, sloping away at a benign angle.

Bernard waded out. The cool water felt slimy through his trouser legs. Suddenly the concrete ended and he was precipitated into deep water. Wallowing, he went right under and then bobbed up, floundering. Instinct told him to turn around and clamber back onto the concrete. Another voice told him to head out.

Flapping and gasping, trying to tread water, Bernard went under again. His sodden clothes were dragging him down. Perhaps, he thought, I have already swallowed so much polluted water I could die of some toxic infection. He was still floundering, but going under now more frequently and taking longer to struggle back to the air. He was no longer certain of regaining the concrete.

A kayak glided up behind Bernard. Two young men grasped Bernard by the collar and armpits and hauled him toward the edge. The kayak ground against the concrete, tipped over, and all three crawled onto the slippery, stinking rocks. The young men escorted Bernard home, mothering him roughly, as if he were a senile bedwetter. He did not dare tell them he was only forty-five and he was too choked with disappointment to enquire why two healthy young men should be out in a kayak on a Saturday night. Verna accepted the miscreant's preposterous account of having tripped into the bay, and the episode did not even eventuate in a chest cold, let alone terminal pneumonia or blackwater fever.

Recollecting, as he iced, the forthright bravery of his teenage saviours, Bernard admitted to himself a predisposition toward the young male. The fantasies he had thus far refused to encourage were always of the young, supple, male body. It was the beauty of these angular rib cages and shins which drew the hands towards them.

Bernard began hurrying through the icing so he could walk over to the high school to watch the junior forms coming out. He meandered through parks watching boys playing and on weekends stood on the sidelines at soccer matches. He asked nothing of his subjects but to be permitted to admire.

Voyeuristic love brought with it tranquillity. Bernard was rendered immune to Verna's malice. He moved, now, as in a mist. His emotion was pure as light, his higher love as virginal as finely milled icing sugar, soft and clinging. He pressed his finger pads into the powder and tasted the sweetness on the tip of his tongue. He longed to run his fingers down a boy's spine, just once.

When Verna moved out, Bernard was suffused with relief. He iced and prowled in a magnificent calm, the strength of his relief obliterating all unhappy flashbacks. After a few weeks, the voice of Verna came back, jibing at him, but so long as she was gone in person he was safe.

Strolling toward the school, Bernard saw there was now no obstacle to his taking a boy. His mother, he had already convinced himself, wanted only his happiness. He imagined, too, the priest at St Brendan's nodding with understanding, the confessional infused with joy. He prescribed himself a daily regimen deserving of a reward: four hours' decorating and fifty *Hail Marys* before he went out.

The initiation with a willing lad was the most difficult step. That done, Bernard learned the right moves with a cunning as wheedling as his mother's.

Mysteriously, Bernard's social prowess multiplied in line with his love-life. At the weekend parties he was a wondering teenager. His eyes felt, at last, fully opened. He saw people, and they addressed him as a distinct individual, and he was able to answer for himself. Conversations went back and forth. Teasing could be conducted without offence. Once, Bernard told a joke and the listeners laughed. He touched elbows without every nerve ending twitching in alarm.

Bernard began to diet. He could not change his shape—broad in the hips, with a drooping backside and a soft little mound of belly below his belt—but he could reduce the pudginess of his chest and upper arms and thighs. Having lost four or five kilos, he felt justified in buying a batch of new clothes, exchanging fawns and tea-browns for lemons and blues. To complete the picture, he swapped his glasses for contact lenses and brushed his hair with a new artifice. Studying his image in shopkeepers' mirrors, he did not know himself, but his cakes got better and better.

In summer Bernard began to go to Mass. He savoured the host, content in anthropophagy.

Since her mother's death, Audrey had been going through her own metamorphosis. She had revived the family company and diversified into the manufacture, import and retail of novelties and partyware. In supermarkets and newsagencies she saw her own name on packages of tinsel and balloons and paper plates and silly hats and caps. There was even the beginnings of a chain of franchised stores selling nothing but Krazee Krautz novelties. In just under five years the business had achieved a steady cash flow, and Audrey and Stan had paid off all the lingering debts, chosen key sites and invested in plant with an eye to capital growth. Stan's ancestry was no disadvantage on the importing side, and as the front-woman Audrey had blossomed into a minor celebrity. Her name appeared in newspaper puffs for her products, and once Bernard was flabbergasted to see her on a midday TV chat show laughing her head off. One Sunday—turning on the TV before Mass—he saw her on a business programme speaking with pride of family enterprise, of her father's fine example, of integrity and application. She sounded like a head of state. She had shrugged off her mother's damning influence and become herself a mother of manufacturing. Her husband rode shotgun for her. Behind them, a secret, silent angel kept the whole enterprise going, injecting funds and advice as necessary. He was the source of their continuing success, and Audrey would do nothing to jeopardise the alliance.

Audrey was now fifty and plucking armfuls of bluebells. She was happy and energetic, marvellous in her confidence. She was as good as anyone and, not only that, she was doing good: her manufacturing set a fan whirling, and the draught wafted success out into the community.

At first Audrey had aimed to seduce her contemporaries: women who were suspicious of anything frivolous, who were sure every item was overpriced, who refused to take into account inflation and metrication, who suspected any product until it was purveyed in *David Jones* and carried the imprimatur of *Belle*. But these women rarely entered Audrey's shops, and, when they did, at their offspring's pleading, their lipstick reddened in instinctive disapproval. Audrey found it was sweeter to enjoy the spontaneous acclaim of young people. She became a mascot for fun events. She was invited to open fairs and go in walkathons and telethons. She dressed youthfully, favouring telegenic bows and makeup and, always, her trademark, funny hats. She approved and condoned where she might have sniffed. Her customers were her realm and she loved them. Her movie theatre and late-night TV advertisements were loud with catchy jingles. Her ghosted newspaper column dispersed chatty hostess advice. Her milieu was a Luna Park of tinkling carousel tunes, beaming teenagers in caps, dinging cash registers, chattering telexes and the smell of hot chips.

Under the exuberance, however, Audrey was zealous to safeguard her name. Her success was dependent on her reputation as an honest merchant. She dealt honestly but shrewdly, without mercy for the weak. She knew how to give a narrow answer to a query. She could mislead while supplying unassailable facts. A rigid backbone ran through all she did. She named her employees' misdemeanours bluntly, even cruelly. Borrowing from the till was theft. Pilfering from the stationery cabinet was theft. Wrongdoers were sacked after the first warning. The unions loathed her. She paid above the award, distributed bonuses to the hardest workers, and sent each employee a personally signed birthday card.

Sometimes she would slip into a branch and request an obscure item.

'Sorry, I don't think we've got it,' the young assistant would say.

'Do you know if one of the other branches might have it?'

'Not really.' The assistant would turn aside negligently.

'I would have thought, young lady, it was your job to get on the phone and find out where I can get it. At once.'

And, looking up for the first time with full attention, the assistant would recognise her nemesis.

Bernard observed his sister's rise with respect and wonderment, but he did not tender his congratulations.

Early in 1983, on his fifty-second birthday, Bernard took into his home a catamite. The boy was a beautiful Maltese with strange, ringed blue eyes and wavy black hair. His skin was the shiny, yellow-green, open-pored casing of a young lemon. Rubbed, it gave off an oily secretion and a tart odour.

The boy swam every morning in Victoria Park and was always taking baths. He lathered and abraded his skin obsessively. Bernard offered to scrub the boy's back and squeeze the red bumps which were the portents of pimples, but the boy refused. He was insistent on modesty in the bathroom and had hammered a bolt onto the door frame to exclude Bernard. He stayed in the bath for an hour at a time, rubbing and towelling to an accompaniment of rock music. When he emerged he was evasive. He hurried through the kitchen, ignoring Bernard's scrutiny and holding his towel secure at the waist. His skin was temporarily dulled, the pores dry and reddened from scrubbing, his hands wrinkled white from immersion. Damp ringlets bounced against his forehead and his eyes were as artificially blue as a chlorinated pool, their black rings as strong but wavery as the painted lane lines on a pool floor.

The boy's background was unclear. Sometimes he seemed nothing but a street-smart kid on the make. At other times he mentioned names which suggested unexpected family or personal connections.

Together, within the house, Bernard and the boy maintained a ritual of intimacy. Outside, they appeared unconnected. Possession of the boy did not reveal Bernard to himself; possession cannot open the owner's eyes as surely as dispossession. While Bernard cooked and iced, the boy went to a private advertising school.

On completion of six months in Bernard's service, the boy asked for an increase in his weekly allowance. Bernard was surprised and annoyed. He reacted as his father had done on the one occasion his employees had got together to petition for a rise. Bernard felt justified in the level of payment he had set. The boy had few needs, since his food, shelter, education and transport were being paid for, and renumeration should surely be in line with need. Refusal induced the lad to sulk and bellow. He behaved, for a day and two nights, like the thwarted teenager he was. Then, putting on his soberest clothes, he went to Audrey's Parramatta headquarters and obtained an appointment for the following day.

At the interview the boy spoke plainly. Enjoyment of malice and avarice made his swimming-pool eyes shimmer. Audrey kept feeling her own attention and good judgment being drawn into these mesmerising pools. Then the savagery of the boy's blackmail hit her like a dousing in chlorinated water. She winced as the water stung her eyes and invaded her eardrums, then shook her head rapidly a number of times, preparing herself to dismiss him. Her public, she told him, had too much trust in her to be alienated by a minor family indiscretion.

Then the boy named the name of Audrey's angel.

Audrey summoned Bernard to Saturday brunch on her balcony. Rolling a pink frosted tumbler between her palms, Audrey invited her brother to speak. Bernard had never confessed his actions or proclivities to anybody. His mind went to his mother, and he allowed his tongue to begin to describe the details of the life he had led with her. He spoke of the years of domineering petulance and then, contrite, of her illness, her passing, the funeral, and the annual notice he placed in the paper. He described too his memories of his father, and spoke of Audrey's day-to-day life before she married. He moved on to the cake-decorating, describing the details of his favourite designs. He alluded to his marriage and from that moved to the solicitude and offhand generosity of the lads he had loved, and the beneficence of his dealings with the Maltese youngster. In all, he spoke for two-and-a-half hours.

Bernard's evocations all had a hazy, rosy, breezy mendacity. He craved Audrey's blessing to go on as he was. I cannot absolve you, Audrey told him, particularly when you are so obtuse and selfish you don't realise the damage your behaviour does to other people.

Bernard studied the spotted tablecloth. Audrey's voice had the quality Verna's had taken on when she had upbraided him for his gutlessness. As Audrey spelled out the Maltese youth's blackmail threat, Bernard looked at her hairline. Her eyes were dark as oily water at night. Tightening her facial muscles, she named Bernard's penalty: he must remove himself. The court of honour had met and passed sentence.

Bernard walked all the way home from Hunters Hill. Pausing on the approach to Gladesville Bridge, he looked along the arching grey concrete to the city buildings. It was an afternoon of perfection.

That night Bernard attended a fortieth birthday party for a greyhound enthusiast, for whom he had concocted a great hunk of cake adorned with rosettes, ribbons, medallions and miniature trophies. Greyhounds lay under the trestles. Others rested their muzzles across laps. When the second keg was broached, Bernard slipped away. In the driveway a dog sniffed gently at his thigh.

The Maltese boy had gone out in Bernard's absence. Bernard went to bed. He lay listening for the wooden gate to creak, but there was nothing to be heard but traffic. At one a.m. he went out into the kitchen to make a pot of tea. Waiting for the kettle to boil on the gas flame, he looked absently at the goldfish bowl the boy had brought with him. One of the fish had been ailing for the past couple of days. It had looked listless and a deeper orange colour than usual. Hanging about at the bottom of the bowl, it had scraped on the lurid flourescent green pebbles. Now the fish was dead, it was certainly dead. It floated almost vertically. Its companion hovered at a distance, gobbling with its thick lips. Whatever grief or loneliness the survivor felt could not be ascertained by an inspection of its yellow flanks. Bernard was not even sure of its gender. Considering the rusted condition of the house's cold water pipes, he wondered whether the dead fish had been killed by the very water it had relied upon.

Sitting on at the table, his hands resting around the teapot, his fingers tracing the raised design of scrolls and draperies, Bernard studied a scrap of angelica and a mist of white icing mix on the lino at the base of a cupboard. He decided a fine white powder would be best. His sister could put it about that he had been ill—with some plague better left unspecified.

Violent Femmes, Gloomy Romeos

It was stinking hot. Di drove like a bat out of hell. The air was dirty grey, flecked with soot specks. The light was searing. Flames crackled a hundred metres from the expressway. We dared not go back. We dared not stop. We tried not to think how quickly fire could run through dry undergrowth, longjump between eucalypts and hurdle roads. Smoke billowed across the bitumen. We wound up the windows and peered ahead.

Di cursed the toll men for letting us onto the expressway, but they could not have known how quickly things were worsening. Behind us emergency sirens clamoured.

We kept going. We stuck to the centre lane and ploughed on at a steady eighty. The temperature gauge was rising and the petrol was below a quarter full. Di berated herself for not having checked the radiator.

By now the old highway would be cut off. It was only two lanes wide for most of the way from Berowra and the bush grew right up to its shoulders. Our choice was to keep going as long as the expressway remained passable, or take the emergency booklets' advice and stop, lie low inside the closed vehicle, and watch the flames sweep overhead. We kept going.

Brooklyn would be cut off by now. At least there one could escape into the water. The people in real danger were the ones deep in the bush, in farmlets and shacks and broken-down cars.

We were coasting downhill now, the smoke parting before us. We came out onto the flat and crossed the Hawkesbury. A haze hung over the water. Behind us the hills were a blur of smoke.

Peat Island appeared untouched. The poor people there, the profoundly handicapped, must be terrified—if they could comprehend what was going on. It would be a hellish job to evacuate them.

'Do you think we should stop here?' I urged as we left behind a grassed stretch beside the river.

But Di was glaring at the rear-vision mirror. I twisted to see a semi gaining on us. At the last second it pulled out and thundered around us, buffeting the car from side to side.

'Let's stick behind him,' Di decided. 'I'll bet he's got a CB radio and he's checked it's OK to keep going.'

The road rose steeply beyond the river. The car strained. The tar was bubbly and blistered; Di said it felt as if it was clinging to the tyres like clag paste. We plugged on up. On the steepest part we overtook the semi. Di lowered her window, inserted her hand into the ferocious air, and waggled it in a gesture which did not increase my serenity. We were now back on our own.

Ahead, smoke rose in columns. There must be recent outbreaks on this side of the water, yet all the firefighters were congregated back south between Mt Kuring-gai and the river. Still we went on.

Old Reliable was holding up magnificently. We had always laughed at big, tall, lusty Di in her succession of sluggish little 1300cc Corollas. She looked so ludicrous with her head grazing the ceiling and her thighs pressing the underside of the wheel. But this one was proving its mettle.

New little fires were springing up, set off by sparks and spontaneous combustion. The hills would be engulfed if the fires merged and got their head.

We had grown up with summer fires. We were used to damp, black tree-trunks in winter and electric green shoots and ground-cover in spring. But this was the fastest moving fire I could remember and the hottest, gustiest day.

We took the Gosford exit. There was no-one to warn us off.

Di kept her foot steady on the accelerator as we careered downhill. I was terrified we'd spin out and plunge into a gully.

'Ease up,' I gasped. 'These bends are awful.'

'Listen to her,' Di snorted. 'Ten years away and she knows it all.'

'Eight,' I corrected. I am prone to pedantry. 'And I haven't stopped getting carsick.'

Di rolled her eyes and shook back her hair. I had declined her offer when she had shaken the ignition key at me. Now she hunched forward and squeezed the wheel. She would keep the car going by sheer willpower. She would run it to death.

I did not actually feel ill, possibly because the new Mooney

Mooney bridge had eliminated half the bends, but that was no excuse for absence of consideration. I let the seat back a couple of notches and, reclining like an invalid, watched the trees approach and recede. We had not seen flames for kilometres but the bush looked dirty and dried out. I tried rolling down the window but it was like having a hairdryer trained on my face.

Fortunatos' fruit stall was deserted, except for a red dog leashed to the bullbar of a truck. At Kariong we turned off the highway and freewheeled down Bulls Hill.

'Eighty, Di,' I pleaded. 'The sign says eighty.'

'That's miles.' She grinned maniacally. 'Old Reliable only works in miles.'

A dozen more bends: I counted them, swallowing nausea. We swept out of the bush and past the abattoir in its shaded, purply glen. When we slowed to turn into the Ocean Beach road, Old Reliable shuddered, the gearstick quaking under Di's palm.

'Five minutes to Meroo Avenue,' Di exulted. Twenty, at least, but I didn't argue.

'Don't relax yet,' Maxine chided as we clambered out of the car. 'There's a ring of fires up in the hills all the way round behind Calga and Somersby. They could easily sweep over to the coast.'

Meredith had the local radio station on, listening for emergency bulletins, and hoses and buckets were ready at the front and back doors. She had hacked away the shrubs around the house and cleaned out underneath. There was nothing she could do about the stubbly grass and crackling eucalypts which waited like camouflaged hand grenades. There had been no rain for weeks and stringent water restrictions were in force.

The house was fibro with hopper windows, a gal roof, a water tank, and magenta bougainvillea covering the weldmesh fences. It had only ever been meant as a weekender. Inside, it was stultifying. We shifted out into the backyard, beside the clump of gums. It was one o'clock, there was no shade, the temperature was over forty, and the air was absolutely still between blasts of hot wind.

As fast as we drank, the fluid poured out of us as sweat. We resorted to sucking ice blocks and holding them against our foreheads. There was a total fire ban, of course, and the barbeque steaks had been consigned to the freezer. Meredith grilled sausages inside and we ate them with the tabouleh Maxine had brought. The salt made us even thirstier.

Those who had forgotten sunhats made coolie shades out of newspaper. We used more newspaper to fold fans and shoo flies. Bronwyn covered her legs with the sports lift-out. Wiping sweat, we smeared out noses with newsprint ink and sausage grease.

In the heat everything looked dulled and blurry. Our faces were as coarse as over-exposed photos. The eucalypts were a shimmering khaki; their leaves seemed to merge. The dirt of the vegie patch was friable and grey. Flowers closed, leaves cringed. Nature drew into herself, and submitted.

We endured it for a couple of hours. The conversation was desultory. I had expected to be the centre of attention, but I had been back since Christmas Eve and they had all phoned me at Mum's early in the piece to try to gauge from my accent how much I had changed.

At three Di proposed a swim.

We picked our way through the caravan park. Patsy, always a shoeless optimist, jigged yelping over superheated paths and scorching white sand. Smug in my thongs, I stubbed my toe on a tent peg.

Meredith led us up a ridge of rocks, tussocks and wind-blasted ti-trees.

'Thalassa! Thalassa!' Bronwyn hailed the ocean. We glanced at her, narrowed our eyes and smiled with compressed lips.

To our right the shallows were that pastel aqua of late-fifties' kitchen accessories. It was here that sea and river bulldozed sand into Patonga Creek.

'It's quite clean,' Meredith assured us in her she'll-be-right way. Patsy was already paddling to cool her soles. Maxine ran her eyes along the houses squatting on piers on the far side of the creek and said: 'I try not to think about septic tanks.'

Patsy had never learned to swim, so I stayed beside her, dog-paddling in half a metre of ripples, trying to keep everything but my head under the surface. It was eight years since I had felt saltwater stringy in my hair. Meredith and Di swam the width of the creek again and again, splashing, kicking, demonstrating strokes and threatening to push me right under. They were not sure enough of me, I realised with regret, to carry out their menaces.

Bronwyn sat high on a clump of tussock grass, slapping at ants on her legs and cupping her hands around her glasses to cut the glare. Maxine had trailed away along the creek's mudflats, examining the brown pearls thrown up by the hiding crabs. As I watched she tripped against an anchor, exclaimed, tripped over a tow line, exclaimed again, skirted a group of youths with bait buckets, and hobbled out of sight around the bend.

Suddenly there was the roar of horsepower: a powerboat came

scudding along the surface of the creek. I screamed and scrabbled towards the edge.

'Mere,' Patsy shrieked. 'Di. Look out.'

The boat thudded over the sandbar and roared off across the open water. Bronwyn hurried down to the edge to expostulate. 'Do you know what it said on the side of that boat?' she demanded. 'Bushfire Brigade.'

'You better not say anything to Maxine,' I cautioned.

'I damn well intend to,' Bronwyn declard. 'The frigging idiots are supposed to be out saving people, not slaughtering them.'

'Hush,' soothed Patsy, always the one for non-resistance. Maxine was on the way back with a treasure cupped in her hands.

'What's the betting it's a crab?' I whispered, but just then Meredith and Di came swooping in around our ankles, trying to drag all three of us under, and in the pandemonium of splashes I forgot to find out.

About four the air freshened and stirred, clouds congealed, and the earth and sea changed from a candy pastel sketch to a fierce work of oils, ink and neon highlighters. The light had an intense purple luminosity. Each tree-trunk was defined against the slopes. Each leaf glinted a different shade of green. The camphor laurels glowed. Charcoal smudges marked outcrops. The ocean was striated in cobalt, aquamarine and grey. Everything trembled.

'Out of the water,' Meredith yelled. 'There'll be lightning any sec.'

We struggled up the dune, sand stinging the backs of our legs. As we reached the top, a billow of sand swept in over the caravans. We gripped each other and stood against the gusts, looking out over a bowl of whirling grit. Canvas was flapping, doors slamming and metal clashing against metal. A beach umbrella spun away, its point a javelin propelled by chance. The first globules of rain slapped bonnets and aluminium roofs. Around our feet droplets indented the sand with coins of moisture. Men shouted and ran and ducked. A boy wrestled with a sailboard. A baby wailed and Maxine shuddered.

Lighting flashed over our heads. 'Count,' Bronwyn commanded. We made it to six before the thunder rumbled.

'Come on, kids,' Meredith instructed. 'Run for it.'

As we scrambled around the caravans, rain pelted down. By the time we reached the road, water was streaming across the bitumen. Dancing on her bare toes, Patsy scampered ahead. Clutching towels around our necks and sploshing in our thongs, we followed.

We showered two at a time, hurrying so the hot water would

not run out on the next pair. Meredith produced enough clean towels to go around and pulled out old tracksuits and sloppy joes.

In the livingroom we settled into the TV chairs and beanbags, pulling them into a circle. The rain had stopped and the garden was radiant with the luxuriant, clarified sheen of a woman fresh from a facial. We sipped our mugs of tea and looked at one another. Freed of jewellery, cosmetics and shoes, simplified to a uniform of baggy clothes and wet hair, we were returned to our girlhood equality. We smiled at each other gently: like satisfied actors, I thought, after the show. Outside there might even be a rainbow.

'Well, what's everyone been doing?' Meredith asked. It was our hostess's prerogative to set the agenda. She already knew the answers to her question. For the past ten or fifteen years she had served as our unofficial pigeonhole.

Meredith's father had been the only big-time builder on the coast. As a gouty sixty-year-old, he took to jogging on the beach below his personal monument, which occupied an entire headland south of Avoca Beach. He pushed himself too hard, as was his wont, and collapsed with a heart attack. None of our group went to the funeral: hypocritical eulogies would have turned our stomachs. Privately we sent notes and cards to Meredith and her mother.

Mrs Dorney did not reply. She had been cowed for so many years, she was dumb with disbelief. As soon as the estate came through she set off on the first of her cruises. The house was left for the most part in the inexpert hands of the younger of the two sons. Mark was the one who had reacted most drastically to his father's edicts. He had withdrawn, rendered himself passive, and opened his mind to whatever rubbish chanced to blow into it. He read indiscriminately—anything from *The Watchtower* to supermarket catalogues—and watched TV and listened to the radio. His only visitors were his siblings, who took turns to do the housework, and the gardener. Meredith and the other brother, Phil, had also eschewed power and possessions. Since school they had subsisted, Meredith in her cottage, Phil in various caravans and shacks, by taking on odd, short-term jobs as the spirit moved. Neither of them had voted in years. They were edgy in formal company, impatient with dress-up occasions. On their own territory they were easy and laconic. They smoked reflectively, picked their toenails and stared into their ring-pull cans. It was their policy never to pass judgement. You could simply turn up, sit with them, and yarn about whatever you pleased. Neither would marry; I'd had to become reconciled to that.

Phil's current shack was up in the bush on Mangrove Mountain.

He kept a few laying fowls, trapped rabbits and watched his pumpkin vines spread. When I was in the early years of high school, I was infatuated with him. He was so good-looking and terse and he had been a Vietnam conscript. He never looked my way twice.

Meredith was packing a small pipe. 'Well,' she observed at last, 'I don't know about you lot, but ah jest bin sittin' here watchin' the grass grow. Pretty soon I reckon I'll have to clear out down south.' She had been saying it for years, but she stayed, tied by loyalty to a runaway mother, a damaged brother, and a mausoleum.

A weaver had lived here with Meredith for a couple of years, on and off. Two of her walls were covered by his hangings: all blues and greens, with protuberances suggesting bits of the female nude or perhaps merely sandstone headlands. Most of us hadn't known him, his sojourns never having coincided with our visits, but we knew about his death and we wanted to hear the story again. Meredith was willing to comply—she lived withour rancour.

Russ had been walking up in the bush above Broken Bay, she recounted. Alone, in summer, in thongs. Not a smart thing to do, but Meredith wasn't the type to tell him how to run his life. He had been looking out towards Lion Island, she supposed, at the shapes, and hadn't seen the snake until he stepped on it. Naturally the poor startled thing reacted by striking at him. He didn't know about pressure bandages. By the time he'd tried to cut the bite with a piece of shale and suck out the poison, and, failing in that, staggered out to the road, it was too late. Not even the Snake Man, Eric Worrell, could help. 'Snake Attack!' the local paper roared, 'Famous Sydney Artist Dies. First Snake Fatality in a Decade.'

That passing had not distrubed our lives. It was in harmony with the natural order. We knew about falls off horses, drowning, all sorts of natural accidents. Decrepitude and sickness, too, we saw all around us in the retirees who congregated on our coast, waiting to cross the bar. It was when we went to the city that we were shocked to find another breed of serpent underfoot: deliberate, man-made depradation.

Meredith got up, tweaking her shorts down over her backside. 'I'm ready for a beer,' she said. 'Anyone else wants anything they can help themselves.' We had exhausted the soft drinks and coolers earlier. It was beer or beer. Patsy remembered she had brought a few casks of red and went out to the Landcruiser to retrieve them. We accepted plastic mugfuls of hot, pungent claret.

'Patsy,' I embarked, 'what've you been doing up in Brizzie?'

'Working for ABC radio.' She twisted her elbows out and

gripped her feet. Her hyperthyroid eyes bubbled.

'Doing what?'

'I'm a PA. Producer's Assistant. I do all the fiddly stuff like timing items and listening to presenters read things through.'

It was a dead cert she'd never be a presenter herself. It was taking all her nervous energy to get this much out.

'Do you like it?'

'I'd rather be in TO.' I raised an eyebrow. 'Technical Operations. That's on the TV side. They monitor all the machines, everything that comes in off the satellite—that's hard to crack, but.'

At primary school she had been adept with mechanical things. She had watched with envy as the boys went off to play with Meccano. In high school she had wanted to do metalwork and technical drawing but was not allowed. In our domestic science lessons her speciality was taming troublesome sewing machines and quirky mixers. At home in the garage she fooled around with a crystal radio and graduated to an elaborate shortwave system. Her father was a Balt. He shook with delight when his Patsy picked up, through the static, a familiar argot. When we visited, we found it fearfully exciting to press around in the dim light watching dials and hearing strange clandestine voices.

Patsy had marched on to do electrical engineering at the Institute and a string of short electronics courses. Yet still, it seemed, she was not working in her field. Her scrawny, pop-eyed fervour did not inspire confidence.

She compensated, I knew, by spending every free hour at home working on her radio system. She spent her nights in the studio she had constructed between the tarred wooden posts holding up her Queenslander. From the cool recess behind the lattice she beamed out the wonder and the mystery. She had constructed her own brotherhood: a network of subversives and radicals and lonely compulsive chatterers, the oddballs of every captive nation. She stood for them as a statue of liberty, the emblem of a free world where the money was easy, women walked unshackled and men were bidden to love.

'Any good blokes up in Bananaland?' Di pressed.

Patsy blinked and shook her head.

Di had always been the ringleader down the back of the school bus. Patsy used to sit a few seats forward and twist her neck to listen in. She had nothing to contribute: no dirty jokes, no prat falls, no encounters behind the sailing club after the school social. She could not even join in the recounting of the previous night's episode of 'Number 96' because they had no TV.

Bronwyn began questioning Maxine about her children. It was the first direct question she had asked. She had never been one to keep up with birthdates, jobs and changes of address. In conversation with parents and children Bronwyn had always missed cues. She would not think to enquire about the consequences of a fall or the outcome of a sporting match. She failed to acknowledge new toys and trophies. She failed to speak directly to children or to admire babies. She would never notice a potential danger or avert a squabble. If she became agitated, it was always a few minutes too late. She was forever a few degrees off square, a few seconds out of cinch, just that bit distrait. Her glasses emphasised this doubleness, and when, for a while, she had adopted cosmetics, the lip-liner was always misaligned and so too the eye-liner, giving her the doubled look of a fuzzy satellite face.

Maxine expanded on her contraceptive difficulties. Being a Catholic with good intentions, and forgetful, and possessed of a lapsed husband, was not a winning combination. Each child had been breastfed for years in a spirit of hope.

'*Que sera sera*,' Bronwyn shrugged.

'Do you remember that song?' Maxine yelped. 'Normie Rowe was my all-time hero.'

She began to sing, her body rising and falling, expanding and contracting, like a squeezebox. Straggling, we joined in as the verses came back to us.

'When I was just a little boy—' sang Maxine, the suckler of little boys, 'I asked my mother . . . '

I took the verse about asking the teacher.

'When I grew up and fell in love,' Maxine crooned, folding her hands and rounding her eyes, 'I asked my sweetheart, what lies ahead?' Four kids was the answer.

Maxine was the eldest of five children, and the only girl. As children we assumed from her grumbling manner that she was spoilt and would grow up to be a real bitch. She never invited us home and did not share her little treasures. We did not give her credit, until we were approaching adulthood, for having endured years of difficulty at home. He mother was an invalid—rheumatoid arthritis, chiefly—and a querulous pain in the neck.

Maxine's tone of voice had come partly from Mrs Fernance and partly from the exigencies of trying to look after the four younger kids. Their father worked long hours as an earthmoving contractor and had no energy for displays of affection or discipline. It dawned on us too slowly that Maxine adored the little boys she complained of and was at a loss without something to touch. At school she was always stroking a pen, biting a paspalum stalk, resting her fingers on a new exercise book or trying to lure a magpie with crumbs. We couldn't stand it.

Finally, Mrs Fernance had to be put into a nursing home. It happened a month before our final exams, and Maxine bombed out completely. In January, when the results were released, Maxine made herself scarce. She surfaced a couple of months later, pregnant to the panelbeater down the road.

Darryl, the husband, was an ordinary, decent fellow. He played table tennis and, for something to do, had joined the volunteer bushfire brigade. Today—the day of our biggest fire in memory—he was at home minding the kids. 'Thank goodness,' Maxine had muttered more than once. Doubtless he was hankering to be out in the action, and feeling humiliated to be babysitting while his mates were doing something manly, but, Maxine's chastising voice implied, '*Que sera sera.*' She had an exaggerated fear of fire and had hated the stage each kid went through of lighting matches and poking fingers into flames.

'What about *Shakin' All Over*?' Di jumped to her feet and began to belt it out, thrashing about with a big carved fork for a guitar.

'Quivers down my backbone—' we roared, catching her spirit.

'I got the shakes in my kneebone.'

'I get a tremor in my sidebone.'

'Shakin' all over . . .'

'Remember,' I rushed on, 'that fantastic one where he was actually crying?'

'Oh yes.' A ripple went round the room as we drew into ourselves, summoning emotional fervour.

'I—' I began, drawing one hand up above my face.

'I who have nothing.'

'I—'

'I who have no-one.'

'Adore you . . .'

Unrequited fidelity radiated from us. We were tragic lovers, noble spirits.

'And want you so—'

We drew our fists up against our chests, closed our eyes, and relived the intensity of teenage infatuations.

'I'm just a no-one.'

'With nothing to give you.'

'But oh—'

'I love you—'

The splendour of a fifteen-year-old's passion.

'He can take you any place he wants,' we snorted, neglecting to adjust the pronouns.

'Fancy clubs and restaurants'

'While I can only watch you'

'With my nose pressed up against the window pane.'

The torment was tangible.

'He—he buys you diamonds.' It was about now we had to simulate sobbing.

'Bright, spark-el-ling diamonds.'

'But believe me.'

'Hear what I say.' The contraltos were doing best now.

We finished in unison, raising our arms ecstatically and then slowly drawing them down around our breasts.

'Oh,' Patsy murmured luxuriously, wiping the inner corners of her eyes. 'Wasn't that wonderful?'

The sharing of a febrile passion had drained us. We lolled back against bookshelves and knees.

Maxine phoned through an order to the good Chinese place at Ettalong. Meredith went out to see how her strawberries had fared. Bronwyn fed the cat, crouching down to watch him eat—I did not remember her as a cat person. Refusing contributions, Patsy drove off to collect the Chinese. I washed up the griller while Meredith wasn't around to forbid it. Maxine phoned Darryl and the children. Di, finding herself ignored, prowled about and finally switched on the radio.

'2GO,' the announcer burbled. 'Voice of the Central Coast. And it's seven fifty-eight on a beautiful Saturday night. I hope you're enjoying our long weekend, folks. Don't forget Valentine's Day next month. Get in early, girls. Drop the hint you'd like a special little something from Marketown Jewellers.'

The news headlines followed. The storm had put out all the coastal fires, but there was still a blaze burning out of control inland behind Peats Ridge. No homes had been lost, but thousands of hectares had been burnt out.

'And now,' the jovial maniac resumed, 'a full hour of golden oldies. Four in a row . . .'

We left the radio on while we ate. Most of the tracks were familiar. We hummed convivially.

Our talk wandered to the girl singers of the sixties.

'Why don't they give the women a look in?' Bronwyn grumbled as the nine o'clock pips sounded. We were all idealogically sound. We had bodysurfed the waves of feminism.

The field was ripe for harvest, and we got stuck into it while

Meredith handed around bowls of lychees and an ice-cream container of melting moments.

'What about Cilla Black?' Bronwyn prompted. She had an exceptional memory for lyrics and names, but not melodies.

'You're my world—' I began.

'You're every breath I take.'

'You're my world—come on you lot, join in.'

'You're every move I make.'

'Hang on, the good bit comes next,' Di cried, leaping to her feet and grabbing a chopstick for her baton. 'Start again from the beginning.'

'With these hands—' we grated, extending our palms, hitting and holding the most horrendously flat note possible.

'Resting in mine'

'I feel a power'

'So div-ine.'

'In the best songs,' Patsy observed, 'the girl's always going to give her all. You know, "I'm nothing, he's everything. He treats me like dirt but I worship him. I'd give the world to be by his side. I'd cross mountains, swim rivers—"'

'You can't swim,' Meredith objected.

Di complained our renditions weren't gutsy enough and launched into a Tom Jones bout of hip-grinding.

'Take me'

'And break me'

'And make me'

'An idol.'

'I'm your's.'

We got our voices way down low. We could do it. These were women's sentiments under a male veneer.

I Will Follow Him came next. 'There isn't a mountain too high,' I led, enunciating extravagantly. 'A river too deep—'

'That can keep'

'Keep me away'

'Away—from—my—love.'

'You'll never know how much I really love you,' Bronwyn declaimed. Again it wasn't a girl's song but we had gone around crooning it.

Patsy discovered she could do a superb Little Millie imitation. 'My boy Lollipop,' she warbled and chirrupped, bouncing up and down.

'He makes my heart go giddy up—'

'Encore,' we cheered.

'He may not be a movie star'

'But when it comes to being happy'

'We are!'

Somehow it led on to Little Pattie's songs, with Meredith stomping in the centre of the circle, her thin tanned legs going like fury, her fingers clicking, her pipe marking time; and then Helen Shapiro's big hit.

'Please don't look at me with hungry lips . . .' Di sang.

'I can't answer for the things I do.'

'I'm not, not, not responsible,' we chorused, belting it out with conviction.

'Not, not, not responsible.'

Di pushed us on to another piece of histrionics.

'Just wishin''

'And hopin''

'And dreamin''

'And prayin'' we listed.

'And so I cry a little bit to be in love . . .' The chorus kept coming back and back, no-one knowing how to bring the thing to a melodious close.

'What's that one?' Maxine hesitated. 'And then he kissed me—'

'I can do a bit of it,' Patsy assured us.

'He kissed me in a way that I'd never been kissed before.'

Hiding smiles, we joined in.

'He kissed me in a way that I want to be kissed for ever more—'

Di set up a counterpoint.

'I'm dreamin' my life away,' she carolled in a falsetto taunt.

'Love is a many splendored thing,' Bronwyn announced.

We tried to join in, but no-one knew the words in the right order. There were fragments about trembling hearts and waiting fingers, interspersed with violin imitations and ribald asides.

Di was calling for me to do my Shirley Bassey medley. I used to be terrific at it. I wore the shortest mini of the lot of us.

'The minute—'

I had only to open my mouth to set everyone clapping and beating out the rhythm. I undulated, growled and wailed, a muddle of Bassey, Eartha Kitt, and every other fading vamp we'd laughed at on TV specials. I looked like an old, daggy cat on heat. They clapped so much I had to do *Big Spender* three times.

'We haven't done my favourite yet.' Maxine sounded querulous. '*Just Call Me Angel of the Morning*.'

'All right.' Meredith snapped to it. 'One, two—'

We obliged. Emotions on call, we launched into another round of wallowing and begging. Look at me, we pleaded. Notice me. Speak to me. Kiss me. Hold me. Tighter. Share my umbrella. Walk me home. Give me a friendship ring. Promise. Say you love me. I'm ready.

'Just one kiss,' we exulted.

'That's all it took.'

'Yeah.'

'Just one kiss.'

We moved on into vows and renunciations: I'll follow you anywhere, give up the world, give anything and everything. Towering emotions, crescendos of loyalty and devotion and grand commitment.

'I will follow him.'

'Follow him wherever h-e-e may go.'

At last Maxine fell back against a wallhanging. 'Oh,' she groaned, 'all this teenage ecstasy when really, you know, oh—' She was breathless.

'We want it all,' Patsy observed, 'Someone closer than a brother.'

Meredith had intended half of us to sleep over at the Avoca house, but no-one felt like moving. We divided ourselves between the two bedrooms, rigging up extra sleeping patches out of sheets and cushions. By unspoken accord the lounge room was left for Bronwyn. She had lived with another woman for the past six or seven years. 'You're sure to read to all hours,' we told her.

Mosquitoes from the water tank patrolled the sweaty little back bedroom. On my top bunk under the creaking galvanised iron I tried to lie still. Below me Maxine was still awake too, unable to settle in a single bed, her body crying out for the tactile goodnight rituals of parents and children. From the next room we could hear Patsy snuffling, gasping, snuffling; she was prone to asthma and hay fever and had been allocated the dusty sandy patch of floor under the window.

A spider web looped across the corner near my head. I could see its shape in the moonlight which seeped in along the edge of the holland blind, but could not see whether it had an occupant. I imagined a tarantula dropping down onto the bed and rushing, on his octopus legs, up onto my face. When I was little I'd call out to my brother and he'd come in with a broom and flush the tarantula down off the wall and whisk it out the front door. I would not let him kill it. When I moved to the city I found cockroaches. They were far more alarming, for, while they were not poisonous, they were tough, shielded, rapid, scuttling and insidious. The hairy, gangling tarantula was more like a mild-mannered gatecrasher; he returned after a polite interval, and allowed himself to be freshly ejected after only a brief, ridiculous show of alarm—like a teenager putting up the requisite show of objection to a parental ruling. He provoked a delicious fear.

Bronwyn had been assaulted when we were all in the first year of high school. I was twelve then, and Bronwyn thirteen. Her mother used to go to the Leagues Club to play the pokies and drink away her pay from Sno–White Laundry. She'd come back to the flat at closing time, flirting in her blurry Welsh voice with some beery local.

The beery locals sometimes stayed. Sometimes they were not locals. The one who attacked Bronwyn turned out to be a Sydney fellow on the run from the police.

Bronwyn turned up at the Dorneys' mansion before seven that morning. It was a glorious morning with the magpies carolling and the water sparkling. Bronwyn was holding her brunchcoat together over stained shortie pyjamas and jiffie slippers with the soles half-off. She had walked all the way out to Avoca from Springfield, trudged out along the roadside in the half-light, the gravel cutting into her soft feet. She was exhausted and wordless. They put her in one of the eight dream bedrooms. After a couple of days she returned to her mother's flat and things returned to our version of normality.

Bronwyn had a younger brother who was profoundly retarded and lived in at Peat Island. He looked out on the world from blank, light blue eyes in the swollen, soft, skin-smelling head of an infant. He was incapable of malice. I saw him occasionally when he had been brought to the flat for a weekend and I was visiting Bronwyn to listen to records. They'd put the boy out on the balcony, strapped into a chair. If the shade shifted before we remembered to move him, he'd stare into the sun. Every woman, we learned, is her brother's keeper.

I woke late and shuffled out to find the others eating toast in the yard. Meredith was in the kitchen cooking bacon and eggs. She was wearing a handprinted T-shirt over her bikini pants and drawing on her pipe between jabs with the spatula.

The phone rang. Maxine scrambled to answer it. She came back after five minutes, her shoulders sullen, grimacing with exasperation. Darryl had dropped the children off at her father's and headed off with the brigade to chase the fire up on the ridge. We said the obvious things to reassure her.

Bronwyn shifted away onto the concrete septic tank to light a cigarette. She jumped up quickly, cursing and swiping at the backs of her thighs, which were the colour and texture of ambrosia cheese. The concrete was aleady warm—it was going to be another scorcher—and ants were swarming over a scrap of coagulated sausage. Muttering 'Septic tanks!' Bronwyn retreated to the back steps.

Maxine was wanting to go home. We howled her down. A day's worrying and snapping at cantankerous kids would build up a full head of resentment, which she would take out on Darryl when he finally staggered in looking for a drink, a shower and a little recognition for the rough-and-ready bravery which Maxine would decry as wilful, selfish bravado.

Meredith poured Bronwyn a second cup of tea and stirred in the sugar. 'Get your duds on, pal,' she ordered. 'We'll hit the Ferneries first.'

Having grown up close to the Ferneries, most of us had never been there before. We meandered along cool, damp tracks coveting the birdsnest ferns.

Di gripped my shoulder and pulled me back. 'What happened to you in the States?' she demanded.

'What do you mean?'

'Well, you've changed in the wrong direction.'

I tried to defend myself, citing the conservatism of everyone in my field. Knowing the political implications, and copping abuse from the activists every time you poke your head up, you learn not to flaunt yourself. If you were ever the kind to do so. It is appropriate that we do so much work below ground.

'What I can't understand,' Di persisted, 'is why—I mean, you used to live with guys. I thought it'd be a real hothouse, shut up with all those men. That's what happens in the spaceship movies. And on subs. You know, Raquel Welch comes out in this white doctor-type coat and starts pushing buttons, and then James Bond comes in, and there's nothing under the coat—'

'When I'm as old as Raquel Welch I might get that desperate.'

'How're your parents? I haven't seen them since they shifted.'

'Not great. They've never got over Neil.'

'We hardly knew anything about it in those days. I remember you saying he couldn't walk any more and me saying why didn't they fix him up with calipers.'

Mum and Dad and I used to go down to Royal North Shore

Hospital every second night. We'd rock down the expressway in the Kombi van. On the way home, Mum would give me the window seat. I'd sag towards sleep, then jolt awake, feeling queasy and disoriented. Counting the final curves was all that held me back from vomiting.

'You know what's wrong with Patsy,' Di pressed, pursuing a line of thought.

'Not entirely.'

'Endometriosis.' She chomped at the syllables with her teeth.

'No wonder she looks so bloody awful.'

'She's bleeding all the time. She's anaemic. She's exhausted. They scrape out all the gunk, and then they've got to go back and chop out the adhesions. And you know what they recommend as the cure, don't you? A pregnancy or a hysterectomy.'

When they told us in Scripture about the woman with the unstoppable flow, we did not think it could be one of us.

'And how are you and Beaver, Di?'

'Terrific. Truly.'

They had always been like brother and sister.

Di kicked a hunk of sandstone bordering the path. Her big, brown body was a picture of frustrated energies. Other people's laments are so melodramatic.

'What've you two been talking about?' Bronwyn's tone was arch.

'Bloody men,' I replied.

'What have men ever done to you?' she asked.

'Very little lately.'

Bronwyn ran a bemused eye over me.

'That's why,' Di proclaimed, 'we're talking about them.'

'Let me recommend brothers,' said Meredith. 'They're a lot less troublesome.'

'In praise of propinquity,' Bronwyn announced.

'Consanguinity,' I corrected. 'Or confraternity.'

'Consorority,' she snapped back.

'Sorority,' I declared. 'No need for the *con*.'

'It's from the Greek,' Bronwyn told me. '*Soros*, a heap.'

'That sounds like a heap of crap to me.'

'Look it up. It's preceded by *sorites*. Simple logic to you. *Brothers are men. Men are benefactors. Benefactors are praiseworthy. Therefore brothers are praiseworthy*.'

I could never tell when she was having me on.

'Or,' she was not done yet, 'a *sorites* can be a sophistical puzzle. *How many women make a heap*? *Is my brother bald because he has only a hundred and one hairs on his head*?'

'Will you two eggheads shut up?' Di bellowed back at us.

We straggled back up to the gates. The ferns curled inward, conserving their wisdom.

While Meredith made a fresh pot of tea and Maxine rang her father, Di flicked around the radio dial looking for a news update. Losing patience, she left it tuned to the ABC. Yet another nostalgia special was filling a hiatus in the cricket. The compositions of Robin and Ranger drifted around us: *Every Little Breeze Seems to Whisper Louise*, *Beyond the Blue Horizon*, *It's June in January*, *Moonlight and Shadows.*

I was up with the lark this morning set us shaking our fingers at Bronwyn, the citified sleeper. *Hooray for love*, sung by a young Shirley Bassey, provoked laughter at my expense. *Love is just around the corner* had us singing along.

'All I want is just one word,' a voice sighed.

'All I want is just one kiss.'

'All I want—'

'That,' Bronwyn pounced, 'reminds me of a Violent Femmes song. It's virtually a parody. I can't sing it, but—'

'Go on,' we urged.

Making her voice belligerent, she began to chant:

'Why can't I get just one kiss?'

'Why can't I get just one screw?'

'Why can't I get just one fuck?'

'Oh please,' a new vocalist was beginning to warble.

'Lend your little ears...'

'To my pleas.'

'Your eyes reveal that you...'

'Have the soul of an angel'

'White as snow.'

'How long must I play the role'

'Of a gloomy Romeo?'

Predictably, the last record was *Thanks for the Memory.*

'Crikey, how I hate that song,' Di snorted, jabbing off the radio. 'They've played it at every piano bar I ever worked in. Thanks for the mammary...'

Our talk wandered into the expense of house improvements. I complained about American plumbers.

'You must be raking in more than the rest of us put together,' Maxine accused. It was quite likely. For all the revolution, most of them were on typically female incomes. Maxine earned nothing in her own right. Bronwyn's work in a women's bookroom she termed a political statement. Meredith's dole money and irregular income—currently from bark collages—all went on paying off her house and keeping her ancient panelvan on the road. Patsy wasn't getting what she deserved. Di's low base wage was supplemented by tips extracted through brazen flirting. I felt a flush of triumph even as I protested about high taxes and the costs of living on the fringe of civilisation.

'Psychic costs,' Patsy corrected. 'I'll bet they give you extra money for living out there.'

'Where is it again?' Meredith yawned.

'Los Alamos, New Mexico,' I recited. 'Institute of Life Sciences.'

'Nuclear bombs.' Bronwyn translated. I did not contradict her. I had given up trying to explain.

Through my Uni years, the others had been patient and generous with me. If I conscientiously added up all the free meals and subsidised holidays, the debt would be in the thousands. I had reciprocated nothing but the odd comp ticket scrounged through my job as a programme seller. I had loved that job, especially the few minutes after the end of the show when everything was put to bed. The way the lights dulled. The way the show music crackled to nothing in the speakers and the transistor behind the bar was turned up. The way the older bar staff lit cigarettes and poured themselves Bacardis; the way the younger ones whisked jackets over their black uniforms and rushed out to hail taxis. The way the caretaker sloped around with chains and padlocks, and the manager swivelled in his cubbyhole, stacking notes and tumbling coins into beige cigars. The way the actors padded out and looked around with bared faces, expectant of greetings. Their foreheads so pale and shiny, their checks hectic, their hair damp at the frills, their bodies still moist and pulsating in loose jeans and shirts, their voices veering between the subdued and minatory. And then the whoops from the bar. And the grill crashing down in front of the box office; the heavy doors wheezing as they closed on that empty grandstand; the storeroom and electrics room clicking shut; a vacuum whining over spilled ash; the glasses rattling to rest in their trays. 'Time, gentlemen,' someone would call in a facetious contralto, and I would go out to meet the John of that year and we would stride home singing through the Glebe.

'Don't you want to share what you've got?' Maxine enquired. 'I mean, sort of settle—'

'With a husband?'

It was impossible to speak to a dependent woman of the satisfaction derived from paying off my second condo or buying a parcel of shares. I had placed my trust in Greenbacks.

'If I were a man,' I protested, stepping into a puddle of silence, 'you wouldn't be attacking me like this.' It was the easy way out.

'You're not wrong,' Meredith conceded.

'I've been to another reunuion since I got back.' I dribbled it in, perhaps to assert the existence of allies. 'Women who were at the same Uni college as me.'

'Women,' Maxine echoed.

No-one chose to appear interested. I was the only one who had gone on to a university, and then only because of a scholarship. Patsy grazed her fingertips on the prickly hairs above her ankle.

'Everyone was either a GP or a languages teacher. We sat there all genteel in our dresses. It was ghastly.'

Bronwyn and Maureen nodded understanding, but Patsy wanted to taunt. 'Why was it ghastly?'

'Half the time they talked about their husbands.'

'Un-huh.' Di spoke the funeral oration for their kind.

'With babies, most of them.' I could taunt too.

Di started going on about her Bevan's generosity.

'Well, what do you want me to do?' I demanded.

'Just ease up,' Bronwyn soothed.

'For instance,' Maxine struck a paying lode. 'You didn't bring a thing this weekend. No food, no drink—' In the suitcases which had weighed down Di's boot sat the electricals I had selected so carefully in duty free and planned to distribute at the end. I could not pay off my critics by producing them now.

'I'll tell you what,' I declared, surprising myself, 'I'll take us all out to lunch.' I had my Amex card.

'And then we go could go to a movie,' Meredith suggested. 'There's a season of terrific old black-and-whites at Avoca.'

It was agreed in a moment. Meredith rang to book a seafood restaurant in Terrigal and Bronwyn thumbed through the *Central Coast Express* to the movie guide.

The others jostled into the bedrooms laughing over the sudden necessity to bring themselves up to my sartorial standard. Bronwyn's jeans were frayed. Catching my glance, she muttered: 'What species are we supposed to be impressing?'

When we were very young, there were no restaurants, not one. In the main street of Gosford there was a milkbar called Country Cousins, and the pubs put on counter lunches. The sixties brought a Chinese, reputed to be the repository of all missing cats, and the first arcade coffee lounge. A real estate agent set up a red plush cavern called the *Moulin Rouge*. It was intended to be the height of sophistication. It folded, of course. We were content with fish and chips and paddle pops. Those were the days when the Musical and Dramatic Society held its productions in the showground pavillion. It was cold as purgatory, and we went along (whenever Mum typed the programme in return for a couple of tickets) armed with cushions, rugs and thermoses. The masonite scenery wobbled. A column fell on a baritone's head. The Messiah had to be transferred to Christ Church when rain thundered on the tin roof. Still, we loved *The Desert Song* and *Annie Oakley*. We whistled *The Surrey with the Fringe on the Top*.

In those days we stomped the pavements with the stenches of small-time agriculture, stenches as sickly and endearing as a baby's milky regurgitations. We kept pigs, then, and chooks and greyhounds and trotters and goats. We mulched our tanging citrus trees, and hoed manure for our vegie plots. Our backyards were littered with smelly dominoes, the rectangles and circles of families accommodating to the land: the 44-gallon drum incinerator, the lavatory, the shed for the kero and horsefeed, the compost mound, the grease trap clogged with a fatty porridge, the corrugated iron tank lapping with soft, sweet rain water.

All around us the rhythms of ripening and deterioration, supply and excess, gave off their odours. Rain set runoff pouring down out of the hills, washing down on top of the slipperydip of the claypan, and flushing through our septic tanks; bronze effluent ran out into the drains we had dug and trickled into the turbid creeks, which sluiced it along with the vomitous emissions of food factories into the Broad Water. At low tide the mangrove swamps reeked. Between the highway and the water, the garbage tip sent up its own eclectic odour. Over-ripe oranges in the packing house and fruitdrink factory thickened the air. At night we gagged on the sweet, rich abattoir stink of burning flesh. At first light the black sanitary can trucks rumbled past, carrying their slopping, rattling cargoes to a hidden valley.

All our senses were green then. We heard the mosquitoes. We felt the caress of flying ants. We entered cobwebs and brushed away huntsman spiders. We were so close to the ground we noticed grasshoppers and fieldmice and trapdoor spiders. We heard our first oratorios from cicadas. We saw the yellow under the wings of cockatoos. We scared each other with droptail lizards and leopard slugs. Our parents photographed us in paddocks of yellow coreopsis flowers. Plovers ran at us. Magpies divebombed us. Our cats retaliated for us by crunching sparrows. In summer the bolder cats brought us their booty: snakes demeaned by breakage and demented by hours of malicious toying. Turning our shovels into weapons, we decapitated. At the wildlife park we studied venomous creatures confined by that cruellest prison, glass, and we failed to find them more exciting than our everyday encounters.

'Look at this,' Bronwyn exclaimed. 'Greta Garbo.'

'In what?' I am always dubious of old things.

'*Queen Christina*. My friend Biff adores that film.'

'Quicksticks then,' Meredith clapped. 'We'll have to get going straightaway.'

One foot in her pantyhose, Maxine hopped to the phone. 'No news of Dad?' she pleaded. 'OK. Tell your Poppy we're going out to lunch . . . Yes, I know. It's a late lunch . . . Never you mind, sticky beak . . . We'll be at the *Lively Lobster* . . . I don't know, about three . . .'

We ate exuberantly, waving our hands, dribbling down our red napkins. 'If only the kids could see me,' Maxine cried. Di signalled, with success, for fingerbowls—culture had reach our coast.

We wandered along the main street opposite the old Norfolk pines. I stopped at a real estate window. Meredith drew me on; her pipe smelt companionable.

Di was way ahead, as usual. She had already reached the rebuilt, renamed Florida. My father used to call at the old hotel on his rounds, and in the school holidays I'd go in with him. While he talked behind a veneer door, I'd trail along passageways, touching the blue flock wallpaper and looking at the framed photographs. One day a cook popped his head out between a pair of swinging chrome doors and gave me a chocolate frog. When I told my mother, she was mortified. 'You mustn't hang round like an urchin,' she scolded. 'People'll think we don't have a brass razoo.'

Mischief shone on Di's face. This was her familiar territory.

'Race you to the top of The Skillion,' she shouted.

Protesting, we followed her to the base of the headland. It was a ritual, something locals never did and visitors were obliged to attempt.

It was a long haul up, as steep and slippery as a grass ski slope. Our leather soles lacked traction. Bronwyn dropped her glasses.

'The view's terrific,' Di yelled from the top.

Above me, bottoms bounced, skirts billowed. Bronwyn had come to a halt, panting despondently. I squeezed her elbow and we slogged on up. My heart was thumping and I could feel a pulse throbbing in my temple.

While the others pointed out surfers and lines of breakers, I crouched on the downhill side of a rock, gripping it with both hands. Our height alarmed me. Below, the surf, the malignant rocks, the long blank vista to the horizon: it tantalised and lured like a mirage; it had killed Meredith's weaver; it could compel you to jump. To the south, Meredith's father's house jutted up out of its private headland.

'Are you missing Lenore?' I murmured to Bronwyn, feeling a sudden affection.

'Biff,' she corrected. I had forgotten the etiquette of changed names. 'Yes, heaps.'

I moved over beside Patsy as we slithered down, but she did not accept the support of my elbow. She did not gasp or squeal when she slipped. There was a red patch on the back of her skirt.

'Do you realise...?' I whispered.

'Oh, no.' She twisted around to look, aggrieved with her body for betraying her yet again.

We walked soberly back to the cars, goose-stepping in formation around Patsy, and drove south in convoy to Avoca.

The day's heat was waiting for us in the foyer of the old picture theatre, a brown snake under a sheet of corrugated iron. The blades of the ceiling fan churned through the sluggish air like a mixmaster striving to blend a thick dough.

Finding myself last in the queue at the counter, I was wondering whether I should push forward and pay for us all when Meredith stretched back, holding out a ticket.

'Here you go, Yank,' she said.

Inside we sat in one row on lumpy red velvet seats. A James Bond theme washed over us: 'All I wanted was a sweet distraction for an hour or two.' The black-and-white film began to roll. 'Aah,' Bronwyn sighed: bliss was imminent.

Interval came after the scene in which Christina takes off her masculine jacket to reveal herself as a woman to the Spanish envoy.

'Thank Christ I don't smoke anymore.' The words burst out of Di. 'I'd have died of longing.'

We ambled towards the beach. The sand was white and grey, each ripple defined by its shadow. A runner in swimming trunks paced along the wavy line of drying foam where the loose sand turned dark and compact. Each footfall left behind it a shallow pool of moisture. The sea simmered and then fell placid. It called like the Lorelei.

Out of nowhere a kelpie, a bitch, came rushing down to the water. She pounded along the waterline, snapping and yelping. At an unmarked point she turned and galloped back, then turned again. In the minutes we stood watching she must have sprinted up and down thirty times.

'We'd better get back in,' Meredith said in a resigned tone.

'She was a beautiful woman,' I breathed to Bronwyn, who seemed to be assaying my earrings. 'Despite Hollywood,' she said.

Maxine looked angry. 'I hope that dog's watching out for sharks.'

At the counter I bought six lime cordials in styrene cups.

'This reminds me of going to the old picture theatre in Gosford,' Patsy said. 'I never cease to marvel...'

'At what?' Di grunted, watching Bronwyn grind out her Silk Cut.

'The whole thing. How we can record pictures and voices. How the telephone works. Satellites. You know.'

'Ask our nuclear physicist,' Bronwyn announced to the entire foyer. I was the enemy within.

'Dad never used to watch the movies,' Patsy mused. 'He'd just go to the Regal to be put into a trance. He'd sit there for two hours visualising his childhood and the sons be never had.'

'Jesus,' Meredith murmured, not unsympathetic.

The drive back to Patonga seemed unbearably long and tortuous. I sat in the front seat with the window open, breathing in coolness and pressing my lips closed to keep in nausea. The gum trunks flashed by like a ghostly chorus-line of naked torsoes. Patsy's Landcruiser bounded over ridges and potholes. Behind us Maxine was silent with preoccupation.

Di's Corolla had beaten us back and Meredith was unlocking the door. Maxine rushed in to the phone.

'Oh,' she was moaning when I reached her. 'Oh, oh, my God, no.'

Meredith stepped across and gripped Maxine around the shoulders. I prised the receiver from her hands. The others stood around us in a semi-circle, breathing shallowly.

I recognised the woman on the phone as Mr Fernance's elderly neighbour. Maxine still called her Aunty Roma. She was a woman who had never learned to summarise. I listened to her story, at the same time watching Maxine's face, registering her jerky, quavering breathing.

'Darryl's in hospital,' I told the others, holding the receiver against my breastbone. 'In Intensive Care. But it sounds like he'll be all right.'

'How do you know?' Maxine flew at me, snatching at the receiver. 'How can you bloody say that?' She fell back sobbing. Meredith pushed her down into a chair and hugged her with both arms around her head.

I rang off, thanking the old lady volubly.

'We'd better get you up to the hospital pronto,' Meredith told Maxine.

'I'll take her.' Patsy was not thrown by calamities.

Meredith and Patsy guided Maxine out to the Landcruiser. Half way up the path she shook them off.

I still felt queasy with car-sickness. Standing at the kitchen bench, I stuffed hunks of white bread into my mouth, gulping them down to quench the biliousness.

Bronwyn and Di dropped into the TV chairs and stared at one another. Meredith stumped in, slammed the screen door, and went through into the backyard. From the kitchen window I watched her examining her strawberries by torchlight. Pincering out a snail, she dropped it on the path and stamped on it.

'What's happening?' Di asked me.

'Well, Mr Fernance and the oldest boy are at the hospital and the old neighbour is in minding the younger three, so I can only give you her version—'

'Get on with it,' Meredith shouted from the back door.

'He's been badly hurt,' I called. 'But it wasn't the fire that got him. They'd given up trying to control it—it was just too widespread—and they were on their way out when they came across some old codger alone in a weatherboard house with drums of kero and God knows what else—'

Bronwyn shuddered.

'Darryl went in to try to reason with him. Apparently the other guys don't know what happened next, but suddenly there was a ruddy great explosion. It blasted Darryl right out of the building.'

'God,' Di breathed.

'What about the old bloke?' Bronwyn puzzled.

'She didn't say.'

'Poor bugger.'

Meredith dumped glasses and a cask of claret between us.

'We'd better go easy,' I cautioned. 'A couple of us will have to go in later to take over from Patsy.'

'You're her oldest friend,' Bronwyn told me. 'You could go in. But I think the rest of us'd just be in the road.'

I let the claret piss into my glass. 'Maxie doesn't need me tonight.' More to the point, she wouldn't want me. All her girlhood allegiance had shifted to Darryl and the children and her brothers and their children, which was only natural. She wrote each birthday, the scratchiest of notes in a Woolworths card.

Bronwyn raised her glass. 'To Darryl—a rapid recovery.' We

drank in unison. Di boasted Beaver had rolled four cars, and crashlanded a plane, and walked away unscathed. Willpower was the essential requisite, she implied.

We began to drink quickly, proclaiming toasts to all and sundry. We ordained handsome lovers, beautiful lovers, fat babies, slim babies, happy weddings and amicable divorces. 'Never-ending free books for Bronwyn,' I proposed. 'Unilateral disarmament,' she retaliated. We were willing ourselves into tiddliness.

Bronwyn was soon uncoordinated. She waved her hands as she talked, splashing wine on the rug and chairs. 'Never mind,' she'd cry, swiping at it with the tissue she used to clean her glasses. Di hooted every time it happened. Meredith kept topping up glasses and knocking her pipe against chair legs. I grew giggly and flushed. Di started on her Helen Keller jokes. We rocked with laughter.

We were making so much noise we didn't hear the Landcruiser pull up. When Patsy opened the screendoor, we were bunched together giggling raucously at a dirty story, with Di ceremonially pouring a libation of claret over Bronwyn's head.

'How could you?' Patsy cried. In a second we were silent.

'They're flying Darryl down to Royal North Shore,' Patsy told us.

'What about Maxine?' I asked.

'One of her brothers is driving her down.'

Bronwyn was struggling to get up off the floor. I grabbed a length of paper towelling from the kitchen, mopped the claret dribbles off her head and shoulders, wiped her glasses, and then sat and pulled her head and shoulders down into the folds of my skirt. She shut her eyes.

'We're going to have to get busy with the salt and soda water,' I said to Meredith.

'Tomorrow,' she said.

I was the only one with any energy. I shifted Bronwyn into a beanbag and began picking up, stacking, putting away and wiping down. Mustering the others into the bedrooms I clapped my hands and called, 'Into bed.' My mother used to clap and call out nonsense as she herded the leghorns into their shed each evening. In the morning when she collected the eggs she'd carol: 'Good girl, good girl.'

I didn't expect to sleep, but I did. Next morning I woke before six. The early light through the hopper barred the ceiling, illuminating the flyspots and spider web.

I hung over the edge of my bunk and, for no reason, looked

down at the empty berth underneath. By common consent the floor-sleepers had elected to stay in their less comfortable possies.

Through the doorway I could see the bottom half of Bronwyn's body swaddled in a travel rug. She shifted slightly, to the sound of a page turning. I squirmed out of the sheets and down the ladder. Whispering 'Good morning,' I snuggled into the beanbag beside her. Outside, the cat was stalking a tiny, hopping wren.

I was blasted out of comfort by the phone. Mrs Dorney's voice crackled in my ear. I carried the phone in to Meredith's bedside table, lifting the extension cord over obstacles. Meredith groaned and settled the receiver between the pillow and her ear. 'Yes mother?' she asked, resigned, ironic. Beside her in the double bed Di groaned, reached across to reassure herself and turned over. On the floor under the window, Patsy breathed in arythmic gasps. I turned to tiptoe out but something made me hesitate. Meredith was struggling up onto her elbow. Her face was sallow. 'Stay there, Mum,' she ordered. 'I'll be right up.' She rolled out of bed and started pulling her tracksuit on over her bikini pants.

'What's wrong?' I hissed, handing her the sneakers from under the desk. She said nothing, but began scrabbling on the dressing table for her keys. I found them with her shoulder bag under Di's discarded clothes.

'I'll come with you,' I said.

'No.'

I ran into the back bedroom, shook off my nightie, pulled on panties and a blouse and skirt, pushed my feet into sandals. Meredith was already in the panelvan. She hadn't unlocked the passenger door. The vehicle began to move. I thumped on the door. Meredith eased off, stretching across to lift the lock. I scrambled in.

'Talk to me, please,' I begged. We were whirling up the hill, slewing through gravel, veering out on corners.

'It's Phil.'

A car crash? Sickness?

'That house, yesterday.'

It hadn't occurred to us. A peculiar old man, yes, but not Phil, not a healthy forty-year-old. He wouldn't stay in a tinderbox shack full of explosive materials in the middle of a bushfire.

'You're sure?'

'We'll see.' She was so ferocious I dared not say any more.

We shot over the Rip Bridge and out through Empire Bay. It was a glorious morning, this Australia Day holiday of ours. Mauve and white watsonia spikes decorated the roadside. The redder mauve of crepe myrtle shrubs hailed us from behind fences. Fuchsia and morning glory and bougainvillea garlanded carports. Pansies bobbed their purple and black faces beside gates. Blue sky and ocean I thought, mixed with the red blood of conquest, plus white, plus black, gives us these tints and shades of settlement.

We grated up the driveway, scattering the flock of plovers grazing on the lawn, and pulled up at an Ionic portico. Meredith pounded inside. I stood on the damp grass, sucking at a broken fingernail. After a while I walked across to the shrubs and rocks at the edge of the headland. The rising sun was so strong I could not see the horizon.

When I turned round to survey the property, I saw a man trudging across the lawn towards me. It was Mark, the younger brother. I wished I had had time to put on a bra. Mark was holding a fern. Soil clung to its rootbound base in a crumbling cylinder.

'I took the petrol up there,' Mark said, handing me the fern. 'There were drums of it here in the garage. Mum didn't need it. I thought Phil could use it.'

'It was very considerate of you. But he shouldn't have stored it in the house.'

'He didn't know it was there. I put it under the verandah while he was out.'

'Didn't you tell him? Leave a note?' Phil must surely have noticed the drums under the verandah. He had been trained to be observant—lives had depended on it.

Perhaps, brooding, he had developed a deathwish. Perhaps he was just sitting there, drawing on a joint, wondering whether chance would toss a javelin in the form of a windblown spark. Perhaps he didn't mind taking Darryl with him—Darryl had been too young to be conscripted. Perhaps he even lit a match and held it, threatening.

'They've got to go in to the hospital,' Mark observed. 'To identify him.' The police and emergency people must have been up in the bush late into the evening, and again at first light, salvaging what they could.

'They'll probably have to get his dental records,' Mark gloated.

A faint noise reached us from the house. The phone was ringing. Most likely the local radio station, news-hunting, or the girls back at Meredith's, wondering what was going on.

I was still holding the atoning potplant. I cupped my left hand under the roots to preserve the last of the soil.

And then, suddenly, I let the fern go, dropped into a squat, fell forward with my breasts flopping and fingers gouging the lawn, and sobbed out deep, ugly vomiting noises until my throat was too dry for the noise to go on and I could feel my gullet closing out the air.

A Double Act

At Uni, the gang who took their coffee and recreation in the English common room knew it would be Glenn who'd make it. He had the charm, the insouciance, the knack of choosing the right subjects, the art of cultivating the right people.

Glenn was always bubbling with anecdotes about big-timers: he had gossiped away the weekend at a professor's ski lodge, had shouted a round for half the Senate, had bumped into an elder statesman at croquet. Sufficient evidence could usually be adduced to support these tales. Glenn had undeniably secured certain names as referees on his research applications; he did indeed hand out freebie theatre tickets (working anti-clockwise around the circle); balding men in academic gowns had more than once nodded to him.

It was advisable to keep in good with Glenn: first, because his *conversaziones* were entertaining and his invitations valuable and, second, because he could be a bitchy adversary, viciously off-hand. He had a polished technique for initiating the exclusion of an offender from the group. 'I'm out every night for the next two weeks,' he would wail; and, then, when the victim commiserated, he'd rejoin: 'I wasn't asking for sympathy. I could hardly expect my social life to be any of your concern.'

Glenn talked as he walked, either rapidly and incisively or with indolent grace. Always, he compelled attention and called the tune. He never helped others to contribute but directed interchanges from a height. He would not accommodate the slow-witted or shy, the non-entities or millstones. They would have to learn in other company; he was not conducting a nursery school. His clichés were forgiven.

He loved or abhored, praised or teased, encouraged or dumped. He could tell a mischievous story against someone he had rejected—an incompetent would-be mentor or lover. He did not hesitate to repeat confidences. He would whisper some ludicrous, murky secret of the bedroom or bathroom and then, turning genteel, elevate his little finger and smack his lips over his *Andronicus* in a delicious moment of self-mockery.

He wore his hair long and wild around his El Greco face, parodying a romantic musician. Yet his clothes were fanatically neat, pressed and close-fitting. He had the custom of lowering his brow, half closing his eyes and inflicting a mock Bogart stare until the unnerved victim squirmed. He should have been an insufferable poseur, but the humour saved him.

He invariably carried a book. Not a paperback forced into a back-pocket—it had to be a lately released hardcover or, better still, an advance copy. He would shuffle through the crisp pages with his bony, manicured fingers, reading aloud the juicier passages in such a manner that they sounded scurrilous. He had only to open a book to intimidate a boring tutor.

There was an edge to Glenn. Even long-time associates could experience a shudder of fear and anticipation—as one may when studying a motionless leopard in a zoo, or watching the family cat stalk a bird. At any minute he might do something awful or, perhaps, magnificent.

A complete lack of musical appreciation was the one shortcoming to which Glenn would immediately admit. Forestalling attack, he boasted of his insensibility to all forms of melody. 'I have no ear for it,' he would announce grandiloquently. 'A congenital defect. Can't tell one note from another and don't want to.'

Dance, he would hurry on to add, was his one abiding passion outside his beloved books. He went to every live dance performance and saw every dance film.

How Glenn could appreciate the dance without the music, or distinguish the dancer from the dance, remained a conundrum.

Helen hovered at the door of the English common room. She had loved Glenn since they were in high school together and remained fascinated by his person however vehemently she reminded herself she despised his conduct.

She was as ponderous as Glenn was lithe. Her body was a superb slab of veined marble, demanding to be stroked with polite awe. The sculptor who dared to take on the marble would have to seek, like Michangelo, to free the spirit within; he would fail, desecrate, if he attempted to hack her into his own image.

Helen always wore loose, dark winter clothes. One wit in the gang said she reminded him of a china cabinet under a grey dustsheet, or an over-stuffed garbage bag bulging with the refuse of others' frivolities, and Glenn did not move to reprimand him. Helen's only ornamentation was jewellery. She loved large, elaborate pieces: earrings, rings, clinking charm bracelets, clanking breastplates. Although she detested hot weather, she would not in even the worst temperatures remove her layers of clothing and jewellery. She hung on to them in the spirit of the child who, pressing her fingers over her eyes, imagines herself invisible. They made her feel bad and good; they induced a luxuriant melancholy.

Music was the one field in which Helen would claim a superior endowment to Glenn's. She possessed several thousand records and every week lay-byed more. Her evenings and weekends were devoted to music, and at Uni she was never without a walkman. In pubs and nightclubs she would dance, stomping her boots, shaking her arms about, wallowing in noise. Her friends recognised her home as an oasis of sound and rhythm in a constrained suburb. There they could bash about and shout above the noise and manufacture happiness as potent as wine. It was a place of drum kits, bare soles, full ashtrays, and bouncing beer cans. Helen's parents had long ago retreated upstairs to the Cape Cod extension.

Intermittently Helen wrote song lyrics and melodies, but she would not let Glenn hear any of her compositions. He did not care about the melodies, but exclusion from her written thoughts infuriated him. It was one of the few areas to which he had ever been refused admission. Helen would not relent. He disturbed her too deeply, and her lyrics were always, however obliquely, about him. He approached his target from every angle, cajoling, complaining, bullying, but she was bullishly immovable and her bulk deterred outright conflict. She weighed sixteen stone and had a trumpeting voice and strong arms from drumming.

Glenn had never seen Helen dance either. Pub bands were so horrendous, he asserted, that even he, the city's most fervent appreciator of dance, would not endure five minutes near one. Helen would not have minded him watching her dance. When she submitted her body to the music she became someone else. The spectacle might have taught him something about himself.

Throughout her university years Helen was constantly depressed. She trudged into black misery claiming she did not want to live past twenty-nine. She would brood and weep for days and then scribble fierce verse and play her most primitive, pulsating records, the wildest banshee screams, the most destructive lyrics. She would puff and inhale, cigarette after cigarette, grinding the butts into a plate, and drink grapefruit juice, and loathe herself. She would stomp around the square suburban rooms, marking out their perimeters—around the livingroom, eating area, bedroom, kitchen, hall, around again, scowling at her possessions, despising her dependence on creature comforts, longing to be freed from her body and her passions. Her love for Glenn was useless and self-perpetuating.

With uncharacteristic generosity, Glenn refrained from exploiting Helen's misery. It was a grief too deep to toy with. He maintained a brotherly, mock-courtly attitude of fondness.

Helen graduated with a BA and began her working life in the university library, where she was required to find books in the Stack and replace books on shelves. The trolleys were so unwieldy she could scarcely push them, the armloads of books so heavy they strained her shoulders and lower back. She trudged through the corridors, head down, wearing out pair after pair of boots.

Glenn was still a student, doing double Honours in Australian History and Archaeology. Whenever Helen spotted him at work in Rare Books she would duck her head, mortified, and thunder past the protective glass with her trolley loaded to overflowing.

Fortunately the other library assistants were amusing. They had learned to make their own fun—uproarious as possible—on the concrete amidst the grey towers of books. They rattled off jokes, sang obscene songs, magnified their life histories, and fantasised about what they would do when they escaped. Helen imagined herself accelerating along an open road on a gigantic Harley Davidson. Since she could not drive, such bravado was patently fantastic and her workmates applauded accordingly. Her aubergine eyes darkened as she smoked and talked of freedom. The others slapped her on the back—her sloping shoulders invited touching, they were so vulnerable and awkward—and said 'Yes, Hel,' and took her out for drinks.

The library people did not mind Helen's miseries. Nobody did. If anything, her friends enjoyed her despondency. It was all so theatrical: the sighing, the heaving chest, the dribbles of tears. She was a colossal clown whom they did not hesitate to tease, confident of her good nature.

Knowing Helen had a degree, work superiors prodded her to apply to do the librarianship diploma or, at least, start a technician's course. She would shudder, blurt out: 'I don't want to work in libraries for the rest of my life. I hate them,' and then, realising she had said the wrong thing yet again, blunder back to her allies in the Stack. Recounted in amplified form, the incident would provide a full afternoon's entertainment.

Work, for Helen, was a means of obtaining cash to buy records. She did not expect to enjoy any job. The library was as good and bad as any workplace. She would not, as Glenn would, create an enchanted, privileged world for herself.

Friends always knew where to find Helen, and she would not betray secrets. In old age, they foresaw, she would make a grand confidante for her sisters' children. Already she was heading that way, transmuting into a monumental old duchess, full of the world's weariness yet ready to listen, ladling out comfort, handing around snacks, entertaining herself and her callers with her music. In time she would settle into an armchair with her music magazines and her beer and her pack of cards and be utterly immovable. She would dress completely in black and chainsmoke putrid cigarettes and admire the oval nails on her pretty, ringed hands. Her aubergine eyes would sink deeper and deeper into her dimpled cheeks, dark with the secrets of an aged warrior-queen. Glenn would slink through her court like a partially tamed leopard. He would pose on the marble at her jewelled toes, or lope about the throne-room disturbing her courtiers. Sometimes he would vanish for months, back into his native territory, the hot plains where he sprinted and hunted and killed for pleasure. He would return sleek and fit, eyes glowering, and permit her to touch his forehead, even stroke his flanks as he moved past, before flinging himself down on the cool marble, growling at the jesters of the court. She would never control him.

Glenn graduated at an opportune time, just as the conservation movement was solidifying into legislation and recurrent funding. He was on the spot as foundations were unearthed, old pubs salvaged, grand redevelopments planned. By his early twenties he was proffering advice, tendering recommendations, and drafting submissions. His preferred employer was the government. For all its cumbersome slowness, it had the power. Better to advise a minister who then in his wilful ignorance brushed aside one's measured submission than to be paid a pittance to further the cause of some strident, no-win protester. Salvation of the state's history was tangential to Glenn's purposes.

As soon as Glenn began work, he thanked his parents for supporting him through university and moved out. At first he boarded with a retired librarian, a choice which Helen interpreted, correctly, as a slap in the face. The house smelt like the water in a vase of dead flowers. Only the books were cherished. They were dusted weekly, and once a month their bindings were treated with British Museum book-dressing. The librarian was something of an antiquarian but could not afford the volumes she coveted. For a time Glenn was the ornament of the collection. He permitted himself to be caressed. He confided archaeological arcana. He produced little gifts, bits of Australiana from digs—bottles and buttons mostly, nothing valuable. He promised to filch a set of convict manacles, but never did. The old girl ate bread at every meal, drank Bundaberg rum, and listened every Sunday afternoon to the Mephisto Waltzes. In the end it was the music which got to Glenn. He slipped away while the old girl was at her ablutions.

The next entry in Helen's address book was for an inner-city flat which Glenn shared with a student of Indian dance, a beautiful boy with wet eyes and long lashes. Amjad was sweet-tempered and thoughtless. He did not pause long enough to be weighed down by anything. He was a vivid, drifting balloon, a silk parachute, a butterfly, and as substantial. He flowed gracefully as a snake. He could make music, too; he played classical ragas and ornamental pieces from the carnatic tradition. Glenn was ravished by the dancing and made discreet use of ear plugs to exclude the music. Amjad was always floating away, like a creature in a Leunig cartoon, while Glenn leapt to snatch at his heels.

About the time Glenn was moving out of Amjad's flat, Helen was taking to the airwaves. She found she was a natural. Her years of preparation stood by her: all those thousands of hours of bashing her drums for an imaginary audience and roaring out her lyrics to the empty room, of playing new releases to her friends and regaling them with obscure information from the overseas magazines, of listening to radio DJs and comperes at pubs and clubs and copying them at home with her microphone.

Helen's voice broadcast well. It was strong and husky, suited to a late-night timeslot. She became a regular with a show of her own, four nights a week. A cult listenership developed: mostly males who shared her musical tastes and appreciated her quirky comments and self-deprecatory asides. Young men sent her cuttings and homemade demo tapes. One wrote demanding to meet her; he seemed to have in mind some supple and sultry beauty off a record jacket. After snorting and crying over a few such letters, Helen composed a stock reply: a snide, tricksy letter which gave away nothing and, in fact, teased and provoked the imagination further. Someone handed a copy around, and she was approached to contribute fillers to a free music newspaper-cum-gig guide. Within a few months she was editing a question-and-answer page. The questions on obscure releases and defunct bands were usually within her ambit, and the resources of the library network were at her disposal. Chasing up answers, she came to speak to trivia buffs, fan-club secretaries, independent producers, even record company executives. She began to review new releases for the paper, and through this came in contact with publicists, distributors, importers, and record-shop proprietors. Most of these people regarded her as a rough-edged youngster, for she did not yet have a recognised, quantified following for her pronouncements. She longed for the day when she would earn enough from the music industry to resign from the library.

Through her radio work and writing, Helen became a minor celebrity in young, inner-city circles. Glenn did not realise this. When she told him, feigning complacency, about her activities, he assumed they were absurd conceits, as trivial as the music which possessed her. 'I won't be impressed,' he insisted in his nicely modulated baritone, 'until you show me those lyrics.' 'One day,' Helen vowed. She was discovering in herself an ambition to bare her soul, whatever the consequences, but did not know whether it was a healthy impulse.

A piano player acquaintance who had heard Helen sing some of her songs offered to play around with the melody lines and work them up into finished products. Apprehensive of Glenn's reaction and afraid she would be betraying him, she declined. Then a band approached her, keen to record her material. They had already put out an EP called 'Raise the Bones of Elvis.' 'Gas!' Helen bellowed. 'Can I play the drums?' Money was scrounged and a single cut. On the A side Helen's rage thundered. On the B side she was more lyrical, celebrating an imagined communion of spirits. It was a good effort by local Indie standards. The trade papers declared it had legs, a scattering of shops took it, Helen's station thrashed it. The big stations, predictably, failed to pick it up. After a month it languished; six weeks and it was finished. Glenn never knew of the record's existence. His current flatmate, a risk management consultant, listened only to current affairs and talkback.

When Glenn next met Helen in the library she studied him with unflinching aubergine eyes. He had never seen her so alert and defiant. 'You haven't lost any weight,' he observed, 'yet you're looking superb. This radio business must be doing you good.' He smiled as a witticism came to mind. 'I'll have to tell my friends I've got a musical encyclopedia for a pal. A full set no less.'

Two days later Helen received a piece of yellowed sheetmusic in the mail. The title was *Egypt! I am calling you* and the lyrics read:

Oh! life is bliss,
I crave a kiss,
One burning kiss from you—
Your laughing eyes
Shall hold a prize
In a paradise for two.
O dreamy Nile,
With your glitt'ring smile,
Roll along to a song ever new,
My desert flower
in God's chosen hour
I shall come to you—

Helen tipped the franked envelope upside down, held its mouth open and shook it. A square of white paper fluttered down. It was a Premier's Department *with compliments* slip, and on it, in his spiralling copperplate, Glenn had written: 'How about a double act? You make the music, I dance.'

But I Keep on Waiting

Jocelyn McLeod née Armitage is your object of contemplation. Proceed in chronological order, comparing, contrasting and highlighting, please, the 1981 incident. I think it is pivotal.

It changed nothing. You're wasting your time, you know.

Allow us to be the judge of that.

Perhaps I can play it as a paper, with slides. My annual presentation to the Cytogenetics Group (New South Wales). Behold, this unlikely looking woman shall conceive by the normal method and bear a child (subtitle: *annunciation*). Behold, this, wise men and women, is the child (footnote: *all functions normal, a bonnie wee mite*). But no, I realise you require a written submission.

I suggest you don't commence with the wedding. That would be fatuous. Go back two years further.

Two years... yes, I've got it. On Boxing Day 1977 Jocelyn brought her man Harry down to Pearl Beach to show him off to Dad and me. I had not seen her in, oh, six years. Her attitute was: 'See, I didn't need your help.' I professed great joy for her. My father, who recalled her as a docile schoolgirl, kissed her and thumped Harry's shoulder.

I took them for a walk and, remarking on the gemstone street names, hinted at the desirability of an engagement. Even as I did it I wondered about the propriety of imposing my beliefs, but there is a right order in this world and we are wise to conform to it. They hugged me, defying me with their happiness.

Harry was pushing sixty, Jocelyn told me in the yard as I picked them a bunch of Christmas bush, and he had not only an ex-wife but two children older than us. We were very conscious then of still being twenty-nine.

Let's skip through to the wedding.

I thought you didn't want the gushy bits.

You can skip the frilly dresses.

There weren't any. Jocelyn wore a white shift which looked remarkably like a lab coat.

Shifts weren't in fashion in 1979.

This wasn't the city. They were living up near Wollombi. Dirt roads—you know? Coal mines, scratchy-looking land. It was only just beginning to be fashionable to own a patch of land up there.

The ceremony was conducted by a celebrant on a patch of turf outside their house. We guests stood on grey, friable dirt. Above us were drooping eucalypts and above them the purple bluffs of the Watagans. Behind us were the castoffs of the previous owner's passion: rusted car bodies. I closed my eyes against the heat haze and heard whipbirds and blowflies and smelt leaf mulch.

They drove away to honeymoon in a tent.

'Better them than me,' I said, making semicircles in the air around my head.

'It does take two,' murmured Harry's son, whom I had sat beside during the meal. My invitation had not included a partner—which I had to suppose was tact on Jocelyn's part.

I went back inside to help with the clearing-up.

Driving away I thought: 'Well, that's it.' Another woman friend had valued my company for as long as it took to shackle a man, and then, with raptured hugs, had slipped the surly bonds of earth.

Confounding my expectations, Jocelyn sent a postcard of a peak called the Breadknife, and kept up thereafter a confetti shower of letters. Her happiness was so unadulterated I felt meanspirited.

Anorexia had crept up on Jocelyn in our last two years of school. By the time we began university, she was gaunt. She rushed between pracs with her jaw thrust forward to support a manic grin. To the unwilling recipient of her obsessive kindnesses it was a sepulchral manifestation, this emaciated creature, the blue veins standing out like cords on her hands, the face unnaturally downy, the pale yellow eyes popping out of black sockets, the big, unused teeth, and that jaw, the jaw of a skull. You have never seen stubbornness until you have seen the jawbone of an anorexic.

She covered her cable neck and broom-handle limbs with ruffled blouses, flounced pinafores, gathered skirts and harem pants. This was at the time when miniskirts were the fashion.

She was continually delivering birthday cakes and tying up gifts of homemade rum balls and coconut ice, while succeeding in consuming nothing but steamed green vegetables, tea, skimmed milk yoghurt, Kavli crispbreads and diuretics. She would employ any subterfuge to avoid eating. At night, I am sure, she dreamed of food with her stomach rumbling and her hip bones gouging the mattress. She begged for love in a Blossom Dearie whine, extending her skeleton fingers to grip her victim's wrists. It was as if a stick insect clutched an animated meal to its belly.

Fear expanded her eyes and nostrils. She knew how far her pubic mound protruded, how frail was her rib-cage, how much of her hair was falling out, how long it was since she had menstruated. But she was obdurate. 'Listen, friend,' she would threaten, 'don't try to tell *me* what to do.'

We fought. My strategy was to wear her down, wear God down, by unrelenting prayer. *Attrition* is the obvious word, did it not also carry the meaning of a defective, imperfect sorrow for one's sins, a repentance based on fear of punishment: I was simply more adept than Jocelyn at covering up atrophy.

I studied conscientiously and graduated with a medal. It had been a matter of applying the brains God had given me: ninety-nine per cent diligence. While I sorted out my PhD topic I worked as a demonstrator.

I could not claim, then or now, to have devised my own life plan. Whatever schema there is has been pre-ordained and God has revealed it to me through human agencies, a chink more each two or three years. Sometimes he has displayed a quirky sense of humour by leaving the revelation to the last moment, but he has always come good in the end.

Mankind's terms of existence are logical and clear. You pursue the tasks set before you as unto God and live in accordance with the rules God has spelled out. You have no option in the long run: God's smarter than you and he'll win in the end, so it's smart to stay on the rails from the outset. I have never entertained any sympathy for the prodigal son. The older brother, resentful or no, is more my cup of tea. If you don't want to get burned, I used to tell my prac classes, keep your fingers away from the bunsen burner.

Certainly cytogenetics produces ethical dilemmas, but that is no reason for a theist to opt out. The microscope merely magnifies what God has already created. The patterns are there for those who choose to perceive. We may tinker, but we cannot create from scratch. A rational system of ethics can be deduced.

Lest this all sound too straightforward, I shall confess to one lapse. I had been elaborating since school the hypothesis that I would marry a fellow scientist and produce twin boys. In 1969 there was a sustained show of interest from an agnostic paleontologist called Damien, and for a while there I wandered off the straight road. Jocelyn—who, if there was any consistency in her, should have been delighted—was furious.

At Christmas 1971 I had my final holiday with my father before I went to Washington to do my doctorate. I should describe my father at this juncture since thereafter he required a weekly letter detailing every intramural machination of which I could get wind and answering a litany of garbled Junior Science puzzles.

Farming never satisfied my father's mind. In retirement, on the edge of a continent on which he had failed to leave a single lasting furrow, he read incessantly and talked incessantly. I know that is a contradiction in terms, but he managed to do both, to the aggravation of the neighbours and the Woy Woy librarian. He ranted like a cabin fever case and paced around the gemstone streets like a yardbound dog.

In appearance, my father is a sunbleached version of me. On him my brindle hair is blanched carrot, my yellow lashes and eyebrows white, my blue eyes cataract dim. My orange freckles are his sun cancers, my sunburn his leather forearms, my ringed neck his waffled rooster's throat. He cannot believe, and I love him so dearly it makes it all the harder to accept the fact of his irretrievable condemnation. When we are together we spat like cockerels.

From Washington I wrote once a fortnight to Jocelyn and prayed for the click inside her head. She reciprocated with illustrated letters describing all her activities in childish simplicity, and handmade gifts: needlepoint bookmarks and rosebuds preserved in Borax.

Since she graduated she had been working at the Dental Hospital. She was and is a thorough clinician, I am sure. What perfectionist is not? She had always insisted on doing every stage of every task, both to be sure it is done correctly and to play the martyr. No doubt she was testy with the nurses, haranguing them—apologetically—on hygiene and double checking. I imagine she was brusque with adult patients: it would not trouble her to plunge a needle into a gum. All things considered, a fearful sight.

Jocelyn held out until we were twenty-six. Then reports began to reach me, through our few mutual acquaintances, of gradual change. There had been no dramatic turning point. My apologies, dear examiner, if you have been hoping for one. No, it was a slow thing, an easing of the sole off the brake, a belated farewell to adolescence.

And how did I react? I, the long-sufferer who had endured ten years of lies, tricks, evasions, embarrassment, abuse and arguments, who had been through all the permutations of despair and anger yet had always come back to exasperated love. I cried. I felt betrayed. I felt deserted and desolate. I felt depressed and diminished. I apologise for the alliteration, but I am telling the truth, and sometimes our feelings cluster around certain sounds, imprisoned by our language.

I never wanted to see Jocelyn again. I detested the object of my pity. I was the spurned lover who destroys letters, reviles his beloved's memory, and lusts to lash out.

I could claim no kudos for Jocelyn's recovery. We had been 20,000 km apart for the past three years. I had not seen the corpse awaking, the skeleton embedding itself in pink baby flesh, the body reupholstered. But I did not doubt my information.

Jocelyn did not thank me for that decade of perserverance. To do so would have been to admit the full awfulness of her behaviour. The humiliation would have been too much. The released prisoner does not care to revisit his jailers, even if they held him back by force from doing injury to himself. Gratitude is displaced by shame and relief. Jocelyn hated me for what I knew.

After Washington, Melbourne on a pittance. My postdoc allowance was small, and I was sponsoring two children in Vietnam (this is 1975 we're talking about, just before Saigon fell and these kids passed 'out of contact'). Frugality was my watchword. I had a single pair of shoes and rarely switched on the heating. Visitors huddling in their cardigans took my miserliness for the absentminded scientist's insensitivity. I was sufficiently provided for; what more could I, in all conscience, expect? Outside work hours I attended courses, played badminton and joined a Reformed congregation. I don't know what Jocelyn did in those years.

I was about to enter the second-last year of my postdoc grant when Jocelyn brought Harry to Pearl Beach. Perhaps it was Harry who brought Jocelyn. Having taken her on, he was determined to complete his healing. He is a vet by trade—have I mentioned that?

No, you haven't. And you've been wandering too much.

A few months after Jocelyn's marriage, I took the first full-time, paying, commercial job of my life. My employer, a pathology practice, required me to help set up and run a prenatal testing lab in Armidale.

On my thirty-second birthday I applied for my first-ever housing loan. I am not in the habit of making long-distance phonecalls, except in the case of birthdays and illness, but, as soon as I got back to the half-house which the practice had rented for me, I phoned my father. He was so delighted he offered to chip in the same amount again. 'Go for an acreage,' he said.

I bought twenty hectares out along Herbert Park Road. Subdivision was a future certainty. The sole 'improvement' on my land was a ricketty kit house. More chilly winters were assured.

Standing on the crest of my land, I imagined dams, orchards, shrubberies, a rose garden, hothouses, shadehouses, and geese. Reverting to parsimony, I did no more at first than sink dozens of bulbs around the perimeter of the foundations and wait for the first green excaliburs.

I had been told the Anglican Cathedral was the best shot for rigorous Bible teaching. I went along one morning, sceptically, and found solid instruction offered hand-in-vellum-glove with High Church sacramentalism. It is a curious thing for a scientist to watch a man in a robe washing his fingers with the aid of a tiny jug and bowl, lifting a veil off a chalice, pouring wine and water out of cruets, trying to wipe the lip of the chalice with a starched cloth, blessing wafers on a silver plate, and raising his hands to proclaim this 'body and blood' effectual for his audience's edification. Still, I stayed. There had been no other ceremonials in my life, apart from the conferring of degrees and other people's weddings.

And now, I think, we have reached the proper time for 'the 1981 incident'.

At last.

On the first Friday evening of that year—a dry, smoky, stubbly twilight with crows calling—I went outside to shift the sprinkler on the lawn I was establishing in front of the unfinished concrete slab designated my patio. A clump of bracken shook and out strolled a tortoise. I spent a delightful half hour squatting watching him waddle around my bulb beds. As that Sunday was Epiphany, I decided to call him that, with Piffle for short. When I announced my household addition over morning tea after church, I used the word 'christened' and received a sharp glance from a canon's wife.

The following Saturday afternoon a taxi ground up my driveway and disgorged Jocelyn, Harry, their infant son, and half a dozen overnight bags. They were en route to a conference in Brisbane—vet or dental, I forget—and their old Volvo had blown something—a head gasket?—just past Uralla. They had been towed into Armidale, but the vehicle could not be repaired at once. Parts would have to be sent from Sydney. They had tossed up between booking into a pub or abandoning the car and hopping onto the first coach north, but something had told them to come out to me. One cannot argue with such a something.

Jocelyn changed and washed the little one, but he refused to sleep. It was too hot. We all shifted out onto the patio.

'Actually, we were going to call in to see you on the way back,' Jocelyn announced, distributing largesse. 'We've got a favour to ask you.' Her eyes were shiny and translucent as the skins of ripe yellowgage plums. Her breast, exposed as she fed her son, was round and veined as a melon. Why do we speak of women as fruit?

'We're going to have a naming ceremony for Timothy,' Jocelyn was saying, 'and we'd like you to be the, you know, sort of godmother.'

After a moment I said: 'I'd be honoured.' I am not intellectually at ease with any form of infant baptism.

In the evening cool Piffle emerged from his bracken retreat and Timothy gurgled at him from the cage of his crouching father's arms and legs. Harry tipped the tortoise unceremoniously onto his back and declared him a healthy youngster.

I whipped up my usual sausage casserole, served it with mashed potatoes and damper, and watched Jocelyn eat. Her upper arms were almost pinchable. Having for so long, so heedlessly, flouted God's laws of commonsense, did she deserve this weight of blessings? I reminded myself this soft new flesh contained all the old failings.

At five the child woke with the birds and bellowed. After church I took them all out to the Falls for a picnic. That evening we went down to the creek to spot wallabies. At midnight the bed in the spare room creaked rhythmically, without tact. At five the child woke and bellowed.

On Monday I went to work, Harry went to spur on the mechanics, and Jocelyn borrowed my car to do some shopping. She bought various child necessities plus a carton of household odds and ends she had noticed I did not possess.

On Tuesday evening they got away, determined to drive straight through to Brisbane and catch the last two days of the conference.

As I walked back up to the house, I felt not that happy relief which comes with a return to peaceful routine, nor that sadness of friends gone, but a vast dissatisfaction with the universe and all its ways.

I grabbed the carpet sweeper and stomped from room to room, bashing into chair legs and skirting boards. Then I pulled down all the curtains, dumped them on the laundry floor, and crammed the top pair into the washing machine, which was set for a cold water cycle. They had come with the house, I had never liked them, and they were tagged 'Dryclean Only'. They would come out of the machine shrunken and creased, dictating a penalty of half a dozen evenings spent stretching, damping down and ironing. If they were badly enough mangled, I would be able to tear them apart for rags.

In the kitchen the orange laminate on the end of one benchtop was curling. With a knife I prised the whole strip free. I had never liked the colour.

The lino tiles also annoyed me. They had a pattern like sprinkled Milo and never looked clean. One was lifting in front of the sink. Using the carving knife I pressed the tile up until it snapped across.

The washing machine had chugged to a halt. I pulled out the tangled curtains and switched on the floodlights which my father had urged me to install after there was talk of a loony rabbit shooter. For my own part I have never been scared of the unseen.

As I was pegging out the curtains I noticed Piffle lying in a clump of portuluca. I carried him inside and put him down on the lino tiles. He blinked, stared around, and then headed away from me in a rapid waddle. I scooped him up and held his snaky little face to my nose. Then I tipped him onto his back. His legs waved and his eyes bulged like a newborn's. The traditional female resorts, I thought: redecoration, travel, fashion, pregnancy, eating, shoplifting. Each engages the outer self, occupies and engorges the body. But the inner—if belief and the intellect are insufficient?

Is that all there is?

No, a final incident insists it be included. There has been a vogue for stories relating visits: a woman visits her ageing parent, a man revisits his hometown, a man and woman visit a relative of one of them. There is a bit of description, a bit of dialogue, a bit of emoting, usually muffled, a symbol (a plant or bird, a gun or knife, vegetable, animal or mineral), a pathetic fallacy or two, and a departure blushed with inconsequentiality.

I have described two visits by Jocelyn to me, and touched on my attendance at her two ceremonies, the wedding and naming. It is her turn, again, for a visit. Make of it, as the formula goes, what you will. I promise there'll be no epiphanies, whether at the hand of priest or lover. I must preserve a remnant of dignity.

On Boxing Day 1984, Jocelyn drove down from the Hunter Valley to call on Dad and me. She had driven down through the worst of the heat, not wanting, she said, to impose upon us for lunch. There was a depth of womanliness about her which I had not noticed before, also the first treacherous white hairs above the ears. My father was obviously delighted by her. He gripped both her wrists and declared what a fine looking woman she was and wasn't her wee lad a brawny young specimen. Timothy was now four and punch-drunk with his own strength. Dad's cat set out for the hills.

We sat out on the patio for high tea. Timothy stripped off and ran in and out of the sprinkler shower. Jocelyn apologised on Harry's behalf: he had stayed home to sink some fence holes. She sighed. Harry had a grand vision, still, for transforming his intractable land into the perfect machine, a concert of irrigation and fences and roads and sheds and clinics and holding yards and agistment paddocks and synchronised crops. But he was sixty-five and slowing down, the land was soaking up his money like spring rain, his practice was still no more than a rough-and-ready first-aid station for the neighbourhood's pets and nags, and the slow payers were also his drinking mates at the *Bellbird*. Jocelyn had imagined a classy equine practice like the biggies around Scone, but Harry confined his dreams to his land. Truth be told, Jocelyn's dental practice in Cessnock was pretty basic too. She scored the school-kids and women and a few courageous, jesting men. Mines were closing and small businesses going under. The boutique wineries folk had their dental work taken care of back home in the city.

Dad started talking. Ignoring my hints, he kept on talking. Having heard every story a hundred times, I interrupted only to correct him on points of incontrovertible fact. Jocelyn listened, and her concentration was not feigned: she found my father delightful. Losing patience I gave her a nod of apology and went around to the backyard to water the fruit trees. After a judicious interval I returned, with a bag of lemons for Jocelyn. Would you have preferred me to present her with a single ripe fig, that symbol of succulence and fecundity? She might have pulled it open in a Lawrentian ecstasy and held it to her mouth. And I might have remarked on the artful white sap running down over her wrists. I'm sorry—figs in that part of the world do not ripen until February, but lemons are always with us.

Dad stopped his yabbering long enough to pat Jocelyn on the knee and remind us all again what a fine woman she was. When they looked at each other, they had that soft, glazed look of people who have confided something special.

Then Dad got stuck into me. 'Tell this girl of mine,' he told Jocelyn, 'to find herself a husband. She's stubborn as a mule. The angel Garbriel himself wouldn't be good enough for her.'

Jocelyn suggested a stroll along the beach. It's changed, I told her. You have to pick your way between the hampers and wine chillers. You must have noticed the cars parked across driveways and the old buttercake cottages disguised by architects' confections, gelato colours, ice-cream skylights, swirls of cream with nuts and *crême de menthe*. At home, Jocelyn said, the heat haze blanches away the colour, but this place glows like topaz.

Timothy sprinted along the tideline to the rockpool. Jocelyn said: 'I'm thinking about a second baby. What are the—ah—risks?'

Would it distress you, gentle examiner, to know I was tempted by spite? I was tempted to multiply the incidence of abnormality, to list a thousand possible complications, to emphasise Jocelyn's medical history and her husband's age. In counselling caution, I could effect death before there had been life. In encouraging risk, I could summon into being a life which would not otherwise have existed.

Cytogenetics, I have often thought, is a peculiarly remote discipline. You test bodily fluids which were compounded just a few weeks before in a panting woman, and then, a few months later, she is panting again, in travail this time. All this, and you usually never meet her. And if you do meet, because the test results are bad, you are deathly silent, in awe of her coming sorrow.

'You're too quiet,' Jocelyn observed. 'Harry goes that way before he has to put down an animal.'

'Plunge in,' I cried, grabbing her hands.

It's melodramatic, I know.

'The bloody body,' Jocelyn muttered and looked out across the water to the Norfolk pines behind Ocean Beach and that horizon of seven hills.

After we had waved them off, I took one of Dad's *National Geographics* and sat out in the backyard. It was eight o'clock; in forty minutes the light would be gone. A mosquito assaulted my arms and legs, returning again and again, mercilessly persistent, however many times I slapped at her.

Come on, how did you feel?

The microscope has shown me the order of things. I know too much to fantasise.

Didn't you sniffle with self-pity?

I told you, there won't be any epiphany tonight. Don't waste your time hanging about. No, you can't hurry love. You'll just have to wait.

The Blackwoman's Underclothes

When I first watched Stephanie coming and going, I wondered why, in our climate, she always wore a high-necked shirt and layers of other unnecessary garments.

Perhaps the high necks were covering something, a goitre or a birthmark.

When we began to chat in the street, I noticed she always had a brooch pinned at her throat. The question became, then, did she wear the high necklines merely so she could support the brooch at the throat, or did she add the brooch to distract from the necessity of the high neck?

I had a professional interest, you understand.

Exhibit A

In my opinion this is odious. It is the foot of a furry animal, with the amputated end sealed by a gold-plated plug. A mink maybe. A ferret? A weasel? In this climate, in this city, one is not too confident of correctly identifying one's furred brethren. There was always an animal's foot at Stephanie's throat, and she fingered the claws as she talked. The fringing fur had grown ratty from exposure and handling, but the claws had taken on the patina of caressed jade or ivory. Every week they seemed to have grown into longer and more lethal scimitars. As the fur fell away, the tiny ankle bones were also asserting themselves. The animals, I fancy, still sought to escape their golden manacles.

Yes, I am a painter, prone to fancy, and occasionally stupid.

Remarks in passing

A woman friend reminded me it was a fashion of the early eighties. I deduced Stephanie would have been new to Europe then and, no doubt suffering in that terrible cold, she would have seized on this layering cult with delight.

That she had retained the layers not out of a prematurely stunted fashion sense but for her own purposes became evident when she accompanied me to an opening. We set out with the layers weighing her down like a baglady's impedimenta, slowing her as do the geisha's stifling gown and pinched feet. In the taxi, the hat and jacket came off. In the gallery, the scarf and gloves and spangled cardigan. In the taxi home, the ankle boots and, in her hall, the totebag and bracelets. She effected all this with the giggles and coy abandon one imagines a courtesan employing, and then she stopped. I stood studying a hobbling leather skirt, a silk shirt with a high neck, and a ferret's foot. The body within, which had seemed insubstantial under all those layers, was sufficiently revealed to affirm its robust solidity. She was, if anything, a little too solid to go on as a model. She was twenty-five and at the end of one career.

Exhibit B

It was not until you were admitted to Stephanie's house that you saw her undergarments. Well, what surprised was that one was forced to address them as she elected to present them: arrayed on airing racks.

The sun was the problem. She did not dare hang them outside for fear of rotting. Why so many scantily impractical items should be in the wash at any one time was a question I could not ask.

It is gorgeous stuff, as you can see. She had acquired most of it in Paris, she told me, and a few bits in the States. The remaining fripperies were the side benefits of photographic jobs in a dozen cities. As she told it, she had been at the top in the modelling of intimate apparel. While she chattered, she fingered one of those awful brooches, and her cats played with the dangling ribbons and suspenders and hooked their claws in the lace.

Smear and innuendo

In the company of her underwear, Stephanie was as bright as a liquorice allsort—black, white and pink. I am assuming you like that sort of lolly. Her black hair swayed in scores of rats' tails secured with pink beads. The whites of her eyes were astonishingly white, with pink veins at the corners. Her lips shaded from grey to pink, rolling inward to press against white teeth and a pink, dimpled tongue. Her hands turned over to reveal padded, pinky grey palms. Her final act of revelation—one rarely conceded, I was to learn—was to undo her hair. The performance took an hour, and the watcher was rewarded at an excruciating pace with an accretion of crimping, rippling black streamers.

It was seeing her this way, immersed in her hair like a nineteenth-century artist's model, which confirmed my resolve.

I had yet to decide how to depict her. In whatever stage of undress one saw her, she set up an opposition between the flesh and the garments. In that voluptuous underwear she could look like innocence betrayed. In a *broderie anglaise* blouse or nightgown she embodied sensuality fighting for emancipation. In all her outer layers she was savagery dressed up in the stoles and tweeds of reputation.

And, in every case, there was the assurity that there were layers still remaining, draperies hiding ritual scars.

Place of residence

Mine is a street in which buyers are sprucing up their clapboard purchases with lattice, pickets and shiny galvanised iron. Stephanie somehow acquired the shabbiest house of the lot at an extraordinarily low rent and then, characteristically, applied her attentions to the interior.

Our acquaintance blossomed when she solicited my stepladder and steady hand to help her rig up a tiffany lampshade over a pink bulb. Within weeks she had created a fairy bower. Every decoration was either fluffy or fragile. Through this haven she flitted and danced and preened, acting out a videoclip of the mission-school girl enticed a decade before by the discos of Kinshasa.

She sprayed the house liberally with Chanel number 19, but from the start nothing could cover the stink of tomcat.

'Note the scent,' she would proclaim in her arch, affectedly Parisian voice, raising a fingertip to forestall attack. 'It comes courtesy of Eau de Chat, Musk Rose and Civet Cuvee.' And, hauling one of the toms onto her lap, she would bend it to take a bow.

These three cats could do no wrong. Stephanie contrived to make her visitors accept even their stench. The house was soon a catalogue, I was pleased to tell her, of their misdemeanours: clawed curtains, furry sofas and marked corners.

'Oh, my poor darling,' she would tinkle as one of the beasts coughed up a fur ball. They were her household gods: selfish, broad-stomached, white buddhas with sunspots on their pink noses and ears. She bought them offerings—snippets of hare, pheasant, quail, lobster—and they spurned her. They were cranky, spiteful things. When she crouched to muzzle up to one of them, he swiped her across the face with open claws, or nipped her wrist and ran away lashing his tail. She enjoyed these rages and nastinesses. Her love was undiminished. She would sit studying her boys' pink noses, their pink scratchy tongues, their pink padded feet, their pointed little white teeth, the white mink on their bellies. They sucked her in. After clothing and rent and perfume, they were her biggest expense. They were endlessly getting cut up in fights, or losing condition, or lacking nutrients, or suffering infected eyes and ears. Treament enraged them. And the more they hissed and struggled, the greater Stephanie's gratification.

No visible means of support

Stephanie told me she had come to Australia with a boyfriend who had been contracted to set up the nightclub in a new casino. She had liked the sound of the words 'Gold Coast'. The boyfriend had jetted on, but she had stayed.

Decent catwalk and photographic work was proving scarce, she claimed, but perhaps she was rationalising. A black face is not a selling point here in department store catalogues, and the clubs which might hire a black hostess to add that uncertain panache are full of fast talkers and slow payers. Sydney beckoned, yet Stephanie stayed, apparently finding something homely about our sweaty young city.

I broached the subject of a portrait by offering to pay Stephanie to sit. She agreed but giggled when I tried to nominate an hourly rate.

In possible mitigation: a prepared statement

Stephanie had acquired the conviction she was frail. She protected herself as if she were an albino. She could speak most affectingly for half-an-hour of a sad history of enforced dieting and enervating steambaths. As she spoke she seemed to turn grey from blood loss and apprehension. But it would end in consolations, of course. What man is not susceptible to a woman's tears?

Another day she would pride herself on never setting out to entice. She would never, she insisted, put herself out to buy homage. Rather, she played her spoilt, sensuous self, and homage came to her. She, as she truly was—guileful, flirtatious, tempting if you will—was the object of attraction. If they chose to come to her, so be it. Too bad for them if they did not obtain what they had hoped; she had perfect mastery of the bait-and-switch technique. Those who turned back, she left to their own devices. She did not wish to win courtiers who were not sincerely willing to be allured. True initiates must elect to love her foibles, indulge her mannered ficklenesses and smile on her luxuries. They must ignore the irrationalities and the mingy strategems which financed the luxuries.

Hunger, for example, was always attendant on the worshipper, as it is on the religiously devout; for while Stephanie stocked her kitchen with delicacies, there were never the staples to accompany them. She would produce a sliver of *Roquefort*, a pot of mustard, a tiny terrine, but no bread or crackers; the feast indefinitely postponed, she would then propose some fresh diversion. In the end it was the admirer who needed the tonics and iron pills.

A favourite trick, I observed, was to refrain from eating for a day or two, pleading some indiposition, and to then swoon into a strong pair of masculine arms, declaring herself so weak and wobbly she was in need of immediate resuscitation at the newest restaurant. After a plate of food, she'd revive and scamper about like a squirrel at dusk. Sometimes she'd declare she could not eat a thing on the menu and, waving aside the maitre d', lead her companion off to Brisbane's sole African place, where she'd hoe into bowls of grainy porridge scooped up with the hand. In the same vein she might suggest an outing to a movie and then, in the middle of the mall, announce herself exhausted and enervated; she'd then bounce into the back seat of a cab, bundling her layers around her like an ancient actress, and swoop away, leaving her escort non-plussed on the taxirank.

She would entertain the merest acquaintance in her bedroom. (I only have this second-hand.) Settling him on the fourposter bed, amidst billows of satin sheets and embroidered, ruffled pillows, she'd leaf through her portfolio, showing off the stills of herself—tittilating ones at times—and, in this fragrant, creased, silken, prickly disarray, feed him pecans and pistachios. Sometimes, halfway through, she'd pull her old trick. Declaring herself bored or fatigued, she'd slap closed the portfolio and dismiss her guest into the night.

Such a fragile constitution required a life arranged around losses and compensations. If one is too intermittently delicate to drive, cook and clean, one must then substitute cab vouchers, restaurant invitations and a cleaning lady. Thus Stephanie freed her time, only to fill it with men: the inviting and chatting and catching up and confiding, the entangling in pink ribbons.

Shadowy background figures

Around the christ or dead bishop the painter traditionally deploys a hemisphere of mourners blessed with the faces of his patrons and clients. He may even pop his own head onto a toga.

To appreciate my subject I needed to watch her in company, even though I would reproduce her in isolation.

It was apparent that those men Stephanie deemed her friends were either gayboys or straight infatuees.

The toy boys appreciated Stephanie for what she was. They applauded the mechanics of her artifice. They liked the highcampery, the layers of frills, the coquetry, the drawn claws. They permitted a stroke of the stubble, the straightening of a tie. They admired her ingenuity. She was generous with favours. She invited them round for cocktails and took them on Teddy Bears' picnics at Lone Pine. They reciprocated with a lesser measure of charm. They bared their bodies just sufficiently, looked into her eyes, and acceded to her considered whims for as long as it entertained them to do so.

Straight men were more ambivalent. The femininity enticed. The pretty weakness evoked masculine thrills of protectiveness. The voice—cleverly modulated—intrigued and flattered. Men desired her company, looked forward to her invitations, but were ultimately baffled and angered. The femininity cloyed.

Once, as I watched, she grew too fond of a man to stop the game in time. He flew away to Sydney. She luxuriated in grief. There were weeping fits, whole days of cursing and rages of aggrievement. There were all the trappings of a doomed, lopsided love affair: the long-distance phone calls, the smudged letter, the telegrams and couriers, the red roses, the snubs, the slighting remarks, the rivals, the bon voyages and au revoirs and go to hells. She loved the self-pity the most of the lot.

Of African males, there are few in Brisbane and those all it seems of the student type. 'Hashed mouse on a bed of rice,' was how Stephanie described the meals they cooked on single hotplates in their bed-sitters. According to her they would propose marriage on the first date, forgetting their benefice of children and multiple wives back home. They never had any cash, they were always late, they were always complaining about the non-arrival of cheques, they strutted and boasted and, at last, departed with armfuls of electricals and wallets of notes with which to bribe the customs men. 'Idiots,' Stephanie said. I smiled. Her own notion of time was alarming, and for the rest I was not equipped to comment.

I need not remark on the paucity of female friends. Stephanie did not chose to cultivate them, and they did not like her artifice. That is my observation.

Once in a while a woman would make a gauche offer of neighbourliness. Stephanie would choose to bristle. She would sniff at the faux pas of a woman made nervous by her beauty, and snap at the woman fumbling over the word 'black'. There was no generosity of spirit toward women, yet for the average male there was an endless store of forgiveness.

Gradually, however, Stephanie did assemble a small coterie of women. They were her third battalion, inferior in rank to the toy boys. She used them to plug the gaps between male escorts. And they tolerated her high-handedness, I suppose for the novelty of experiencing such an exotic alliance. We are a small, gullible city.

The hostile witness

It was the delight of hearing another French-speaker which brought them together, although their accents were not remotely alike, even I could tell that.

Berthe talked like an animated art journal. However slowly she articulated an idea in her accented English, I could not grasp it. Her thinking was too highbrow and convoluted. She had a European cast of thought which baffled. Everything was shot through with philosophy. She walked around thinking out pure maths conundrums and questioning the laws of physics. As a child, she told me, she had wanted to invent a perpetual motion machine. One afternoon she harangued Stephanie and I for a solid hour on the need for a feminist mathematique. When we at last rebelled, Berthe shook her electrified curls in anger and exclaimed: 'The sun has fried your brains.' We laughed, your Honour.

Berthe was not only a theoretician. I was amazed and mortified to learn from a portfolio she produced one day that she had practised the art of sculpture. Her exhibition pieces and commissions were works of a salutary satiric wit; even someone of my reactionary spirit was drawn into laughing with them and thumbing the nose. Each, you understand, was notionally a piece of furniture. May I consult my notes? A yellow étagere sprinkled with twinkling lightbulbs; an armchair—a *fauteuil*—with no seat, just an exposed chamber pot; a painted harpsichord with spikes for keys; an upside-down table ('for indoor picnics,' she said); a desk with fig-leaf modesty panels; a wardrobe with see-through doors; a table marblised on its underside; and an aluminium chair which converted into a ladder. Nothing pretended to be useable.

Berthe had been at the Sorbonne for the riots. She had been in Milan and—well, you name it. Now, she was an emigrée for reasons never fully clarified. She had come via Uruguay, where the culture had intrigued her but not the currency. She had moved on to Brisbane with a man, George Boubeta, who was emigrating for economic gain and to escape the effects of the seventies upheavals. She had come in as his de facto wife and obtained permanent residency. She lived alone in a flat under a big old house in Clayfield, and supported herself by that usual concomitant of art: teaching. In her case it was French imparted in accordance with some feminist dialectic which went way over my head. Stephanie showed no inclination to sign up for a course. Periodically Senor Boubeta reappeared to claim his quasi-conjugal rights and Berthe, for reasons unexplained, complied. On lonely afternoons she would drop in on Stephanie, armed with her own coffee beans, and Stephanie, unwilling to bear it alone, would call me in.

A prejudicial account

Andrew was Stephanie's latest lover. Sufficient to say, he raised my hackles. He was emblematic of a past I thought had safely passed.

It was Andrew in jeans which aggravated me. His hair at once seemed to grow longer, his body lost its flesh, the shape of his glasses changed, a bong sprang into his hand, and I could see the part he had chosen in that back-packer decade. What I had kept out of, for self-preservation, he had embraced, for self-promotion.

What did I not like?

The freedom purchased with selfishness. That spiritual promiscuity. That long road movie promising a buzz of revelation. That 'hit the road' responsibility. That 'fuck you' generosity. That tolerance for others of the same impulse. Those households. That bludging. Those discussions. That mumbling. Those depths. That frappant decade. It petered away into crime and property.

Ah, Andrew would respond, but we had brotherhood. We shared a tramps' alphabet. We left our secret signs on gateposts. We wore a uniform, sure. We had our idols, true. But we were an army of liberation, not mercenaries. We stole the North Side's milkbottles to give them to the black babies.

What restitution, then, I ask you, for the acidhead who roams these streets—leather jacket, beard, flared jeans, bare soles? We give him the benefit of our reformed laws and our tolerance. We refrain from calling the cops when he shits in our front yard. I'm sorry . . .

The Moonstones and Tamsins are with us too. They are

changing their names and, shouldering on their own back-packs, heading out to pillage in their own fashion. They are making records of their attenuated lives on Super Eight. They are running road movies at speed and adding their own dialogue. Look, here come Dennis Hopper and Peter Fonda roaring backwards, home, across that bridge.

Ah, that implacable tolerance. But we lived our ideals, Andrew argued. We let our dangling crystals direct us. Our grass was healthier than their beef. If our women's bellies are swollen now, it's only temporary, a side-effect of their ligations. We pay the doctor in Indian silver.

In his contemporary person Andrew is not particularly offensive. Indeed, he is a junior member of the circle which commissions my work and I am given to understand we attended the same school. St Peter's. Indooroopilly. Yes, I am several years his senior.

In a suit he fiddles with his jacket button, pulls in his belly, squeezes his tie-knot, closes his hands with his signet ring uppermost, and addresses his audience with a pithy self-satisfaction, as if he had been trained as a little boy to deliver miniature homilies to impress guests. He is handsome in that way which evokes suspicion. He looks well-fed, and worried by the strain of remaining himself. Reality, he once told me, was what you could trade: it fluctuated in kind and value. He was all for *realpolitik*. He spoke of spilling, rolling, stoushing, stitching up, doctoring, liquidating and blowing away. He maintained, however, that he had no desire to accrue a fortune; if he had, he'd be getting a cut of all the rorts he knew about. He takes vicarious pleasure in observing others' unsavoury dealings. He backlights the city's moral turpitude, and collects his broking fees. His favourite lines of approbation are: 'He's not a moralist' and 'He's Simon Pure, for sure'. He calls women 'ma'am'.

Of course there is a decent woman in the background, waiting to lay out the body. A subdean this one, fortyish also, large, with photos of nieces and nephews in her wallet. Her father was a police inspector.

From the outset Stephanie played Andrew with tragic gestures. She fluttered her hands, closed her eyelids and crumpled a white lace-edged handkerchief in her palm.

'Isn't he grand company?' she would acclaim at her soirées, hugging his head to her belly. 'He's great,' the few women present would agree. They talked as if the man were a decorated cake or a chocolate dildo, something to be handed around at a lingerie party.

'Know your talent,' he would respond with a flattered smirk. The knife was never far from his back.

Stephanie instinctively took a pastel-pink role with him. She drew his head down to her breast; he lowered his face like a child blowing apart the fur on a pet's belly. She entertained select little groups in pink lounging pyjamas. About ten she would go into the bedroom, slip out of her narrow jewelled Indian scuffs and come out in a pair of fluffy children's slippers with cat's faces on the toecaps. Bead eyes, black felt noses and nylon whiskers, Your Honour. She would snuggle up on the floor beside Andrew's legs and pretend to listen to whatever story he was partway through. When he faltered, she would take his hands and draw them towards her. They were big, spotted hands. She would examine them as if they were sewing machine attachments or a crab's pincers. His palms and fingers were rounded and there were scar lines on the tops of his hands between the brown hairs and protruding veins. While he talked, she composed and anticipated. She was like a callgirl with a client who thinks himself a capable lover.

Naturally the subdean was not present at these soirees. Yet on more than one occasion Stephanie suggested to Andrew he bring her to afternoon tea at my place. She could never resist formenting a mischief.

No, I chose my words unwisely. That would not be the same as creating a public mischief.

A witness impugns herself

Months passed. I made a couple of false starts on the preliminary sketches. Stephanie worked selling records for a marketing man outside a long-running black American musical. She learned a pretty convincing American accent. I wondered about her long-term plans, and determined to press on with the painting. Berthe and Andrew came and went, but never together: Stephanie policed her self-serving apartheid.

Stephanie began to complain Berthe's behaviour had deteriorated. I took it to be the common disillusion of closening acquaintance. Berthe was clearly not an easy ally. Her enquiries were too forensic, her tongue too scathing.

Each time I encountered the Frenchwoman she was angrier and skinnier. She would tear into her friendship with Stephanie. She was not strong enough to rip it apart—her arms were too scrawny—but she kept worrying at the fabric of it, teasing out threads, pulling at the selvedges. She cried out over the trivial annoyances the rest of Stephanie's court tolerated. She whined for special attention.

After a spat with the owners upstairs, Berthe was evicted from her flat. She came to sleep on Stephanie's floor. At the time Andrew was safely absent in Chicago and staying up all night so he could phone Stephanie at the hour which suited her. Berthe was, as Stephanie reported it, an ungrateful, vicious guest. She would get up early, for instance, and bash about, ostentatiously cleaning and tidying. Letting the cats out, she would tell them—loudly—what a neglectful, selfish owner they had to endure. You can imagine the scene. The cats snickering their tails. The Frenchwoman thumping cushions into shape or picking cat fur out of crevices. And Stephanie stumbling out, naked, pulling on a pink silk robe, rubbing her eyes, hauling back handfuls of unravelling rats' tails—a picture of delightful *déshabillée*.

Inadmissable admissions

The portraitist can go on sketching forever, but the time presses when he must commit himself to oils and the discovery of his interpretation.

All through the mornings Stephanie had slept in the house across from mine, behind the Austrian blinds, slept off her late-night partying with the black Southerners and her trysts with Andrew, and I had worked on my commissions. Then in the afternoons she had sat for me: unpaid, as she insisted. I could not understand why she should sit so freely, except that to sit in the company of a man, any man, was better than solitude.

While she chattered, I sketched, discarded, and tried again.

Normally I am commissioned to immortalise board-room knights in pinstriped corsets and parliamentary knights in laundered shirts, to freeze grammar-school grandchildren under boaters or flatter the young wife of a pressure-pack hairdresser. I have even been called upon to revivify a dead chinchilla from a single polaroid. In all these trials, I do not retouch too flagrantly. But Stephanie lured me into drawing her classically beautiful, when in reality you may observe she has the model's bland, malleable planes. I kept getting the eyes wrong. The lenses came out bulbous and plastic, deflecting the light and magnifying the irises. The problem was her eyes were never still. She could not bear to be unanimated in the presence of a male for longer than it took to click a shutter. I resorted to using a camera. I should have realised from the start it was the only way.

I am not a life painter. My usual subjects would look risible without their public uniforms. But Stephanie remained so elusive, even in front of the tripod, that I got angry and thought perhaps I would have to paint her naked. She asked to be exposed, to be stripped of her obscuring layers. They were all she amounted to, perhaps, but the viewer would not be satisfied with such an interpretation. The painter is required to delve. But I could not love her sufficiently to do it. I began to want to hurt her.

In fairness I must add Stephanie did not care for my ways. She found me, if I am translating her correctly, a precisian, a formalist, costive. My few jokey affectations—my four Bs: the beard, the bowties, the Bombay bloomers, the bicycle—she failed to find endearing. Still, she invited me in to her soirées, displayed me as a nineteenth-century colonial dabbler, and watched the gayboys' reactions. I was her mockturtle.

I would go home from her praises and rebukes stripped of the serenity I had so slowly garnered. One does not care to be teased or admired for what one has taken on out of necessity. A person like that, well—there is always a foolish maiden wanting to borrow the oil of the wise. Dull virtue is hard to defend. To have chosen it is made to seem perverse, while to have lapsed into it is pathetic. To have a holiday fling is to invite both approval and criticism; and the approval reduces like fairy floss into sticky lumps while the criticism resounds in the ears of the solitary. So, one withdraws further into self-reliance. The world becomes stolid virtue opposed to flibbertigibbet enchantment. And it is consistent outward virtue—plus judicious conniving—which gets one the repeat business.

The events in question

Your Honour, I went one evening—January the fourteenth I believe, a Friday—with Stephanie and Andrew to a concert. African music: drumming, Caribbean reggae, and other styles I had never even heard of. Stephanie told me the names. Actually, she shouted them above the din. Highlife, afrobeat, I forget the rest. It was all very hot and exciting. At least, Andrew tried to get excited, and I, well—that's irrelevant. Afterwards, I saw them home to Stephanie's front door.

No, I do not drive. Andrew drove—in one of his partnership Peugeots. A 505. Stephanie asked me in for a drink. I refused—I would have thought my reasoning was self-evident. She was being a tease, you know. I stood on the front verandah chatting with Andrew about a mutual acquaintance, a departmental secretary. I agree it would be wiser not to name him. Well, sir, it was cooler outside and there was the smell of mangoes and the passionfruit vine, and I was trying not to walk away too abruptly. The verandah boards were rotting, incidentally.

Stephanie had gone on inside to say hello to her cats. Yes, that was her custom. She always ran on ahead calling out 'How are my boyboys?' or something like that. No, she was not afraid of the dark. With respect, I wouldn't think that was a characteristic of all Africans. Anyway, the next thing that happened was she screamed, howled really. I thought she must have found one of the cats dead. It was that sort of wail—a bereavement wail.

Yes, Your Honour, I have. Both parents. And my wife. She was quite young, indeed. That was in 1976.

Had I any designs? Once you have painted someone, you give them away, if you see what I mean, dispossess yourself. So—to answer your implication—no, I was neither father nor husband to her.

To either woman. I'm sorry. I was a husband to my wife, of course, but—I don't think we should . . .

Andrew and I ran inside. Andrew was first. We saw—all right, I saw—Stephanie, the accused, standing in the middle of the lounge—yes, the livingroom. She did appear distressed. Sobbing, weeping, shaking. To my mind the cause was not immediately evident. I walked across and looked in the bedroom door. Every drawer had been up-ended. There were toiletries and clothes and perfume bottles strewn all over the floor. I assumed it was thieves looking for money. Andrew at this stage was trying to comfort Stephanie, and looking into the other rooms to see what else had been disturbed. Both, at once.

I did not, in fact, realise what had been stolen until Stephanie pointed at the drying racks. These racks were normally arranged all around the livingroom with her underclothes on them—as I said earlier. Yes, I should have noticed straightaway. Perhaps I did but my subconscious told me they were bare because everything was in the wash.

Who did I . . . ? The subdean? Oh no, that would have been unthinkable.

Stephanie was still very distressed at this point. It was like the dismay of a woman who is bruised on the face or breast and has not realised until then how greatly she trades on her attractiveness. Possibly, it might have been feigned. But I did not think so at the time. Naturally, when I realised it was only the underthings missing, I thought the Frenchwoman was responsible. I left Andrew attempting to soothe the—Stephanie.

I did not know Stephanie intended to notify the police. I thought she might well flay Berthe's reputation at her next soirée.

That sort of thing was more in her line than calling the police. It was my impression that she did not care for the gendarmerie. Possibly owing to some past boyfriend's skirmishes with the law. Are you positive it was she who phoned with the complaint?

I considered it a private matter. A piece of vindictiveness on Berthe's part. No, really, it seemed petty to me. I did not know the underwear was so valuable, hence the profit motive did not occur to me. I admit I did testify it was all gorgeous stuff, but it is some years since I have had any experience of paying for such items. My expertise, you understand, is limited to paintings. Yes, I do deal, in a small way. Chiefly Australian sea-scapes. Allcot I'd recommend, to start with. My own house has alarms, and portable insurance.

No, I can't imagine Stephanie would have had her undergarments insured. She was no longer modelling. Although, admittedly, they were still her tools of trade. I do not think fraud of that kind entered her head.

The following morning she came in to see me. Nine o'clock; I was up to my second pot of tea. She asked me to go with her and Andrew to try to recover—find, she said—the stolen goods. I believe she thought two men would be better than one. Personally I consider the subdean, Janet, would have made a fiercer ally.

We went first to the Frenchwoman's last known address, the flat I mentioned earlier. The owner, upstairs, began harangueing us about unpaid bills and strange callers and going out at two a.m. to the autobank. Unfortunately familiar. She had phoned the owner with her new address so he could forward her mail. I did not notice whether Stephanie appeared to recognise this second address.

We drove there. It was another big old house, this time on a block sloping down to the river. Paradise Street, West End. Indeed. The front door was open, so no-one could stop us. Stephanie barged on in and started poking her nose into each of the doors opening off the hall. She was dressed in her usual manner. Which particular underwear? I could not possibly say.

It appeared to be a student household. Bohemian. Unemployed. What you would expect: dirty seagrass matting, mattresses on the floor, mounds of dirty clothes, heaps of paperbacks, a lot of records. Yes, everything seemed to be on the floor. Such places never have enough cupboards. Let us say their recreational pursuits were obvious enough: bongs, saucers, little bowls with a grey-green haze in the base. Yes, feasibly it was a squat.

It was a young man who interrupted our search. We *were* actively searching, I suppose. We did not place much reliance on the police; the notion of a search warrant had crossed my mind.

Anyway, this young man—typical really. Thin, as they all seem to be. Rough hair. Pale. No shirt at all. No shoes. Just tightish black jeans, and a belt undone at the buckle, and the waist stud of the jeans undone. Dressing, undressing, or merely relaxing. About eleven o'clock by this time. On a Saturday. Not everybody shops, as His Honour would know.

Stephanie got in first. Launched into him with the story. He called out 'Berthe'. We heard footsteps coming up stairs and the Frenchwoman came in the back door. Dishevelled, I suppose. A T-shirt, with no bra, and a skirt, twisted at the waist. Bare feet. A bit hazardous, I agree, on such littered floors. I expected them to scowl and go for each other's throats like cats. Instead they each made little apologetic, conciliatory noises, the way feuding women will sometimes. I could not understand the undercurrents, I freely admit it. Then some sort of indication passed between Stephanie and the young man. She said: 'May I have a word, in private?' And he replied: 'Sure,' in that young man way—and he led her out the back door and down the stairs. I could see her head bobbing down, a step at a time; she would have been bunching up her skirt and picking her way on her heels; they were steep old wooden stairs, down to some form of flat. Andrew did not intervene. We gathered we were required to wait. We spread out in the hall. Berthe went into one of the rooms. A bedroom I presume: it contained a mattress, a lot of personal effects, and a wardrobe without any doors. About twenty minutes we waited. I left it to Andrew to keep checking his watch. No sounds. The first indication was when I heard Stephanie tapping back up the stairs. She pushed the screen door with her elbow and stumbled in with her arms full.

A faded Indian bedspread—reddish—enclosing a bundle of underwear. Bits were hanging out, suspenders and so forth. She marched through the hall and out the front door. She said only: 'Come gentlemen.' We obeyed. We did not attempt to say anything to Berthe.

The police came the following day. A Sunday, yes. They did strike me as zealous. They questioned Stephanie at length. Or, I should say, they were in her house for at least an hour. Then they spoke to me, and to Andrew and Berthe, I believe. And then they laid this charge. I gather they thought she'd been mucking them about.

No, I haven't been able to work out how Stephanie could have hidden her underwear in that house. It would have been possible, certainly. Women have been accused of stranger things. But I do not consider it probable. She is not an exhibitionist in that sense.

I am fond of her only in an objective way, as any artist grows fond of his subject.

The outcome

I have not been able to get anywhere with the portrait. I went back to sketching Stephanie from memory. I tried the head alone, that splendid black face, but the skin had stripped off, those troublesome eye sockets were empty, the pink lips had caved in, and I was left with a grey skull and a mess of rats' tails. The clothing was all still there. Those voluminous outer layers seemed to have taken on the likeness of a cape. The mink's foot was there too, but it had slipped down onto her breast, where it was clawing at the folds of cloth. Around her neck there was now a puritan's collar. White, but spattered with red. The smeared plastic collar of the man lugging the carcass over his shoulder into the butcher's shop.

From my window I still saw Stephanie coming and going. When we bumped into one another, she bemoaned her lot. But within a few weeks she was looking buoyant again, and a satin camisole—new I presume—was stirring on the drying rack nearest the front door

Andrew was reported to be humiliated. Stephanie had had as much of him as she wanted. Someone else could lug away the carcass to boil down into soup.

'Put him out of his misery,' the gayboys advised, as if the man were a crow-pecked lamb. 'Set him up with Berthe.'

An open verdict, if that were possible.